To my awesome beta team. Thanks for being my biggest cheerleaders!

STEPHANIE FAZIO

HEX KITCHEN SERIES BOOK 3

BLOODY DELICIOUS

Syafant Press

New York, New York

Copyright © 2022 Stephanie Fazio.

Cover designed by Keith Tarrier

This book is a work of fiction. Names, characters, places, and incidents either are the product of the author's imagination or are used fictionally, and any resemblance to actual persons, living or dead, business establishments, events, or locales is entirely coincidental.

Stephanie Fazio

Visit www.StephanieFazio.com

Library of Congress Control Number: 2021915768

ISBN 978-1-951572-27-3

CHAPTER 1

KENZIE

Kenzie snuck a surreptitious peek at Braxton. His shirt was draped around his neck, and his bare chest gleamed with perspiration. She watched a drop of sweat trickle down his golden skin and roll over his defined abs.

"Kenzie."

"What?" she asked. It came out as more of a shout than a question.

Smooth one, Ashner. Way to play it cool.

"Can you repeat the question?" Kenzie asked at a much more reasonable volume.

Braxton sighed. It wasn't a happy, contented sort of sound. It was more of a frustrated, I-need-you-to-get-with-the-program sigh. He leaned back against a tree and crossed his arms.

"Why did Sofia abandon me in a field and make me run eight kilometers back here?" Braxton asked.

His tone was patient, but a vein throbbed in his temple. He mopped more sweat off his glistening chest with his damp T-shirt.

"Um…." Kenzie bit her lip.

How to tell your boyfriend that you helped his sister get herself arrested….

"So, I kind of did my Culinarian thing on her," Kenzie began.

Okay. She could do this. She could totally do this.

"I mean, it was consensual," she forged on. "Actually, Sofia kind of threatened me if I refused to give her magic. Then, she stole your recipe that changes a person's appearance—really creepy by the way—and made herself look like Graham. And then she drove off and got arrested. Well, I presume she got arrested. I obviously don't know for sure, since she's there and I'm well, here…."

In the time that had passed between Sofia driving away and Braxton returning to the cabin, Kenzie had practiced the explanation she was currently in the process of delivering. And she was getting the distinct impression it could be going better.

Braxton covered his face with his hands and swore. A lot.

"Will you two keep it down?" Aralia whisper-shouted from above them. "Our uninvited guests will be here any minute."

According to Aralia, someone had tripped her magical motion sensor at the end of the private, unpaved road that led to the cabin. If they were lucky, it was just some overly-ambitious Jehovah's Witnesses. The far more likely scenario—and the reason why they were all currently hiding in the woods behind the cabin—was that the Gourmands were on their way to kill them.

Fun times.

Aralia was perched in a leafy oak tree, straddling one of the branches like a female Tarzan. Her blonde braids and the feathers she'd stuck into them hung over her shoulders. She had her bow looped around her arm and a quiver of arrows strapped to her back. And, dear God, who the hell had told that girl it was acceptable to climb trees in a miniskirt without underwear…?

"How could you do this to me?" Braxton demanded.

The accusation and betrayal in his voice made Kenzie forget all about Aralia's unfortunate undergarment choices…or lack thereof. When Kenzie turned to Braxton and saw the expression in his emerald eyes, her stomach felt like she'd swallowed pickling brine, all sourness and gut clenching.

When it had just been her and Sofia, everything they'd decided had seemed so logical. Braxton's magic was on the brink of collapse because of how hard he'd been pushing himself. So, Sofia had decided to take Braxton's place in the bargain he'd made with Aralia.

Sofia had transformed herself into looking like Graham before leaving the cabin. Her plan was to get arrested for a double-murder Graham had committed nearly a decade ago and go to jail for his crimes.

"How could you do this to me?" Braxton asked in a ragged voice.

"Braxton—"

"You know she's the only family I have left," he interrupted before she could stammer out anything else.

His animosity wasn't, in context, entirely unreasonable. And yet, the accusation radiating off him stung.

"I was trying to protect you," Kenzie said, her voice rising with her growing anxiety. She dug her nails into her palms hard enough to form little half-moons. "We both were."

"Ashner, lower your voice," Chef Levy hissed.

The ex-Mossad and prior Hex Kitchen judge was somewhere nearby, but she was too camouflaged for Kenzie to spot. The woman's full name was Elyannah Levy, but Kenzie referred to her as *Chef Levy*, even inside her own mind. Someone who wielded a gun as comfortably as most people handled forks should be first-named solely at the user's peril.

The temporary quiet was broken by a humming that rose into actual words.

"Rosemary and thyme and basil and coriander and caraway and dill," Rosemary sang.

Rosemary stepped out from the tree she was hiding behind as her superfood song rose in volume. She stroked her food charm necklace in time with the words.

"Same goes for you," Chef Levy told Rosemary, clearly on a roll. "Don't give me even more of a reason to put a bullet through your brain."

"You're not killing her," Kenzie informed Chef Levy, not for the first time.

"And if the Gourmands get their hands on her?" Chef Levy retorted. "Need I remind you what will happen if Rick gets the superfood recipe?"

Kenzie winced. Rick becoming the single most powerful person in the world of culinary magic was terrifying enough. Kenzie really didn't want to think about what would happen if he gained access to a recipe that could spontaneously imbue someone with magic. And if Rick got its sister recipe, the anti-superfood, then he'd have the ability to take away culinary magic from anyone he wanted.

"Enough of this," Braxton muttered to himself, clearly not having heard a word anyone else was saying. "I'm going after Sofia. Maybe she hasn't turned herself in yet. I know this recipe—"

The squeal of tires drowned out the rest of Braxton's sentence. Kenzie and Braxton backed deeper into the foliage as three black SUVs barreled up the driveway and screeched to a halt in front of the cabin.

"Only three?" Aralia grumbled. "I'm insulted Rick thinks that's all it'll take to kill us."

As Gourmands spilled out of the cars, it seemed to Kenzie that Rick hadn't underestimated them at all. The air was practically electric with magical energy.

Kenzie searched each person who stepped onto the driveway, looking for Rick. The last car door slammed shut, and still, he didn't appear. She'd known he wouldn't—after all, Rick had recently become the Gourmand leader and had an army of minions to do his dirty work for him. Still, she'd hoped. It would have been so easy to end this here and now.

The Gourmands tossed handfuls of what appeared to be sunflower seeds into their mouths. The hoods of their crimson robes shrouded their faces, which gave them an even more sinister appearance. Not that they needed any help in that department.

The Gourmands crunched down on their sunflower seeds and spat the shells onto the ground. Magic surged through the air.

It smelled like burnt sugar and felt sticky. Acrid.

These sunflower seeds weren't like the magical ingredients Sofia had gotten from the Reaper. Those ingredients were bursting with a steady flow of natural power. These sunflower seeds left an erratic, unpleasant residue in their wake. That was how Kenzie knew they were of the synthetic variety.

Kenzie had felt this kind of magic before in Cutthroat Cuisine, when Benedict had introduced her to the synthetic magical ingredients he was producing. That was when Kenzie had learned the steep price that was required to make each and every one of those synthetic ingredients.

Kenzie clenched her fists tight enough for her knuckles to crack.

"Ashner, you're up," Chef Levy whispered.

"Hey," Braxton said, giving her a little nudge. "You okay?"

Since losing her shit wasn't really an option at the moment, Kenzie nodded.

She reached down to the leftover container on the ground by her feet. She pinched a piece of cedar-smoked trout out of the container and put it in her mouth. Her palate filled with a woodsy flavor that was at once homey and rustic. Just like the cabin itself.

The trout reminded her of nights gathered around the long table that Graham and Aralia filled with enough naturally-sourced food to feed a small army. Kenzie could almost see all of them sitting down to dinner together. She heard their mostly good-natured squabbling, tasted the food on her tongue, and felt Braxton's hand resting on her leg under the table.

Kenzie's magic snapped into place.

Voices began to float out from the cabin's open window, even though there was no one inside. The phantom speakers sounded exactly like Kenzie and Braxton.

Kenzie adjusted her magic, making it appear as though shadowy figures were moving around inside the cabin. She was not ashamed to say she'd totally channeled Macaulay Culkin from *Home Alone* when she came up with this recipe.

The Gourmands signaled to each other, quietly congratulating themselves as they converged on the cabin.

The Gourmands drew guns from their cloak pockets. Kenzie had just enough presence of mind to register that the guns they were holding were made out of chocolate.

A thunderous sound split the air. Bullet holes appeared in the cabin's beautiful wooden frame. Chocolate or not, the damage they inflicted was the same.

Kenzie's body flinched reflexively, even though she knew the cabin was empty. Beside her, Braxton tensed.

The gunfire stopped.

One of men kicked in the cabin's door. He moved so fast, his leg was a blur.

Wood splintered. The Gourmands stormed into the cabin.

Kenzie quickly adjusted her magic, tugging on the invisible strands and creating the illusion of dead bodies inside. She created one for each of them.

Nausea surged through her as she envisioned a dead Aralia…a dead Rosemary…a dead Braxton….

"Five bodies," one of the Gourmands called. "All dead."

"Mr. Santiori will be pleased," one of the Gourmands standing outside replied.

"Now we can get back to our real job," a third said. "Magic needs to be protected at all costs. We have to tell Mr. Santiori—"

"I'm going to kill them all," Aralia growled, reaching back for one of her arrows.

"You're not going to do a damn thing," Chef Levy said in a low voice. "Your bow-and-arrow routine is no match for their magic guns."

"I don't believe in guns, magic or otherwise." Aralia sniffed. "Do you have any idea what kind of toxic metals come off spent bullets? Besides, any idiot can shoot a gun. These take actual skill." She lovingly caressed her arrows.

"Look," Kenzie whispered, interrupting the two of them before they could really get going. She pointed to the driveway.

The Gourmands' robes fanned out behind them as they darted around the driveway with preternatural speed. Magical speed. They were like red blurs across Kenzie's vision, zipping back and forth between their cars and the cabin.

Rosemary made a whimpering noise and buried her face in her hands.

"What are they doing?" Kenzie asked, trying and failing to track their rapid-fire movements.

"I have a feeling we're about to find out," Chef Levy replied in a low voice.

The wind shifted, carrying gray wisps of smoke and the scent of gasoline. Seconds later, flames began licking their way up from the cabin's chimney.

"No," Aralia whispered.

There was a slight tussle as Aralia started forward, and Chef Levy held her back.

The forest around them was oddly silent. The birds and other creatures had made themselves scarce. Even the wind had stopped rustling the leaves.

The eerie quiet was abruptly broken by the crackling and popping sounds of a blaze coming to life. Kenzie watched in open-mouthed horror as flames began to devour the beautiful house.

She was dimly aware of the Gourmands chatting amiably among themselves as they got back into their cars and drove away.

She was nowhere near the cabin, and yet, Kenzie could feel the flames' heat wafting across her face. Pitch-black smoke was pouring out of the cabin's open doorway.

"I'm so sorry, Aralia," Kenzie said, her voice hoarse from a combination of smoke inhalation and witnessing their refuge burn to the ground.

Aralia cleared her throat. "Wasn't like we could stay here now that Rick knows about the place, anyway." When she dragged her gaze away from the cabin, there was a suspicious gleam in her eyes.

"I never wanted to bring my shit with the Santioris to your home," Braxton said, glancing between Aralia and the burning house.

Aralia let out a choked laugh. "Don't kid yourself, stud. You're not the only one who has beef with the Santioris'."

"The loss of your home is unfortunate," Chef Levy said in a businesslike tone. "But it'll buy us a little time, at least. It won't be long before Rick figures out we duped him, though. We can't linger." She leapt out of her tree and landed lightly on her feet. "Everyone toss your phones on the ground."

Without asking why, all of them did as they were told.

Kenzie yelped when Chef Levy pulled out her handgun and started firing bullets into each of their phones. Then, she stomped on the screens for good measure.

"Better safe than sorry," Chef Levy muttered before turning and walking away.

None of them spoke as they trooped over to the van they'd packed earlier and hidden under a mountain of dead leaves. Even Rosemary had stopped humming her superfood song under her breath.

Their van was stuffed to the gills with clothes, Chef Levy's weapons, magical food, and Kiwi's habitat. There was barely enough room for them to squish in and buckle their seatbelts.

"You okay, bud?" Kenzie asked her chameleon.

Kiwi opened his eyes and yawned. When Kenzie reached into his habitat to adjust his heat lamp, Kiwi's long tongue darted out to give her hand a comforting smooch. Or taste the remnants of trout. Either way.

Chef Levy started the engine and backed slowly out of the pile of leaves. The winding driveway brought them around the side of the cabin, giving them an up-close view of the smoldering wood. Kenzie could feel heat pouring off the blackened boards.

There was a dull creak, followed by a groan as the cabin's roof caved in. The whole house shuddered like it was a living being. Then, it collapsed on itself.

Aralia sniffed and quickly wiped at her eyes. Chef Levy hit the gas.

"Where are we going?" Kenzie asked, her throat thick for reasons that had nothing to do with the noxious smoke.

Throughout their harried discussions, that part of their plan had always remained vague. If a middle-of-nowhere wilderness retreat wasn't safe from Rick and the Gourmands, then where could they go?

"We're going to hide in plain sight," Chef Levy said. She smirked into the rearview mirror. The expression on Chef Levy's face made Kenzie grateful the two of them were on the same side.

"I don't know about the rest of you," Braxton said, speaking for the first time since they'd gotten in the van. "But I'm going after Sofia. Before it's too late."

Kenzie wanted to reach for his hand but didn't dare. She had helped Sofia, knowing full well how angry Braxton would be. And, while she had been telling the truth about wanting to protect him, her intentions hadn't been completely selfless, either. Sofia had promised to try and end up at Rikers Island, where Kenzie's dad was also imprisoned. If everything went according to plan, Sofia was going to help Kenzie's dad escape.

"You're not doing shit," Aralia informed Braxton, her pleasant tone belied by the way she caressed the daggers strapped to her belt. "Sofia is going to jail so the cops will stop searching for my brother. I'll kill you before I let you interfere."

"You're welcome to try," Braxton snarled.

"Children," Chef Levy snapped. "That's enough. You can fight about this once we get to Manhattan. You're giving me a headache."

"We're going to Manhattan?" Kenzie asked, feeling a familiar tightening in her chest at the mention of the city she'd once called home.

"Yep," Chef Levy said. "But not because of anything to do with your petty family dramas. I don't give a crap about any of that."

"Noted, Chef," Braxton muttered.

"Where in Manhattan are we supposed to hide without Rick finding us?" Aralia asked. "I didn't just watch my home burn down so we could turn ourselves over to the Gourmands."

"No one's getting caught." Chef Levy's lips twitched. "There happens to be a vacancy in a rather large building. A magical food bank with an attached hotel, formerly owned by a one, Polly Berrywhite."

A few moments of silence passed while they all absorbed that nugget of information.

"We're going to find a way to overthrow Rick and the Gourmands," Chef Levy continued. "And we're going to do it right under their noses."

Now, that was a plan Kenzie could get on board with.

CHAPTER 2

BRAXTON

Six hours later, they pulled into the underground garage beneath the Manhattan building that had been Polly Berrywhite's pet charity project.

Braxton was ready to crawl out of his skin.

The news was all over the radio. The infamous cop killer, Graham Malyung, had been apprehended. According to the headlines, Graham had turned himself over to the authorities and been transported to Manhattan with unprecedented speediness. He—or *she*…if Braxton was thinking in technical terms—was awaiting trial. In Rikers Island Jail.

Braxton's little sister was a prisoner in one of the toughest jails in the world, and there wasn't a damn thing he could do about it.

Damnit, Sofia.

"We'll figure it out," Kenzie said giving his arm a tentative pat as they followed Chef Levy and Aralia to the elevator.

Braxton couldn't manage anything more than a tight nod. He knew none of this was Kenzie's fault; when Sofia made up her mind about something, nothing and no one could stop her. But he was still fucking furious with Kenzie for helping her.

Instead of stepping inside the most famous culinary magic food bank in the world, the elevator brought them into a sparse hotel lobby. It was brightly lit and completely devoid of people. The air smelled a little stale, like the place had been closed and vacant for some time.

"Polly's boutique hotel," Chef Levy explained, putting her duffle down on a glass coffee table. "Volunteers who came to help out at the food bank were required to spend a minimum of two nights here." Her mouth twisted in disgust. "The proceeds supposedly went directly to the food bank."

"Where did they actually go?" Kenzie asked.

"Diamonds and top-shelf liquor," Chef Levy replied tersely. A bitter smile curved the corners of her lips. "I called in a few favors and started a rumor that this place is full of asbestos. Between that and Polly's estate being locked up in legal trivialities, we should be safe here for a while."

"Rosemary is tired," Rosemary announced. She was holding Kiwi's habitat and leaned down so she could press her lips to the glass next to the reptile's face. Kiwi didn't look impressed.

"You and you," Chef Levy pointed to Rosemary and Aralia. "Bring our bags up to the rooms." She reached behind the check-in desk, grabbed keys, and tossed them to Aralia.

"I'm not a bellhop," Aralia grumbled, but even she wasn't brave or foolish enough to put up more of a challenge beyond that.

Chef Levy might have been shorter than anyone else in their group, except maybe Kenzie, but what she lacked in size she made up for in her intimidation factor. Her spiky hair, straight nose, suspicious glare, and commanding presence combined for one hell of a mess-with-me-at-your-peril attitude.

"You and you." Chef Levy indicated Kenzie and Braxton. "With me."

"Aye aye, Captain," Kenzie muttered.

"I can't," Braxton said.

Chef Levy turned slowly and gave him her one eyebrow raise that would have turned a lesser man into stone. Braxton held firm.

"My sister's in Rikers," he said. "I have to get her out."

"We have bigger problems than your sister, McKaid," Chef Levy said.

"Respectfully disagree, Chef," Braxton shot back, not at all respectfully. "And I'm not asking for permission. I just need—"

"Come," Chef Levy barked.

Her angry footsteps stomped puffs of dust from the floor as she strode down the hall. She didn't wait to see whether he and Kenzie would follow, seeming certain they would.

"Let's just see what she's up to," Kenzie whispered anxiously. "Then I'll help you figure out what to do about Sofia. Promise."

Braxton was about to argue, but then he made the mistake of looking into Kenzie's pleading, gunmetal gray eyes. There were a dozen emotions there that she made no effort to hide. Sighing, Braxton reached out with his thumb to smooth the little crease of worry that had formed between her eyebrows.

"Fine," he relented, and then had to stop himself from leaning in to kiss the relieved smile that broke out across her cherry-red lips.

They followed Chef Levy to the end of the hallway to a door that opened automatically. The three of them stepped into the food bank that had been Polly's pride and joy. Or at least her ticket into the culinary magic socialite scene.

Unlike the slightly-unkempt atmosphere of the hotel, this room looked more like a ballroom than a food bank. The floors were polished wood. Bright pink wallpaper was dotted with pastel-blue cupcakes. There were no windows, but velvet drapes hung over enormous portraits of Polly in various ball gowns and posing with baked goods. Not one, but three gaudy crystal chandeliers hung from the ceiling.

Circular tables covered with pink-lace tablecloths bordered the room. Instead of flowers or candles as the centerpieces, each table had a towering cake sculpture made out of solid gold.

"Well, this is…exactly what I would have expected from Polly," Kenzie said with a grimace.

"Indeed," Chef Levy replied. "Like unicorn puke."

Braxton snorted.

"This food bank did service some needy families," Chef Levy acknowledged, "but its main function was holding upscale dinners for Polly's ritzy friends. Hence the décor."

"Wow, about time you all decided to show up," someone called.

Braxton tensed, not having realized anyone else was in the room. Two people sitting at the far end of the room stood and started toward them.

"Is that—" Kenzie began.

Philippe, Braxton's former Hex Kitchen competitor and friend, jogged across the room and caught Kenzie up in a bear hug.

Philippe looked mostly the same as the last time Braxton had seen him, although his wild hair and beard had been tamed a bit. And a new platinum wedding band stood out against his dark mahogany skin.

"Ohmygosh!" Kenzie squealed, when she caught sight of Raina, Philippe's girlfriend. Raina's arms were tucked protectively around an infant. "You had the baby!"

A few seconds later, they were all tangled together in a laughing, hugging pile. Braxton hung back, unable to drum up even a fraction of the enthusiasm appropriate given the situation.

The last time Braxton had seen Philippe, it was after Hiroto had been killed. Philippe had taken part in Hiroto's death. Even though Rick had threatened to kill Raina if Philippe didn't do whatever he was told, Braxton still couldn't forgive him.

"What are they doing here, Chef?" Braxton murmured to Chef Levy, who stood beside him and seemed utterly unsurprised by Philippe and Raina's appearance.

"Look around, McKaid," Chef Levy said, motioning to the empty room. "You see people lining up to help us take on the Gourmands?"

"I haven't exactly been asking around," Braxton replied, giving her attitude right back to her.

"Well, I have," Chef Levy retorted. "And all I got for my time was a bunch of *fuck you's*. Except from them." She gestured to Philippe and Raina.

Braxton found that difficult to believe. Philippe hadn't been willing to go up against Rick when he'd been nothing more than a powerful mobster. Now, Rick was the Gourmand leader. And it was clear Philippe had even more to lose now than he had back in Hex Kitchen.

Finally separating from Kenzie, a smiling Raina came over to Braxton and stretched up on her toes to kiss Braxton on both cheeks.

"So good to see you, Braxton," she said in a heavy French accent. "Glad we could be here."

"Good to see you too, Raina," Braxton said, feeling himself soften. "And congratulations." He nodded to the baby, who was babbling happily and squeezing his chubby fist around his mother's finger.

The baby had dark skin like both of his parents, as well as a cap of black fuzz covering his tiny head. His brown eyes were wide and expressive. When he smiled, he sported dimples just like Raina. He was wearing a onesie that said *Culinary magician in training*.

"Did you have to bring the infant?" Chef Levy grumbled.

"We considered leaving him behind." Raina grinned at Chef Levy. "But he hasn't quite learned how to change his own diaper, yet."

"Pity," Chef Levy replied.

"But he does know how to make a mean Coq au Vin," Philippe said, beaming with fatherly pride.

"Seriously?" Kenzie said.

"No." Raina laughed as she shook her head. "Philippe just puts the spoon in Hiroto's hand and moves it around so they both think—"

"Hiroto?" Braxton interrupted. "You named your baby…Hiroto?" He didn't speak loudly, but everyone else went silent. Even the baby stopped gurgling.

Philippe and Raina exchanged a nervous glance.

"Let's talk over here," Philippe muttered, gesturing to the kitchen area, which was partitioned off from the dining room by a wall of glass.

Braxton stomped after him, mind still reeling. He could feel Kenzie's disapproving gaze and Chef Levy's impatient one burrowing into his back, but he ignored both. Fury pulsed through his blood.

As soon as they were alone, hidden from view by a stainless-steel fridge, Braxton faced Philippe.

"Not to be rude or anything, mate," Braxton said, "but are you out of your fucking mind?"

Philippe tugged on his collar as though it were strangling him.

"I know you're still mad about what happened at Hex," he began.

Braxton laughed humorlessly. "You betrayed Hiroto…the real one…and got him killed," he seethed. "And then you had the nerve to name your baby after him? Who does that?!"

Philippe pulled at his collar again and then started to fidget with the buttons on his cuffs.

"Raina and I wanted to do something to honor Hiroto's memory," he said, looking down at his shirt. "Naming our baby after him was just the start of it." He stopped fiddling with his shirt and looked up at Braxton. "We realized Hiroto would want us to live the best version of our lives. So, that's what we're doing. We got married. We're saving up to open our own farm-to-table restaurant. And now we're here." He waved a hand at the empty room. "You think I wanted to bring my wife and our baby to this sorry excuse for a rebellion?"

"Then why did you?" Braxton shot back.

"Because Chef Levy said you needed help," Philippe replied. "And it's what Hiroto would have done."

Braxton could feel his head beginning to throb.

"This is so fucked up," Braxton muttered.

"You know what?" Philippe leaned forward, jabbing a finger into Braxton's chest. "I'm not going to stand here and defend myself for protecting Raina, when I know you would have done the same damn thing for Kenzie. And furthermore—"

"Stud!" Aralia shouted from the other room. "Get in here."

"Now," Chef Levy commanded, when Braxton didn't immediately comply.

Braxton and Philippe exchanged a glare before returning to the others, who were crowded around a large, flat-screen TV tucked between two portraits.

"We're here in Times Square," a reporter on the screen was saying, "and—"

The microphone was wrenched out of her hand. The camera wobbled slightly and then focused on the person now in control of the microphone. Rick Santiori.

"Thank you, Amber," Rick said with his trademark smirk.

"Is it just me," Kenzie said, "or is his suit a little much?"

Rick was wearing a plum three-piece suit, complete with a folded pocket square. It swallowed him, suggesting that it might have been his father's.

Rick's brown hair was slicked back, and his pointy chin was raised in full douche pose. Excitement glittered in his beady eyes.

"I've got a treat for all of your viewers today," Rick drawled.

Braxton had no idea where Rick was going with this, but he could feel his muscles seizing up. Anything that had Rick this excited couldn't possibly be good news.

"Mr. Santiori, please," a voice said off-camera.

Kenzie made a distressed little sound as the frame panned to include Benedict Vandermeer, the former leader of the Gourmands. He was leaning on his cane, and looked paler and more drawn than the last time Braxton had seen him. His goatee was also less pristine and more salt than pepper.

Without taking his gaze off the TV, Braxton moved close enough to Kenzie that he could rest his hand at the small of her back. He still didn't know everything that had happened to her during Cutthroat Cuisine, but the expression on her face made Braxton want to forget about everything except for warping straight to Benedict Vandermeer. He wanted to strangle the man with his bare hands.

Rick swatted at Benedict the way he might a troublesome fly. He reached into his coat pocket and drew out a brown envelope.

Braxton's heart turned to stone and plummeted all the way to his toes. That envelope looked just like the ones that held the Reaper's magical ingredients. The ingredients Rick had stolen from Sofia.

"I'm here today to reveal a secret that's been kept from the world for centuries," Rick said. He slowly slid his finger under the envelope's seal.

"What secret are you referring to?" the reporter asked, making a feeble attempt to reclaim control of the interview.

"Magic." Rick said the word in a hushed voice and waggled his eyebrows.

He overturned the envelope.

The camera zoomed in on the corn kernels that fell out of the envelope and onto his palm. Rick tossed the kernels into the air. Between one blink and the next, the kernels transformed into solid gold bars.

The bars hit the pavement with resounding *thunks.*

Rick grinned at the camera, which panned around to show a gathering crowd.

"Just in case you think this is some kind of trick," Rick said, reaching into his jacket pocket and taking out another envelope, "I'm going to prove it isn't."

This time, he removed a single, shriveled spinach leaf from the packet and put it in his mouth. He chewed. Swallowed.

"I suggest everyone get out of the way," he said in an ominous tone.

With another smirk at the camera, Rick rested his palm on an empty bus parked next to him. He gave the bus a little shove.

There was a screeching sound. The bus scraped sideways across the pavement, its tires tearing up ribbons of asphalt.

The bus skidded into a building—empty, thank Christ—and kept going. The vehicle crashed right through the wall.

Glass shattered. People on the sidewalk screamed as they threw themselves out of the bus's path.

Kenzie grabbed Braxton's shirt as they watched the bus hurtle toward a baby carriage. They all released a breath of relief as a woman on the street yanked the baby out of the carriage before the bus plowed into it.

A second later, the bus came to a smoking, squealing stop against a concrete pillar.

"Oh my *God!*" the reporter shouted. "Did you see that? Dear God. My heart." She clutched at her chest.

The on-screen image was bouncing all over the place as the cameraman and reporter ran over to assess the damage. Onlookers were shouting. Sirens had started to blare.

Inside the food bank, everyone had gone completely silent. Braxton imagined that, like him, they were all trying to wrap their heads around the shit storm Rick had stirred up with his little magical demonstration. Even with the shoddy camera work, the Vanillas' reactions were plain as day.

They weren't awed or inspired. They were fucking terrified.

A firetruck appeared onscreen and began blasting the bus, which had become nothing more than a hunk of twisted metal.

"Those are Sofia's ingredients," Braxton said, his voice unsteady from the pent-up rage that had nowhere to go.

"Which Graham told her not to bring to Tennessee," Aralia unhelpfully pointed out.

"For centuries, we have been forced to hide our magic from the world," Rick said into his microphone. "My predecessors believed culinary magic should be hoarded and suppressed. I, on the other hand, think it should be celebrated." He threw his shoulders back and looked straight into the camera. "Which is why I'm hosting a culinary magic exhibition in Times Square on Saturday. Anyone's welcome. Culinary magicians—bring your ingredients, and more importantly, your magic. Let's give the world a show they'll never forget."

Right before Chef Levy clicked off the TV, the camera panned to Benedict. He was staring at Rick with an expression of utter horror. There was too much noise from the people who were fighting each other to reach the gold bars on the ground for Benedict's words to be audible, but Braxton could read them on his lips.

What have you done?

CHAPTER 3

SOFIA

en. Are. Pigs.

*M*Sofia was shuffled down yet another hallway that stank of urine and worse. The mud-brown jumpsuit she wore itched and smelled like BO. Not hers, obviously. And she was wearing plastic flip-flops. With socks.

Oh, the indignity.

"Eh, bab-ay!" a prisoner shouted, sticking his hand out of his food slot and banging on the metal. "You lookin' fi-iiine."

Sofia had assumed that, by wearing Graham's body, she'd be safe from sexual harassment. Not so much. It would seem she wasn't the only one who found Graham attractive.

She could imagine telling him about it—could almost see him itching the back of his neck the way he did when he got embarrassed. She felt her lips curving into a smile without her consent and quickly schooled her expression.

Don't be ridiculous, Sofia chided herself. Firstly, she was in jail and unlikely to cross paths with Graham anytime soon. Secondly, even if they did cross paths, he wouldn't want anything to do with her. She'd led him to the cops. She'd betrayed him.

And now you're paying the price.

Be the Robot, Sofia counseled herself. There was no sense in moaning about past errors she couldn't take back. All she could do now was keep moving.

"Come on." A sharp jab in Sofia's back made her shuffle forward. She almost tripped over the chains around her ankles.

She let out a pained *oof* as her shoulder struck the metallic edge of a doorway, and then hissed out a curse as her forehead knocked into the top of the frame.

"Watch it," her escort said, about four seconds too late.

Sofia tried to rub her throbbing temple before remembering her wrists were shackled together. The magical pea soup she'd drunk the previous day had transformed her body into Graham's, and she kept forgetting how big he was.

Sofia could feel strength coiled in her solid calves and hard-as-rocks biceps. As men behind their cell doors jeered and cursed at her, it was a comfort to remember that she wore Graham's skin like armor.

Doors buzzed open just long enough to allow her and her entourage to pass through. Around every corner, there were correction officers with stun guns, pepper spray, and truncheons.

Sofia noted every turn, every guard, every camera.

She'd done as much research as she could before getting arrested, but the no-cameras rule inside the jail meant the Internet didn't offer much in the way of preplanned escape routes.

"In here, Malyung," the correction officer said. "Malyung!"

Oh, right. That's me.

Graham Malyung. 26 years of age. African-American mother, Caucasian father. Accused of murdering both parents in their own home before fleeing.

The correction officer led Sofia-as-Graham into a cramped office. The CO connected Sofia's handcuffs to a metal ring on the wall.

"This is Graham Malyung, Warden Smith," the CO said, addressing a military-looking man sitting behind a desk strewn with papers. "He requested to speak with you."

The man behind the desk stood. Disregarding Sofia, he glared at the CO. "And we're just granting prisoners' requests now, are we?"

"No, Sir, we aren't." A puzzled expression came over the guard's face. His eyes were glazed, the same way they'd been ever since he ate a bite of the sugar cookie Kenzie had given Sofia before she left the cabin. The CO shook his head, as though trying to clear it.

Sofia fumbled with her bound hands and managed to extract the last piece of sugar cookie she'd been hiding in the cuff of her jumpsuit.

"Give this to Warden Smith," Sofia said to the guard, holding out the cookie. She startled at the deep timbre that came out of her throat. She still wasn't used to hearing Graham's smoky voice instead of her own.

While the CO and the warden exchanged words, Sofia caught a glance of her reflection in a chrome sculpture hanging on the wall. Sofia's heart gave a small, absurd leap as Graham's whiskey-rimmed eyes stared back at her. She could see his light dusting of freckles, which she'd once traced with her fingertips between brain-melting kisses. His close-shaved dark hair, corded muscles, and thick eyebrows made him the sexiest man she'd ever seen.

"Greg, what ya doing?" the warden demanded as the guard strode up to him.

With a muttered apology, the CO stuffed the crumbly bite of cookie into the warden's mouth.

Sofia watched with satisfaction as the warden closed his eyes and made a contented *Mmm* sound. When he blinked, his eyes were ever-so-slightly glazed.

"What can I do for you, Mr. Malyung?" the warden asked.

Thank you, Kenzie.

"I would like my assigned job to be in the jail kitchen," she said.

The magical pea soup that had turned her into Graham was supposed to last about a week. Sofia had no intention of being in this hellhole for that long, but her situation was precarious. The whole point of this venture was to make sure the real Graham Malyung would be able to live the rest of his life without fearing retribution from the authorities. That meant Sofia couldn't simply escape.

She had a plan for getting out of here *and* making sure Graham stayed free, but she wasn't entirely sure she'd be able to pull it off. Regardless, whatever she ended up doing, it would involve magic. And that would require ingredients and a kitchen.

"Is there anything else I can do for you, Mr. Malyung?" the warden asked. He licked his lips in search of any stray cookie crumbs.

"As a matter of fact, yes," Sofia replied. "I want my cellmate to be Walter Ashner."

* * *

Sofia felt strangely naked now that the sugar cookie Kenzie had given her was gone. From here on out, she had only her own magic to rely on.

Well, it wasn't really her magic. It was the magic Kenzie had gifted her. Sofia could feel it, rattling around inside her, like a transplanted organ…something the rest of her body was fighting to reject.

She'd expected it to feel like it had when she'd used Qiang Lee's magical ingredients: energizing and powerful. Instead, Sofia felt unsettled and, honestly, a little nauseous. Or maybe that reaction was just a consequence of her current residence.

Sofia was led through more locked doors and past more shouting inmates. She knew they were nearing their destination when an offending stink of low-grade cafeteria food assaulted her nostrils.

Sofia was herded into a puce-colored kitchen. The metal countertops were stained with grease remnants. At least, she hoped those were grease stains.

It was a good thing Sofia had taken her brother's place here, because if Braxton saw the state of this kitchen, he'd probably have a heart attack on the spot.

Vats of mystery meat bubbled away in canned tomato sauce that made a frightful glugging sound. Sofia lamented that her hair was going to stink like this kitchen for weeks, before she remembered that she didn't have long hair anymore.

Prisoners stood on both sides of a long metal table, chopping vegetables with rubber knives bolted to the counter. Most of the inmates didn't so much as glance at Sofia as a CO parked her in front of a rusted sink filled with dirty dishes.

Her handcuffs were removed, and with a cursory order to *stay in your lane*, her guard retreated inside a fortified box in the center of the kitchen.

Sofia looked around, surveying her new…domain.

Ugh.

She started forward and knocked her head into a low-hanging range hood.

"Son of a bitch," she growled.

"You talkin' to me?" an inmate barked in the heaviest New York accent Sofia had ever heard.

And people said Aussies talked weird.

The inmate stood over a giant, metallic vat of something that vaguely resembled meatballs…in shape, if not smell. He raised his rubber soup ladle in a menacing gesture.

"No," Sofia grumbled, reaching up to rub her head. This was becoming a height discrimination issue. Maybe she should file a complaint.

"The fuck you look' at?" the inmate demanded, clearly itching for a fight.

"Nothing," Sofia replied. "I'm here to work."

She made eye contact with the bloke, letting him know she wasn't intimidated. She also flexed her courtesy-of-Graham biceps.

"Big shot, eh?" The bloke chortled. "Maybe I'll teach ya a lesson."

This was not off to a promising start. Sofia looked around, just in case she needed a quick escape. Or a weapon.

"Who's learnin' a lesson?" a different voice asked.

A skinny inmate with an ugly scar down the side of his neck poked his head around the corner. The smile he gave Sofia wasn't at all encouraging.

"I don't want any trouble," Sofia said, backing up a few steps until she hit the wall.

"Boy, you sure do talk a lot," the first man said. "Don't he, Lars?"

The second one—Lars—nodded.

Two more prisoners came over from their work stations, their jail-issued sandals almost silent against the tiled floor.

"Someone givin' you trouble, Murphy?"

"Just some fish." The first man smiled at Sofia, displaying a mouthful of gold teeth.

"Leave me alone," Sofia said with a calm control she definitely wasn't feeling.

"You hear this mother fucker?"

The men laughed as they closed in around her.

An overhead speaker system sputtered to life.

"Get back to your stations!" a CO ordered.

The semi-circle of men around Sofia didn't obey. They moved closer.

"Stay away from me," Sofia said.

Graham's voice cracked as it came out of her throat. If she'd been in her own body, it would have squeaked. Her prison uniform clung to her as sweat gathered on her skin.

"This one definitely needs a lesson," Murphy decided. His gold teeth flashed. Then, he pounced.

Sofia didn't have a chance to react before she felt her legs being kicked out from under her. She hit the ground so hard a tile broke beneath her skull.

Thank God Graham had a hard head.

Sofia thrust out wildly, landing a lucky punch in someone's groin.

"You're a dead man, fish!" Lars shrieked.

Sofia felt herself hauled off the floor.

Do something! she ordered herself. If she got shanked, Braxton would be so pissed.

She struck out with her fists, landing a blow in one man's stomach and across another's cheek.

Damn, Graham was strong.

If she'd been in her own body, her half-punches wouldn't even slow these men down. But with Graham's weight and muscles, she was kicking arse. Literally.

She lost a sandal, but managed to send one of her attackers sailing into the vat of meatballs.

"Get back to your stations!" a guard roared.

Sofia crouched down as all her instincts fired on high alert. She didn't so much as blink as an inmate barreled toward her. Something glinted in his closed fist.

Shit.

Sofia twisted to the side, managing to avoid the worst of the pointy, metallic object that would have gone right into her chest. She heard fabric tear. Heat bloomed across her ribcage. Sofia spun and kicked the man in his kneecap.

Crack.

She experienced a wave of satisfaction when she felt the give of bone, followed by the man's shriek of pain.

It was possible Sofia had a touch of sociopathy in her.

"Disperse!" a voice shouted over the loudspeakers. "Disperse!"

Alarms were blaring. Smoke started to fill the kitchen.

Sofia's eyes and throat began to burn from the smoke. She retched as the smoke invaded her lungs, making it impossible to breathe.

She struck out blindly, her fists making contact with flesh and hard bone as the other prisoners continued to come for her. All around, she heard shouts. The whistling alarm was making her head pound.

Someone grabbed her from behind. Sofia snapped her head back as hard as she could.

She couldn't breathe. Holy shit. She couldn't breathe.

She kept coughing and coughing, but no air would come into her lungs.

"Come on," a choked voice said.

Someone grabbed her arm. Sofia jerked up with her elbow, smashing her attacker in the face. He collapsed on the floor.

Through the smoke, she saw that the man she'd just punched in the eye was elderly.

Oops.

Sofia found herself surrounded again. This time, though, it wasn't a group of inmates. A vicious blow landed on her lower back as a CO shoved her against the wall. He was screaming in her ear to stand down as he wrenched her arms behind her back. The man used enough force to bring tears to Sofia's eyes.

She gasped and wheezed as she forced tiny streams of air into her starved lungs. Next to her, one of the guards was helping the old man to his feet.

Sofia found herself with her face pressed to the wall, her arms pinned behind her back as her cuffs were locked in place. The old man was next to her in a similar position.

"You shouldn't have hit me," the old man wheezed. His voice was low, but he somehow managed to pack more threat into it than all the blokes who had come at her shouting their heads off.

Sofia was relieved when she was dragged out of the kitchen and marched back through the prison's hallways. Sofia was too busy trying to breathe to notice anything else, until she was slammed into a tiny cell with bunk beds, a dirty sink, and dirtier toilet. She turned around in time to see the old man who'd threatened her being shoved in behind her.

"Wait a second," Sofia said. "This is a mistake. I'm supposed to be rooming with Walter Ashner."

"Yep." The guard gave her an evil smile. "So you are." To the old man, the guard said, "Give this fish hell, Walt."

The guard backed out of the cell. The door slammed shut with a resounding clang.

CHAPTER 4

GRAHAM

Graham crouched behind the dumpster, willing himself to melt into the shadows. He scratched at the two days' worth of beard growth on his cheek, wondering when he'd get to shower again. Probably when he got caught and dragged off to prison.

He needed to call Aralia and tell her he was alive before she went on a killing rampage. He needed food and water.

The issue was that he didn't have a phone or so much as a dime in his pocket. He was a six-foot-three man who happened to be a wanted criminal…so going up to random strangers and asking for help wasn't exactly an option.

He watched another car pull up to the gas pump. This one had an elderly couple, both of whom got out and went into the mini-mart. It looked like they'd even left the keys in the ignition.

This was what Graham had been waiting for, but he couldn't bring himself to steal from old people. Not yet, anyway.

His stomach growled so loudly he was surprised the people inside the mini-mart didn't hear it.

Somewhere down the street, a siren began to wail.

Sweat gathered under Graham's arms. The collar of his sweatshirt began to choke him.

He had to get out of here, but his legs had turned to rubber. He couldn't move.

Graham tugged up the hood of his sweatshirt to hide his face. He tried to burrow deeper into the fabric to shield his identity and give himself some breathing room. It didn't help. He was suffocating.

A strangled sound he didn't recognize came out of his own throat. His ankles gave out on him. He collapsed in an oily puddle next to a bag of rotting garbage.

The sirens were coming closer.

Graham's vision started to flicker out. Another sound was added to the siren. Graham heard his father's rumbling laughter.

Bile rose from his stomach and burned his throat.

"I've had enough of your shit," a harsh voice said, cutting through the sirens and laughter.

Graham gasped in a lungful of air as his senses returned. The sirens faded away until they disappeared altogether.

Still sweating and trembling, Graham used the lip of the dumpster to haul himself to his knees. The old couple had driven away and been replaced by a rusty old truck. A man in grease-stained overalls and a very pregnant woman were leaning against the truck and shouting at each other.

"You hear me, S'mantha?" the man slurred, taking a stumbling step toward the woman and jabbing a finger in her face.

"Fuck you, Mike," she shouted back.

A slap rang out, although Graham couldn't tell from his position behind the dumpster who had hit who.

The two of them continued to berate each other as they headed for the mini-mart.

Graham waited until he could no longer hear the sound of their arguing. Then, keeping his hood pulled high over his head and his face turned away from the security cameras, he walked quickly to the truck.

The doors were unlocked and the keys were in the cupholder. The gas tank was full, and there was even a fifty-dollar bill and half-bottle of water scattered among the empty beer cans.

Graham guzzled the water as he made his escape as fast as he could without drawing attention.

Once he was on the highway and his adrenaline started to wear off, it occurred to him that he had no destination.

He couldn't go back to the cabin and risk leading the cops back to Aralia. He might be the one who had murdered his parents, but if Aralia were caught hiding him, she'd become his accomplice.

Besides, even if going back to the cabin wouldn't put Aralia in danger, it would bring him face-to-face with the one person he wasn't sure he could ever bear to see again. Sofia McKaid.

Sofia. The most incredible woman he'd ever met. The woman he'd believed wanted him as much as he wanted her.

You're a goddamn fool, his father's hateful voice said in the back of Graham's mind. *Why would someone like her even look twice at someone like you?*

Graham kept driving. He'd drive forever if it meant he could get Sofia's beautiful face and his father's awful voice out of his head.

He headed north, figuring he'd just drive until his strength gave out. Minutes blurred into hours. He stopped only to refuel and then kept right on going. His eyes felt gritty and his mouth was dry as sandpaper. He was looking for somewhere he could pull over and rest when he saw a sign for Acadia National Park in Maine. Before even processing the decision, he took the exit.

For better or worse, he had a destination.

CHAPTER 5

SOFIA

Sofia was standing next to Walter Ashner in the jail kitchen as they both prepared a heap of vegetables for lunch. Well, Walter was prepping the vegetables. Sofia was mostly just standing in front of her station and pretending to chop vegetables.

She was cranky. She'd spent the night in a tiny cell that was not made with Graham's bulky frame in mind. And she'd undergone a communal shower situation that was as unpleasant as movies made it seem. Now, she was back in the smelly kitchen.

At least she'd managed to avoid being murdered on her first night by her cellmate…who also happened to be the man she was supposed to break out of this hellhole. The man who also had a serious shiner on his left eye courtesy of Sofia's right-hook.

The two of them had come to an understanding once Sofia revealed that she knew Kenzie. After that, they'd gotten along just fine. Or as fine as two people stuck in Rikers Island could. They'd spent the rest of the night discussing Sofia's admittedly precarious escape plan.

"Let me get this straight," Walter said as he used a knife bolted to the counter to slice his way through a pile of raw carrots. "My daughter gave you the ability to perform magic. On food."

"We call it culinary magic," she explained. "Those who are born with the ability can infuse power into certain recipes to produce magic. There are also magical ingredients, which carry their own inherent power and don't need the chef to do anything."

Blood rushed to Sofia's head as she thought about the crates of magical ingredients she'd had and lost to Rick Santiori.

She steadied her breathing before she succumbed to her urge to run screaming through the nearest wall…cinderblocks be damned.

"Your daughter is especially…special," Sofia continued. "She's a Culinarian, which means she can bestow culinary magic on others, as well as take it away. She's the only one of her kind."

Sofia tried to will away the thrum of jealousy that surged through her. It just wasn't fair that Kenzie should have so much power when Sofia had been born with none at all.

Sofia scratched the back of her neck, realizing after the fact that it was a distinctly Graham-like gesture. She let her arms fall to her sides.

"There's also a superfood recipe," Sofia forged on, not even sure why she was telling Walter all of this. From the glazed expression on his face, she'd lost him back somewhere around *Culinarian*. "The superfood is a recipe that can allow any culinary magician to do what your daughter does, if they have the recipe."

Thus far, Rosemary and Benedict Vandermeer were the only non-Culinarian people alive who had ever had possession of the recipe. Now that Benedict's only copy of the superfood recipe had been burned to ashes, Rosemary's mind—or more so her song—was the sole record of the recipe. If Chef Levy got her way, Rosemary would die, and the superfood recipe would die with her.

"I'd like to believe you," Walter said. "But the truth is, this all sounds a little far-fetched." He reached under his glasses to rub the bridge of his nose.

Sofia took the opportunity to glance at Walter's profile.

As far as Sofia could tell, he shared more personality traits with his daughter than physical ones. Unlike Kenzie's stunning black hair, gray eyes, and flawless skin, Walter would sooner melt into a crowd than turn heads for his appearance.

He wasn't fat, but his entire body lacked definition. His skin had a yellowish tinge, probably from too much time spent indoors. Between the wrinkles around his eyes and mouth, a sizeable bald spot, and glasses he wore perched diagonally across his nose, Walter looked like an old man. Either he'd had Kenzie late in life, or jail had seriously taken its toll on him.

Then again, after everything he'd been through, Sofia supposed Walter was in remarkably good condition.

"And you're telling me that you're not really a man?" Walter asked out of the corner of his mouth. His knife was a blur as perfect, coin-sized chunks of carrot piled up on his board. If Sofia tried to do that, she'd probably slice off her fingers. Even with these blunt knives.

"Correct," Sofia said. "Which brings me to the part that requires your help. I'm going to need some unsupervised time to cook a magical recipe." She glanced pointedly at the other prisoners and barred-off section where the guards observed their every move. "As soon as I start cooking more magic, this," she gestured to her body, "is going to go back to normal."

Walter's eyes widened behind his glasses. "The last time my daughter and I spoke, Kenzie mentioned that strange things were happening. I'm just finding it difficult to wrap my head around all of this." His gaze darted away from her, making it clear he was more than a little skeptical. Not that Sofia could blame him.

A buzzer sounded nearby, startling Sofia. She turned, whacking her head on a metal exhaust hood.

Damn Graham for being so tall.

"Alright?" Walter asked, his brow wrinkling in concern.

"Fine." Sofia scowled as she rubbed her head, which was definitely going to have a bump.

The overhead loudspeaker crackled to life. "Malyung," the guard in the cage barked. "Get to work."

Sofia fumbled for one of the knives and started hacking at an onion. Beside her, Walter cringed.

"Might want to peel that first," he suggested.

Oh. Right.

"Am I supposed to call you Sofia or Graham?" Walter gave her an apologetic half-smile. "I really would like to believe you. It's just…."

"Call me Graham," Sofia told him. The last thing she needed was for the other prisoners to hear someone calling her by a girl's name. Talk about a reputational hazard.

Walter nodded. "Alright, then. I can't say I'm completely on board with everything you've told me, but if you really are a friend of Kenzie's, I'll do whatever I can to help you."

Sofia swallowed the first sarcastic response that rose to the tip of her tongue. If their roles were reversed, she wouldn't believe a word she was saying, either.

"Can I ask you something?" Walter asked, smoothly sweeping several onions out of her pile and into his. "Why are you doing all of this? I mean, it seems like an awful lot of trouble." He gave her a wry smile. "And I'm not presumptuous enough to think rescuing me was your primary objective."

Sofia didn't know what it was about this man. She was supposed to hate him—had hated him for the last five years. But there was a kindness in his eyes that made her want to trust him.

And Sofia didn't trust anyone.

Without her consent, the weight of all the thoughts Sofia had been suppressing bubbled to the surface. She had to tell someone. She glanced around, just to make sure no one was eavesdropping.

There was one other prisoner standing nearby, but he seemed fully focused on a murky vat of what might have been baked beans.

"This bloke." She motioned to her body, which was the spitting image of Graham's. "We were…close."

Sofia tried not to remember his small kindnesses, and the way he'd held her when they kissed, and the trust that had shined in his eyes when she asked him to go for a drive….

And then the pain when he realized she'd betrayed him.

Be the Robot, Sofia.

She relayed a quick version of what had happened. All the while, Walter continued methodically slicing vegetables. He gave her little nods and made encouraging sounds whenever she stopped to catch her breath. Every time she told herself to stop talking, the story continued to pour out of her.

"And then I hurt him," Sofia finished. Her voice broke a little. Hearing her confession spoken in Graham's voice somehow made everything worse.

"There's nothing in the world that's worse than hurting someone you love," Walter said.

"I don't love him," Sofia sputtered.

Walter gave her a knowing smile and went back to his onions. "Assuming you aren't pulling my leg," he said, "this is a very brave thing you're doing."

It wasn't bravery. It was making sure her reckless, honorable brother didn't have to pay for her fuck-up. And it was penance for betraying Graham.

"Anyway." Sofia pulled another onion toward her and half-heartedly started chopping it. This emotional chitchat was liable to give her hives. "You'll need to do something to clear the kitchen for half an hour."

Walter made an incredulous sound. "How on Earth do you expect me to pull that off?" He motioned with his chin at the guard cage and the dozen-or-so other prisoners who were working in the kitchen.

"I don't know." Sofia waved her knife. "Pay off a guard? Make a few pointed threats?"

Walter chuckled. "This isn't television, you know."

"So, you're saying you can't do it?"

Sofia felt the beginnings of panic sink their talons into her. She wouldn't be able to put her plan in action without some private cooking time.

Walter opened his mouth but didn't have a chance to speak.

"I might be able to help with that."

Sofia whipped her head around at the new voice.

The baked beans bloke had somehow sidled closer without Sofia or Walter noticing. There was an evil smirk on his face.

The man was almost as big and muscular as Graham. His chin-length hair was artfully-tousled. Unlike Walter's sallow appearance, this man could have just come off a week on the beach with his tan skin and days-old stubble. He had a cleft chin and cheekbones that looked sharp enough to cut stone.

The bloke gave Sofia's body a long, lazy perusal. It wasn't unfamiliar—Sofia was used to men checking her out. Except the assets that normally drew men to her—the blonde hair, long legs, boobs—were gone. She looked like Graham.

"Leave him alone, Zack," Walter said.

Zack met Sofia's gaze, held it, and ran his tongue along his top lip in an unmistakable invitation.

"Couldn't help but overhear something about cooking up an escape," Zack said, his gaze darting to the guard station before sidling closer.

Shit.

"Didn't know there were any other culinary magicians in here," Zack continued.

Sofia jerked at that. "You're a—"

"Shh," Zack said, giving her a wicked smile. "Never know who'll overhear you in this place."

Walter looked from Zack to Sofia with an expression of mild shock. His grip faltered, and an onion went skittering across the counter. Walter didn't even notice.

"You believe you're a magician, too?" Walter asked Zack.

"A *culinary* magician," Sofia corrected automatically, even though Walter's skepticism was the least of her worries. The prickling sensation at the back of her neck confirmed what she'd known from her first glimpse of this man: Zack was trouble.

"I'm not very good at keeping secrets," Zack said. He cocked an eyebrow and flicked his hair in a move that oozed sensual confidence.

Sofia could only imagine how many broken hearts—of both genders—this man had left in his wake.

"Try," Sofia said stiffly.

"Aww, baby," Zack said in a seductive purr. "You could make me be quiet." Zack did something suggestive and complicated with his tongue.

Oh, hell.

This whole encounter would be complicated enough without the unwanted come-on. To make matters weirder, this man wasn't hitting on her…he was hitting on Graham.

When had her life gotten so bloody complicated?

"First off, I don't actually have a dick," Sofia informed him. Well, technically she did, since the pea soup had transformed her entire body. But she had been trying really hard not to think about—or look at—those parts. "It's just magic that's making me look like I do."

Surprise flashed across Zack's handsome face, followed by revulsion. Sofia almost laughed.

"In that case, offer rescinded," Zack said, moving back to the baked beans. He tilted his head toward her. "At least the sex part. I'm still escaping with you."

How wonderful. Thanks so *much for that clarification.*

"Better decide quick." Zack flicked his hair and somehow managed to indicate the guard cage in the same motion. "I'd hate to have to tell them you're—what are they calling us now—a *food witch*?"

Sofia had never heard that term before. It must be some kind of prison lingo. Regardless, this problem wasn't going away.

"Very well, Zack," Walter said, holding up a hand to stop Sofia's squawk of protest before it could leave her mouth. "You can come with us under one condition."

"Name it," Zack said immediately.

Walter slid a warning gaze to Sofia before turning his full attention on Zack. "You're going to cause a distraction that'll clear the kitchen for my friend, Graham."

"Done," Zack replied, grinning like a maniac. He winked at Sofia before going back to his baked beans, stirring them with enough vigor that brown sauce splurted out of the vat and onto the wall.

"What the hell?" Sofia hissed at Walter.

"Five years in this place has taught me a thing or two about people," Walter replied calmly, returning to his vegetables. "Sometimes, the best way to get what you want is to give someone else what they want." He gestured in the direction of Zack with his bolted-down knife.

"But how do we know we can trust him?" Sofia persisted.

"You don't have a choice, do you?" Zack said, making it clear the man had annoyingly-good hearing.

That observation would have served Sofia a lot better if she'd made it ten minutes sooner....

"I could break your jaw," Sofia countered. "Then we could see how easy it is for you to go tattling."

Zack laughed. "It takes more than some threats from a pretty boy to scare me. If you knew my cousin, you'd understand."

Sofia was about to show him just how scary her threats could be, but his words stopped her.

"Who's your cousin?"

He gave Sofia a crooked smile. "Rick Santiori."

Sofia felt her whole body go rigid. This jokester was Rick's cousin?

Just hearing that name made Sofia want to punch through the nearest wall. With Graham's strength coursing through her, she could probably do it, too.

And then she'd get mobbed by a bunch of correction officers, stun-gunned, and tossed back in her cell.

"If you're Rick's cousin," Sofia asked out of the corner of her mouth as she worked on her vegetables, "then why are you locked up in here?"

The Santioris knew enough people and had greased enough palms that they could get away with murder...literally...and never have to pay the price.

Zack chuckled. "Let's just say my cousin and I have never been close."

Those were the most reassuring words out of Zack thus far.

"Ah," Zack said, his shrewd gaze reading whatever grimace she hadn't been quick enough to hide. "I can see the feeling's mutual."

"Rick has something that belongs to me," Sofia said stiffly.

Five crates' worth of Reaper Qiang Lee's magical ingredients, to be specific.

There was probably a million questions Sofia should be asking this man. In fact, she should probably be figuring out how to tell him to fuck off without him blabbing to the COs. Instead, she asked, "When are you going to start this distraction so I can cook?"

A smile ghosted across Zack's handsome face. "No time like the present, eh?" He pulled something out of his pocket.

"Sofia!" Walter said.

The warning came too late. Sofia saw the flash of metal. And then stinging heat bloomed across her throat.

She'd allowed herself to get shanked on her second day in jail?!

She couldn't believe her death was going to be so mundane. Braxton was going to be furious.

It was her last thought before she hit the floor. She didn't feel a thing, but she heard the smack of her head against the unforgiving tiles.

Something pressed against her lips. Sofia turned her head, trying to fight the intrusion, but she couldn't move. Sticky molasses flooded her mouth, choking her.

Sofia saw blood spray in an arc as Walter's body collapsed beside her. Then, she saw nothing at all.

CHAPTER 6

KENZIE

Kenzie guzzled coffee while she stirred activated charcoal into her anti-magic lemonade with her free hand. Because she rocked multitasking when one of the activities involved drinking coffee.

The activated charcoal lemonade was her Culinarian version of the anti-superfood recipe, which Benedict had created so he could take away people's magic at a whim.

On the other side of the kitchen, Rosemary was frantically combining ingredients as she hummed her superfood song and intermittently stroked her charm necklace.

The only time Rosemary was ever truly focused was when she was cooking the superfood. From what Kenzie could tell, the woman had an almost druglike addiction to cooking the dish over and over.

Unfortunately, the recipe was also unstable to the point of having driven her a wee bit crazy.

Rosemary rummaged around in a cupboard and produced one of those insulated lunch totes that were popular back when Kenzie was in elementary school. This one was covered in dust and had a god-awful floral pattern, reaffirming that it was at least a few decades past its expiration date.

Rosemary unzipped the tote and tipped the ruby-red contents of her saucepan inside.

Kiwi sat on top of his favorite rock in his habitat, munching on some waxworms and presiding over the general bedlam with a cool confidence that Kenzie wished she possessed.

Out of the corner of her eye, Kenzie watched the giant TV screen set up in the food bank's dining room.

"…holding emergency parliament sessions to determine what to do about the food witches," a reporter said in an English accent.

"Food witches?" Kenzie snorted.

"I like it," Raina said, tucking her baby closer against her side. "It sounds less pompous than culinary magicians."

"Yeah, it sounds good now," Philippe said dubiously. "But I'm concerned about what happens when the Vanillas decide we're more of a threat than a curiosity."

Baby Hiroto was idly gumming the corner of the channel changer and giggling to himself. He was wearing a tiny T-shirt with a picture of melted cheese and the words *Bring my diapers just in queso.*

"Hopefully, Rick will be out of the picture and we'll be able to take control of the narrative before that happens," Raina replied.

"Hear, hear," Kenzie muttered, toasting Raina with her coffee mug.

It was T-minus two hours before Rick's culinary magic exhibition in Times Square, and the world was going nuts.

It was almost time to initiate Operation *Take Down Dickhead Rick.* Kenzie couldn't freaking wait.

They all returned their attention to the TV.

"Government officials are trying to find out more about the food witches," the reporter narrated. "Is it genetics? Training? A clever trick?

"There are conflicting opinions about what to do with these unique cooks."

"*Cooks?*" Philippe scoffed. "Now, I'm offended."

"In the meantime," the reporter continued. "Citizens are urged to maintain their distance until the authorities know more about these individuals. They could be…dangerous."

The breathy pause, and calculated widening of the reporter's eyes, managed to convey just how dangerous these alleged food witches were.

From the way they were being described, Kenzie half-expected to sprout fangs and a furry chest.

"Ashner," Chef Levy said, coming into the kitchen and giving Kenzie's lemonade a critical frown. "It's time we talk about what happened to you in Cutthroat Cuisine."

"W-what?" Kenzie squeaked. Her whole body flushed with intense heat, followed by intense cold. This was one conversation that could very well send her over the edge.

Braxton, who was stirring serrano peppers into a fiery sausage stew, jerked his head up at the sound of her obvious distress.

"I don't think now's the time, Chef," Braxton said, coming to Kenzie's defense.

"Now is precisely the time," Chef Levy replied in a clipped tone. "We're going up against the most powerful forces in our world with a paltry band of misfits. We need to know what we're up against."

Kenzie gulped.

Braxton had made it clear he wouldn't push her to recount her harrowing experience in the arena, and she'd been more than happy to repress the memory. Now, it seemed like her little hiatus was at an end.

Kenzie stared down into her coffee as she haltingly recounted her time in Cutthroat Cuisine, and everything she'd learned about the Gourmands' ruthlessness during her time as a prisoner.

She couldn't bring herself to look at Braxton as she described the atrocities she'd witnessed and perpetrated.

When she'd finished, Braxton was the first to break the silence.

"Fuck," he whispered. "This is my fault."

Kenzie couldn't help but laugh at that. "Your fault?" When she stole a glance at him, his expression was full of self-recrimination rather than the disgust at her she deserved.

"I should have been more specific when I ate that wish truffle," he muttered, more to himself to than to her. "I was so obsessed with saving your life that I didn't even consider how else you might need protecting." He dug his fingers into his thick hair and shook his head. "Fuck! I'm so sorry, Kenz."

A lump formed in Kenzie's throat, preventing her from speaking. She rested her head against his arm, hoping it conveyed all the things she couldn't find the words for, especially in a room full of other people.

When Braxton looked at her, his eyes were blazing with fury. "I'm going to kill them for what they did to you."

His sexy Aussie accent wrapped around Kenzie, making her feel all kinds of safe and warm and…loved.

"Good plan," Chef Levy said, her voice dripping in sarcasm. "And then, on the very slim chance you survive the ordeal, you can spend the rest of your life in prison for committing murder."

Braxton made a low growling sound in the back of his throat.

"The Gourmands took my Hanna from me, and I want revenge on them as much as anyone," Chef Levy said. "But we have to be smart. This venue is too public for any outright killing. Besides, murdering a bunch of people in broad daylight won't help convince the Vanilla population that culinary magicians aren't a threat."

"So what do you suggest?' Braxton ground out. "That we do nothing?"

"Not at all," Chef Levy replied. "We need to cut them off at the knees. That begins with taking away their best weapons: their magic, and their magical ingredients."

Chef Levy turned to Kenzie. "Talk to me about the superfood. Is it something we can use against the Gourmands?"

Kenzie shook her head slowly. "In normal culinary magicians, it can enhance the magic you already have, but the cost isn't worth it." She thought about the manic light that had come into Rosemary's eyes after she'd consumed the superfood. Her magic had zipped around her erratically, and then left her in an unconscious heap after she ate the anti-superfood. "The recipe is unstable."

All eyes turned on Rosemary, who dipped her bare finger into a hot pan and yelped as the liquid burned her.

"Enough said," Braxton muttered.

"We need to kill her before she falls into the wrong hands," Chef Levy observed, still watching Rosemary.

"No, no, and no," Kenzie replied. "You're not killing Rosemary."

Sheesh. She was feeling like a broken record with this refrain.

"We can't leave her here alone, because she'll just wander off," Chef Levy said.

"We'll have to bring her with us," Kenzie decided, cringing at the onslaught of *Are you serious's* the statement garnered.

"If Rick gets ahold of her, he won't just have magical ingredients." Chef Levy planted her hands on her hips. "He'll have the superfood recipe."

"I'll take full responsibility for her," Kenzie hastened to offer.

"Listen to me," Chef Levy said. She didn't yell, which made her scarier. "I want only one thing: to give the Gourmands what they deserve. They killed my Hanna, and I want to make them pay. If they get the superfood recipe, that'll never happen. Do you get me?"

"They're not going to get the recipe," Kenzie said with confidence she didn't feel.

She was saved from having to argue further when the door between the hotel and dining room opened.

"Phew, traffic was a bitch," a female voice with an Aussie accent declared. "Are we late? Oh shit, we're totally late."

They all turned to face the intruder. She looked to be in her late thirties or early forties. She was on the heavy side but wore it voluptuously rather than as added weight. Her hair fell in thick auburn ringlets down her back, and she had deep laugh lines around her eyes that matched her friendly smile. She also had her right arm in a sling.

"Natalie?" Braxton said, an incredulous laugh flying out of his mouth. The woman jogged over to Braxton and engulfed him in a one-armed bear hug.

"Sous chef at the McKaid's flagship restaurant," Chef Levy explained to Kenzie.

"What are you doing here?!" Braxton asked Natalie, returning her fierce hug. "And what did you do to your arm?"

"Got a call from Elyannah Levy," Natalie said, her voice a little muffled because her face was mashed against Braxton's shirt. "And burnt myself trying out a new recipe. Hurt like the fiery pits of Hell, but that crème brûlée was a thing of beauty. I have no regrets."

"Braxton!"

"There you are, mate."

"McKaid!"

More and more people were entering the room. They surrounded Braxton, exchanging hugs and back pats and filling the dining area with chatter. There were twenty newcomers in all.

"Holy shit." Braxton laughed, disappearing in a four-way hug. "What are you all doing here?"

Kenzie found herself smiling too, even though she'd never seen any of these people in her life.

"Chef Levy called us," Natalie explained. "Said you needed help."

"I…wow…" Braxton stammered, looking at Chef Levy in bewilderment. "I mean, thank you."

"I didn't do it for you," Chef Levy snapped. "I did it because I'm not ready to die, and even if I was, I wouldn't want your ugly mug to be the last thing I get to see."

"Okay, Chef," Braxton said, chuckling. He gestured his friends over to Kenzie. "Come meet my girlfriend." As soon as the words were out of his mouth, he caught Kenzie's gaze and blushed.

It was freaking adorable.

Kenzie's heart did a pirouette in her chest. She smiled at him, letting him know it was okay he'd called her his girlfriend, even though they'd never explicitly had *the talk*.

More than okay.

Introductions were made, and that was how Kenzie came to discover that everyone in the room was a former waitress, busboy, or chef at a McKaid restaurant. And all of them had come halfway around the world for Braxton.

"Look at us," Natalie said, beaming. "We might be a small lot, but we're fierce." She punctuated the statement with an elbow to Braxton's ribs.

"Thank you for coming," Braxton replied, sounding a little choked up as he scanned the group. "I can't tell you how much I appreciate it."

Someone must have found Polly's liquor cabinet, because bottles were being passed around. No one bothered with glasses—everyone just took a swig or two and then passed the bottle on without missing a beat.

When Kenzie slipped her arm around Braxton's waist, he immediately leaned into her.

"I can't believe they came all this way to help us fight the Gourmands," he murmured. "I didn't realize anyone hated Rick as much as we do."

"They don't," Kenzie said. "They're not here because they hate him. They're here because they love you."

Braxton swallowed. "Aidan would have loved this."

Kenzie tightened her hold on him, trying send comforting vibes from her body into his. "This is like your brother's legacy, then."

Braxton turned to look at her. "How's that?"

Kenzie swept her hand around the room, indicating all the people chatting and drinking.

"All these people have memories of him and your parents," she said. "It's like they're carrying tiny pieces of your family."

Braxton stared down at the floor, taking a few seconds to gather himself.

"You have no idea how right you are," he said, his voice rough with emotion. "Aidan didn't give a damn about the restaurants themselves. It was the cooking he loved…and the people he cooked with and for.

"We're with you, Braxton!" someone shouted, pounding a liquor bottle on the table for emphasis.

"We're going to fuck the Gourmands up!" someone else called.

More whoops and table-pounding ensued. The sounds warmed Kenzie to her core.

The battle cries were interrupted by a bloodcurdling scream. Kenzie had never heard so much agony contained in a single sound.

"What the—" Braxton began.

Aralia burst into the dining room. She was a bedraggled, haggard shell of her usual self. She was wearing a faded T-shirt that reached to her knees. Her platinum-blonde hair was free of braids, beads, and feathers. It hung in limp strands across her cheeks, which were tearstained.

Aralia was crying.

"What is it?" Chef Levy demanded, immediately taking charge of the situation.

"Graham." Aralia made a keening sound and sank onto the floor. "He's dead."

Kenzie blinked, trying to make sense of those words.

"How do you know?" she asked, when she finally found her voice.

"Because they fucking called me!" Aralia shrieked. "They fucking called me and told me my brother's dead!" She threw her head back and howled.

"Who called you?" Braxton demanded. He crossed the room and wrenched Aralia to her feet. He pulled her hands away from her face and shook her. "Who called you?!"

Kenzie couldn't move. She'd lost feeling in her limbs. A horrible suspicion was worming its way into her brain.

"Rikers fucking Island!" Aralia yelled back.

Kenzie felt all the air leave her body at the same moment she saw understanding dawn on Aralia's ruddy face.

"Oh," Aralia said, sinking back against the wall and pressing both hands to her chest. A harsh laugh shuddered out of her. "Graham isn't at Rikers, is he?" Her laughter cut off abruptly as understanding dawned on her face. "Oh, shit. Sofia."

Aralia said something that sounded sympathetic and devoid of her usual mockery. She got to her feet and staggered back the way she'd come, disappearing through the sliding door that led to the hotel.

Everyone else in the room had gone silent in a combination of horror and grief. Kenzie didn't spare them a glance. She didn't have eyes for anyone except Braxton.

He stood in the same place he'd been, his arms hanging loose at his sides, his expression vacant. His mouth moved. Even though no sound came out, Kenzie recognized the shape of the word.

Sofia.

His sister. The last family he had in this world. Sofia had gone to Rikers Island disguised as Graham because Kenzie had helped her.

"Braxton?" Kenzie began. She reached out and touched his arm.

"It should be me," he said in a choked voice. "Christ. It should be me."

Braxton wrenched away from her and raced for the bathroom. He didn't even make it to the toilet before he was retching all over the floor.

Kenzie didn't know what to do. She knelt on the floor next to Braxton, saying nothing, just being there.

Natalie, Philippe, and some of the others clustered around outside. Their expressions were filled with the same helpless grief that was making Kenzie mute.

"McKaid," Chef Levy said, coming to stand in the doorway. "I know it's the last thing you want to think about right now, but if we're going to this exhibition, then we need to leave now."

Kenzie gave the chef a *Really?!* glare.

Chef Levy winced. When she spoke again, her voice had softened marginally. "I understand how you feel better than most. I also know that your sister wouldn't have wanted Rick to get away." Chef Levy crossed her arms. "Don't you think we owe it to Sofia to take away his power?"

Braxton didn't say anything. Kenzie didn't even know if he'd heard Chef Levy. The nothingness in his expression was scaring her more than if he'd been raging.

"Let's do this for Sofia," Philippe said, coming into the bathroom and crouching on Braxton's other side. "I only met your sister a few times, but I know she was brave as hell." He squeezed Braxton's shoulder. "Let's take down Rick and the Gourmands in her honor. Because it's what Sofia would have done."

"For Sofia," someone else said.

The sentiment was echoed by others.

Philippe offered Braxton his hand and hauled him to his feet.

"Philippe." Raina, who was standing in the bathroom doorway and holding Baby Hiroto, bit her lip. "Mon amour, do you really think this is a good idea?" She looked down at the sleeping child in her arms. "It'll be very dangerous."

"We said we were going to live the life that would honor Hiroto's memory." Philippe went over to his wife. "We said we'd be the kind of people our son would grow up to admire." Both of their gazes softened as they looked at their son.

The two of them devolved into a whispered conversation in French.

"I'm coming with you," Philippe said less than a minute later, switching back to English. He looked at Braxton. "It's what Hiroto and Sofia would have done."

"It won't change anything that's happened," Braxton said in a lifeless voice that squeezed Kenzie's chest.

"That's true." Philippe nodded. "But I'm going to do whatever I can to honor their memories."

Braxton didn't say anything.

"Alright," Raina said. "Then, I'm coming, too."

"But, Hiroto," Philippe began.

"I'll babysit him," Natalie offered. "With my bum arm, I'd just slow the rest of you down anyway. Besides, I'm a kickarse babysitter." She belched, and then chased it with a sip of whiskey. "Baby Hiroto and I will hold down the fort. Along with the diabolical little chameleon."

"Then it's settled," Chef Levy said. "Kenzie will use her lemonade to take away the Gourmands' magic. The rest of us will destroy Rick's magical ingredients. Any questions?"

"How do we know Rick will bring the ingredients with him?" Raina asked.

"He'll bring them," Chef Levy and Braxton both said.

"He wouldn't let them out of his sight," Braxton added in a dull voice. "He doesn't trust anyone except himself to keep them safe."

"That's good news for us then, right?" Raina asked.

The dining room door opened, and Aralia came sprinting in. She was holding a landline phone, which she'd ripped right out of the wall. The cord dangled behind her, looking oddly like entrails.

"Number Eight."

There was no teasing or mockery in the way Aralia said those words. When Kenzie looked at the other girl's face, she knew.

Kenzie's knees buckled.

"I'm sorry, Number Eight."

Kenzie felt the wetness on her cheeks, even before the next words were out of Aralia's mouth.

"Your dad is dead."

CHAPTER 7

GRAHAM

Graham wasn't quite sure how he found the road to the Reaper's house again. He'd been there once before, but Qiang Lee's hut was ten times more remote than his and Aralia's cabin. Without a map or phone or anything else to guide him, Graham had expected to run out of gas somewhere in the middle of Acadia National Park. Instead, he found he was being directed by some inexplicable pull inside him, which guided him better than any GPS.

With every mile he clocked, the tautness inside him eased a fraction. The crisp air blowing through the open window smelled like fresh pine and mist rising off the nearby lake. By the time his stolen truck crunched up the unpaved drive that led to the hut, he felt almost serene. The only other time in his life he'd been so at peace was the last time he was here. He was struck with a visceral memory of healing Reaper Lee's garden while Sofia knelt at his side, her warm hand curled in his.

Dusk was falling, and a soft light filled the hut's single window. It beckoned him.

Graham got out of the truck and…collapsed.

He must have blacked out, because the next thing he knew, a tiny pair of arms was hauling him to his feet while their owner talked at him incessantly. Graham blinked, registering the person who went with the arms and voice.

Clementine, he remembered. Reaper Lee's assistant.

"Graham. Sweetheart." Clementine's eyes filled with tears as she tugged on him, trying to get him to the hut. She was less than half his weight. Graham struggled to hold himself up, afraid he'd crush her if he leaned against her.

"The boy's starving and dehydrated," a surly voice said from the hut's entryway. "Bring him inside, and we'll get him fixed up."

Graham forced himself to focus. "Wait," he told Clementine. His voice was so thin and ragged he barely recognized the sound. "You should both know…." He sucked in a breath, trying to generate the energy it would take to speak in a complete sentence. "The police are looking for me. If you let me in, you'll be in danger."

The Reaper stared at Graham for long enough that Graham was starting to slip back into unconsciousness.

"I'm having a problem with one of my trees," Qiang Lee said, bringing Graham back to semi-alertness.

The Reaper turned on his heel and went into the hut.

Clementine gave a little squeal of delight, directly into Graham's ear.

"That's Reaper Lee-speak for *you can stay*," Clementine announced. "Now, let's get you inside. We'd be very bad hosts if we let you starve to death on our doorstep."

CHAPTER 8

BRAXTON

Braxton felt like he was underwater. His body went through the motions of gathering ingredients and preparing for the exhibition, but his mind was in a fog.

Sofia. His little sister. She was gone.

No matter how many times he thought the words, he couldn't make sense of them. Sofia was too strong...too fierce...too damn stubborn to die.

I'm sorry, Aid. I'm so fucking sorry....

That niggling, persistent thought, that it should have been him instead of Aidan, returned with a vengeance. If he'd died five years ago in Ashner's, then maybe Sofia would still be alive right now.

At the very least, he wouldn't have to live with the knowledge that he'd failed the one person he should have protected above all others.

If his parents knew he'd failed to save his sister...the last member of his family....

"You with us, McKaid?" Chef Levy asked.

Their little group of rebels poured out of the subway and onto the busy street.

"Yeah," he managed to scrape out. "I'm with you."

Braxton had been in Times Square dozens of times over the years, so he thought he'd known what to expect. Despite the fact that only a day had passed since Rick's announcement, the place was almost unrecognizable.

"This is fun," Aralia said, looking around.

"It's like New Year's Eve on steroids," Kenzie said. "My dad would have loved—" She broke off and lowered her head.

Braxton reached for her, as much to make sure they weren't separated by the crush of people as to offer comfort.

"It's a goddamn circus, is what it is," Chef Levy grumbled. "Won't take long for the Vanillas' curiosity to shift to something far more dangerous."

All the billboards had been transformed into an homage to culinary magic. There were advertisements for various culinary magic schools—some legit, some very much not—throughout the tri-state area. Some of the most upscale culinary magic restaurants in the world had taken out ads for their establishments. There were videos of culinary magicians showing off their creations on a loop. One billboard was filled with an image of Rick's smug face.

A stage had been set up where various culinary magicians were cooking. They were using simple recipes that every culinary magician learned within a year of discovering his or her power.

There were deviled eggs that had sprouted horns and were carrying red tridents as they chased weeping slices of angel food cake. Wheels of cheese were shrieking and cursing as they were rubbed against a grater. A sushi roll was doing complex acrobatics as it tumbled and flipped on its bamboo mat. A pancake, the size of a flying saucer, was casually floating through the air.

Braxton used his elbows to forge a path through the madness. In one corner of the square was a tent with a sign that said *Exhibition Registration*. Another tent was labeled *Ticket Sales*. According to the sign posted outside, standing-room tickets were being sold for five-hundred bucks a pop.

Gourmands were gathering behind a cordoned-off arena where four makeshift cook stations had been arranged. The arena was surrounded by ten-tiered bleachers, which were already bursting with spectators.

The air buzzed with magic.

All the sights and sounds and smells were making Braxton sick.

"Alright, everyone," Chef Levy said. She didn't yell, but somehow her authoritative voice carried through the madness that surrounded them. "Ashner, Rosemary, and Raina, you're with me."

To Braxton, Philippe, and Aralia, she said, "Find those ingredients and get rid of them." She turned to the other chefs who had come all the way from Sydney to help them. "The rest of you, get ready to stage a massive distraction so Ashner can get close enough to use her lemonade to take away the Gourmands' magic."

"Those red-robed bastards won't know what hit them," Philippe said, cracking his knuckles.

"Let's do this," the sommelier from Braxton's dad's first restaurant said. "For Sofia and the rest of the McKaids."

"For the McKaids," someone echoed. "And for us. Let's get these Gourmand sons-of-bitches."

They put their hands together and fist-bumped, like they were athletes about to start the game of their lives. Which, in a way, they were.

As everyone else started to separate, Kenzie held Braxton back. Beside them, Philippe and Raina were wrapped around each other as they made out.

"Please don't do anything…reckless," Kenzie told him.

"I won't," Braxton answered mechanically.

"I'm serious." Kenzie gripped his hand tight enough to make his bones grind together. "I know that after…everything, you probably don't care about yourself anymore…but I do. I can't lose you."

Braxton didn't have anything to say to that. Clearly, Kenzie knew him better than he gave her credit for.

Kenzie stretched up to kiss him, but an overeager tourist with a camera hanging from his neck knocked into her. She would have gone down if Braxton didn't have a hold of her. The interruption gave Chef Levy a chance to turn back and see them.

"I don't have time for your teenage romance!" she hollered loud enough for all of Times Square to hear.

"We're not teenagers," Kenzie was saying as she disentangled herself from Braxton and rolled her eyes at Chef Levy's back.

Kenzie kissed the tips of two fingers and touched them to Braxton's chest, right over his pounding heart. Then, she was gone, swallowed up by the crowd.

"What's the plan?" Philippe called. He gave Raina's arse a squeeze as she ran off, laughing, to join the rest of their distraction-generating chefs.

"Split up," Braxton ordered Philippe and Aralia, who were looking at him in a way that made it clear he was in charge. "We need to find those ingredients."

"They'll be somewhere the Gourmands can keep tabs on them," Aralia said. "Which conveniently narrows down the options."

She was right. The Gourmands, who were easy to spot courtesy of their red robes, were consolidated in a few locations throughout the square.

Braxton moved off toward the VIP tent, where a dozen Gourmands were milling around. Aralia went toward the McDonald's, where more were congregated. Philippe took the far side of the tournament arena.

Braxton shamelessly elbowed his way through the crowd until he was steps away from the VIP tent. Gourmands surrounded it, and anyone who got too close was shooed away with a combination of harsh words and harsher shoves. No one was actually allowed inside except the Gourmands. Sunflower seed shells littered the ground outside the tent.

When an especially enthusiastic observer made an unsuccessful attempt to barrel her way into the tent, a scuffle ensued. The woman knocked into the tent wall and, for just a second, the flaps billowed opened and Braxton caught a glimpse inside.

"Bingo," Braxton whispered.

There were Sofia's ingredients. Five crates, stacked one on top of the other.

Braxton reached into his pocket and pulled out a small container. He uncapped the lid and tipped his head back, swallowing the spicy sausage stew he'd made earlier.

Dijon mustard, cayenne pepper, and chili powder tickled his nose as he drew in the peppery broth. With the first bite, his senses were suffused with an intense heat from the Cajun seasoning he'd liberally used on the sausage. The rich, dark spices sat heavy on his tongue even after he'd swallowed.

Braxton let magic flow through his senses. He tugged and twisted the strands until he had them right where he wanted them.

The recipe was a generic one that he'd modified to make stronger and faster-acting.

While Aidan had always been more interested in creating new recipes from scratch, Braxton had found his knack in modifying recipes that already existed and making them better.

You'd like this one, Aid, Braxton thought as the magic locked into place inside him.

Braxton strode up to the tent flap. As soon as the Gourmands caught sight of him, they tensed.

Oh, yeah. These blokes knew who he was.

"G'day," Braxton said.

"Y-you," one of the Gourmands stammered. "I saw your corpse. How did you survive?"

If Kenzie were here, she would have come up with a clever retort. Braxton was too tired and heartsick to bother.

"I don't suppose I could convince you to walk away from this tent?" he asked the Gourmands.

One of the men murmured into a walky-talky. Braxton didn't imagine the man was saying anything complimentary.

"Mr. Santiori wants him alive," one of the Gourmands said, holding his walky-talky to his ear and wrinkling his brow as he tried to make sense of the staticky voice on the other end.

The Gourmands swarmed him.

Braxton grunted as several pairs of hands latched onto him. They moved so fast, he hadn't even seen them coming.

"Those sunflower seeds are something," he managed. "Worth all the chefs you had to kill to make them?"

That earned his hair a vicious yank.

"How did you survive our attack on your little cabin hideout?" one of the Gourmands demanded. "Never mind," he snarled before Braxton could reply. "By undermining Mr. Santiori, you've put all of culinary magic at risk."

"Look around you," Braxton scoffed. "Pretty sure your precious Mr. Santiori is risking culinary magic all on his own."

It was difficult to tell with the way their hoods shadowed their faces, but Braxton thought he detected some uncertain looks being exchanged among the Gourmands. He didn't wait for them to say anything else. He closed his eyes and focused on his magic.

He let the molten serrano peppers rise to the tip of his tongue. He inhaled stifling summer air and felt sticky humidity dampen his palms.

He opened his eyes. And exhaled.

A geyser of fire erupted from Braxton's mouth.

The Gourmands shouted and let go of him as fire engulfed the tent. The fire was the same bronze color as the sausages Braxton had eaten.

He exhaled another gust of wildfire at the tent. The acrid stink of burning chemicals filled the air as the plastic tent walls curled up and vaporized. Braxton caught sight of the crates before the fire swallowed them up.

The fire burned unnaturally fast…magically fast. It devoured the tent without spreading. In seconds, everything inside the tent was charred beyond recognition.

Regret flared through Braxton. If Sofia knew he'd just destroyed the magic she'd worked so hard to procure, she'd never speak to him again.

Sofia is dead, he reminded himself.

Sickness descended on him, and Braxton had to concentrate on getting oxygen into his lungs.

At that moment, Braxton's deepest desire was to be rid of his magic.

If it wasn't for magic, Sofia wouldn't have been able to go to jail in his place. She wouldn't have gotten herself killed.

While the Gourmands were busy shouting into their walky-talkies, Braxton started back in the direction he'd come from. He broke into a jog when he saw another column of sausage stew-induced fire spurt up from the McDonald's.

What the hell?

"Oy, stud!"

Braxton almost ran headlong into Aralia. She was grinning, even as she batted a flickering flame from the ends of her blonde hair.

"I got them," Aralia crowed. "All five crates. Poof!"

Braxton cocked his head. "No," he said slowly. "The crates were in the VIP tent. I just destroyed them."

"You better get your eyes checked," Aralia replied, flicking her singed hair back. "Because *I* destroyed those crates."

They looked at each other.

"We need to find Philippe and the others," Braxton said. "Right the fuck now."

He started pushing his way through the sea of unfamiliar faces, all of whom were shouting about the fires. What had previously been something like controlled chaos was quickly devolving into pandemonium.

The registration tent, he told himself. That's where Kenzie had gone. And the others would be with her.

"Braxton!"

He followed the sound of Kenzie's voice, his heart starting to beat again when he found her. She was standing with Chef Levy, Rosemary, and Raina.

Rosemary, who had a lunch bag slung over her shoulder, was guarding the thing like her life depended on it. Every time someone in the crowd jostled her, she bared her teeth at them.

"Where's Philippe?" Raina demanded as soon as Braxton and Aralia reached them.

"He's not back yet?" Braxton asked, even though he could see that Philippe wasn't. He tried peering in the direction Philippe had gone, but there were too many people for him to see anything.

"No, and neither is anyone else," Kenzie said, rising on her tiptoes and scanning the crowd. "They were supposed to create a distraction so I could get close to the Gourmands, but no one's—"

A speaker system crackled to life. People groaned loudly as squeaky back feed filled the air. The irritating sound cut off abruptly.

"Ladies and gentlemen." Rick's loathsome voice filled all of Times Square, making it seem like he was everywhere at once. "The fires have been contained. If you'd all please gather around, we can begin the opening ceremony for the first *public* culinary magic exhibition in history."

A giant screen next to Braxton flickered. All at once, the screen went from black to showing a podium that had been set up alongside the arena. Rick, wearing his characteristic haughty expression and a three-piece suit, stood on top of the podium.

Rick offered the camera an indulgent smile as raucous applause filled Times Square. He held up a hand, and the noise quieted down.

"I know those of you who are new to culinary magic have many questions," he said. "How is such a thing possible? Is it all just a hoax?" He gave the camera another smile. "I promise you that by the end of today, all of your questions will be answered."

His statement was met with more applause.

"As for my own people, who have expressed concerns about my decision to expose magic to the Vanillas," Rick began. His gaze moved to the side, where Benedict Vandermeer and the rest of the Gourmands stood. "I want to assure all of you this isn't a decision I made lightly." He paused to sip from a water glass, clearly enjoying the way everyone waited for his next words with baited breath. "Culinary magicians have always hidden in the shadows. Now, it's our time to shine." He stood taller.

"Methinks someone's got a chip on his shoulder," Kenzie muttered.

"No kidding," Braxton replied.

For someone who had lost Hex Kitchen twice and never managed to live up to his father's expectations, Rick had to know all about living in shadows.

"I intend to be as honest and straightforward with all of you as I possibly can be," Rick said, like the magnanimous leader he had convinced this audience he was. "In that regard, I would like to address a nasty rumor that's been circulating." He waited a beat. "Rumors need to be quashed as soon as possible before misinformation spreads. Isn't that right, McKaid?"

Braxton startled at the sound of his own name. When he looked at the screen, it felt as though Rick was staring right at him.

"Ladies and gentlemen," Rick continued. "I'd like to introduce someone who planned to deprive you of the beautiful magical ingredients you've come from far and wide to see today."

Boos filled Times Square. The screens set up all around the square flickered, and then Rick disappeared. Braxton's own face filled the canvas screens.

"I'm pleased to say this man's arson attempts were a failure," Rick said.

The cameras moved off Braxton and focused on five open crates, all of which were full of magical ingredients. Before Braxton could take note of where the cameras were, they shifted back to Braxton.

"I've been clear on the gifts my supporters can expect," Rick said. "Many city officials have already received their own magical ingredients, which is why we were able to pull together this exhibition so quickly and efficiently."

Rick paused for a sprinkling of whoops and applause.

"I have rewarded people who help me," Rick said. "Similarly, I feel it's only right for there to be consequences for those who oppose me. Don't you agree?"

The onlookers responded with raucous applause.

"He even talks like his father, now," Aralia said, rolling her eyes. "Daddy issues are the biggest turnoff." She raised her voice several decibels and added, "Well, that and disappointingly average-sized cocks."

They were far enough from the podium that Rick shouldn't have been able to hear, but his upper lip curled in a sullen expression.

"You fools," Rick hissed into his microphone. "Did you really think I would leave the ingredients somewhere you could get to them?"

Braxton's feeling of apprehension was growing by the second.

"Where's Philippe?" Raina asked again, her voice high with barely-concealed panic.

There was a disturbance as two Gourmands made their way through the crowd. The men were carrying a single crate between them. It was larger than the ones that held the ingredients, but otherwise it looked the same. The two men were obviously straining against the burden they shared between them.

The Gourmands lowered the crate to the ground right in front of Braxton.

An ominous silence filled Times Square.

Moving as one, the two Gourmands lifted off the crate's heavy lid. Wood creaked and splintered as the lid toppled onto the ground.

A videographer standing beside Braxton stuck his enormous camera into the now-open crate so everyone watching the screens would be able to see what Braxton was seeing.

Inside the crate was Philippe.

Philippe was crumpled on a layer of bloodstained straw. His face was turned up to Braxton. Dried blood was crusted along his hairline, and there was a slash mark across his throat. His dark eyes were open and glassy.

The silence was broken when Raina started to scream.

CHAPTER 9

SOFIA

Sofia groaned as she shifted around on the flat surface where she was lying. Her throat hurt, and her mouth was filled with an awful, sticky flavor.

Damn. How long had she been out for? It felt like the crick in her neck might be permanent.

With that thought, she came fully awake, and her mind flooded with memories. Zack had *shanked* her. She should be dead.

Why wasn't she dead?

When Sofia opened her eyes, she found herself in a room she hadn't seen before. There were cinderblock walls and a metal ceiling with harsh white lighting. She took in the metal gurney she was laid out on, the metal lockers surrounding her, and the overwhelming smell of formaldehyde.

A morgue. She was in a bloody morgue.

Letting out another groan that made her feel a hundred years old, she sat up. A label hanging off her ankle identified her by Graham's name, birthdate, and prison ID. She looked down at herself and let out a little yelp.

She was staring at Graham's naked body.

The bright side was that her magic had held while she was unconscious. The bad part was that she was now lusting over herself. This was so goddamned wrong in so many ways.

Was that really what he looked like, or had her subconscious filled in the blanks for her magic? It must be the latter, because no one was actually that…perfect.

The squeak of metallic hinges, followed by a pained grunt, gave Sofia an excuse to stop ogling herself. Next to her, on a gurney identical to her own, Walter was waking up.

"What happened?" Walter wheezed. He reached up to touch the nasty-looking mark across his throat. The skin was puckered and angry. Sofia imagined if she had a mirror handy, she would see a similar mark across her own neck. She could feel the same spot burning unpleasantly.

"How did we get here?" Walter persisted. "How are we—"

Alive? The word hung unspoken between them.

They both turned to the third occupied gurney. Zack, who had a matching, partly-healed gash across his throat, began to stir.

"Fuuuuuck." Zack sat up and rubbed his throat. Dried blood flaked off and fluttered to the floor. "The recipe notes didn't mention how much that was going to blow. And not in the fun way."

Sofia hopped off her gurney with an agility she hadn't been expecting. She wrapped one of her big hands around Zack's injured neck and squeezed until he made a gurgling sound.

"What the hell did you do to us?" she demanded, her threat coming out in Graham's low voice.

She loosened her hold on Zack enough for him to answer.

"Magic sticky bun," he croaked. "I had one stashed in the kitchen because some assholes were threatening me. I had to guess at how much to feed both of you." He let out a nervous little chuckle. "If I'd gotten it wrong, we wouldn't have woken up before they cremated us."

Sofia gaped at Zack.

"Magic sticky bun," she repeated. So, that was where the overwhelming taste of molasses was coming from. "What did it do to us?"

"The sticky bun congealed our blood and put us in a temporary coma," Zack explained.

Now that Sofia was no longer choking him, Zack took in her—well, Graham's—naked body looming over him. Zack's heated gaze swept all the way up and then back down.

"Don't even think about it," Sofia said nervously, looking around for something to cover herself.

"Oh, I'm thinking about it," Zack replied.

Sofia's quick exploration of the morgue turned up their uniforms, which were balled up in a plastic garbage can. She fished them out and pulled hers on before tossing the others to Walter and Zack.

"I can't believe it," Walter murmured, reaching up to run his fingers along his neck. "It's really real."

"I told you it was," Sofia grumbled.

"I know," Walter said. "And I wanted to believe you. I just—" He shook his head, clearly at a loss for words.

"It was the easiest way I could think of to get us out of our cuffs and give us free reign of the place," Zack said. "Now, we just need to get gone."

"Easier said than done," Walter pointed out. "There are cameras everywhere, and even if we make it out of the jail, we're on an island."

Zack pffed, like those were insignificant details. And, between his and Sofia's magic, they probably were. Or would be, if it weren't for the complexity of Sofia's situation.

The whole point of this jail excursion was to give the real Graham his freedom. If she escaped now and the medical examiner or whoever came back and found Graham's body missing, Graham would go right back to being a wanted criminal. He'd never have true freedom as long as the authorities were hunting for him. That meant Graham needed to stay dead. At least as far as the Rikers personnel were aware.

Zack's magic sticky bun stunt had changed all of Sofia's plans. There was no doubt he had provided them with an opportunity. Now, she just had to figure out how best to leverage it.

Sofia's mind churned through possibilities and recipes.

"First order of business," she said, her plan still fitting into place, piece by piece. "I need to get back in that kitchen."

"There shouldn't be any guards in the kitchen right now," Walter said, pointing to a digital clock that noted it was 2:00 AM. "But the cameras will be a problem, and we obviously don't have the keycodes to unlock the doors."

"I'll deal with those parts," Zack said, pulling a screwdriver out of a drawer and holding it up in triumph. To Sofia, he said, "You just focus on the magic. Those sticky buns knocked the stuffing out of me."

Fortunately, Zack turned out to have a far more delicate touch with a screwdriver than with magical sticky buns. The three of them managed to sneak back to the kitchen without setting off any alarms.

"Told you I made a better friend than enemy," Zack boasted as he made a grand gesture with his hand and opened the kitchen door for them.

"Where did you learn how to do this?" Walter asked as Zack pocketed his screwdriver.

"When your uncle is a mobster," Zack replied, "you learn things."

"You never mentioned why you fell out of your family's good graces," Sofia said.

Zack grinned at her. "The night Rick was planning to lose his V-card, I filled his room with magical popcorn that exploded right when things started heating up. Rick shit his pants in front of the girl."

"No fucking way," Sofia said, pressing a hand to her mouth to stifle her laughter.

"Way." Zack's smile broadened. "I was pretty much excommunicated from the family that night, but man. It was so worth it."

"You have to tell my brother that story," she said, still chuckling. "You'll make his day. Possibly his week."

As soon as they were inside the kitchen, Sofia got down to business. She had perused hundreds of magical recipe books before leaving the cabin, and she'd memorized several recipes she thought would serve her well during her incarceration. Now, she knew precisely which one she wanted to cook first.

Sofia began rattling off the ingredients she needed to Walter and Zack. Instead of rushing off to gather everything, the two men just stared at her.

Zack began to laugh, which devolved into full-belly guffaws that were loud enough to wake up the entire jail.

Walter elbowed Zack before turning to Sofia.

"This is jail," Walter said in a gentle voice. "We don't have access to loin of pork or baby spinach." His lip twitched, like he was trying hard not to join Zack, who was crying he was laughing so hard. "And we definitely don't have access to pancetta or parmesan."

Beside him, Zack let out a snort and slapped his thigh.

"Well, how the hell am I supposed to make magical meatloaf?" Sofia demanded, feeling panic begin to take hold.

"I don't know anything about magical meatloaf," Walter said. "But I make a jailhouse loaf that is quite palatable, if that'll suffice."

Sofia considered that. Magical recipes were finicky, and only the most powerful chefs could make adjustments without having dire consequences. Then again, she had Kenzie's magic inside her and a lifetime of observing her brothers cook. She could do this.

"Okay," Sofia relented. "Show me how to make it."

Jailhouse loaf, as it turned out, was a disgusting amalgamation of ingredients that were nothing like any meatloaf Sofia had ever encountered. The basis was crumbled Ramen noodles, followed by mystery meat pilfered from the industrial fridge. It was held together with copious amounts of mayo, lukewarm water, and topped with a Cheetos crust.

It was possible Sofia might never want to eat again.

Walter talked her through each step of the process, since she needed to be the one to actually make the loaf if she expected the magic to have any hope of sticking.

"We work with what we've got," Walter said, indicating that she should add another sprinkle of fluorescent-orange crumbles to the top of the loaf.

Sofia vaguely wondered whether her fingers would be permanently stained orange.

"I can't believe I'm going to have to eat this," Sofia groaned as she manipulated the blobby loaf into the shape of a human hand and popped it into the oven.

When the loaf had cooked, Sofia was hit with a hearty burst of steam that smelled far more akin to actual meatloaf than its ingredients would have suggested. The Cheetos crust had darkened to a more tolerable brown. If she used her imagination, she might be able to convince herself it was a breadcrumb topping. The umami Ramen seasoning complimented the meat, and the mayo helped keep the entire concoction from drying out.

It didn't look half bad. At least, that was what she told herself.

"You sure you can make this work?" Zack asked.

Not even a little.

Sofia rolled up her scratchy sleeves and focused on the hand-shaped loaf. She inhaled, getting a lungful of Cheetos dust. She forced her mind to focus on the file folder she needed but had no idea where to find.

Tiny, translucent wisps of magic began to emerge, hovering over the meat. Sofia pressed harder on the magic until the threads multiplied. They wriggled over the meat, dangling like strings of a spider web.

In her mind, the magic began to transform from nonsensical threads to something usable. Just like when she was presented with a spreadsheet full of numbers, and she transformed it into cash flow analyses, income statements, and balance sheets.

Sofia knew it was working when she looked down at herself and saw that her body had begun to change. The color of her skin was lightening from a rich brown to her natural tanned skin tone. Her body shrank, reminding her of just how much larger Graham was compared to her. The prison jumpsuit that had left Graham's body with little wiggle room hung off her. She felt an added weight on her head as Graham's buzz cut transformed into her long blonde hair. The ends fell limply against the puce of her jumpsuit.

As soon as she got out of here, she was getting a trim and deep-condition.

A sharp gasp beside her had Sofia turning. Walter was staring at her, wide-eyed and slack-jawed.

"I—" he began. He swallowed, and when he reached up to adjust his glasses, Sofia saw his hand was trembling. "How is this even possible?"

"Kind of hard to fake this," Sofia said, startling a little at the sound of her own voice. She'd gotten used to Graham's smoky rumble coming out of her mouth.

"You were so much hotter before," Zack complained. He crossed his arms and gave her a petulant look, like he was a little kid who had just opened a present expecting to find a puppy and instead received a bag of kale.

Pure nerves and the magic coursing through her system made Sofia start to giggle. She quickly finished with the magic in her meatloaf before she lost her focus.

"Oh my." Walter stumbled backward as the meatloaf began to quiver.

Sofia gripped the counter as she gave the magic another fierce tug. She felt sweat dampen the back of her jumpsuit as the meatloaf hand lifted itself off the pan. Her creation balanced itself on its meaty fingertips. Then, using its index and middle finger, the meatloaf hand began to walk.

The more confident Sofia became with her magic, the more control she had on her creation. The meatloaf hand scuttled across the counter, hopped down, and shot across the room. It slipped through the partly-open door and disappeared down the dark hallway.

"Was that…supposed to happen?" Walter asked.

Sofia didn't answer. She squeezed her eyes shut and concentrated on the magic. She could feel her connection to the meatloaf hand straining the farther it got from her.

She rearranged threads, tightening here and deleting there. Just like she did when she had taken a restaurant's profits and stretched them until all the bills got paid. It wasn't always neat and pretty, but in the end, she'd always gotten it done. This time was no different.

Sofia had no idea how much time passed. All she knew was that she was breathing as hard as if she were in the middle of a grueling workout, and her hair was drenched with sweat. She was seconds away from collapse when the meatloaf hand reappeared in the doorway. It was clutching three file folders in its beefy hand.

"That is extraordinary," Walter said, looking as dazed as Sofia felt.

"Anyone have a pen?" Sofia asked tiredly.

"Oh, let me," Zack said, producing a writing implement from his pocket and grabbing the folders out of the meatloaf hand. "I'm the shit at forging. If there'd been a major for it in college, I might have stayed longer than a semester."

A few moments and strokes of Zack's pen later, the three of them were deceased. Officially.

Then, there was more sweating and straining as Sofia directed the meatloaf hand to take their files back to wherever they'd come from. By the time she was finished, her limbs felt like jelly.

"Oh, no you don't," Zack said when Sofia sagged against the counter. "We need to find replacement corpses and get off the Island pronto. The COs are going to start clocking in at any minute. If they find us wandering around unsupervised, we'll be toast."

With a small groan, Sofia roused herself and gathered the scattered remains of her energy. She'd heard her brothers complain about magic hangovers, but this was the first time she'd ever experienced one for herself. They were the worst.

"What are you thinking?" Zack asked.

At the moment? That she could use a hot bath and warm bed. Preferably with a memory foam mattress and 800-thread count Egyptian cotton sheets.

She wiped her sleeve across her sticky forehead and refocused.

"I found a good recipe for magical wine. Once we drink it, anyone who looks at us will get temporarily confused. The effect should be strong enough to let us get back to the morgue without drawing any attention."

"What happens once we get to the morgue, Blondie?" Zack pressed.

Sofia looked at the conglomeration of ingredients spread out on the counter.

"I'm going to burn it down," she said. "Everyone will assume our bodies got incinerated with everything else." Sofia scowled. "And don't call me Blondie if you enjoy having your head attached to your shoulders."

Zack put up his hands and backed away from the counter, looking more amused than contrite.

"Don't you think that's biting off more than you can chew?" he asked.

Sofia gave him the finger before turning to Walter. "I don't suppose you have the makings for sangria around here, do you?"

Walter's face lit up. "Pruno," he said.

"Excuse me?" Sofia replied.

Zack just chuckled.

"Prison wine," Walter clarified. "I make an excellent one, if I do say so myself. It's got apple juice, melted butterscotch candies, maple syrup, cornbread, and prunes of course—that's where the name comes from. The sauerkraut is what helps the fermentation process. You can barely taste it. I've got a batch ready, in fact. I'll be right back." With that, Walter hustled out of the kitchen.

"It's actually pretty tasty," Zack offered. "If you can get past the fact that it's chunky."

Sofia very much doubted she could. More to the point, she wasn't sure she'd be able to magic a recipe she hadn't had a hand in cooking.

She ran out of time to fret about it, because Walter returned with a large tomato juice can cradled to his chest. He proudly presented the container to Sofia.

The purple liquid smelled like the powdered fruit juice she and her brothers had drunk when they were kids…with an added bonus of gasoline.

Sofia turned to Zack, who had been cooking magic far longer than she. "What do you think?"

Zack lifted a shoulder. "It's a risk, Blondie. If you can get it to work at all, you'll have less control over the magic."

"What are my other options?" she asked.

Zack glanced at the clock over the oven and shook his head. "Go back to your cell and admit defeat."

Not a chance.

She was a goddamned McKaid. Cooking was in her blood.

Sofia poured some of the pruno into a cup and drank. And immediately began coughing.

Walter thumped her on the back as her eyes watered and her insides shriveled. It was the most singularly sweet and sour concoction she'd ever ingested. She imagined a purple hole forming in her esophagus.

"It's a bit of an acquired taste," Walter said apologetically.

"Get going on the magic before you wake up the whole jail with your hacking," Zack advised.

After shooting him a look that promised death, Sofia did just that.

The magic appeared instantly, but the threads were strange. They flickered like pixels on a computer screen. As soon as she reached for one, it slipped away. She took another sip of the vile brew in the hopes that it would strengthen her connection. She worked quickly, trying to strengthen the magic before it dispelled.

No matter how much effort she exerted, the threads frayed and rebelled against her.

"Something's wrong," Zack said.

"Yeah, no shit!"

She'd have to unravel the work she'd already done and start again. Except, when she tugged on the threads to loosen them, they just got more tangled.

God, was it just her, or was it hot as an oven in here? And what the hell was that annoying sound?

Glug. Glug, glug.

The pruno was boiling. There was no source of heat beneath the can, but the liquid had gotten so hot it was beginning to foam.

Purple bubbles spurted out of the can and flicked onto the cinderblock wall. The stone sizzled and eroded.

"Fuck," Zack said. "We gotta go."

"But—" Walter began.

"*Now.*"

Zack grabbed Sofia and Walter, roughly yanking them away from the can of pruno.

A dollop of wine spurted out of the can and blasted straight up to the ceiling. Sofia jumped as a lightbulb shattered. Then, another burst. And another.

In the darkness, Sofia heard a sizzle, followed by an electric pop. There was a shower of fiery sparks.

A chorus of beeps, blares, and alarms began. Sofia covered her ears in a useless attempt to drown out the sounds. Her nose burned with the acidic stench of fermented prunes.

"Oh shit, oh shit, oh shit!" Zack yelled.

Almost as quickly as it began, all the sounds cut off.

For several seconds, Sofia heard nothing beyond her own harsh breathing.

"Power's gone out," Walter said. "The backup generator should kick in soon."

Wine arced out of the can and through the barred window.

"Should we—" Walter began.

BOOM!

All three of them jumped as something huge and metallic flew into the air outside the window. It erupted in an array of blue-and-orange sparks before crashing back down.

"RIP backup generator," Zack announced. "Phew. It's already hot as Hades in here." He ripped open his jumpsuit and tore the top half, making a sort of makeshift belt. It actually looked deliberate, in a grungy, prison-chic sort of way.

"Oh, God," Walter said. "If the electricity is out, then that means—"

"The chickens have flown the coop," Zack said grimly. He reached into his pocket and pulled out his screwdriver.

Shouts filled the dark corridor outside the kitchen.

"We're free, motherfuckers!" someone screamed. "Let's burn this shit down. Burn it down, burn it down!"

Sofia hurriedly tucked her hair into her jumpsuit and started looking around for something she could use to hide her face. And she was definitely going to need to do something about her boobs....

"We're trapped in here," Walter said, his calm voice replaced by something tight and unrecognizable. "The only way out is through them."

The scents of smoke and sweat were heavy on the air. More screams and raucous whoops filled the hallway. And then prisoners burst into the kitchen.

CHAPTER 10

KENZIE

Kenzie stared at Philippe's broken body as Raina's screams filled Times Square. All Kenzie could think about was Baby Hiroto. That adorable child was fatherless now, thanks to Rick. And Raina was a widow.

Kenzie gripped her canteen full of anti-magic lemonade more tightly. If only she could get close enough to Rick and the Gourmands to use to it on them. Something must have happened, because the distraction all the other chefs were supposed to orchestrate never came.

The crowd of onlookers seemed frozen in shock. Parents were covering their children's eyes. Everyone else was gaping at Philippe's body on the projected screen with a morbid kind of curiosity. No one seemed able to look away.

As Kenzie stared at the Gourmands, all she could think was that these were the people who had thrown rotten tomatoes at her as she was forced to cook to the death in Cutthroat Cuisine. These were the sickos who had cheered as she snapped Brute's neck. When she stabbed Scarlet with her own bread dagger.

Kenzie's entire body began to tremble with the need to do violence to the people who had kidnapped her…who were responsible for the nightmares she'd no doubt have for the rest of her life.

Beside Kenzie, Rosemary was chanting her superfood song and clutching the lunch bag slung over her shoulder. Aralia was gripping daggers hidden under her shirt. Chef Levy was wearing a murderous expression.

Kenzie saw her own sense of helplessness reflected on each of their faces.

"Your other friends are dead too, McKaid," Rick boasted. "Killed every one of them."

"Rick, you bastard!" Braxton yelled. He launched himself through the crowd.

Kenzie hurried after Braxton, knowing there was no stopping him. Hell, Kenzie didn't want to stop him. In that moment, Kenzie didn't give a flying fig what happened to her, as long as she took Rick down with her.

Sunflower seed shells crackled under Kenzie's sneakers as she approached the wall of Gourmands that separated her from Rick.

With lightning fast-speed, the Gourmands drew chocolate guns from the depths of their robes and aimed them at Kenzie and Braxton.

"I cooked these chocolate guns myself," Rick announced to the rapt audience who was watching all of this like it was a play rather than real life. "I thought it would be a good opportunity to demonstrate to the world what culinary magic is truly capable of." He peered down his nose at Kenzie and Braxton from his podium. "This is also my response to the terrorists who started those fires in the hopes of inciting chaos and killing as many of us as possible."

Terrorists? Really? That seemed like a bit much to Kenzie, but the audience was eating Rick's words up.

"Kill 'em!" a random person in the crowd shouted.

Fear had turned to fury, and in just a few words, Rick had managed to turn the entire crowd onto Kenzie's group.

More shouts came from the audience that seemed to be practically salivating over the idea of ripping Kenzie and her friends to shreds. There were shouts of *kill the terrorist food witches!* and *we should burn them alive!*

Rick dipped his chin in a subtle nod.

The Gourmand closest to Kenzie raised his gun high. He pulled the chocolate trigger. A loud *crack* sounded through the speaker system.

Kenzie saw a chocolate bullet strike the vinyl screen a mere two inches from her head. The screen began to wobble from tiny vibrations coursing through it.

The vibrations increased in intensity until the entire screen ruptured. Shreds of vinyl and chunks of plastic flew in every direction.

The Vanilla onlookers oohed and ahhed and applauded. Freaking applauded.

Before Kenzie could regain control of her fluttering pulse, another gunshot rang out. The canteen Kenzie was holding began to shudder. It shook with such intensity that she had to cling to it with both hands.

A chocolate bullet was stuck to the lid.

Kenzie knew what was about to happen but was powerless to stop it. The vibrations traveled all the way up Kenzie's arms. Then, the canteen burst apart.

Wetness splattered through the air. The fresh scent of lemons rose up as the activated charcoal lemonade spilled onto the pavement. The liquid was instantly absorbed into tiny cracks in the cement.

"No," Kenzie gasped, looking down at the wet smear on the ground.

The Gourmand smiled and blew on the tip of his chocolate gun, which was smoking.

"Mr. Santiori is our leader now," the Gourmand said. "Any attack on him, or on those who serve him, will be viewed as an act of war against all culinary magicians."

There were a few whoops from the audience, although Kenzie couldn't tell if they came from culinary magicians or Vanillas who were simply enjoying the show.

"Screw you," Kenzie snarled at the Gourmand.

Admittedly, it wasn't the world's finest comeback, but her heart was still racing from the chocolate bullets that had come within striking distance of her.

"I've gotta hand it to you, Dick," she said loudly. "You're a better showman than I gave you credit for. Kudos to you."

All of the chocolate guns were aimed at her and Braxton. It would take only a single word from Rick, and then she and Braxton would be history.

A desperate, broken cry tore out of Raina, who was hurling herself through the crowd. Her fingers were curled into claws, and her hair was a wild mass around her face.

Kenzie tried to stop her, but Raina barreled right past.

"You took my husband!" she shrieked.

Braxton caught Raina around her waist and held her back, turning his body so he was between Raina and the guns.

"He murdered Philippe! He murdered him!"

Braxton had to pin Raina's arms to keep her from raking her nails across his face.

"Calm down," Braxton said, struggling to hold her without hurting her. "You're going to get yourself killed."

Raina wrenched around in Braxton's grip until she was facing him. "This is your fault," she told Braxton, her voice hoarse from shouting. "Philippe wouldn't have gotten himself killed if he wasn't trying to prove to you that his life was worth something."

Braxton's entire body seemed to freeze up. He didn't move, except for a muscle that was pulsing below his clenched jaw.

When Raina gave him a hard shove, Braxton didn't try to hold onto her. He didn't seem capable of moving.

"Raina," Kenzie said in a sharp voice.

The other girl paused long enough for Kenzie to get a hold of her shoulder to make sure she didn't go barging into the line of chocolate guns.

"What'll happen to your son if you die, too?" Kenzie asked Raina. It was harsh, but there wasn't time for gentleness. Their lives were hovering on a knifepoint.

Kenzie knew it was the right thing to say, because some of the blind fury drained out of Raina. She sagged against Kenzie.

"Go back to Baby Hiroto," Kenzie said, smoothing Raina's hair back from her forehead. "You don't want your son growing up without a mother. Trust me. I'd know."

Images of Denise flashed through Kenzie's mind before she shut down the poisonous thoughts. If she was about to take a chocolate bullet to the brain, she didn't want her last thoughts to revolve around her abandonment issues.

Raina sniffed and nodded. She turned and melted into the crowd.

"Let her go," Rick told the Gourmands, loud enough for the microphones to pick up his benevolence. He offered the cameras a smile that was as genuine as the zero-calorie iced tea Kenzie had served back at *Good Ol' Apple Pie*.

"As you can see, there are good and bad food witches," Rick said into his microphone, stopping the Vanillas, who were veering into panicking territory again. "However, you have nothing to fear. I will make sure you're protected."

Kenzie could practically see the stars appearing in people's eyes. They looked at Rick like he was a king. Or a god.

Kenzie wanted to be sick all over Rick's polished shoes.

"As the greatest threat to magic-kind," Rick said, staring down at Kenzie and Braxton. "It's my duty to eliminate you." A glittering malice filled his gaze.

"This is between us," Braxton said, his voice cracking with a combination of hatred and desperation. "Leave Kenzie alone."

"Can't do that," Rick said with an idle shrug. "Say your goodbyes, because in about three seconds—"

"Stop," a voice ordered, cutting Rick off before he reached the apex of his threat. "Enough, Mr. Santiori."

Kenzie knew that polished English accent. The sound of it made her simultaneously want to commit murder and cower on her nonexistent cot.

Benedict Vandermeer, former head of the Gourmands, stepped out in front of the others.

Instead of his usual tailored suit, Benedict wore a crimson cloak with the hood thrown back. He leaned heavily on his cane, both of his hands curved around the ivory handle, as his ice-blue eyes found Kenzie's.

"Stop this violence at once," Benedict said, addressing Rick.

Kenzie didn't know if it was her imagination, but outside of the confines of Cutthroat Cuisine, Benedict's voice seemed to hold less authority. His whole persona seemed…smaller. He was more hunched. His goatee made him appear less refined and more elderly. And the billowy cloak gave him an air of frailty that was at complete odds with the man who, until a few days ago, had controlled the most powerful organization in the world of culinary magic.

Kenzie's attention was diverted from Benedict when her other nemesis, Nurse Ratched, wedged her way through the Gourmands until she stood at Benedict's side.

Nurse Ratched's white sneakers were as freakishly white as ever. Her hair was pulled back in an extra-tight bun. She wore the same green scrubs she'd had back in Cutthroat Cuisine. And she had on the same self-important expression she'd worn every time she drugged Kenzie before hauling her back into her cell.

"You don't give the orders around here anymore," Rick hissed at Benedict. "I do."

In affirmation of his words, the Gourmands moved away from Benedict and toward Rick. Their red cloaks undulated around them, giving them an even more ephemeral appearance. The group of them pooled around Rick like smoke. Or blood.

Benedict dipped his head in acknowledgement. "Forgive me, Mr. Santiori."

Kenzie almost choked at the way Benedict pandered to the weasel.

"But if I might impart a singular piece of advice," Benedict said. He went on before Rick had a chance to speak. "The Gourmands have protected the secret of culinary magic for generations because we have always understood the fundamental nature of people. We all want what we cannot have."

Benedict turned away from Rick, scanning the throngs of people who were hanging on his every word. His features contorted in disgust. He continued, "History has proven the necessity of secrecy and a ruthless defense of our laws. If we devolve into petty rivalries and personal vendettas, then we've already lost. I urge you not to make this grave error."

Rick pffed, which came out sounding even more petulant because it was blasted out of more than a dozen speakers.

"You talk too much," Aralia said.

Kenzie hadn't even noticed Aralia sneaking around to her other side.

"I should kill you for kidnapping Number Eight," Aralia growled at Benedict. She reached for the dagger tucked into her belt.

A rush of warmth went through Kenzie. She was about to go for a high-five or something, when she remembered that all of Aralia's loyalty couldn't save them now. They were screwed.

"Kill them," Rick said.

Crap.

The Gourmands raised their chocolate guns.

Movement blurred as people converged around Kenzie. Braxton and someone else moved in front of her, blocking her from the Gourmands.

Rosemary, Kenzie realized.

Rosemary, who had stepped in front of Kenzie, was fumbling at the lunch bag hanging off her shoulder. She was singing her superfood song in a shrill voice that seemed unnaturally loud in the tense, waiting silence that had descended.

"Wait!" One of the Gourmands threw himself in front of the others and put up both of his arms.

The man moved fast enough to make his hood fall back, revealing a messy shock of orange hair that was the same shade as Rosemary's. The man was younger than Kenzie would have guessed a Gourmand could be—he looked barely out of his teens. He was almost as skinny as Kenzie and not much taller. He had a baby face, which probably made him look younger than he actually was. His blue eyes were rounded and fixated on Rosemary.

"Mom," he choked out. "Oh my God. Mom!"

Beside Kenzie, Rosemary made a jerky motion. A hiccup-sob came out of her and was magnified because she was standing next to one of the mikes.

Rosemary shook her head. "No," she said.

"It's me," the boy called, his voice tinged with desperation. He took several steps closer.

"No," Rosemary said again. She was stroking her charm necklace and clutching her lunch bag. She didn't so much as look at the Gourmand.

"Please, Mr. Santiori," the Gourmand said, never taking his eyes off Rosemary. "Benedict is right. The Gourmands are supposed to be better than this. Haven't enough lives been lost?"

Rick didn't so much as acknowledge the young Gourmand. He just gave the rest of the red robes a chin-tip that meant only one thing: Kenzie's people were going to die.

The smell of cocoa filled the air, but it wasn't at all comforting.

Kenzie felt Braxton reach for her hand. She tangled their fingers together and squeezed.

Kenzie turned to the side, hoping inspiration would strike her before a chocolate bullet did, and locked gazes with Benedict. He was mouthing a single word. It took her a few tries to figure out what he was saying.

Culinarian.

Kenzie furrowed her brow. What did that have to do with anything? She was still staring down the barrel of a gun.

A magical gun.

Duh!

Something inside her jolted to life. Kenzie didn't need her lemonade or any other magical food. All she needed was herself. Because she was a freaking Culinarian.

When she focused, she could see the shimmery threads of magic woven through the chocolate weapons. There they were…like strings on an instrument, waiting to be plucked.

So, pluck she did.

There were a lot of Gourmands, and hence, a lot of chocolate guns. It took her only a second to understand the magical mechanism in the guns that turned the chocolate bullets into deadly missiles. Once she did, she was able to grab whole fistfuls of the magic—mentally speaking, of course. She gathered up the tendrils of magic as though she were holding the strings of a hundred wayward balloons. Then, she let go.

She heard gasps and muffled shouts as the guns began to melt in their owners' hands.

Kenzie didn't stop there.

It felt weird and unnatural, but she reached inside the Gourmands with mental fingers and grasped for their magic.

Gotcha.

She could almost see her translucent, magical talons yanking up the Gourmands' magic.

No mercy.

Kenzie wasn't exactly sure how she was doing it, and figured it was better not to think too hard about it. Methodically…painstakingly…she drew pieces of the Gourmands' magic up and out of them.

Their magic clung too tightly for Kenzie to unwind all of it, and she got the sense that if she tried, she'd kill them. But there were parts that were free and ripe for the picking. Those she extracted quickly. Ruthlessly.

"No," Rick said, as soon as Kenzie started tugging at the magic winding through him. "What are you doing? No!"

Mine now, she thought as she swept his magic into her growing pile with all the rest.

There were hundreds of culinary magicians in and around Times Square, and once Kenzie started drawing out magic, she found she couldn't stop.

"Kenzie?" Braxton said.

His face was a shimmery mirage, clouded by all of the magic that was surrounding Kenzie.

She was beginning to feel the way she had the night she'd done fire and ice shots with Braxton, loose and pleasantly floaty. She was punch-drunk.

No. *Magic*-drunk.

The tingling warmth inside her began to turn searing. The magic she'd drawn away from others wasn't dissipating on the wind.

Why wasn't it going away?

The answer struck her with sudden, all-consuming clarity.

The magic had congealed, and it was flowing straight toward her. And then it was flowing *into* her.

Kenzie was absorbing all of the magic she'd taken away from those guns and the culinary magicians who wielded them. It was inside her. And it was eating her alive.

CHAPTER 11

SOFIA

Prisoners burst into the kitchen, hollering and smashing everything they could get their hands on. Pots and pans clattered across the floor. Glass jars shattered. The bedlam was deafening.

This couldn't be happening.

Sofia had always believed that having magic would help her fix broken things…that it would make her strong. Now, she was in the weakest position she'd ever been in, and it was all her magic's fault.

Thousands of testosterone-charged criminals had been freed from their cells, and a swarm of them were now blocking the only way out of the kitchen.

"Come and get me, motherfuckers," Zack said, flipping his screwdriver around in his hand and crouching down.

Walter yanked a rubber knife free from the counter. Sofia clenched her fists and waited for the inevitable moment when the inmates stopped tearing apart the kitchen long enough to realize they weren't alone. It didn't take long.

The men took one look at her and lost whatever was left of their minds.

"All for one," Zack said sardonically. "And one for—"

The other inmates started howling like mad dogs. Wolf whistles, filthy cat calls, and lewd gestures came at Sofia. And then the men were actually coming at her.

The first bloke to reach her was familiar. It was the one who had threatened her the first time she set foot in the jail kitchen. *Lars*, she remembered. And his pal was—

"Murphy," Lars called to the man at his side, who was holding a long, rusted screw. "Looks like we're gettin' lucky tonight! Hold her down while I fuck her, and then we'll switch."

"Nah, you hold her, first," Murphy argued. "Then I'll hold her for you."

They were so busy arguing about who was doing the holding and who was doing the fucking, they didn't notice Zack come around behind them.

Zack leapt onto Murphy's back and impaled his screwdriver into the bloke's neck over and over again. Blood spurted up, coating Zack's face. Murphy screamed and clawed at the air. He bucked, but Zack hung on and continued to stab him until Murphy's legs gave out.

Lars turned to Sofia, his teeth bared in a feral snarl.

Walter tried to stop him, but Lars just bowled right over him. Walter fell to the ground, his rubber knife flying out of his grip.

When Lars got within striking distance, Sofia swung. Her punch bounced off his muscular shoulder. It didn't even slow him down.

Lars grabbed at the front of her jumpsuit. There was a ripping sound, and then Laws was pawing at her chest. She kneed him in the balls.

Lars howled and reared back. Sofia didn't wait for him to recover. She smashed her fist into his face.

Sofia felt the bones in his nose give and heard a satisfying crunch. She waited for Lars to hit the floor, and then she kicked him in the ribs. She kicked him over and over again. When he curled in on himself to protect his lungs, she went for his skull.

Blood was thick on the air, and it turned the inmates into ravenous beasts. Everyone was tangled together. They were a mass of flying fists and makeshift weapons. Screams of rage and agony filled the kitchen. Blood slicked the floor.

Someone had turned on every burner on every stove, and people were shoving whatever flammable objects they could get their hands on into the fire. Inmates were running around with torches, burning everything and everyone that crossed their path.

Zack killed a second inmate with his screwdriver. Sofia downed another with an old frying pan.

"This way," Walter gasped, taking Sofia's arm and pulling her through a gap that had opened up in the fighting. It looked like two rival gangs were facing off, and they were too busy with each other to notice the three of them as they shot out of the kitchen and down the corridor.

They didn't get far. Three COs, keys jangling from their belts and truncheons gripped in their hands, rounded the corner.

"Get down!" one of the guards shouted. "Get down on the floor!"

Walter started to obey, but Sofia yanked him back up.

While she waited for the officers to reach them, her mind flipped back to the first time she'd been alone with Graham. She'd been pummeling a bag of flour in his storage shed, and he'd taught her the right way to throw a punch.

Use your core, she heard Graham's gentle voice advising.

Motion comes from your hips.

Then, the COs were on them.

Sofia's fist flew. She caught one of the guards in the jaw as his truncheon glanced off Sofia's head. Starbursts danced across her vision.

Walter put out his foot and tripped one of the other COs. Sofia spun to face the third in time to find Zack pulling his screwdriver out of the man's throat. He was dead.

"You killed him," Sofia choked out.

Prisoners like Lars and Murphy were one thing, but these correction officers were just doing their job.

"They saw our faces," Zack grunted. He bent down next to one of the unconscious bodies and, before Sofia could stop him, plunged his screwdriver into the man's neck.

Zack shrugged off Walter, who tried to stop him, and gave the third CO the same treatment. "We're supposed to be dead, remember?"

Sofia stood, dumbstruck and sick, as Zack started undressing one of the guards.

"Help me!" he ordered. "We need their clothes if we're getting out alive."

He was right.

Sofia shook herself out of her stupor and started stripping one of the others. She tried to ignore the stench of fresh blood and the wetness seeping into the man's uniform.

After a moment's hesitation, Walter did the same with the other CO.

They'd just finished donning their new uniforms when prisoners poured out of an adjoining hallway.

And now the three of them looked like correction officers. They may as well have signs painted on them that said *Please kill us slowly and painfully.*

Sofia stood shoulder-to-shoulder with Walter and Zack. If she was going down, it wouldn't be without a fight.

Another sound joined the inmates' death threats. Heavy booted footsteps were pounding toward them.

A metal cannister rolled around the corner. Acrid smoke began to fill the hallway, making Sofia's lungs instantly feel like they'd been lit on fire. She doubled over, coughing.

"Disperse!" a voice shouted through a megaphone. "Disperse immediately!"

Police holding shields and wearing gas masks flooded the corridor.

Walter, who was hacking up a lung beside her, pressed a cloth to Sofia's face. The material smelled like harsh prison laundry cleaner, but it helped give her some relief from the tear gas.

Together, the three of them somehow managed to weave through the police, who were tangling with the inmates. They ran blindly through the smoke.

Walter led the way. Zack brought up the rear, pushing Sofia forward when her lungs threatened to shrivel up and surrender for good.

"Morgue first," Sofia gasped as the three of them dragged themselves out of the last streams of tear gas.

It took them forever to reach it, but at least the place was empty. The morgue was probably the only place that hadn't been touched by the night's violence.

Still coughing and dry-heaving, Sofia managed to get the cremation furnace on and running. Then, using a makeshift torch she made out of a roll of paper towels and a metal rod, she set the place on fire.

"I feel pretty good for a dead person," Zack announced as he used his screwdriver to take a handle right off the door and let them outside.

Sofia took deep gulps of fresh air as they wound their way around the building, moving away from the sounds of sirens and screams.

"This way," Walter said, leading them through a hole that had been cut through the chain-link and barbed wire fence.

"How did you know this was here?" Sofia asked as she scrambled through the opening, careful not to let her hair or clothes snag on the bits of protruding metal.

"Same way I find out anything around here," Walter replied, crawling through the hole after her. "I keep my eyes and ears open."

Their luck held when they came across a parking lot that was full of cars but nary a person in sight.

Sofia went from one vehicle to the next, jiggling door handles and searching for open windows.

"Hey, Blondie!" Zack poked his screwdriver into the nearest car's door. There was a soft *click*, and then the door opened. He searched around, letting out an *Aha!* and producing a set of keys from the glove compartment.

He grinned at Sofia. "Ladies and gentlemen. Your chariot awaits." He swung himself into the driver's seat. "Now let's get the fuck outta here."

CHAPTER 12

GRAHAM

Graham rested his cheek against the tree's rough bark. He felt, rather than heard, the tree's whispers. It was agitated.

Graham could sense that the tiny, shriveled apples dangling from the uppermost branches would taste sour if he bit into one. He could also tell that what little magic the anemic apples contained was draining away. It was trickling weakly down the leafless branches, down the trunk, and into the soil where it was lost.

Graham was struck with a sudden urge to give his own energy to the tree.

He wasn't exactly sure what he was doing, but it felt right. It was nothing like all the times Aralia had tried to teach him how to cook with magic. That had always felt strange and wrong. This felt—

A sharp sting landed across his forearm.

"Ow!"

Graham turned to see Qiang Lee standing next to him, his pipe dangling from his mouth and a willow switch grasped in his hand.

"What was that for?" Graham asked, rubbing at his smarting skin. A welt was already appearing on his forearm.

"If you keep pouring yourself into every ailing plant, there'll be nothing left of you," the Reaper groused. He scratched at a mole on his chin that was sprouting a plethora of white hairs.

"If I don't, the tree will die," Graham argued. He wasn't entirely sure how he knew, but his certainty went beyond the point of doubt.

That earned him another smack from the willow branch.

Qiang might look as aged and gnarled as this tree, but the man had attitude to spare.

"You cannot let yourself be drawn into its power," the Reaper cautioned.

Graham almost laughed at that. Maybe if he'd gotten the advice a little sooner, he wouldn't currently have a Sofia-sized hole in his heart.

"Healing this tree is beyond even my skill," the Reaper said.

The cloyingly-sweet smell of Qiang's pipe smoke was making Graham woozy.

"What is this tree's magic?" Graham asked. "You never told me."

"No, I didn't," was the surly reply.

In the short time he'd spent living with the Reaper, Graham had come to learn that Qiang only gave cryptic and terse answers to questions…except when it came to the garden. Then, he expounded for minutes and sometimes even hours about the intricate nature of each plant.

This was the first time the Reaper had flat-out refused to discuss something garden-related. And it happened to be the part of the garden that interested Graham the most.

"Come."

Qiang crooked a finger at Graham before hobbling over to neat little rows of magical celery. Qiang sank down onto the ground with more creaks and groans than a dead tree during a storm. He adjusted his poncho and kicked off his shoes, which were full of holes.

"Well?" the Reaper barked.

"Magical celery," Graham recited, knowing by now what was expected of him. "Takes two-and-a-half years to mature. In optimal conditions, one stalk in fifty will be magical. Magical properties include water purification and mold eradication within a five-mile radius."

Thanks to Clementine's tutoring and his own exploration, Graham was familiar with just about every plant in the garden. Except for that damn apple tree.

The Reaper grunted, which was the closest he ever came to praise. He'd been quizzing Graham like this every second he'd been awake since Graham arrived.

Graham didn't ask why—he was simply grateful for any excuse to spend time in the garden. So long as he was here, his magic and his head were at peace.

For a chronic insomniac who was plagued with night terrors when he did manage to fall asleep, peace was the last thing Graham had expected to find after the whole Tennessee fiasco. And yet, after Clementine had fed him and given him a tour of the garden, Graham had sat down at the base of a birch tree and fallen asleep. He'd woken up eight hours later.

"This celery won't be ready for years," the Reaper grumbled, motioning to the plants with his pipe. "Since Clementine gave all of my mature crops to that girl, I have nothing to harvest this season." He made a disgruntled sound in the back of his throat.

Graham didn't have to ask who the Reaper meant by *that girl*. Sofia.

"Ah," the Reaper said, regarding Graham through one slitted eye. "Finally some emotion out of you. I was beginning to think you had none."

"I have them," Graham mumbled. He just usually didn't let them get the best of him.

Unable to sit still any longer, Graham gave in to his urge to return to the ailing apple tree.

"That will never work," Qiang growled, getting slowly to his feet and limping over. "You have to—"

Graham waited, but when nothing else came, he pulled his attention away from the tree and turned to the Reaper.

Qiang blinked at Graham, seeming disoriented.

"W-who are you?" Qiang demanded.

"Um, what?" Graham glanced to either side in bewilderment.

Had he missed something?

Qiang scrambled back from Graham. The Reaper tugged on the long wisps of white hair on his chin as he regarded Graham with a mixture of confusion and fear.

"Get out of here!" the Reaper reached for a stick and waved it in Graham's direction like it was a weapon. "Get out. Get out!"

Clementine burst out of the hut and came running toward them. Graham put his hands in the air as though to show he was unarmed and hadn't done anything to hurt the Reaper, who was growing more agitated by the second.

"Intruder!" the Reaper shouted.

"It's alright, Reaper Lee," Clementine said in a soothing voice. She gently but firmly pressed Qiang's thrashing arms down to his sides. She pulled a dish towel off her shoulder and held it to the Reaper's nose, which was bleeding.

"Let's get you inside, Reaper Lee," Clementine said, leading him toward the hut. "I'll fix you your tea, and then you can take a nap. You'll feel so much better."

As she steered the Reaper past Graham, she gave him a small smile and shake of her head before the two of them disappeared into the hut.

Unsure of what had just happened and whether he should try and help, Graham just stood there until Clementine came back out. She fussed with the chunky bracelets on her wrist before giving him a smile that didn't quite meet her eyes.

"Fancy a trip to the supermarket with me while Reaper Lee is resting?" Clementine threaded her arm through Graham's and started leading him toward the driveway. "Reaper Lee might be able to subsist only on ingredients from his garden, but there are some kinds of magic that just can't be grown. Like gummy worms." She giggled. "And donuts. With *sprinkles.*"

"Clementine." Graham stopped walking. "What was that?"

Clementine's sunshine attitude wavered for only a moment.

"Oh, Reaper Lee just gets tired sometimes. He's got a lot on his mind."

Graham was about to point out that people with a lot on their minds didn't get bloody noses and amnesia.

"Please, Graham," Clementine begged. "Can we not talk about this?"

The way her bottom lip wobbled convinced Graham to drop the issue. He gave her a stiff nod.

"Supermarket," Clementine said. "You. Me. Gummy worms. It'll be a party."

She gave his arm another tug.

"I…can't," Graham said, hanging back.

"You don't want to go with me?" Clementine jutted out her chin and made a pouty face.

"It's not that," he hastened to say, not wanting to upset her any more. "I just can't…go out in public."

Please don't ask me why.

"Oh." Clementine's face brightened. "No worries. Reaper Lee makes a salve from magical jicama that can temporarily change your skin and eye color to whatever shade you choose. That should be enough of a disguise, right?" She didn't wait for an answer before forging on. "I think we've got a single dose left."

"Clementine—"

"I'll go get it. Be back in a flash!"

Clementine returned moments later with a pot of cream. She smeared the goop onto Graham's face, talking all the while about how he had nothing to worry about.

"I really don't know about this," Graham tried in a final attempt to evade this outing.

Clementine's only response was to dig her sparkly nails into his biceps and hauled him along with her. What she lacked in size she made up for in pure determination, and Graham had no choice but to let himself be dragged in her bubbly wake.

"It's good to get out of here every once in a while," Clementine said as she climbed into the large box truck she'd driven the first time Graham met her. "Otherwise, you're liable to go as crazy as me!" She laughed again, but this time, it sounded forced to Graham.

A check in the side mirror revealed that Graham's skin and eyes had become more bronze than brown, and the distinctive gold rim around his irises had disappeared. It was probably enough that no one would recognize him. It wasn't enough to quell the feeling of dread that tightened his insides into knots every time he went into public.

While Graham tried to slouch down in the passenger seat, Clementine kept up an endless stream of chatter.

"You're the handsomest man I've ever met," Clementine declared as they pulled into the grocery store parking lot. "And you're sweet. Like, you're like the whole package." She giggled and brushed her lacquered nails across his arm.

It took Graham several seconds for her words' meaning to register.

"I'm…not," he stammered, feeling his cheeks grow uncomfortably hot. He looked around, desperate for a change of subject.

"Do you have a girlfriend?" Clementine asked, unperturbed by his awkwardness.

An image of Sofia filled his mind before he could lock down his traitorous thoughts. His desire to see her…touch her…was a physical ache that made it difficult to breathe.

"No," Graham replied.

Had any of it been real for Sofia, or had it all been a ruse to get him to trust her? To convince him to blindly follow her right into the cops' trap?

His father's mocking laughter filled Graham's mind until there wasn't room for anything else.

"Oh," Clementine said, sounding far happier about that response than Graham felt. "Would you—"

Graham got out of the truck and slammed the door with unnecessary force.

He kept his shoulders hunched and his head down as he followed Clementine through the parking lot. He almost had a heart attack when someone put a hand on his shoulder and shoved a piece of paper in his face.

"Excuse me, but would you like to join the Hunters?" the man asked.

Graham shrugged out of the man's grip and glanced up just enough to see that the man who had addressed him was wearing all-white. It was very KKK, and if he hadn't been so concerned about drawing any amount of attention to himself, Graham might have laughed at the irony of someone wearing all-white asking him to join their club.

"What's this?" Clementine asked. She leaned around Graham to read the paper he'd unwillingly received.

"We're food witch Hunters, ma'am," the man said. "Tasked with finding and eradicating them folks who sell their souls to the Devil to do funny things with food. It ain't natural. And the Bible says—"

"Come on." Graham gave Clementine a little push toward the automatic doors, sidestepping the man who was still proselytizing.

"God will punish them," the man said in an ominous tone. "But in the meantime, the Hunters will help."

"That was weird, huh?" Clementine whispered.

Graham could only nod. That knowing sense of dread he'd always gotten as a kid right before his father came home was churning in his gut. He just wanted to get out of here and go back to the Reaper's garden where it was safe.

"Would you rather chicken or steak for dinner?" Clementine asked, perusing a selection of pre-cleaned and packaged meats.

"Doesn't matter," Graham muttered, turning his face away from a security camera perched overhead.

"Of course, Reaper Lee won't approve of me buying something that was mass-produced." Clementine held up a package of chicken. "He says we live in a world of excess, and it's going to be our doom." She giggled. "He's such a fatalist."

That made a smile touch the corner of Graham's lips, because it was the exact kind of thing Aralia would say.

"You haven't heard from my sister, have you?" Graham asked Clementine.

He'd tried calling Aralia from Clementine's phone twice, but both times, it had gone straight to voicemail. Knowing his sister, she'd disappeared on one of her hunting trips and hadn't brought her phone.

Either that, or she'd gone on a mad rampage with the goal of destroying anyone she felt was responsible for Graham's disappearance.

The thought was almost enough to make him get in his stolen truck and drive straight back to the cabin.

He stopped himself by remembering that if anyone could defend themselves against Aralia, it was Sofia.

Clementine shook her head. "Our service is really spotty in Reaper Lee's house, so it's possible she called and I haven't gotten it. Can you believe we don't even get Internet on the property?" She blew out an aggrieved breath. "I also tried texting her and Sofia, but I haven't heard a peep from either of them. You're still friends with Sofia, right?"

Graham tried not to let it show on his face that his heart was tripping over itself at the mere mention of Sofia's name.

"Oh my *God!*" someone in the next aisle shrieked.

The cry was followed by others. People were running away from the bread aisle.

Graham and Clementine looked at each other.

"Come on," Graham said, abandoning their cart and taking Clementine's hand so they didn't get separated by the shoppers making a beeline for the exit.

They came around the corner as someone knocked over a towering display of cereal, giving them a view of what had caused the commotion.

Clementine cried out and buried her face in his shirt. Graham could only stare.

Three bodies lay crumpled next to a display of artisan breads. Blood was still trickling out of the corpses' bodies. One of them was a child.

Graffiti had been spray-painted on the wall next to the bodies. *Die, food witches,* was scrawled in red paint.

"We need to call the police," Clementine said in a wobbly voice.

That snapped Graham out of his mindless stupor.

"No," he said, sharply enough that Clementine flinched. "No police."

"He's right," said another voice.

Graham whipped around. A woman wearing a white apron and a nametag that said *Margaret* came to stand beside them. She glared at the bodies.

"They were food witches, and the Hunters took care of them." She sniffed like she'd smelled something distasteful. "This isn't the cops' business."

"What do you mean?" Clementine asked, even though all Graham wanted was to get away as quickly as possible.

There were three dead bodies in a grocery store, which meant the cops would arrive any second. Graham needed to leave. Now.

"Haven't you heard?" Margaret asked. She snapped her gum. "The President made an announcement this morning. Food witchery is a crime and punishable by a minimum of five years in jail if they don't register themselves or some such."

"What are you talking about?"

This time, the question came from Graham. A wretched hot-cold sensation was prickling along his skin.

He assumed that, by food witchery, Margaret was talking about culinary magic. Graham just couldn't figure out why the President or anyone else was talking about it publicly.

"You look like you'd make a good Hunter," Margaret said, eyeing Graham's muscular body. "Here." She pushed a pamphlet into Graham's hand and tapped her finger on an address. She leaned in and lowered her voice. "We're having a meeting there tomorrow tonight to talk about our next hunt. Next time, it won't just be three food witches. It'll be three-hundred."

"Wait," Clementine said. "Are you talking about culinary mag—"

Graham clamped his hand over Clementine's mouth.

"Thank you," Graham told Margaret tightly as he stuffed the pamphlet into his back pocket. "But we need to be going."

He half-dragged, half-carried Clementine out of the store. As soon as they were in the car, Graham turned on the radio and flipped around until he found a news channel.

"Food witches have taken over New York City," the radio voice reported. "Twenty of them were recently killed in an ongoing situation in Times Square.

"The food witches are considered to be extremely dangerous and should be avoided at all costs. The President is asking food witches to present themselves—"

"Ohmygod, we're not aliens," Clementine groaned. "And how in the world did the Vanillas even find out about us?"

"World leaders have been cautioning citizens about these extraordinary individuals," the radio voice continued. "A growing number of vigilantes and neighborhood watch groups calling themselves the Hunters are banding together to provide protection from magic individuals. It's not yet clear how much of a threat these food witches pose or what the best defense against them might be. This is still a developing story…."

"Reaper Lee needs to hear about this," Clementine said, stepping on the gas and screeching out of the parking lot. "He'll be able to fix this. I know it."

They made it back to the hut in half the time it had taken to get to the grocery store.

"Reaper Lee!" Clementine called before the truck had even come to a stop.

Graham followed more slowly. He waited until the cream Clementine had put on his face wore off, remembering the way Qiang had reacted before Graham had left with Clementine. Even once he looked like himself again, Graham hesitated in the hut's doorway.

The Reaper, who was sitting at the table with a mug of tea in front of him, waved his pipe in Graham's direction.

"Come sit down and tell me what's got my grandniece all in a tither," he ordered.

Graham blew out a breath, not realizing until that moment how worried he'd been that Qiang would stick to his earlier demand that he leave.

Graham leaned against the wall next to the potbelly stove and motioned for Clementine to take the only other chair. Then, they filled the Reaper in on everything they'd seen and heard.

"We have to do something, Reaper Lee," Clementine said, squirming around in her chair and gesticulating with her hands.

The Reaper took a sip of his tea. When he set his chipped mug back down, Graham noticed his hands were shaking.

"What are we going to do, Reaper Lee?" Clementine asked.

"Nothing."

"Nothing?!" Clementine squeaked.

"Nothing," Qiang repeated. "I am the Reaper. I grow and harvest magical ingredients. I do not concern myself with politics."

"This isn't politics," Clementine argued. "It's murder."

"Not our business." Qiang rapped his pipe on the table. "And even if I wished to get involved, I could not. Against my explicit instructions, you gave all of my mature ingredients to Sofia McKaid."

"What do you care?" Clementine asked, bursting out of her chair. "You would have just destroyed them like you do to all the ingredients when they're full-grown."

"It is a Reaper's duty to ensure magical ingredients are not misused." He glared at Clementine. "There is no telling what kind of long-lasting harm will come about because of your foolish choice." He stood up, waving away both Clementine and Graham's offers of help. He picked up his pipe and pointed it at each of them. "You will work in the garden during the day and spend your nights in this house. You will not get involved in this madness that has the rest of the world in a frenzy. We will speak no more about it."

He waited for a nod from each of them before shuffling off to his room and slamming his door.

Clementine spun on her heel. Just before she closed herself in her own room, she turned to the side. Graham recognized her expression, because he'd grown up with Aralia as his sister.

That was the face of someone who had been told not to do something and was going to do it anyway…consequences be damned.

CHAPTER 13

BRAXTON

Everyone was yelling.

Rick was ordering the Gourmands to kill Braxton. The problem was that their chocolate guns had melted. Rick was shouting something about his magic.

Braxton barely noticed. Something was different inside of him. There was a sense of weightlessness, like a thousand kilos had been lifted off his shoulders. Like he could drift away with the softest of currents. He was almost giddy with the sense of lightness.

That was when he realized what was missing. His magic.

Not all of it—he could still feel a cushion of power around his core—but the bulk of it was gone. He didn't think he could cook even the simplest recipe.

That revelation should have been, at the very least, concerning. Instead, it was liberating. Braxton didn't have enough magic inside him to do anything. He couldn't use it to save or hurt anyone. He felt...normal.

Somehow, amid the surrounding bedlam and his own euphoric discovery, Braxton heard Kenzie's soft groan. He turned in time to see her eyes roll back in her head.

"Kenz!" He caught her before she hit the pavement. "What's wrong? What happened?"

"Hurts," she murmured.

Did one of Rick's people shoot her? Braxton hadn't heard anything, but there was so much noise….

He frantically checked her over, searching for blood and chocolate.

Kenzie didn't have any injuries he could see, but Christ, her skin was burning. Braxton could barely stand to touch her. When he pulled his hand away, his palm was red and blistered where it had pressed against the side of her neck.

"Braxton." Kenzie writhed in his arms. "It's too much."

"What's too much?" he asked, growing more desperate by the second. "Tell me what's wrong. How do I fix this?"

She didn't answer. She was delirious, and just kept repeating *It's too much* as she started to claw at her own skin.

"McKaid, what's wrong with her?" Chef Levy demanded, squatting down beside him.

"I don't know!" Braxton was wild with terror.

"Stud." Aralia appeared on his other side. "How's your magic?"

"Barely there, but it doesn't fucking matter," he shouted, even though Aralia was right next to him. "I need to help her!"

"My magic's weak, too," Aralia said. "You don't think—"

"My magic!" Rick shrieked. He gesticulated wildly as he jumped around on his podium like a madman. His hair had broken out of its gel hold and was plastered across his face. He looked as untethered as Braxton felt, although presumably for very different reasons. "What did you do to my magic?!"

Braxton felt his jaw go slack. He turned to Kenzie, who was crying out in pain as she convulsed on the ground.

"We need to get out of here," Chef Levy said. "McKaid, get your girl. This is about to turn into a bloodbath."

Sure enough, the Gourmands were tossing magical sunflower seeds into their mouths. Braxton and the others needed to disappear before the seeds' magic initiated.

Kenzie screamed when Braxton hoisted her into his arms.

"I'm sorry," he said, tucking her carefully against him and wincing when he touched the bare skin at her midriff. It felt like grasping a cast-iron skillet hot out of the oven.

"Hang on, baby," he begged her. "We're getting you out of here."

And then what? he wondered. He had no idea how to help her.

"It's her Culinarian ability," a voice said at Braxton's ear. He whipped around to find Benedict Vandermeer beside him.

Benedict's face was sheened with perspiration, and he was gripping his cane hard enough that his knuckles had gone white.

"I thought my earlier threat was a clue to stay away," Aralia said, whipping a dagger from her belt and holding it under Benedict's chin. "Guess I need to be more explicit."

Benedict's nurse—the woman dressed in green scrubs who Kenzie had called Nurse Ratched—whimpered.

"Mr. Vandermeer, we have to leave," she pleaded, tugging on the sleeve of his robe.

Benedict didn't pay her any notice. He didn't seem concerned by Aralia's threats, either. All of his attention was on Kenzie.

"It's inside her," Benedict told Braxton. "No one can hold onto that much and survive. She needs to expel it, or it will devour her."

"No one can hold onto what—" Braxton stopped himself as realization struck, sudden and fierce.

He and the other culinary magicians had lost the bulk of their power. And Kenzie had turned into a human inferno.

"She absorbed our magic into herself," he said, looking down at his girlfriend, who was sweating and writhing in his arms.

"She needs to expel it," Benedict said again. "It's the only way for her to survive."

"How do you know any of this?" Braxton demanded.

After everything Kenzie had told him about this man, Braxton wasn't inclined to take him at his word.

Benedict offered a wry smile. "I was the Gourmand leader for thirty years. I have been privy to centuries' worth of culinary magic records."

"Fine. Whatever." All Braxton cared about right now was Kenzie. "How do I get the magic out of her?"

How do I help her?

Several ominous, simultaneous clicks prevented Benedict from answering. When Braxton tore his gaze off Kenzie, it was to find that they were surrounded by the Gourmands.

The men were holding guns…real ones.

Adrenaline coursed through Braxton until he thought he was made of the stuff, but there was nothing for him to do with it…no way for him to fight. A sea of red, undulating cloaks surrounded them. Guns and more guns were aimed at their small group.

A small path opened in the circle of Gourmands to let Rick in.

"What did you do to my magic?" he snarled. "If you don't fix it right now, I swear to God I'll make all of you wish you'd never been born."

Braxton held Kenzie tighter. Fear flooded through him when she didn't make a sound. She wasn't fighting against him anymore, and he realized it was because she'd passed out.

Kenzie's skin was growing hotter by the second. It was like trying to hold onto a furnace.

"Kill us, and you'll never get your magic back," Chef Levy told Rick.

"Fuck that," Rick snarled. His whole body was quivering with pent-up rage. "Whatever recipe you used to pull this little stunt will die with you." To the Gourmands, he said, "Kill them all."

"Mr. Santiori—" Benedict began, but his voice was cut off by the sound of gunfire.

Braxton tensed, expecting a bullet to rip through his body.

Instead, the Gourmands began to fall.

Rick shouted something indecipherable. The Gourmands moved with magically-enhanced speed. One second, they were surrounding Braxton and his friends; the next, they were meters away.

As the Gourmands retreated, Braxton got his first glimpse of their saviors. They were wearing all white and carrying assault weapons.

Who the hell were these people?

The Vanillas who had come to Times Square for the exhibition were realizing they'd gotten way more than they'd bargained for. Everyone was fleeing…or attempting to flee. Braxton was getting a mental image of those religious pilgrimage stampedes that periodically showed up in the news.

Rivulets of blood were streaming across the pavement as the soldiers in white faced off against the Gourmands.

"The food witches are a threat to humankind," a voice boomed through the speaker system. "If we don't stop them, their black magic will drag us all down to Hell."

The man who had taken Rick's place on the podium was dressed all in white. He was tall and reed-thin, and he was holding a sign with *Death to food witches* written in bold red.

"We are the Hunters," the man said. "We're going to root the food witches out and send them back to the Devil that made them!"

Braxton could only watch as the soldiers in white took over the square. The Gourmands were fighting for all they were worth, but they were outnumbered.

"Mom!"

The young Gourmand with ginger hair reached a hand out to Rosemary.

Rosemary, who was sitting on the ground and clutching her lunch bag to her chest, didn't so much as raise her head.

"Mom!" he called again, just before a gag was stuffed in his mouth. A soldier in white slapped handcuffs on his wrists and wrenched him away.

"What the actual fuck is going on right now?" Aralia asked, whipping Braxton in the face with her braids as she turned her head from side to side.

"I don't want anything to do with this," Nurse Ratched was saying. "I don't want to die!"

She elbowed her way past Benedict and others in her way. She leapt over a dead Vanilla on the ground before being swallowed up in the insanity.

Kenzie shifted in Braxton's arms. Everything else fell out of focus as all of Braxton's awareness centered on her.

"Hurts," Kenzie gasped. Her eyelids fluttered. Her muscles tensed, and she cried out in pain.

Braxton had never felt more helpless.

"I told Rick Santiori not to reveal magic to the Vanillas," Benedict raved, thumping his cane on the asphalt. "I told him if they found out about us, it would spell our doom." His mad gaze swiveled onto Kenzie, who was still delirious. "She is the only one powerful enough to save our people."

"She can't save everyone else if she dies right now," Chef Levy snapped. "Why don't you do something useful and help us get her out of here?"

Braxton had no idea what a bloke with a bum leg could do in this clusterfuck of a situation, but he was willing to try anything if it might give Kenzie a fighting chance.

Two more Gourmands dropped, which opened a narrow path in the fighting.

"Come on," Chef Levy ordered. She bent down to haul Rosemary, who was rocking and humming to herself, to her feet. To Benedict, she shouted, "Lose the cloak, you goddamn fool!"

Benedict, seeming shell-shocked, contemplated the order for several crucial seconds before dropping his cane and stripping out of his cloak. He was just bending down to reclaim his cane when a Hunter spotted them.

"Uh-oh," Aralia said.

Kenzie let out a small moan as she raised her head. She stared at Benedict through glazed eyes.

"Save magic," Benedict told her. "Save us all."

"You're under arrest!" the Hunter called. He tucked his gun under his arm and began unwinding a length of chain he had slung over his shoulder. "Come quietly and you'll be permitted to live until your trial."

"Tempting," Aralia replied. "But I think not."

Sensing he was in the midst of a predator more dangerous than himself, the Hunter stopped fiddling with his chain and reached for his gun.

"Go," Benedict said out of the corner of his mouth.

Then, with a quickness Braxton never would have expected from someone with a bad leg, Benedict threw himself at the man in white. He cracked his cane across the Hunter's head. Benedict grappled with the man as two shots fired off.

Benedict's body slumped. His dead weight fell forward, taking the Hunter down with him.

"Come on!" Chef Levy yelled.

They ran.

Braxton turned back in time to see the Hunter thrust Benedict's corpse aside. The man, his face streaked with blood, raised his gun. He fired at Braxton's group.

There was a *ping* as the bullet struck the metal siding of a nearby building.

They kept running until Braxton had lost count of how many blocks they'd put between themselves and Times Square. His calves burned, and Kenzie had gone quiet again. The sounds of fighting were barely audible.

"Braxton," Kenzie groaned. "Hurts so bad."

He stopped running, his chest heaving. He turned all of his attention on her.

"I know, baby," he told her, lowering both of them down to the sidewalk. He cradled Kenzie's head in his lap. "I need you to let go of the magic. Can you do that for me?"

He looked down at her beautiful face, flushed red from the magic that was eating her alive.

"I—" she began, looking confused and frightened.

"Let go of the magic, Kenz," he coaxed. He wished more than anything that he could do it for her.

Not for the first time, he cursed himself for not having been more specific when he ate that wish truffle. If he had, maybe he could have spared her all of this agony.

"Let it go," he said, raising his voice over the tumult of regrets clambering around in his head. "Just let it go."

Heat flared through Kenzie, singeing Braxton even through the layers of clothes that separated them. She cried out.

Then, he felt it.

Magic began pouring out of her. It shimmered on the air in a dense cloud as it rushed skyward.

Braxton followed the strands with his gaze. They exploded overhead in a shower of multicolored sparks. It looked like an explosion of diamonds. It was blinding in its intensity.

The magic began to fall back down in glistening, shimmering strands.

Braxton gasped as power zinged back into his body. It fused to the small amount that had remained nestled around his heart and lungs, filling up the places that had been absent for a short, blissful time.

Aralia and Rosemary were clutching their chests and breathing hard as magic rushed back into each of them. More magical threads zipped off in every direction, presumably returning to their rightful owners.

Finally spent of all her excess magic, Kenzie let out a shuddering sigh.

"You okay, baby?" Braxton asked.

In answer, she fell boneless against him.

CHAPTER 14

SOFIA

Can't this hunk of junk go any faster?" Sofia gritted out.

"This hunk of junk saved our asses," Zack replied affably from the driver's seat. "So what if her radio's shot and her carburetor's a little saggy? She's still a MILF. Or would be, if I were into women." He caressed the car's dashboard.

"What makes you so sure the car's a *her?*" Sofia scoffed.

"Fact," Zack replied sagely. "And I'm naming her Zelda."

"We're not naming a stolen car," Sofia said.

"What's a MILF?" Walter asked from the backseat.

Zack snorted. "How did you survive five years in Rikers, bro?"

"Not easily," Walter said. The seriousness of his reply shut Zack up, at least for a minute or two.

Sofia groaned when they hit a red light.

"Be grateful we're not going that way," Zack said, jerking his thumb at the opposite side of the road, where cars were stopped in bumper-to-bumper traffic.

"Strange," Walter said. "It's early for rush hour."

"It's New York," Zack observed. "It's always rush hour."

"It's not usually this bad," Walter said. "Something must be going on."

Zack gave them a few minutes of peace before he opened his mouth again.

"You sure we can trust this friend of yours?" he asked, drumming his fingers on the steering wheel. "I didn't go through all this just to go back to the can."

"She's not even going to be home," Sofia replied.

They were heading to an apartment that belonged to Sofia's old roommate from uni. Sofia had stayed with her during Hex Kitchen and remembered the keycode to access the unit.

Sofia's friend had recently inherited the apartment from her grandmother and hadn't gotten around to redecorating yet, which meant the apartment was the only residence Sofia knew of that still had a landline. Since the three of them didn't have a penny between them, it seemed like their safest option for getting a hold of Braxton.

"You're not even going in," Sofia assured Zack. "I just need to call my brother and tell him to come get us."

After everything that had gone down, Sofia knew that Chef Levy would have forced everyone to abandon the upstate New York cabin. But aside from knowing where Braxton wasn't, she had no idea where he and the others might have gone.

They were on 7th Ave heading toward Midtown. They were two blocks from Times Square when all the traffic disappeared. Like, they were the only car on the road, disappeared.

"Okay, now I'm freaked out," Zack said.

"Agreed," Walter replied. "This is probably the strangest thing I've seen, and I grew up in New York."

There were no pedestrians on the street, no tourists taking photographs, no doormen standing outside the hotels. It was like they were driving through a ghost town. Sofia wouldn't have been surprised to see tumbleweeds blowing past.

"Are we in the Twilight Zone?" Zack asked.

They reached another red light, but there wasn't a single car or pedestrian to stop for.

"Shit," Zack said. "Do you see that?"

Sofia craned to see out the dusty windshield into Times Square.

"What on Earth?" Walter whispered.

"Did someone drop an A-bomb while we were breaking out of jail?" Zack asked. He pulled the collar of his officer uniform over his nose and mouth.

Sofia rolled her eyes. "All the buildings are still standing, in case you haven't noticed. And I don't think that," she twirled her finger at Zack's partially-covered face, "is going to protect you from radiation."

"It might," Zack said, his voice muffled from behind the fabric. "You don't know."

Sofia had a smart response, but it caught in her throat as they cruised past the next block.

Times Square was full of bodies. Dead ones.

Sofia wrenched open the car door and stumbled out.

"Bad idea, Blondie," Zack said. "The radiation—"

She ran over to the nearest cluster of people. Three bodies were stretched out on the ground. Flies buzzed around them.

The weirdest part was the smell emanating from the corpses. Instead of blood or rot, Sofia could have sworn she smelled chocolate.

"I know him," Zack said, coming up behind her. He kept his collar over his nose and mouth as he pointed to one of the bodies. "And him." He nudged another corpse with his toe. "They worked for my Uncle Veneziano."

These were Santiori's men? Then, was this some kind of gang thing?

A cool breeze stirred a pile of trash on the ground. Sofia stepped to the side to avoid getting struck by the refuse swirling across the ground, when a piece of garbage caught her attention. It was a crumpled brown envelope that she recognized at once. It was one of Qiang Lee's magical ingredient envelopes.

Fury and longing surged through her as she picked it up. It was empty, of course.

Oh God. Was this massacre some kind of war over the ingredients? *Her* ingredients?

"Look at this," Walter said, pointing to graffiti that had been spray-painted across a billboard that was advertising a Las Vegas culinary magic restaurant. The graffiti said, *Die, food witches. The Hunters are coming....*

Below that were the words, *Cane will save us.*

"They say the world changes while you're in prison," Zack said. "But I didn't realize a three-month possession charge would leave me so out of the loop. Since when are culinary magic restaurants allowed to advertise in public?"

"They're not," Sofia replied, trying to comprehend what she was seeing. "At least, they weren't as of a few days ago."

This was Rick's doing. It had to be. He had her ingredients, and as the new Gourmand leader, he was the only person powerful enough to change centuries' worth of secrecy in the blink of an eye.

"Your cousin is a real piece of work," she told Zack.

He let out a humorless laugh. "You're telling me, Blondie." He cocked his head at her. "You think Rick caused all this?"

"I know he did," Sofia said.

"Not even my cousin's stupid enough to drag our world out into the open like this." Zack shook his head. "Can you imagine the chaos if the Vanillas got a load of what we're really capable of?"

"I imagine it would look something like this," Sofia replied grimly.

"We should check to see if there are any survivors," Walter said, looking around doubtfully at all the dead bodies.

"No chance, man," Zack said. "And we should get outta here before whoever got these suckers kill us, too." He started to retreat toward their car, but huffed and doubled back when he realized no one was following him.

Sofia walked carefully among the dead, searching for clues about what had happened.

A number of the corpses were dressed all in white. This was seeming more and more gang-related by the minute. Except, Sofia didn't know of any culinary magic gangs that rivaled the Santioris in strength. And now that Rick was the Gourmand leader, she couldn't imagine anyone being stupid enough to go after him.

"No one survived," Zack announced. "Time to get gone. Seriously."

That was when a familiar face caught Sofia's eye. She started to jog, and then sprint.

She skidded to a halt and fell to her knees beside a man—a boy, really—who had been a dishwasher at the fanciest of her family's restaurants. He'd been a tireless flirt and an aspiring chef. Now, he was dead.

Sofia touched his cheek, noticing the melted chocolate and blood that were still oozing from a hole in his forehead. Sofia turned her head, trying to swallow down the emotion that was threatening to spill over, when she noticed the corpse stretched out next to him.

Sofia knew this man, too. He'd been a sommelier at one of her family's restaurants.

Part of his skull was missing, and his brain matter was smeared across the pavement.

As Sofia's breaths grew shallower, she registered there was a row of twenty-or so dead bodies lined up. And every single one of them was familiar.

"Friends of yours?" Zack asked quietly, putting a hand on her shoulder.

"They worked in my family's restaurants," she said, her voice coming out thin and barely recognizable. "I don't understand."

"Is there a reason why my cousin might have a vendetta against you?" he asked.

That got a bark of humorless laughter out of Sofia. It was either that or devolve into hysterical crying, which wouldn't help anyone. Especially the people who had paid for their association to the McKaid family with their lives.

"Time to go," Zack said.

This time, he didn't give Sofia a choice in the matter. He practically dragged her back to the car.

"You drive," he said, when she started for the passenger side.

"Fine," Sofia said, not in the mood to argue. "But don't complain if a few curbs get jumped."

"Take it up with Walt," Zack said, pulling his screwdriver out of his pocket and jogging over to an abandoned Mercedes SUV.

Sofia's jaw dropped. "Aren't you coming with us?" she demanded.

He got the Mercedes unlocked before he deigned to answer.

"Nah. This is the end of the road for the Three Musketeers, Blondie."

"Seriously?!" She stomped her foot on the ground out of sheer irritation.

"I'm getting out of here while I still can." Zack gave her a rueful smile. "I've got a pal in New Jersey I can crash with until all of this blows over."

"Go then," Sofia said, getting into her own car and dismissing him.

She didn't know why she was disappointed when the Mercedes sped away, except that she'd gotten used to having Zack around. And he was good with tools, and decent in a crisis, and….

And they'd been through hell together.

"Good riddance," she muttered.

Walter was giving her a sympathetic look, which she pointedly ignored by screeching out of their parking space.

"Honey, would you like me to drive?" Walter asked, after the second time Sofia hopped a curb.

Damn things should be banned.

"Don't call me honey," she retorted. And then almost crashed into a light post on the next turn. She really was a rot driver.

She was about to give up and let Walter take over when she spotted a group of people crumpled on the sidewalk. At first, she thought they might be more Times Square victims, but then one of them lifted his head.

Sofia's heart stopped.

She forgot to put the car in park, and Walter fumbled with the controls as she hurled herself out of the vehicle.

"Braxton!"

She ran across the street but stopped when she was a few paces away. Her brother was standing but made no move to close the short distance between them. He was staring at her like she was a ghost.

"Brax, it's me," she said, like a bloody idiot. But, really, what was wrong with him?

"I thought—" Braxton swallowed. His face was getting paler by the second. He looked like he was in serious danger of passing out.

"Dad!" Kenzie cried. She stood, a little wobblily, and ran to Walter.

That got Braxton moving. He made it to Sofia in two long strides and gripped her shoulders. Sofia could feel tremors shuddering through him as he bent to look her in the eye.

"Sofia," he choked. "Oh, Christ. I thought you were—" His voice caught. Then, he was crushing her against him.

"Brax," Sofia squeaked, flailing her arms. "I can't breathe."

It took at least a full minute before Braxton loosened his grip. Even then, he didn't let her go. He took several, stuttering breaths as he leaned into her, trying to get a hold of himself.

"I thought I lost you," he said, his voice muffled against her shoulder. He sounded so tortured it brought a sting to Sofia's throat.

"It was just jail," she said, giving her brother's back a few awkward pats.

"I thought you were dead!" Braxton pulled away so fast Sofia almost lost her footing.

Braxton wiped quickly at his eyes, which were red.

"What?" Sofia blinked at her brother.

"Aralia got a call that Graham died, but I knew that you'd gone to Rikers in his place, so I thought—"

"Oh, Brax."

This time, she was the one to latch on and squeeze the life out of him.

"I'm sorry," she said. "I assumed I would be out of there before you heard anything about it."

It just figured that the one time the Rikers Island admin got their shit together and actually processed paperwork in a timely fashion, it resulted in that look on her brother's face.

"I'm sorry," she said again. "Brax, I'm so sorry."

Until that moment, she hadn't really considered how her choice to go to jail in Braxton's place would affect him.

"Will it make you feel better if I promise to never get arrested again?" she asked, trying to ease the haunted expression in her brother's eyes.

Braxton huffed out a laugh. "Yeah. That'll definitely help."

"Alright, then." She reached up and pinched his cheek.

He glared but couldn't completely hide his smile. Shaking his head, he ruffled her hair the way he'd done when they were kids. Then, he hugged her again.

They'd barely separated when Kenzie latched onto Sofia and began squeezing the daylights out of her.

"Thank you, thank you, thank you for freeing my dad," Kenzie gushed.

"You're welcome," Sofia said, getting more uncomfortable by the second. All this emotion overload was giving her hives.

She managed to peel herself away from Kenzie, who Sofia was beginning to suspect might be part-monkey.

"How'd my magic work for you?" Kenzie asked.

The question, Sofia knew, was meant innocently enough. But it rankled her. It was a reminder that the power swirling inside her didn't belong to her.

"A little watered-down, actually," Sofia replied breezily.

Kenzie just laughed, not seeming offended in the least. "The magic I gave you works a little differently from the kind people are born with," she explained. "It's still the same power, but yours isn't connected to the core of your very being. That's probably what you're feeling."

Kenzie smiled, not realizing how those words were like a rusty knife to Sofia's gut.

Sofia had spent most of her life wishing for culinary magic. Now, she had it, but it wasn't really hers. And she still felt every bit as powerless as she'd been before.

A tap on Sofia's shoulder drew her attention away from her self-pity and onto Aralia.

"Glad you're alive," Aralia said, offering a little chin dip of recognition.

Sofia was grateful the other girl didn't go in for a hug, since her hug quota for the month had been very much exceeded.

Chef Levy and Rosemary were standing behind Aralia, looking cranky and shell-shocked, respectively.

That was when Sofia noticed the last member of their party. A dark-skinned woman who seemed familiar but who Sofia couldn't immediately place was sitting on the curb with her knees drawn up to her chest. Her face was turned away, and she didn't so much as bother to look at any of them.

"Did you do it?" Aralia asked.

The statement was vague, but Sofia knew what she meant. She nodded.

"Graham and Walter are officially dead," Sofia said. "As long as they don't get arrested and fingerprinted, no one will ever come after them again. They're free."

"Good." Aralia nodded.

Sofia wasn't fooled by the terse response. She could see the relief, bordering on jubilation, that had Aralia bouncing in place.

"That was an incredibly brave and selfless thing you did," Walter told Sofia. "I know you didn't do it for me, specifically, but thank you, nonetheless."

Braxton muttered something under his breath. Sofia caught the words *send me to an early grave.*

Walter gave Braxton a sympathetic look. "Making a sacrifice for a person you love is the greatest gift you can ever give," he said.

Braxton released a heavy sigh. "I get that." He turned the full force of his stare on Sofia. "But if you ever pull shit like that again, I will kill you myself."

That made her laugh. "Love you, big brother."

Braxton draped a heavy arm across her shoulders. "Love you more, little sis."

Kenzie and her father exchanged another tight hug.

Rosemary made a small whimpering sound and started stroking the avocado charm on her necklace. Chef Levy wrapped an arm tightly around her, although it appeared to be more of a restraining kind of hold than a comforting one. When Chef Levy tried to unwind the lunch bag that had gotten tangled around Rosemary's neck, Rosemary slapped her hand away.

"I hate to break up this vomit-worthy emotional display," Chef Levy said dryly, "but I'd like to get the hell out of here before we end up dead on the street like the rest of the chefs we came with."

Everyone's mood sobered at that.

Sofia followed Braxton's gaze to the woman sitting on the curb. That was when her identity clicked into place. It was Raina—Philippe's girlfriend.

Sofia had met the girl a couple of times. On both occasions, Raina had been one of the most annoyingly friendly and happy people Sofia had ever encountered…at least until Sofia had met Clementine.

Sofia hadn't seen Philippe's body among the dead, but one look at Raina's expression, and she knew. Sofia cursed quietly.

"Rick?" she asked, even though she already knew the answer.

Braxton's expression darkened with a combination of grief and fury. "Let's get back to the food bank," he said.

"Food bank?" Sofia repeated.

"We'll need two cars," Chef Levy said, before Braxton could answer. "You imbeciles think you can manage to find your way back while I procure another ride for the rest of us?"

Sofia led the way back to her stolen car, with Braxton, Kenzie, Walter, and Rosemary following behind. Chef Levy broke into a van with almost as much finesse as Zack.

Just the thought of Zack sent a short burst of resentment through Sofia before she quickly tamped it down.

He's a criminal, she told herself. *What did you expect?*

"This thing doesn't look very safe," Kenzie observed, knocking on poor Zelda's rusted hood.

"This thing has a name," Sofia said. "It's Zelda." In a rare show of generosity and safety-consciousness, Sofia swung herself into the passenger seat and told her brother, "You can drive."

CHAPTER 15

KENZIE

*S**ave magic. Save us all.*

 Those had been Benedict's last words before he threw himself at the Hunters so Kenzie could escape. So she could be culinary magic's savior.

No pressure or anything. Sheesh.

It still seemed impossible that the man who had kidnapped her and been the bane of her existence during Cutthroat Cuisine had saved her life.

And then there was the fact that Kenzie had absorbed every culinary magician's power in a two-block radius. She'd managed to figure out how to release the magic back to its right owners before it ate her alive, but it had been a close call.

Kenzie felt like she'd been put through a heavy-duty laundry cycle. She had no idea which way was up.

But she had her dad back.

She was in the kitchen with him now. Yummy smells filled the air, and the rhythmic *clack clack clack* of her dad's knife on his board was as familiar to Kenzie as the thrum of her own pulse. In spite of everything going on in the world, Kenzie felt an overwhelming sense of contentment.

An egg timer on the counter binged, and Kenzie skipped over to her hot-out-of-the oven mac and cheese. The parmesan breadcrumb topping was perfectly golden. Cheesy goodness oozed between the bubbling macaroni. Sharp white cheddar perfumed the air, along with creamy gruyere and peppery asiago. Because one could never have too much cheese.

She was pretty sure there was an ancient Chinese proverb about that, or something.

Beside her, Aralia was spatchcocking a frightening number of chickens for dinner. Sofia was opening reserve-label bottles of wine from Polly's liquor cabinet. Chef Levy was alternately drinking straight out of a bottle of vodka and setting the table. Braxton and Natalie, his sous chef friend, were having a hushed conversation in the corner of the dining room. Kiwi was presiding over all of them from the top of Rosemary's head.

Raina had disappeared to the hotel with Baby Hiroto as soon as they'd gotten back. She hadn't spoken a word to any of them.

Kenzie's heart ached for what the other girl had lost. She made a mental note to make a plate for Raina and leave it outside her door in case she got hungry.

"Should we start calling you something different, now that you're important?" Aralia asked, oblivious to Kenzie's melancholy thoughts. Aralia bent down to her chicken and, in a single motion, yanked out its spine.

"Absolutely not," Kenzie replied, horrified by the thought.

"Crafty Kenzie, the Culinarian?" Aralia suggested.

"No." Kenzie glared at her.

"Your Royal Culinariness?" Aralia batted her eyelashes innocently.

Out came another chicken spine.

"*No*."

"You're so boring, Number Eight." Aralia yawned.

"Number Eight?" Kenzie's dad asked, cocking his head.

Kenzie sighed. "Don't ask."

She couldn't begin to process how weird all of this must be for her dad. He was even newer to the world of culinary magic than she was, and he hadn't exactly gotten a favorable introduction.

She looked at her dad, who was scooping out the tender pumpkin flesh from two halves he'd roasted. Kenzie took up a position beside him and prepared an egg wash for the pie pastry. The scents of cinnamon, ginger, and nutmeg filled the air as her dad made the filling.

"Remember that year we went pumpkin picking and then made a whole pumpkin-themed menu for Ashner's?" Kenzie mused.

"It's one of my favorite memories," her dad replied. "The florist did leaf arrangements for all the tables, and we got the hearth repaired so we could have a fire going during service." He closed his eyes and smiled. "That pumpkin hot chocolate you came up with was so popular we had to keep it on the menu through spring."

"I was so proud of myself for that," Kenzie said, smiling at the memory.

"I was so proud of you, period," her dad replied. "Still am."

He touched the tip of her nose with a knuckle that was covered in flour. She flicked a crust crumb at him.

As they continued to reminisce, tendrils of magic shimmered into existence above the pie.

"Want me to cook some magic?" Kenzie asked.

Her dad's hands paused in their work for only a moment. He nodded.

Kenzie began to weave the strands of magic together. Compared to the complex feats she'd been trying to accomplish over the last several days, this was effortless. It was energizing rather than exhausting. She barely even needed to think about it.

The pie was ready for the oven, but Kenzie was distracted by the sound of Braxton's raised voice.

"I'll be right back," she said, wiping her hands on a towel and slipping out of the kitchen and into the dining room.

Braxton's back was to her, so he didn't see her approach.

"I'm not fucking kidding, Natalie," he growled. "You're leaving. Tonight."

"I'm not afraid of you, Braxton McKaid," Natalie replied, planting her hand that wasn't wrapped in a sling on her hip. She glared up at him.

Atta girl, Kenzie thought. Whatever Braxton was trying to bully her into, Natalie was having none of it.

"You're not going to make me believe you're a curse," Natalie continued.

"Tell that to everyone I got killed in Times Square!" he whisper-shouted.

Kenzie's heart stuttered. She bit her tongue, wanting to jump in and defend Braxton against himself. Instead, she continued eavesdropping.

"I'm not abandoning your family when you need help the most," Natalie insisted. "It's just too bad for you, because you're stuck with me. If I die helping a friend, then so be it."

Braxton's whole body stiffened.

Uh-oh.

"I don't want you here, Natalie," Braxton said, his voice going eerily flat. "You're not anywhere near powerful enough to be useful. You're a liability, and you're going to get my sister and me killed."

Yep. Kenzie saw that one coming.

"Find somewhere safe to hide out until all of this is over," Braxton continued in that cold monotone. "Stay the hell away from me. I don't want to see you again. You get me?"

"I get you, Braxton. Loud and clear."

Natalie spun on her heel and stalked out of the room.

As soon as she was gone, Braxton's shoulders slumped. He turned and caught sight of Kenzie standing there.

"Not a goddamn word, Kenz," he warned.

Kenzie mimed zipping her lips.

"Kenzie, honey," her dad called from the kitchen. "Is this pie supposed to be doing something magical? Because it's not." He paused. "Although it does smell darn good."

Lacing her fingers through Braxton's and tugging him along with her before he could do any more damage to himself or others, Kenzie rejoined her dad in the kitchen.

Kenzie's dad took one look at Braxton's face and immediately asked, "Are you alright, son?"

Kenzie freaking loved her dad.

Braxton gave him a sharp nod.

Taking her life into her hands, Kenzie explained, "Braxton's beating himself up because a lot of his friends came to Times Square for him, and he thinks their deaths are his fault."

"Thanks for that," Braxton muttered.

Kenzie's dad put down the knife he'd been using to chiffonade basil.

"You aren't responsible for their deaths," her dad said.

Braxton gave him a sharp nod and turned his face away.

Kenzie's dad leaned over the counter and put a hand on Braxton's arm.

"Do you know how many times I brought Kenzie's mother to the hospital after she overdosed?" he asked.

Emotions Kenzie thought she'd managed to bury began rising to the surface. She felt Braxton's chest at her back, and she leaned against him.

"Countless," her dad said, answering his own question. "And every time I sat in that waiting room to find out whether that would be the time she didn't make it—" He paused to clear his throat. "—I blamed myself. I always tried to figure out what I could have done differently to keep her from hurting herself.

"You know what it took me more than a decade to finally realize?"

"That there was nothing you could have done," Braxton said in a rough voice.

"Precisely," her dad agreed. "Because everyone is responsible for their own choices." He gave Braxton's shoulder a quick squeeze. "What happened to your friends is heartbreaking, but it isn't your fault."

Braxton released a shuddering sigh, and Kenzie felt some of the tension ease out of him.

Her dad offered both of them a kind smile that melted Kenzie a little. "Now, tell me how we're going to make this pumpkin pie magical."

After that, Kenzie lost herself in the joy of cooking with her father and boyfriend.

Kenzie cut a generous slice of freshly-baked pie and plated it with a dollop of whipped cream. She handed the plate to her dad along with a fork.

"What do I do now?" he asked, looking at the pie like it might grow fangs and bite him.

Kenzie giggled. "Take a bite."

Cautiously, he did.

"Okay," Kenzie said, concentrating while she put the final touches on her magic. "Touch something."

Looking at her like he feared for her sanity, her dad tapped the counter.

He yelped and hopped backward when a pyramid of heirloom squashes shimmered into existence in the place where he'd touched.

"Well, I'll be," he murmured.

"Keep going," Kenzie urged.

Her dad took another bite of pie and then brushed his fingers along the wall. All at once, the white-washed surface turned a burnt-orange color. Leaf arrangements, just like they'd had at Ashner's that fall, grew right out of the plaster.

"Unreal," her dad said. He took off his glasses, looked around, and then put them back on.

"Don't stop there," Kenzie said. She was having way too much fun with this. Even Braxton was smiling a little.

By the time her dad finished the slice, the kitchen had been transformed into an autumn wonderland.

Clusters of burning candles appeared next to a tower of lit jack-o-lanterns. A cornucopia full of winter vegetables bloomed into existence on top of a cake tray. An empty wall became a fire hearth that was crackling merrily. Baskets of yellow, red, and orange flowers appeared in every corner of the kitchen. There was even a bale of hay with a scarecrow sitting on top. The air was filled with the warm smells of roasted marshmallows and burning leaves.

"This is—" Her dad twirled his hand in the air, searching for the word.

"Magical?" Kenzie supplied.

Her dad nodded, still staring around the transformed room like he couldn't believe his own eyes.

At the awe on her father's face, an idea occurred to her.

"Would you like to be able to do this yourself?" she asked. "I could make you one of us."

Braxton said something under his breath. Kenzie couldn't be sure, but it sounded like *You can have mine.*

Her dad reached out and touched her cheek. "Thank you, hon, but no. Cooking is already plenty magical for me."

Kenzie gave her dad a distracted nod. She wanted to ask Braxton what he'd meant, but his posture had gone rigid. Raina and Baby Hiroto appeared in the doorway.

"Oh, sorry," Raina said. "I thought maybe everyone else would be asleep by now." Her eyes were red and puffy, and Kenzie noticed she was wearing a man's shirt that was much too big. It must be one of Philippe's.

Just the thought made Kenzie's heart hurt. She had to stop herself from clinging to Braxton.

"What can we do for you?" Kenzie whispered.

"Gah!" Baby Hiroto said. He was wearing a flannel onesie with a smiling tomato and a speech bubble that said *I'm loved from my head tomatoes.*

Raina pressed her lips together and shook her head.

"Can I hold him?" Kenzie's dad asked.

"Gah!" Baby Hiroto agreed, reaching his chubby hands out to her dad. He scooped the little guy up and brought him over to the cornucopia.

Braxton muttered an excuse and fled from the kitchen. That left Kenzie to try to find the right words to comfort Raina.

"Um," she began awkwardly. "Want some coffee?"

In Kenzie's world, there was no better way to express love and comfort. Raina shook her head. And then she started to cry.

Kenzie engulfed the woman in her arms and held on tight.

"Hiroto will never know his father," Raina choked. "He'll never know how wonderful Philippe was."

"Yes he will," Kenzie said firmly. "Because everyone who knew Philippe is going to tell him." She gave Raina another squeeze. "Hiroto's going to be loved by so many people we'll give him a complex."

That made Raina let out a snuffly laugh.

They both jumped when a voice barked, "What is this nonsense?"

Chef Levy stomped into the kitchen and surveyed its transformation. "First of all, it's May not October, so this gaudy display is seasonally inappropriate. Second of all, you have more important things to do with your magic than be a Martha Stuart impersonator, Ashner."

"Sorry, Chef," Kenzie said, trying to keep a straight face.

Chef Levy threw up her hands and said something in Hebrew that Kenzie could only assume was a prayer of thanks for Kenzie's general awesomeness.

"If you're finished messing around," she growled, stomping back to the dining room, "there's something you should see."

Kenzie got Raina a mug of coffee and slice of pumpkin pie before they joined the others in the dining room. They all crowded around the TV, which was displaying image after disturbing image of what had happened in Times Square.

It was almost worse this time around, because when Kenzie had been in the midst of it, she'd only been attuned to a tiny piece of the horror. Seeing a bird's eye view of the carnage was almost unbearable.

The footage switched to a reporter standing outside the Brooklyn Museum.

"We're live in Brooklyn with Cane Solominck, the self-proclaimed leader of the food witch Hunters," the reporter said.

There was a weighted pause, and then a man appeared onscreen. Kenzie recognized him as the tall, thin man who had gotten up on Rick's podium and been shouting anti-magic propaganda in Times Square.

The man's skin was almost as pasty as his white clothes. Even his blue eyes had a milky quality to them.

"Mr. Solominck," the reporter said. "Can you tell us why you're so intent on apprehending food witches?"

"Call me Cane," the man said in a voice that was as thin and reedy as the rest of him. "My daughter was killed by one of these food witches." He paused to allow the reporter to suck in a surprised breath. "That's why I'm dedicating my life to protecting normal humans from them. Food witches are a threat to our entire population. If we don't stop them, they'll kill us all."

"Is that true?" Kenzie asked the room. "The part about one of us killing his daughter, I mean."

"No," Sofia replied. She had a cell phone in each hand and was scrolling madly across both screens. "Looks like the girl ate contaminated food while the family was travelling abroad. She died from salmonella septicaemia."

"Translation, Sofe," Braxton said.

"Food poisoning," Sofia said. "The bloke's daughter died of food poisoning."

"And now he's using that loss to turn the whole world against us," Chef Levy murmured.

"Now, Cane," the reporter said. "Isn't it true that one of the reasons folks are so spooked is because food witches look like regular people?"

"We are regular people, you cunt!" Aralia shouted.

"That's absolutely correct," Cane said. "Fortunately, one of our supporters has intimate knowledge of the food witches."

The sly smile Cane offered the reporter made warning goosebumps rise on Kenzie's arms.

"What do you plan to do with all of the food witches your followers are capturing?" the reporter asked.

Kenzie held her breath, along with everyone else in the room.

"I'm sure you heard about the unfortunate power outage at Rikers Island that led to the mass prison break," Cane replied.

Sofia pressed a hand to her mouth, stifling a groan.

"We've received permission from the mayor to use Rikers Island to incarcerate all food witches until Congress approves an appropriately severe penalty for their crimes," Cane continued. "These people have kept their black magic a secret from the rest of us. They've used it to cheat and gain unfair advantages over the rest of us time and time again. They've even used it to get away with murder.

"The food witches need to be punished accordingly."

"Holy shit," Sofia said. "Holy shit."

Braxton leaned closer to her and said something, but she just shook her head and kept saying *Holy shit.*

Rosemary started to cry.

"We have to do something," Kenzie said.

Braxton nodded.

"And what, precisely, would you like us to do?" Chef Levy asked.

Sofia surged to her feet. In that moment, the resemblance between her and Braxton was more pronounced than ever. It must have been the pure determination on Sofia's face.

"I'm going to recruit the most powerful culinary magician in the world," she said. "Aside from Kenzie, of course."

Kenzie had to stop herself from squirming uncomfortably. She definitely didn't feel like the most valuable weapon in their arsenal. If anything, she felt like a liability.

"And who would that be?" Chef Levy demanded.

"The Reaper," Sofia replied. "I'm going to recruit the Reaper."

* * *

Kenzie had barely fallen asleep when she was rudely awakened.

"Wake up," Chef Levy ordered.

Kenzie opened one eye, saw that it was three AM, and closed it again. She yelped when the blanket was yanked off her.

"What if we weren't dressed?" Braxton grumbled.

"Please, McKaid," Chef Levy scoffed. "Difficult as it may be for you to imagine, seeing you in the nude wouldn't be so much as a blip on my radar."

"Hmph," Braxton said, tugging on his shirt.

"It would be way more than a blip on mine," Kenzie assured him.

"Aww, thanks baby."

"That's enough," Chef Levy announced. She finished turning on every lamp in the room. For reasons unknown, a fan was also whirring. The cold air was making Kenzie's skin prickle and her tattoos shrivel.

"Rick put out an announcement on all the culinary magic channels," Chef Levy said. "Anyone who wants to fight the Vanillas is meeting at the old Hex Kitchen venue to discuss battle plans."

"And we're going?' Kenzie asked, dumbfounded. "To a place crawling with Gourmands?"

She was pretty sure Chef Levy hadn't forgotten those people had tried to kill them yesterday. Like, multiple times.

"We're going," Chef Levy confirmed. "I sent Aralia out for your outfits. She'll be back soon."

"You sent Aralia out," Braxton said slowly. "For our outfits…?"

He exchanged a look full of horror with Kenzie.

Yep. No chance of that going horribly wrong. No chance at all.

CHAPTER 16

GRAHAM

Graham leaned back against the mossy ground and stared up at the stars.

There was a spare bedroom in the Reaper's hut, but Graham rested easier in the garden.

After all the magic he'd expended in the garden and all the knowledge the Reaper had tried to cram into his skull, he should be exhausted. Instead, he could feel the ailing apple tree tugging at him, willing him to do something. No matter how many times he'd prodded, neither Qiang nor Clementine would tell him what the tree was for. Clementine had hinted that, if Graham could heal the tree, it might help with the Reaper's mysterious illness.

Earlier that day, Qiang had gotten three nosebleeds. He'd also fallen for no reason and forgotten where he left his watering can…which he'd been holding at the time.

Graham sat up, rubbing his face. Knowing sleep was a lost cause, he stood and started to walk.

The night-blooming jasmine reached out and tickled his arms with their delicate blooms. Their heavy perfume filled the air, bringing him right back to his first night in the garden. The same night he and Sofia had shared their first kiss.

That single thought brought on a barrage of memories Graham had been trying with all his might to suppress.

He saw Sofia's smile. He felt her body press against him as their tongues met in a scorching kiss.

He saw her standing next to the police in the moments after she betrayed him.

Aralia had warned him to stay away from Sofia. His sister had said he'd get nothing from a McKaid except trouble. He'd heard all the warnings and ignored them.

When he'd first met her, Sofia had been encased in ice: perfect and impenetrable. After a few conversations, though, he'd realized that was only her surface. Underneath, she was vulnerable and desperate to do right by the people she loved. And a little lost.

Just like him.

Sofia was brave and smart and beautiful. She was…amazing.

That's why you shouldn't be surprised, his father's voice sneered. *Why would a woman like her ever want a weakling like you?*

The rumble of an engine was a welcome distraction, until Graham looked through the trees and saw Clementine's truck peeling away from the hut.

There was only one reason she would be driving out of here at this hour.

He'd known Clementine was planning to go against the Reaper's orders to stay away from the Hunters. He just hadn't expected her to act so soon.

"Clementine!" he shouted. "Stop!"

The truck's brake lights disappeared over the rise of a hill.

Graham cursed and sprinted to the hut. He dug in the garbage and fished out the pamphlet that woman at the grocery store had given him. He found the address at the bottom of the front page and then raced back to his stolen truck.

With her head start, and the fact that she knew the roads out here far better than Graham, Clementine reached her destination long before he caught up.

He killed his headlights and parked behind Clementine's empty truck. He'd left the garden in too much of a hurry to think about weapons, but a quick check of the backseat revealed a heavy wrench amid all the empty beer cans. It would have to do.

As soon as he got out of the truck, he heard rowdy shouts and smelled smoke.

He kept to the shadows, slinking along as he followed the sound of voices.

Graham crossed a lawn that was in dire need of mowing. He'd almost made it to the bonfire at the center of the activity when his feet stopped working.

Ten corpses were laid out on the ground, just beyond the flickering firelight. Every one of the dead was naked, and the words *food witch* had been carved across their torsos. Three of the dead were children.

Lightheaded, Graham bent and grasped his knees, trying to swallow down the nausea that threatened to overtake him.

"You're all monsters!" a voice in the distance cried.

Clementine.

That got Graham moving.

He gripped his wrench as he ran blindly toward the bonfire, where a group of eight Hunters were standing in a circle. They each held a long length of chain, and they were taking turns striking their chains against whoever was in the middle of the circle.

"You're all Devil-worshippers," a Hunter growled. "Murderers!"

Graham heard the clank of the chains, followed by a whimper.

One of the Hunters moved to the side to get a better arc on his chain, giving Graham a view into the circle. Clementine and another woman were cowering on the ground, naked. The other woman was covered in blood.

"Leave her alone!" Clementine cried.

"Shut up, witch," one of the Hunters commanded. "You're next." He raised his chain.

Graham sprang.

He cracked his wrench across the man's lower back.

The Hunter stiffened, his chain rattling as his back bowed.

"Argh!"

Graham struck again. And again. He welcomed the blood that slicked the wrench and coated his hands.

He caught another Hunter's chain around his bare hand and used it to haul the man right into him. Graham head-butted the man. And then punched him in the gut.

As soon as he fell, Graham brought his foot down on the back of the man's skull.

Graham whirled around. He ducked beneath a length of chain that came at his face. He smashed his wrench into another Hunter's mouth. He felt his knuckles split when he knocked out a man's two front teeth.

Graham broke legs and ribs. He slammed his wrench against elbows and spines.

"Please," one of the Hunters begged, his chain clinking as he held up bloody, trembling hands. "Let us go."

Graham strode up to him and yanked the chain out of his unresisting grip. Then, he took hold of the man's jaw and gave it a vicious twist.

Crack.

Graham didn't wait for the lifeless body to hit the ground before he moved to the next one. He didn't stop until every one of the Hunters was dead.

Graham kicked aside one of the bodies and ran over to Clementine.

"Are you okay?" he asked, peeling off his jacket and wrapping it around her.

Clementine, who was curled on the ground and shivering, didn't answer.

"Clementine, are you okay?" he asked again as he scanned her for injuries. She wasn't hurt as far as he could tell. At least, not physically. She was clearly in shock.

Graham started to pull off his shirt to give to the other woman, when he realized she wasn't moving. Or breathing.

He checked her pulse, even though he knew it was pointless.

"Is she—" Clementine hiccupped. "Is she?"

Graham crouched in front of Clementine, careful to keep his hands behind his back and maintain several feet of distance.

"Did any of those men touch you?" he asked.

Even saying the words out loud made him want to bring the Hunters back to life so he could kill them again.

Clementine shook her head back and forth as silent tears streaked down her cheeks.

"I w-wanted to h-help," she gasped, her panicked gaze flitting to the dead woman.

"I know," Graham said gently. "Can I take you out of here?"

Clementine tucked his jacket more firmly over herself before winding her arms around his neck. She buried her face against his shoulder when they passed the pile of dead culinary magicians.

A little too late, Graham's father whispered in his mind. *That's your modus operandi, isn't it?*

If you were quicker, you could have saved them. You could have protected your sister from me.

They had almost reached the road when Graham heard the sirens.

"Graham?"

He heard Clementine's worried voice, but all he could see were the red and blue lights.

The police had found him. They had come to take him to jail for the crime he'd committed eight years ago. He'd spend the rest of his life rotting in prison. Because he'd murdered his child-molesting parents.

Graham couldn't breathe. He felt dried grass beneath him, but he couldn't see anything except the lights.

"Graham?" Clementine asked again. She said something else, but the words were drowned out by the sound of the sirens. And then that sound was muffled by his father's laughter.

A little too late, Graham. A little too late....

CHAPTER 17

SOFIA

Sofia was awake before the sun made an appearance. She didn't like the idea of Braxton and Kenzie going into the wolves' den without her, but if they didn't take a divide and conquer approach, they wouldn't accomplish anything.

She was travelling light these days, so it took only moments to throw her few outfits—most of which were borrowed from Aralia—into a bag with toiletries she'd pilfered from the hotel.

She grabbed her phone off the table—one of several she'd bought on her drugstore run the day before, and shoved it into her bag. At least this way, she'd have a means of keeping in touch with her brother while they were separated. Kenzie had taken one look at the purchases and declared them *badass burner phones*. Since they were officially outlaws.

Kenzie had then proceeded to hug Sofia without her consent and declare that they were friends *whether Sofia liked it or not*.

Sofia could go so far as to admit that Kenzie was growing on her. Like a congenial fungus.

But friends? Future sisters?

Even if Kenzie and Braxton stayed together forever, Sofia would never fully let her guard down.

Kenzie Ashner had killed Aidan. It was an accident, but it happened. And that was something that would always hang between Sofia and any friendship she might try to form with her brother's girlfriend.

Sofia rode the elevator down to the lobby. She expected it to be empty on account of the hour, but she heard a soft rustle on one of the lounge chairs.

Raina stood slowly, careful not to wake the sleeping baby in her arms.

"You're leaving," Raina said, her gaze dropping to Sofia's duffle bag and the keys to Zelda.

Sofia nodded.

"Can we come?" Raina blurted out.

"Um," Sofia said, thinking of Qiang Lee's sparse hut. "I don't really think the place I'm going is baby-friendly."

"Please," Raina begged, her voice hoarse with desperation. "I have to get out of here. I have to get away."

Sofia could understand that. After Aidan died in a Manhattan restaurant, Sofia had sworn to herself she'd never return to New York again.

"Fine." Sofia tossed Raina the keys, which she managed to catch even while holding a sleeping baby. "But you're driving."

* * *

"So, what's the plan?" Raina asked as she navigated the winding road through Acadia National Park.

"First, we convince Qiang Lee to let us use his magical ingredients to protect culinary magicians from the Hunters," Sofia replied. *Provided he doesn't kill us for trespassing.* "Then, we ask him to help us find and destroy Rick's stash of ingredients."

Sofia massaged her chest with her free arm that wasn't wrapped around Baby Hiroto. The tea she'd drunk during their drive had turned to pure acid inside her. Just saying Rick's name out loud conjured images of Mum's bloody, lifeless body.

Rick had taken Sofia's mum and her ingredients. Sofia was going to destroy him if it was the last thing she ever did.

She directed Raina to park their car on the rise just before Qiang's hut came into view. She figured it might soften the blow of her appearance if they didn't drive up like they owned the place.

Sofia handed a now-awake and grinning Hiroto to his mother. Hiroto's outfit for the day had a smiling marshmallow and the words *Nothing s'more cuter than me.*

Sofia found herself holding her breath when she knocked on the Reaper's door. Raina stood quietly beside her. To her credit, Raina didn't say anything about the downgrade in accommodations she'd unwittingly signed on for.

Sofia was starting to see stars from oxygen deprivation, and still, no one answered the door. She pressed her ear to the wood but didn't hear any movement coming from inside.

"Maybe he's in the garden," Sofia said, gesturing for Raina to follow her around the side of the house.

The narrow footpath brought them to a border of tall trees that offered them some cover as they peered into the garden. Beside Sofia, Raina gasped.

Sofia had only ever seen the garden at night, so it was almost as new for her as it was for Raina.

The sunlight sparkled over everything, making the colors less luminous but more intense than they'd been in the dark. The air was perfumed with fruity nectar and rich earth.

The air felt thick…charged.

Sofia realized it wasn't the light that was changing the way she was perceiving the garden. She was different. The last time she'd been here, she hadn't been able to sense the garden's magic. That wasn't the case anymore.

The borrowed magic swirling around inside her was agitated, but in a good way. It was like a kid in a candy shop situation…wanting everything and not knowing where to look first.

At least, until she saw him.

Graham. He was here.

Everything, including her magic, stilled.

Graham was standing with his forehead lightly pressed to a black-as-night tree. A few sad-looking apples dangled from the leafless branches. A light sheen of sweat was making Graham's face sparkle in the sunlight. His eyes were squeezed shut and his lips were moving as though he were talking to the tree.

He was wearing ripped jeans and an undershirt that molded to his bulging muscles. He was turned to the side, which gave Sofia a mouthwatering view of the way his shirt had ridden up to reveal a sliver of his V-cut abs.

Blood surged down to her toes, readying her body to sprint straight to him and throw herself into his arms. And yet, she didn't move. The knowledge of what she'd done to Graham kept her rooted in place.

Sofia had many strengths. Apologies weren't one of them.

"Uh-oh," Raina said under her breath.

Sofia had forgotten anyone else in the entire world existed. She turned to the other girl, who was bouncing Hiroto on her hip and giving Sofia a little smirk.

"I know that look," Raina said.

Sofia grimaced. "Is it that obvious?"

Raina gave her a little nudge. "Quit standing here with me and go get him."

Sofia clenched her fists, like she was a boxer about to go into the ring.

I knew telling the police about you was wrong from the minute we pulled up to that intersection, she began in her head. *I should have had more faith in you. I was afraid....*

Her internal gears ground to a halt as Clementine's high-pitched and overenthusiastic voice filled the garden.

"Gra-ham," she sing-songed.

He opened his eyes and turned to face the petite bundle of joy. She was wearing a pink miniskirt that would have given Aralia's style a run for her money in terms of length...or lack thereof. She was wobbling around in sandals that would have been cute in a bar setting but were completely outrageous in a garden.

When Clementine practically fell into Graham's arms, Sofia stopped paying attention to the girl's outfit. The two of them leaned toward each other as Graham's hands came to rest on Clementine's waist. Sofia caught the low, smoky rumble of Graham's voice, although she couldn't hear his words.

Clementine thrust her arms up, encircling Graham's neck. And then—

They were kissing.

Sofia's stomach lurched. She turned away quickly, swallowing down the unpleasant burning sensation that was tearing through her insides. She really needed to lay off the green tea so early in the morning.

"It's fine," Sofia snapped at Raina, who was giving her a look full of unwelcome sympathy. "I honestly couldn't care less."

The only reason she'd wasted even a nanobyte of brain space on Graham was because she felt guilty for betraying him. She could see now that her guilt had been unwarranted. Graham clearly wasn't hung up on whatever had gone down between them. He'd moved on.

Now, she could too.

Be the Robot, she ordered herself.

Sofia was here for a reason, and that reason had nothing to do with Graham. She scanned the rest of the garden, careful not to look in Graham and Clementine's direction again. Finally, she found what she was looking for.

Qiang Lee was kneeling on the loamy ground beside a bubbling spring. His pipe was dangling out of his mouth as he yanked weeds from the soil.

Sofia raised her chin and took a centering breath. Then, she went to go talk to the Reaper.

CHAPTER 18

GRAHAM

What are you doing?" Graham tore his mouth away from Clementine's.

One second, he'd been reaching out to steady her before she tripped on those ridiculous shoes she was wearing. The next, she was mauling his face.

"Wow," Clementine said dreamily. "You're a really good kisser."

"Um." Graham shook his head, trying to think of the right way to let her down without hurting her feelings. He knew for a fact he hadn't kissed her back. "Clementine, I'm sorry if I gave you the wrong impression, but I can't. We—can't."

"But," Clementine reached for him again. "I think I love you."

Graham moved away so quickly Clementine almost toppled over again.

"No, you don't," Graham said stupidly.

He'd spent all morning trying to connect with the ailing apple tree and doing his best to forget about the murders he'd witnessed—and perpetrated—the previous night. Now, his sluggish brain was trying to come back to the real world. It wasn't ideal, given the way this conversation was progressing.

"You saved my life," Clementine said, taking a wobbling step closer and putting a hand on Graham's chest.

He shrugged away from her.

"I'm your friend," he said, needing to say something to take that look off her face. "I think you're great. It's just…me." He cringed at using that trite line.

"I'm twenty years old and I've never had a real kiss," Clementine said, her chin quivering in a way that made Graham feel like a monster. "I just thought—I mean—" She shook her head. "I'm so stupid."

"You aren't," Graham insisted. He wanted to pat her shoulder or something, but given the circumstances, he kept his hands very much to himself. "You're going to find someone perfect for you. It just can't be me."

Clementine blinked rapidly and regarded him. "Are you in love with someone else?"

Graham felt his face get hot. Clemetine disappeared from his view and was replaced by green eyes and blonde hair.

He gave Clementine a helpless shrug, desperate for this conversation to be over.

"It's Sofia McKaid, isn't it?" Clementine said, startling Graham and making him wonder whether he'd spoken her name out loud.

Yeah, it is, he wanted to blurt out. His mind rebelled against the idea, but his chest throbbed at the memory of what he'd almost had with her…almost had, and lost.

His father's grating laughter filled his ears.

"I thought maybe there was something going on with you two," Clementine continued, her voice getting higher and more agitated. "But when you came here without her, I figured I was wrong. At least, that was what I hoped…." She trailed off.

Graham tried to think of something to say. He looked around, as though the shrubs and trees would give him some guidance. His gaze caught on a woman standing at the other end of the garden. She was talking to the Reaper, so her back was turned to Graham. For a second, he convinced himself it was Sofia, live and in the flesh, standing in his garden. His mind had to be playing tricks on him.

Was it possible to want someone badly enough to conjure a phantom of them?

The sunlight glinted off her hair, making it look like spun gold. She was so beautiful it made him ache.

Normally, Graham could tell the difference between reality and the warped thoughts inside his own head. But he could have sworn she was standing *right there*.

"Ohmygosh, Sofia?!" Clementine shrieked. She bounded across the garden and threw herself at the woman, who, as it turned out, wasn't a figment of Graham's imagination. Sofia was here.

As Clementine hugged her and chattered in her ear, Sofia looked over the top of the other girl's head and stared at Graham. The emotion in her stunning eyes gutted Graham. It was hatred.

CHAPTER 19

KENZIE

Kenzie did a little twirl in front of the mirror. The gray sheath dress fanned out around her before settling back against her curves like a second skin. A lacey, expensive second skin.

Kenzie had been more than a little nervous knowing that Aralia was the one picking out her clothes for a black-tie event. Okay, fine, she'd been terrified. But *damn*. Kenzie looked fantastic. If she did say so herself.

The dress was a lighter shade of gray than her eyes, which made her irises appear even brighter.

She wasn't sure she felt like the savior of culinary magic-kind that she was supposed to be, but this dress was doing wonders for her confidence. Less so with the shoes. While they were sex-on-four-inch-spikes, Kenzie admittedly didn't have the best balance even in sneakers.

As if tonight wasn't going to be dangerous enough, she was going to have to worry about tripping and falling on her face. Joy.

"Ashner!" Chef Levy rapped on the door. "Get moving. We're trying to make a point, and fashionably late isn't it."

Kenzie took ten-thousand teeny steps across the room and opened the door.

Chef Levy was standing right there, wearing a navy pant suit and her trademark pissed-off expression.

The elevator dinged, and Braxton stepped out. He was carrying a tin foil package and wearing a tuxedo.

Kenzie swooned, although it was possible the shoes had something to do with that.

Braxton's green eyes did a slow sweep of her from bottom to top. He let out a low whistle.

Kenzie laughed. "You look edible too," she told Braxton. "I think we should hire Aralia to be our personal stylists after this."

Provided they all lived through the night.

"Fuck that, Number Eight," Aralia said, coming out of the elevator behind Braxton. She was wearing a black cutout dress that was classic Aralia—all cleavage and daring slits. She'd paired the dress with a white fur coat, because it was Aralia. "You have any idea how much material wastage the textile industry produces? If you're asking me...."

"We clean up nice," Kenzie observed, mostly to interrupt Aralia's tirade before she really got on a roll. "We should go out more often."

"This is not a social visit." Chef Levy heaved a tortured sigh. "And keep your knife hidden," she snapped at Aralia. "If that blade catches the light, you're going to light up like a goddamned menorah."

"I think everything's going great so far," Kenzie said, probably a little too loudly.

On their way through the lobby, Kenzie said a quick goodnight to her dad and Rosemary, who were staying behind for this particular adventure. Then, she followed the others out to the car Chef Levy had procured. Braxton unwrapped the tin foil packet, filling the car with the smells of roasted garlic and sweet cherry tomatoes.

"This will make our faces unrecognizable to other people for the next couple of hours," Braxton explained to Kenzie as she looked down at a charmingly misshapen heirloom tomato galette.

Kenzie took a bite, enjoying the crunch of the garlicy crust followed by the soft give of tomatoes.

She passed the galette to Aralia, who took an enormous bite and proceeded to chew with her mouth gaping open. Braxton closed his eyes, and magic shimmered into place over each of their heads. As Kenzie watched, her companions' appearances changed.

It wasn't a full transformation like the pea soup Sofia had made when she impersonated Graham. They all still looked like themselves, except for some subtle changes that made all the difference. Aralia's striking white-blonde hair turned light brown and lost the beads braided into her locks. She'd also dropped several inches' worth of height and had become almost diminutive.

Braxton's nose was now comically large and hooked, and his luminous green eyes had become drab and unnoteworthy. Chef Levy's spiky hair had become a sleek bob. She also had accumulated a little extra pudge around her midsection.

"Car's out front," Chef Levy said. "Let's go."

When Kenzie looked down at herself, she saw that her tattoos had disappeared. A glimpse of her reflection in the window showed a woman with an eyebrow, lip, and nose piercing. She also had black lipstick and waist-length blue hair.

Bad. Ass.

"Ashner, quit making googly eyes at yourself and get in the car!" Chef Levy roared.

"Better do what she says, baby," Braxton said in her ear. "Because you are looking so damn fuckable, I'm about to bend you over the nearest—"

"McKaid!"

There was a thunderous blast, and then something pinged off a metal sculpture two inches from Braxton's face. Kenzie was pretty sure it was a bullet.

Holy crap.

"Jesus, Chef," Braxton said. "You could've killed me."

"We should be so lucky," Chef Levy barked. "I suggest you hustle before I have time to reload."

They hustled.

The car pulled away from the curb in a swirl of exhaust before Kenzie had even shut her door. At least the rest of the ride to the Empire State Building was blessedly uneventful.

"Never thought we'd be back here again so soon," Aralia said as they got out of the car and wound their way through the hidden underground garage.

"Rick has been busy," Braxton observed as they stepped into the newly-renovated space that had formerly been the Hex Kitchen complex.

No kidding. Instead of the dome and audience seating that had been blown to pieces by Kenzie & co., they stepped into a pristine, red-carpeted hallway. They followed the other people in black tie to a fancy schmancy marble staircase that looked like it belonged in an old-fashioned opera house. Craning her neck, Kenzie could see there was a ballroom at the top of the staircase. Magic shimmered on the air.

Kenzie wondered if any of Sofia's magical ingredients had been used to help reconstruct this space.

A crimson-robed Gourmand stood menacingly in front of the staircase, which had resulted in a bottleneck of people waiting to enter. The man was holding a large book he consulted with every person he let pass.

"What's all this?" Kenzie asked, nerves fluttering around in her stomach.

"Checking culinary magic lineage," Chef Levy said in a low voice. "All of you keep quiet and let me do the talking."

The trio of women ahead of Kenzie's group reached the front of the line. The women gave their names, which the Gourmand verified in the giant book he was balancing on his open palm. Then, he gestured to a crystal bowl on a small table beside him. The bowl was full of Brazil nuts.

Kenzie could feel magical heat wafting up from the nuts. There was something slimy about the magic, though. Instead of tight strands of power woven into the Brazil nuts, this magic slithered around like it wasn't quite sure of its purpose. A slight burnt sugar aroma hung on the air.

That was how Kenzie knew this magic was synthetic. And not entirely stable.

The first woman in line took a nut, put it in her mouth, and chewed. The guard watched her for a few seconds and then nodded. The woman walked past him and started up the marble staircase.

The process was repeated with the second woman. The third plucked a nut out of the bowl and tossed it in her mouth. She chewed for a few seconds before looking at the Gourmand. He nodded and stepped aside to let her pass.

She took a single step and then stopped. She groaned and doubled over, clutching her stomach.

Kenzie yelped and hopped back as the woman's long hair began to fall right out of her head. A tuft, held together by a piece of bloody scalp, landed at Kenzie's feet.

There was a soft clatter as the woman's shimmery purple fingernails fell onto the floor.

"Yuck," Aralia said with little interest.

"We have to do something," Kenzie gasped, but Braxton held her back. He pulled her close to him so he could whisper, "selenium toxicity. Brazil nuts have it naturally, but these ones have been magically enhanced to have more."

"Selenium—what?" Kenzie hissed back.

By this point, the woman was writhing on the floor. Her two companions had noticed and were racing back down the stairs, crying out.

The Gourmand shoved the twitching woman against the wall with his shoe so the doorway wasn't blocked.

"What is this?" one of the woman's companions demanded as she crouched down by her shrieking, squirming friend.

"Magical Brazil nuts," the Gourmand replied in a bored voice. "Kills anyone without enough magic to fight off the selenium."

"She's a culinary magician," the woman argued in a frantic voice.

The woman on the floor was gagging. Bits of nut and bloody saliva spewed out of her mouth.

Braxton tightened his hold on Kenzie—whether it was to stop her from running forward and trying to help, or to keep himself steady, she didn't know.

"Not enough of one, clearly," the Gourmand said.

"That's bullshit, mate," Braxton said, stepping forward. "Your own law states—"

"The Hunters have necessitated a change in the laws," the Gourmand replied, cutting him off. "This is for the protection of all culinary magicians. Mr. Santiori hopes you understand."

Braxton started to say something else, but Chef Levy gave him a warning glare and shook her head.

The woman on the floor had stopped spluttering and writhing. It took Kenzie a few heartbeats to realize it was because she was dead.

"Next," the Gourmand barked.

No way. They were going to turn their well-dressed butts around and get the hell out of here. Kenzie started to do just that when Chef Levy stepped forward.

"Name," the Gourmand repeated.

"Frommet Blum," Chef Levy replied without a moment's hesitation.

Kenzie's knees had started to knock together, which made the tiny beads woven into her dress clink together. Braxton put a steadying hand on her lower back and nudged her forward until she had a front-row view of the Brazil nuts-of-doom.

The Gourmand leafed through his tome. With the added height her heels provided, Kenzie could see family trees written out in elegant script on the creamy pages.

The man's gaze scanned a page that was crammed with so many words it was impossible for Kenzie to read any of them.

"Says here all three of your siblings died in the Times Square massacre," the man said, giving the rest of their group a critical look. The hand he wasn't using to balance the tome reached down to where a gun was poking out of his waistband.

Kenzie got ready to bolt before remembering she could barely walk in these shoes. They were so screwed.

"Well, it's a good thing these aren't my siblings," Chef Levy—sorry, *Frommet Blum*—said without any of the feeling of someone who had actually just lost three siblings. "They're my…children." Chef Levy managed to hide her grimace. Mostly.

"Three different fathers," Chef Levy continued, since apparently the only way out was forward.

The man frowned as his finger traced down the page. "There's no notation about children on that side."

"There wouldn't be," Chef Levy replied. "They were all born at home, and this is the first time I've brought them out in public. They've got a fair amount of magic, but it's taken time to iron out their kinks." Then, she pointed to Kenzie's fake-pierced face.

Kenzie fake-resented that.

"Ah," the Gourmand said, still seeming uncertain but apparently not enough to challenge Chef Levy. "Alright, then." He gestured to the bowl of Brazil nuts.

Kenzie muttered a little prayer and took one of the nuts. She didn't breathe a sigh of relief until all that remained of the nut was the slightly-bitter aftertaste on her tongue. A quick check of her hair and fingernails confirmed that she was still in one piece. So were Braxton and Aralia.

All three of them turned to Chef Levy.

"I'll wait for all of you out here," Chef Levy said, eyeing the Brazil nuts and taking a step back. "Behave yourselves and don't do anything foolish…darlings."

"Whatever you say, Mother," Aralia said in a saccharine voice, adding a gratuitous wink at the Gourmand as she sashayed past him.

"Hang on." The man put a beefy hand on Aralia's shoulder. "You're all related, but there are at least three different accents between you?"

They all froze.

"Boarding school," Chef Levy said, gesturing again to Kenzie's face piercings.

Kenzie was really starting to get annoyed at her fake mother's judgment. It was a good thing her tattoos were under wraps, otherwise Frommet Blum would have even more reason to nag her.

"Hmm." The Gourmand was seeming to finally come around to the fact that their family wasn't exactly kosher. All brawn no brains, this one. "Only way out is that way," he said, motioning with his pointy chin at the staircase beyond.

Chef Levy and Aralia slipped their hands into their pockets. The Gourmand pulled out his gun and clicked off the safety.

"Whoa whoa whoa." Kenzie held up her hands like she was a cop directing traffic. "Our mom was just kidding around. She's got a weird sense of humor." Kenzie picked up one of the nuts between her fingers and held it out to Chef Levy. She bugged her eyes like Kiwi did whenever he was trying to convey the meaning of life to Kenzie.

Unfortunately, Kenzie didn't have that same nigh-telepathic connection with Chef Levy as she did with her chameleon.

"Darling," Chef Levy said through gritted teeth.

"Trust me," Kenzie insisted. "Mother."

The Gourmand adjusted his grip on his gun. The people behind them had begun muttering angrily.

In the time it took for Chef Levy to put the nut in her mouth, Kenzie grabbed hold of the slippery magic and gave it a fierce tug. Mentally speaking, of course.

The magic unraveled, leaving the nut inert and poison-free as it passed between Chef Levy's lips.

"Move along," the Gourmand said, seeming disappointed when Chef Levy didn't start decomposing on the spot.

None of them spoke until they'd climbed the stairs and stood outside a grand ballroom.

"I should be dead," Chef Levy said, her face pale and her usual kickass expression replaced by something closer to fear. "I don't have enough magic in me to make magical toast." She whirled on Kenzie. "How did you do that?"

"Took the magic out," Kenzie replied. She refrained from saying anything more, because another Gourmand was waiting outside the ballroom. This time, instead of doling out semi-poisonous nuts, he was announcing each person's name as they entered the ballroom. It made Kenzie feel like Cinderella…if Cinderella had face piercings and was going to a war council instead of a dance. So, like, it was practically the same thing.

"Mrs. Frommet Blum and her children," Chef Levy muttered to the man, who proceeded to make the announcement into a tiny microphone clipped to his lapel.

Kenzie was about to step into the ballroom, when the man who had just introduced them gripped her elbow in an overly-familiar way.

"Do I know you?" he asked. He leaned in way too close and breathed out a lungful of 100-proof air into Kenzie's face.

"No," Kenzie squeaked in a way that was not at all suspicious.

The man continued to paw at her elbow. "Wait a second," he said, his face lighting up. "You cooked at my birthday party last weekend, didn't you?"

"Uh, yeah," Kenzie replied.

Thinking on her feet wasn't Kenzie's strong suit. Especially when she was wearing stilettos.

"Damn, that oyster pie was something." He chuckled as his gaze dropped to her chest.

What the hell kind of magic had been in that pie?

"Want to have a repeat?" he asked, making it clear that the chef he was confusing her with had most definitely given the birthday boy more than pie.

"Not on your life, mate," Braxton growled, wrapping a possessive arm around Kenzie and cupping the side of her boob.

The man's hazy expression cleared, and his brow furrowed. "Isn't she your sister?"

"Come along," Aralia said, herding them into the ballroom.

Kenzie batted her eyelashes at Braxton. "I'm so glad that didn't take a turn for the weird."

"Focus, you imbeciles," Chef Levy said. "Let's do what we came here for before you get us all killed."

"Yes, Mommy," Aralia said.

"Sure thing, Frommet," Kenzie added.

"That's Chef Blum to you," Chef Levy retorted.

The ballroom was something out of a magazine—polished wood floors, crystal chandeliers that were each bigger than Kenzie's entire Tennessee apartment, and towering red-rose centerpieces on every table. The scent of magical food hung heavily in the air.

Rick was easy to spot, since he was sitting at a table full of red-robed Gourmands, and their table was raised on a dais in the center of the room. A freaking dais.

At that moment, Rick stood up and took a microphone that one of the Gourmands passed him.

"Ahem," Rick said.

Kenzie and the others quickly found a place to sit as the ballroom went quiet.

"I've gathered all of you together because culinary magic is under threat," Rick said. He paused to let the weight of that dramatic, but not inaccurate, statement sink in. "Hundreds of our people are locked up on Rikers Island, and more are getting slaughtered on the streets by the hour." Rick's face contorted. "And the US government has made it clear they're on the Vanillas' side. We're in talks with some international groups, but we need to take steps to protect ourselves in the meantime."

Kenzie had to give Rick credit—he sounded like the leader he'd become. Every pair of eyes in the room was riveted on him. It was like everyone had forgotten that he was the one who had caused this entire shitshow in the first place.

"I just received word that the Hunters broke into a school and slaughtered ten culinary magic children. *Children*." Rick held up a hand to quiet the furious murmurs filling the room. "For that reason, I've decided to gift a magical ingredient to anyone who provides proof of killing a Hunter."

Whoops and cheers of Rick's name filled the ballroom.

Aralia let out a low hiss. "Going around and killing Vanillas isn't going to help us convince the world to accept culinary magic."

Kenzie seconded that assessment.

"We are the most powerful people in the world, and we're being slaughtered like cattle," Rick continued. "The time to try and appease the Vanillas is over. Now, it's time to fight. It's time to show them how dangerous we really are!"

His words were met with thunderous applause from most of the audience. Kenzie noticed, however, that more than a few people were exchanging anxious glances. It was clear that not everyone at this meeting was eager for a genocide.

"Your move, Ashner," Chef Levy whispered, giving Kenzie a little push.

"Okay," Kenzie muttered, rubbing her hands together and standing up.

"We've got your back," Braxton said, staying close by her side. Chef Levy and Aralia flanked them.

Kenzie was a little wobbly on her feet. This time, she was fairly certain it was due to nerves rather than her shoes.

At least the four of them had their disguises to hide behind if everything went south. Not that a few face piercings and new hair styles would protect them from bullets....

"I have a better plan," Kenzie said in a loud voice that drew everyone's attention. "I think we should focus on showing the Vanillas that we aren't dangerous. If we can convince people that we're not a threat, then the Hunters won't have anyone to support them. We can get the government to pass laws on our behalf, and—"

"If you saw those dead kids, you'd be singing a different tune." Rick's lip twisted in disgust. "Furthermore, you aren't our leader. I am."

Kenzie resisted the urge to admit defeat and slink back to her chair.

"You won't be our leader for much longer, if I have anything to say about it," she said, sounding calm and in control. On the inside, she was freaking out.

Please, please, please *don't let me throw up in front of everyone....*

"And why would you have anything to say about it?" Rick asked, smirking.

Titters came from the audience that was absorbing this unexpected source of entertainment.

"Because," Kenzie said, letting the word linger. "I'm the only living Culinarian." *Breathe.* "And I'm challenging you for the right to lead the Gourmands."

CHAPTER 20

KENZIE

If you were a Culinarian," Rick said with a dismissive wave of his hand, "then I would have heard about it before now." He raised an eyebrow as he regarded his audience, like they were all in on a joke at Kenzie's expense. "I think we all would have." He raked his calculating gaze over her, taking in her piercings and blue hair. "I don't even know you."

As Rick studied Braxton and Aralia's slightly-altered appearances, his certainty wavered. Kenzie didn't give him time to puzzle it out.

"Sure you do," she said with a confidence she wasn't even close to feeling. "Remember when I was supposed to compete against your father in the Cutthroat Cuisine finale to become the next Gourmand leader? You know, the one where you impersonated me and killed your father in my place…the one you cheated your way through?"

The amused gleam in Rick's eyes turned to fury. Gasps and exclamations filled the ballroom.

"Do it," Chef Levy murmured. "Now."

Beside Kenzie, Braxton's muscles tensed. The air around them shimmered. Their magically-altered appearances slid away.

Kenzie looked down and saw that her tattoos had reemerged on her arms.

"McKaid," Rick said, his voice dripping in contempt. "How the fuck did you get in here?" He whirled on the Gourmands surrounding him. "How the fuck did he get in here?"

"Hey there douche canoe," Aralia said, wiggling her fingers at him.

"Seize them," Rick ordered the Gourmands.

Chef Levy and Aralia drew their weapons. Braxton pulled another foil-wrapped packet out from his jacket.

"Aw, come on, cousin," said a man sitting at one of the tables below the dais. He had dark brown hair and blue eyes, and was movie star-handsome.

For some reason, the guy was holding a screwdriver, which he was rolling around his fingers in a way that was mesmerizing. If Kenzie tried that, she'd end up stabbing herself.

The guy had something tucked under his other arm. Kenzie caught a sliver of brown paper before it disappeared under the table. She couldn't be sure, but she thought it might be one of Sofia's magical ingredient envelopes.

"Shut your mouth, Zack," Rick hissed.

"Hear her out," the guy—Zack—persisted, still doing crazy screwdriver acrobatics. "We all know you're the most powerful culinary magician alive. This little pipsqueak's just trying to make you look bad."

Pipsqueak? I'll give you pipsqueak....

A tense look passed between Rick and his cousin. It would seem even his own family didn't get along with him.

Gee. Who woulda thunk.

"There's an easy way to see if I'm just full of hot air or telling the truth," Kenzie said sweetly. "I propose a cook-off between you and me."

Excited murmurs filled the room. One of Rick's eyes began to twitch.

A little thrill went through Kenzie. She'd always wanted to make someone's eye twitch.

"Fine," Rick said. He stood up from his table.

He reached his hand behind his back so one of the Gourmands could give him something. Probably a magical ingredient that would flay Kenzie alive, if she knew anything about the way Rick's twisted mind worked.

"I think I saw some portable grills in the kitchen," Zack said, hopping up from his seat. "I'll go grab them, and then we can get this party started."

Rick glared at his cousin. If looks could kill....

Kenzie barely had time to regulate her breathing before Zack was returning with kitchen staff in tow. Two portable grills were set up, along with folding tables. A variety of fresh produce and meats appeared. There was also a spice rack and other cooking staples.

The other culinary magicians in the room began gathering around. Some were even pushing and elbowing each other to get a better view.

"No funny business," Chef Levy told Rick as he walked down the dais steps.

Don't bother, Kenzie wanted to say. She could feel magic oozing from whatever magical ingredient was clutched in Rick's fist. She also caught a hint of that burnt sugar aroma. The smell that trailed off the synthetic ingredients didn't exist with the real ones from Qiang Lee's garden. That was how Kenzie could always tell the difference between the two.

Kenzie gave the magic a tug, unraveling it. Whatever the ingredient was, Rick was going to get a nasty surprise when it didn't do whatever evil thing it was supposed to.

Hah.

As Kenzie finished dismantling the ingredient's magic, she was assaulted with a memory of the day Benedict showed her how the Gourmands made their synthetic ingredients.

Kenzie's mind filled with an image of Cookie, her friend and fellow kidnappee in Cutthroat Cuisine, being stretched out on that medieval torture machine. Kenzie remembered the way the machine had literally squeezed the magical essence out of Cookie's corpse.

Had the magical ingredient in Rick's pocket been made from Cookie's essence?

The ingredient in Rick's hand was inert, but Kenzie didn't stop there. After all, as she'd just explained to the entire room, she was a Culinarian. All the magic she required was inside her.

Rick was too busy insulting Kenzie and working up the crowd to realize that the competition had already begun. She reached imaginary talons inside Rick, seeking the magic that pulsed inside him.

Kenzie began to draw his magic out. She felt the air around her grow heated as his magic collected around her.

Let's see how tough you are without your power, Kenzie thought as she continued to draw magic out of him and into herself.

This time, she limited her magic thieving only to Rick rather than drawing from everyone in the room. She didn't want to have a repeat of what had happened in Times Square. And instead of only taking his excess magic, she intended to take it all.

She could feel the strands of power attached to his life force. They wove in and around his organs, as much a part of him as his blood or bones. It occurred to her that if she removed all of his magic, Rick would die.

Kenzie hesitated. She'd killed before, but this seemed wrong. If she killed him this way, she'd be as bad as Rick.

Even as that thought struck her, Kenzie remembered the way Cookie's dried-out husk of a body had looked after she'd been sucked dry. Cookie was dead, and yet Rick was still alive? Where was the justice in that?

And what the hell was the point of Kenzie's magic if she couldn't use it to give people what they deserved?

Kenzie reached deeper into Rick for the very energy that gave him breath.

She could feel it, pulsing bright and fierce within him. She could wrap her invisible hand around it and rip it right out of him and—

A commotion from the doorway rocketed Kenzie out of her furious haze. With her concentration interrupted, the magic started to seep back out of her and return to Rick.

People dressed in white were swarming into the ballroom. They wielded wooden clubs and lengths of chain, which they cracked across anyone who got in their way.

"Hunters!" someone yelled.

The cry was taken up by others. The ballroom became a whirl of sound and motion.

Rick opened his fist, revealing the shriveled vegetable he'd been planning to use against Kenzie. He threw it at the Hunters clustered in front of the door.

Rick's victorious smirk slipped off his face when nothing happened. Because Kenzie had stolen the magic right out of the ingredient.

Rick turned tail and raced back to his table, where the Gourmands had clustered together. They were bending over a burlap bag and grabbing handfuls of whatever was inside.

Sunflower seed shells began covering the ground at the Gourmands' feet.

The room filled with the heavy tang of synthetic magic. The Gourmands' red robes fanned out around them as they crossed the ballroom fast enough that they were nothing more than red blurs.

The two opposing forces collided. Red versus white. Magical speed against chains.

The Hunters grunted as they hurled their chains from side to side. The Gourmands dodged, leapt, and flipped with an agility that would put Olympic gymnasts to shame. The Hunters' chains couldn't touch them.

"Come on," Chef Levy shouted, pulling a gun out of one of her hidden pockets while she herded the rest of them toward the ballroom's exit.

Unfortunately, everyone else had the same idea.

About a thousand people were fighting to reach the exit—which was blocked by the clashing Hunters and Gourmands. Errant chains smacked against culinary magicians who didn't have the luxury of sunflower seed-enhanced speed.

People fell to the ground and were trampled before they could regain their footing. Others were doubling back in search of loved ones, which only added to the mayhem. Everyone was screaming. The iron tang of blood was heavy on the air.

Chef Levy shot down two Hunters who came for them. Aralia threw a dagger that caught another in his throat. The man gurgled and clawed at the air before falling face-first onto the floor.

Kenzie didn't think things could get worse, but then everyone at the exit began falling back. An ominous quiet began to spread through the crowd that had been shouting their lungs out moments before.

The silence was scarier than the noise had been.

When Kenzie saw the new source of panic, she understood. Soldiers dressed in military fatigues marched into the ballroom. There were at least twenty of them, and each one carried a machine gun. And they were blocking the only way out of the room.

"No one else needs to die," a voice announced.

Everyone turned to look at the man who had climbed onto one of the tables.

Cane. The tall, skinny man who had gone on TV and told the world that culinary magicians had murdered his daughter. In five seconds flat, he had taken control of the room.

This wasn't boding well. At all.

Cane kicked a crystal champagne flute off the table. He stepped on top of a man who was slumped over his plate. A bloody trail was soaking through the tablecloth.

"How did you find us?" Rick demanded, his voice coming from behind a wall of Gourmands.

Cane offered a thin smile.

Kenzie choked on air as a white pair of sneakers squeaked across the ballroom floor.

"Nurse fucking Ratched," Kenzie growled.

Her scrubs were now white instead of green, which made her pink lipstick stand out like a pair of clown lips. Her hair was pulled back into a tight bun, which gave her entire face a stretched appearance.

"Didn't I tell you, Cane?" Nurse Ratched asked, crossing her arms over her chest and nodding in approval. "Cul—I mean, food witches—are creatures of habit. I'd wager all the most powerful ones are in this room right now."

Nurse Ratched raised her overly-plucked eyebrows at Kenzie.

"Must have been so easy for you to switch sides," Kenzie hissed at the evil nurse. "Didn't even need to change your sneakers."

Either Nurse Ratched didn't hear her or chose not to react.

"You're trapped," Cane told the room, his milky eyes roaming across the group of terrified chefs. His smile was even more evil than Rick's.

Kenzie hadn't thought such a thing was possible.

One of the braver Gourmands launched himself at Cane.

The magical sunflower seeds made him fast. The soldiers' guns were faster.

Blood sprayed. The Gourmand slumped to the floor.

"Now, then," Cane said, crunching across shards of glass as he paced across the table. "You will all be brought to Rikers Island to await your trial. Any who resist will be killed here and now."

Everyone shifted on their feet. Some of them looked to Rick for guidance. When he was nowhere to be found, they turned to Kenzie.

Panic surged through her. This wasn't the battle she'd been expecting to fight. Nevertheless, she had to do something. She had to protect these people.

"Put down your guns," she heard herself tell the soldiers. "Please."

"Shut it, Ashner," Chef Levy growled.

Too late. A million pairs of eyes landed on Kenzie. Sweat was trickling down her back.

Don't pass out, she ordered herself. *Don't you dare pass out.*

"Put down your guns," Kenzie said again. "If you do, you can have me."

"Kenz, shut up," Braxton said.

"And who are you, my dear?" Cane asked.

The way he said *my dear* made Kenzie shiver.

"I'm the one you need," Kenzie said. "You hate magic? Well, I have the power to take it away from everyone in this room."

Behind her, Braxton sucked in a breath. He tightened his grip on her until her vision began to go spotty.

Cane turned so he was facing Kenzie. At the same time, one of the culinary magicians nearest the door rushed the soldiers.

Gunfire erupted.

"Fuck this," someone muttered.

It was Zack, Rick's cousin. He emerged from under a table with the brown envelope Kenzie had seen him holding before. There was soft crinkle of paper. Dust that smelled strongly of cinnamon poofed into the air.

For a few seconds, nothing happened. Then, the red-brown dust began to settle.

That was when the real panic set in.

CHAPTER 21

BRAXTON

The air was filled with a cinnamon fog. Within seconds, it became impossible to breathe.

Braxton buried his face in his collar, which made it feel a little less like his entire head was on fire. He was so consumed with his own discomfort that it took him several seconds to realize Kenzie was doubled over and coughing beside him.

Braxton held his breath and squeezed his eyes closed as he tore off his jacket. He wadded up the fabric and pressed it to Kenzie's face.

She fought him at first, but then she relaxed a little.

"This way!" Rick's crazy cousin ordered. He had taken off his shirt completely and had it wrapped around his nose and mouth like a bandana. He waved frantically as he led them through the murky haze to the back of the ballroom.

They were heading away from the door, where Hunters and culinary magicians were tangled up as everyone fought to escape. Gunshots rang out. Magic zipped from whatever ingredients the Gourmands still had.

Knowing it would be useless to try and get out that way, Braxton followed the bloke he'd met about ten seconds ago and trusted not at all.

Braxton hooked one arm around Kenzie, half-supporting and half-dragging her with him. Chef Levy and Aralia were right behind them.

They made it into the kitchen, where bubbling pots and half-opened champagne bottles lay abandoned. The further they went from the main ballroom, the easier breathing became.

"You trying to kill us all, mate?" Braxton demanded. It came out as more of a whisper because his throat was wrecked. Tears were streaming from his burning eyes.

"Nah, man," Zack said, his voice as hoarse as Braxton's. "Truth be told, I didn't know what this shit would do when I pinched it off my cousin."

"And so you just decided to dump out the whole bloody thing?!" Braxton demanded. "Christ. You really could have killed us all."

"Oh, relax." Zack waved a hand. "It's like seasonal allergies on steroids."

Seasonal allergies, my arse.

"Where are you taking us?" Chef Levy demanded.

Of all of them, she seemed the least affected by the magical cinnamon. Braxton wondered, not for the first time, whether there might be a touch of cyborg in that woman.

"Found another way out when I was poking around earlier," Zack said, leading them into a narrow pantry and pulling himself up onto one of the shelves. He took a screwdriver out of his slacks pocket and went to work on an overhead panel that blended into the rest of the whitewashed ceiling. "Hazard of doing time in the big house, I guess. Can't go anywhere without immediately searching out escape routes." He gave his screwdriver a hard jerk, and the panel clattered to the floor. He grinned.

"Name's Zack, by the way," he said, jumping back down to the floor and dusting off his hands. "Where's Blondie?"

"Blondie?" Braxton squinted at him in confusion.

"I'm blonde," Aralia purred, reaching out to stroke Zack's muscular chest. She did something with her elbows that made her boobs lop over the front of her dress. It was kind of horrifying.

"Tits aren't my thing," Zack told Aralia. "Thanks anyway."

"No one's ever said that to me before," Aralia mused, seeming more puzzled than upset by the brushoff.

"Your sister," Zack said to Braxton. "The other McKaid."

"You know Sofia?" Braxton said.

It shouldn't really have been surprising, since Sofia knew everyone. But between the cinnamon and the fact that they were fleeing for their lives, Braxton's brain wasn't exactly firing on all cylinders.

"Yep. Recognized you because of the eyes," Zack said. "Your sister was hotter as a dude."

With that disturbing comment, Zack made a sweeping motion with his hand toward the opening in the ceiling.

"Huh," Chef Levy said, climbing up the pantry shelves and poking her head through the open panel. "Ventilation shaft. Clever."

Braxton waited for Aralia and Kenzie to go through the small opening ahead of him.

When it was his turn, he hauled himself into the narrow metal tube. He stayed motionless and gave his eyes a few seconds to adjust to the dimness. When he saw what they were in for, Braxton let out a low curse. Chef Levy and Aralia were already climbing up the air shaft like spiders, with their hands and feet braced on either side. Braxton and Zack would barely be able to fit in the air shaft, let alone comfortably climb. Kenzie had no trouble fitting, but the combination of a dress and her endearing lack of coordination were giving her a world of problems.

"I swear to God I'm going to start an exercise plan when we get out of here," Kenzie gasped. "Glutes…quads…the works."

"You're looking damn fit from this angle," Braxton replied, catching a glimpse up her dress and almost falling back down the air shaft.

"Focus, McKaid," Chef Levy said, her voice reverberating off the tinny sides.

Fortunately, it wasn't far to the top, since the ballroom wasn't deep underground. Aralia and Chef Levy heaved Kenzie up and out before doing the same for Braxton and Zack.

They were all wheezing from the remnants of cinnamon in their lungs and their climb, so it took them a few scrabbling seconds to right themselves.

"Think anyone else escaped?" Kenzie rasped.

"I'm certain they didn't."

The voice didn't belong to anyone in their group.

Cane and the nurse—Nurse fucking Ratched, as Kenzie had called her—were waiting for them. Five soldiers stood behind them. All of them had guns, which they were aiming at Braxton's group.

"Now," Cane said, his thin lips twitching in victory. "What was this you were saying about being able to remove food witches' magic?"

Braxton wanted to kill the man for the covetous way he was looking at Kenzie.

Kenzie didn't say anything.

Cane nodded to his men. "Take her."

Braxton grabbed Kenzie and thrust her behind him.

The soldiers fumbled with their guns as they each tried to be the first to make the arrest. For the space of a few heartbeats, no weapons were trained on any of them.

"Not happening, you fuckers," Aralia snarled. She whipped out two hunting knives and held them in front of her. "If you want her, you'll have to go through me."

Chef Levy's gun was out of bullets, but she still had her own knife. Zack was holding something that looked like a knife at first glance, but which was actually just his screwdriver.

The steady clip of footsteps on pavement had all of them looking down the street, where at least fifty of Cane's Hunters were marching their way. Every one of the white-clad maniacs held a wooden club or length of chain.

They were never getting out of this alive. Unless—

Braxton felt around in his pocket for the small container he'd brought and hoped he wouldn't need to use.

"You can have me as long as you promise to let my friends go," Kenzie said, stepping forward. Braxton yanked her back.

He turned to the side so no one would see when he opened the container that held a squished egg-and-spinach omelet. He gulped down a bite and started to weave the magic.

This recipe was stupidly simple to make and convenient, since the magic was added after it had already been cooked. That meant the dish hadn't interfered with any of the other magic Braxton had cooked earlier in the night.

The problem with this particular dish came after it was eaten.

Braxton didn't have time to be nearly as precise with his magic as he'd like, but it was enough to do the job.

The soldiers surged forward with their handcuffs.

"I'll hold them off," Braxton said.

"No way," Kenzie said.

They didn't have time to argue. Braxton pushed Kenzie at Aralia.

"Go!" he shouted.

Aralia glanced at the dish Braxton shoved back in his pocket, and the remnants of omelet inside. He could see recognition pass across her face, followed by hesitation.

"Braxton," she cautioned.

There was no more time. One of the soldiers was reaching for Kenzie. The others were right there.

Braxton threw himself at the soldiers.

"Wait—" Kenzie began.

Braxton didn't wait. He punched one soldier at the same time he elbowed another. He felt a nose crunch and a larynx collapse.

A gun went off.

Braxton saw the hole appear in his slacks. He saw the blood oozing down his pantleg. He felt nothing at all.

"Braxton!" Kenzie cried.

"Go!" he yelled again.

Braxton plowed into the next man. He heard at least a couple of ribs crack, but again, he felt nothing. The man's skull met Braxton's fist. Braxton's knuckles split and bones in his hand gave way. He didn't feel a thing.

Adrenaline gave him strength. Magic took away his pain and kept him on his feet.

"Devil," one of the Hunters gasped, staring wide-eyed at Braxton's bleeding leg.

"They aren't human," Cane said from somewhere nearby. "That is why we need to kill them all."

Out of the corner of his eye, Braxton saw Aralia pick Kenzie up and toss her over her shoulder. Chef Levy threw a knife behind her, getting a soldier right between the eyes.

The man fell, and his gun hit the pavement beside him with a clatter. Bullets sprayed. The chaos gave Braxton a few seconds to disarm one soldier and take down another.

He turned to gauge how far his friends had gotten. They were halfway down the block. From the looks of it, Chef Levy had punched right through a car's window. Zack was squirming into the driver's seat.

Hurry up, Braxton silently urged them. He could feel the magic he'd ingested beginning to eb, and with it, an onslaught of pain began to take hold.

Cane and the nurse had disappeared back into their horde of Hunters. Braxton kept fighting. He was surrounded.

A chain whipped across his back as he knocked another Hunter to the ground. Braxton took a club to the stomach as he broke a soldier's elbow. He whirled around and smashed two Hunters' heads together and threw them to the ground.

He punched and kicked and fought until the last gleams of magic faded. All at once, the numbness receded and the pain of his injuries hit him at full force. Braxton roared.

He felt everything…from the bullet lodged in his right kneecap, to his three broken ribs, to his torn ACL. His body was shredded. Bleeding. Broken.

Braxton saw a club coming right at his face, but could do nothing to stop it.

He felt an excruciating jab of pain. Then, he felt nothing at all.

CHAPTER 22

SOFIA

"Everything that is happening your fault," Qiang growled. "I gave you those ingredients to balance out the harm the Gourmands were wreaking, not enable them. Now, look." He sliced his pipe through the air. "Chaos everywhere."

Sofia closed her eyes and counted to three, forcing herself to calm down before she said something she couldn't take back.

"I will admit things didn't go as planned with the ingredients," Sofia said in as calm a voice as she could muster. "I had no intention of losing the ingredients Clementine gave me."

Qiang scoffed. "Clementine is a fool. You are dangerous."

Calm, she ordered herself. She'd come here to ask the Reaper for help. Flying off the handle wouldn't get her what she needed.

Swallowing her pride, Sofia said, "I'll take responsibility for whatever you want to blame me for, if you'll help me rescue the culinary magicians locked on Rikers Island."

"Absolutely not," Qiang said, looking as insulted as if Sofia had demanded that he hand over his firstborn child.

"I'm not asking you to give me any more ingredients," Sofia clarified. "I'm asking you to come with me and help get those people off of Rikers Island. I have my own magic now, so—"

"Yes, I can feel your magic," Reaper Lee spit. "It surrounds you like a stolen cloak. It reeks of desperation."

Sofia faltered. She had nothing to say to that, because it was precisely how the magic felt inside her.

"Sofia?"

She didn't have to look to know who that smoky voice belonged to.

Great. Bloody terrific. Because Graham appearing right now was absolutely the icing on her shit cake. Maybe he could start making out with Clementine in front of her again, just as an added *fuck you*.

Sofia spun and gave him the coldest glare in her arsenal.

"Yes?"

She wouldn't have been surprised if the man turned to stone on the spot.

He flinched at her tone, and Sofia didn't feel bad. Not even a little.

A flash of anger, followed by hurt, passed across his face.

"Can we talk?" he asked.

"No," Sofia and Qiang both said at the same time.

At least the two of them had finally found something to agree on.

"She is leaving," Qiang grumbled as he began stomping back toward the hut.

"Reaper Lee, that's not very nice," Clementine chided. "Shouldn't we at least—Ohmygosh, baby!" Clementine almost bowled Sofia over as she sprinted to Raina and Baby Hiroto.

Within seconds, Clementine was cradling Hiroto in her arms and was chattering to both mother and baby in what sounded like fluent French. Because Sofia needed another reason to hate her. Damnit.

The universe took pity on Sofia at that moment, because her burner phone began to ring. Since the only people who had the number were Braxton and Kenzie, there was little mystery about who it could be. She gave Graham another icy glare before stepping to the side and answering.

Kenzie's frantic voice filled the line as soon as the call connected.

"Just slow down," Sofia said. "Tell me what happened."

Kenzie babbled incessantly for another few seconds before her voice cut off and was replaced by Aralia.

"Sofia?" Aralia said.

"I'm here," Sofia said, stomping her irritation into the garden's flagstone path. "What happened?"

"The Hunters got your brother," Aralia replied. "He—" She paused just long enough for Sofia to lose her mind. "He used some powerful magic so the rest of us could get away. He's going to be in bad shape, if he's alive at all."

Sofia must have briefly blacked out, because the next thing she knew, she was leaning against Graham—where had he even come from?—and he was talking into the phone. Sofia couldn't make out his words; all she could hear was Aralia telling her that Braxton might be dead.

Graham and Aralia talked for what felt like forever. By the time Graham ended the call, Sofia had mentally boxed up her panic and was in triage mode.

"Do you think Qiang will let me use his kitchen?" Sofia asked without waiting for the sympathy on Graham's face to transform to actual words. "I can get my own ingredients. Where's the nearest grocery store?"

And where the bloody hell had Raina put the keys?

"Slow down for a second," Graham said.

"Haven't you been listening?" she screeched. "The Hunters have my brother. I have to—"

"Easy," Graham said, taking her flailing wrists and gently lowering them before she did harm to herself or others. He didn't let go right away, and it was an indication of Sofia's distraction that she didn't wrench away.

To think, just a short while ago, she'd been preoccupied by Graham and Clementine's kiss. Now, they could start humping each other in the middle of the garden and she wouldn't give a damn.

"Listen," Graham said, rubbing his thumb in small circles along her inner wrist. It was oddly comforting. "Aralia said she and Kenzie are going to cook enough magic to break into the prison. We're supposed to meet them at the Rikers Island Bridge tomorrow at noon."

Sofia hated the idea of her brother spending even a second longer than necessary in that hellhole, but she understood the logic behind the decision. They couldn't storm the prison without a shit-load of magic…which had been the entire reason for her trip up to Maine in the first place.

"Okay." Sofia took a few gulps of air to try and calm her racing pulse. It didn't really work. "Okay."

She mentally flipped through every cookbook she'd ever read, sifting through recipes that might be useful for rescuing her twit of a brother. Couldn't he stop trying to be the hero for one goddamned minute? Was that seriously so much to ask for?

"I still need a kitchen," Sofia said, continuing through her mental consideration of various recipe options.

"Whatever you need," Graham assured her. He glanced around at the garden, his whiskey eyes taking on a thoughtful and faraway look. "I wish more of these ingredients were ready to be harvested, but some of them might still be useful."

"It doesn't matter." Sofia massaged the place in her chest where acid was beginning to eat its way back through her esophagus. "Qiang said he won't help." She laughed bitterly. "He'd rather burn this whole garden to the ground than give me a single ingredient."

"We'll see about that." Graham took her hand in his. It felt so good that Sofia briefly forgot why she was supposed to wrench her hand away. "Come with me."

CHAPTER 23

GRAHAM

Qiang Lee was inside the hut with Clementine, who was bustling around the small kitchen and preparing food for their new guests. The baby was banging a wooden spoon on the table. His mother, a petite woman with sad eyes, gave Graham a small smile before returning her attention to her child.

"Reaper Lee," Graham said. "Sofia's brother was taken hostage, and I'd like your permission to harvest some of your ingredients to help rescue him."

The garden didn't have much to offer since most of the plants were months from full maturity, but half-grown magical ingredients were better than nothing.

Reaper Lee scowled. "I do not like repeating myself. My answer is *no*."

Graham felt Sofia stiffen beside him. He moved closer, trying to silently communicate that he wasn't going to give up so easily.

He wanted to be angry for what she'd done to him, but mostly, he wanted to do whatever it took to draw that pained expression from her face.

Graham stole a glance at Sofia while her attention was elsewhere. Only a few days had passed since the last time he'd seen her, and yet, something was different. She was harder…colder…but there was something else, too. It took Graham a few more seconds of trying to study her without being obvious to figure it out.

Sofia had magic. And not in the carrying-magical-ingredients-on-her-person way. She felt like a culinary magician.

"Graham, you still with us?" Clementine prompted.

Remembering that he had a reason for being here beyond puzzling out the enigma that was Sofia McKaid, he shook himself.

He met Qiang's gaze and asked, "Do you still want me to heal your apple tree?"

"Of course." The Reaper's frown deepened.

"Then, I'm asking you to help us," Graham replied.

Clementine stopped stirring sugar into a mug of tea and let out a tiny gasp. "Graham, you don't know what you're saying."

"I'm not trying to be disrespectful," Graham said, feeling abashed. Qiang and Clementine had taken him in without any questions or strings attached. And here he was, resorting to threats. And he was doing it for a woman who had betrayed him…who was doing nothing to hide the fact that she was repulsed by him.

How pathetic could one person be?

Keep talking, Graham, and you'll find out….

"If you help her," Qiang said, motioning to Sofia with his pipe, "I will un-name you as my successor."

Whatever Graham had been expecting the Reaper to say, it wasn't that. "What?"

"You heard me." Qiang lifted his chin. "You have the magic and the dedication. That is why I want you to be my successor," he said.

Graham could swear he felt a crackle through the air.

"Oh, Graham," Clementine whispered. "This is such an honor." She pressed a hand to her chest.

Graham turned to Sofia. She looked as stunned as he felt.

"You were meant for this," the Reaper told him. "You belong here."

Graham wondered if Qiang had any idea how much those words affected him. He'd spent the better part of his childhood knowing he wasn't enough. He was a culinary magician, born to culinary magician parents, and yet he couldn't cook the simplest magic.

In a few words, the Reaper had just offered to fill that gaping hole Graham had carried with him for so long he barely felt it anymore.

"When you become the Reaper," Qiang said, watching Graham carefully, "everyone will want some of your magic. You need to be strong enough to resist." His hawklike gaze slid to Sofia. "Her appetite for power is unquenchable. If you go on this quest with her, it will be the death of you and everyone she's so eager to save. You must make a choice. You can take up your rightful place as my apprentice and train to become the most powerful Cultivator ever to live, or you can help this woman in her fruitless quest. You cannot have both."

Graham's blood turned to lead as the Reaper's words sank in.

A minute that seemed like eons passed. When Graham spoke, it felt like his throat was lined with gravel.

"I appreciate your offer," Graham said. "But I can't accept it. I'm going to help Sofia."

The Reaper's eyebrows drew together as a stormy expression passed over his wrinkled face. Clementine bit her lip as though she were trying not to cry. The baby actually was crying.

"Are you kidding me?" Sofia demanded, speaking for the first time.

The anger radiating off her wasn't the reaction he'd been expecting, nor, if he was being honest with himself, was it the one he'd been hoping for.

"I know I should shut my mouth," Sofia continued, "but how could you give up this opportunity?"

Graham didn't say anything. If Sofia hadn't figured it out by now, he wasn't going to humiliate himself more by spelling it out for her. He kept his gaze fixed on the Reaper. He said, "I'd still like to heal your tree, if I can. In exchange for any help you can give us to get Sofia's brother out of jail."

Qiang made a sound of disgust as he stuffed leaves into his pipe with so much force that most of them ended up crumbling onto the floor.

"None of the ingredients in my garden are ready," he said, refusing to so much as look at Graham. "However, when I was younger, I got it in my head to build my garden at the highest altitude in this park. I began cultivating the ingredients before I realized the soil was too poor for everything I wished to grow." He pulled a cloth out of his pocket and dabbed it to his nose, which had started to bleed.

"Reaper Lee," Clementine began, but Qiang shooed her away.

"Most of the ingredients are probably dead and the climb is not for the faint of heart," Qiang continued. "But if you can manage to hike all the way up without breaking your necks, you can have whatever is still there." He shuffled across the creaky floorboards to his bedroom.

"Thank you, Reaper Lee," Graham said, unprepared for the bone-deep ache he was experiencing for disappointing a man he'd begun to see as his mentor.

Qiang didn't say anything else before he slammed his door shut.

"He'll come around," Clementine said, offering Graham a brave smile. "In the meantime, let me get you some things to help with the climb, otherwise you'll never make it." She hurried around the kitchen, gathering supplies and tossing them in a burlap sack before giving the whole thing to Graham.

"Good luck," Clementine said, reaching up and brushing her hand across his cheek.

Beside him, Sofia's posture stiffened and her expression turned murderous. Graham wasn't sure if it was jealousy or disgust or something else entirely.

"Raina, Hiroto, and I will hold down the fort until you both come back," Clementine said in an overly-cheery voice. "Don't get into any trouble, you two."

As soon as Graham and Sofia were out in the garden alone, she whirled on him.

"What the hell is wrong with you?" she demanded.

Without waiting for a response, she added, "Are you really willing to pass up becoming the next Reaper just to help me?"

Graham didn't even need to consider his answer.

"Yes."

"Bloody why?"

Feeling an unwelcome rush of heat to his face, Graham did something he knew would infuriate Sofia. He answered her question with a question.

"What happened to all those ingredients Clementine gave you?"

Sure enough, fury and indignation darkened her eyes and brought out a pretty flush along her neck. He wondered how far down that flush went....

"Rick stole them from me." She straightened to her full height and gave him a challenging look. "Go ahead and say it."

"What?" Graham asked, genuinely not knowing what she expected from him.

"Tell me it's karma for turning you over to the cops."

"I don't believe in karma," Graham said. "But I'd accept an apology. If it was being offered."

"Why bother?" Sofia said in her blunt way. "It's not like it would change anything. Besides, you seem to have moved on just fine."

Anger Graham rarely allowed himself to feel surged through him. He slung the burlap bag Clementine had given him over his shoulder and turned his back on Sofia. The sun would start setting in a few hours, and they still had a long hike ahead of them.

* * *

"Which way?" Sofia asked when they crested a hilltop.

It was the first time either of them had spoken in hours.

The view was exquisite. Spruce and pine trees dotted the sloping green hillside that overlooked the bay below. The setting sun gleamed off the blue-green water. It was a view that, normally, Graham would have been happy to stare at for hours.

Now, he barely registered it. Instead, he watched Sofia as she took in the landscape. The setting sun kissed her cheekbones and the column of her throat. Her hair fanned out behind her in a wave of gold. Graham ached to run his fingers through the strands.

"Graham?"

"What?" His jaw clicked shut, and it occurred to him that his mouth might have been hanging open.

"Which way?" she asked again with a note of impatience.

"Um." Graham fumbled with the map Clementine had drawn them, which consisted of a bunch of intersecting lines and a few unrecognizable landmarks.

"If I'm reading this correctly," Graham said. *And there was a very good chance he wasn't….* "We need to climb straight up, follow the cliff line to the left, and then—" He didn't really know what.

"It's pretty steep," Graham hedged, knowing Sofia wouldn't appreciate any suggestion that she might not be up to the climb. "If you want me to go up, you can—"

"Forget it," she snapped. "Try and keep up with me, if you can."

With that, she gracefully leapt onto a narrow ledge and started to climb. Shaking his head at her sheer grit, Graham shouldered his bag and followed her.

"Wait up," he said, mesmerized by this city girl who was turning out to be a more proficient rock climber than he was. No matter that he'd spent the last decade of his life in the wilderness. At this point, Sofia's least surprising quality was her ability to constantly surprise him.

"Need a break?" Sofia asked, peering under her arm to give him a challenging glare.

Unable to suppress a chuckle, Graham hauled himself onto a narrow ledge beside her and sat down.

"We should eat these before we go any farther," he said, taking a handful of fresh dates from his bag.

The dates weren't fully ripe, and he hadn't exactly asked permission to pick them, but their magic would be useful since Graham didn't have any climbing equipment. He reasoned that the Reaper wouldn't be happy if he and Sofia both died on this hike. Not that Qiang would ever admit it.

As soon as they both ate the magical dates, the climb got easier. Their fingertips were sticky enough that they could grip the sheer rock face even when there was nothing else to hold onto.

The only time Graham faltered was when he looked up and got distracted by Sofia's lithe body scaling the cliff.

They spent the next hour clambering up sheer granite ascents, punctuated with the odd spruce tree that offered them a place to rest briefly before continuing their climb. They weren't following any trail made by the park, which meant they didn't encounter anyone else during their climb.

They didn't speak again until they'd both pulled themselves over the cliff's lip and fallen onto solid ground. They both lay on their backs, panting.

Graham heard the soft rush of wings on an air draft, and he raised his head.

"Look," he said, pulling Sofia's arm so she sat up. He angled her shoulders so she was facing the bald eagle, which was gliding across the sky. Sofia sucked in her breath when the eagle dove.

They lost sight of the magnificent bird as it was swallowed up by the dusk.

Sofia tilted her head to the side, which brought their faces inches apart. Graham could see the gleam of sweat on her flawless skin and the flecks of light and dark green in her eyes. Graham didn't move a muscle.

His brain was urging him to move away…to put distance between them before he was pulled in by the sheer, inexorable magnetism of Sofia's presence. The rest of him stayed still out of fear of breaking the spell of this moment. He didn't even think his heart beat.

Graham let Sofia decide what would happen next, since he was too conflicted to make a move.

Sofia blinked. Then, she jerked back, shrugging away from him.

Graham swallowed down his disappointment and stared out at the darkening sky.

"I don't regret killing my parents," he blurted out.

He had no idea why he'd said that, except that if Sofia already thought he was a monster, she may as well know how deep the stain on his soul went.

"You shouldn't," Sofia said with a ferocity that surprised Graham.

"You mean, you're not…troubled by what I did?" he asked, now more confused than ever.

"Of course not," Sofia replied. "Aralia told us what happened. What you did was brave and necessary and—"

"Aralia told you?" Graham asked, floored.

Aralia never talked about that day. Ever. She never even talked about it with Graham.

"Yes." Sofia turned away, but not before Graham saw her cheeks color with something that looked very much like shame. "I may have made some assumptions about you, and Aralia set me straight."

It wasn't quite the apology Graham had been hoping for, but it was something.

"Then, why," Graham began, not quite sure how to verbalize his question. "I mean…. What's changed? Between us, I mean."

Sofia let out a scornful laugh. "I don't know what you take me for, Graham, but—"

Before he could overthink it, he reached for her hands and entwined them in his own.

"Can I ask you something?" Graham asked, heartened by the fact that she didn't immediately pull away.

"Hm?" Sofia didn't look at him.

"How did you manage to keep my sister from killing you after you—" *Betrayed me. Made me think I mattered and then tossed me away like garbage.* "—did what you did."

Sofia made an indecipherable noise. "Didn't Aralia tell you?"

"Tell me what?"

"I just assumed she said something when you were on the phone with her earlier," Sofia said.

Graham shook his head. "We didn't talk about much except for Braxton getting taken by the Hunters. I mean, she wanted to know that I was safe, but beyond that, there wasn't time for catching up."

"Oh." Sofia drummed her fingers along the rock, refusing to meet his gaze. "Well, the thing is—" She stopped and raised her face to the wind. "Do you smell that?"

Graham's senses were too full of her to process anything else. He inhaled, trying to get control of his jumbled emotions. That was when he was assailed by the heavy scents of mint and magic. The place inside him that came alive in the Reaper's garden pulsed in recognition.

Home that feeling seemed to say.

"It's this way," Sofia said, taking off at a run across the clifftop.

Graham got up to follow her. He made it only a few yards before a small cluster of new mint growing amid the rocks caught his attention. Graham knelt down and pressed his fingers to the ground, letting his own magic out until it connected with the plant.

An icy shock spiked through his system.

"Sofia, wait," Graham called. "Don't touch anything."

He hadn't even finished speaking before he heard Sofia scream.

"Sofia?" he called.

No answer.

Graham began to run.

CHAPTER 24

BRAXTON

Braxton sat against the cell wall and tried to will away the pain. His body was shattered. He'd used his shirt to stem the bleeding in his leg, which had gone blessedly numb. His ribs, on the other hand, were making every breath a chore. He couldn't see out of his left eye thanks to the beating he'd taken to the head. And he had more torn muscles than he wanted to count.

But Kenzie and the others had gotten away. In the end, that was all that mattered.

To add insult to his myriad of injuries, Braxton was surrounded by a hundred starving, panicking culinary magicians. They'd been stuffed into a holding cell that was meant for a quarter of their number.

"Here, man," a voice said, startling Braxton out of his morose musings. A small carton of chocolate milk hovered in front of his face.

The milk was attached to a pale arm dusted with coppery hair, which belonged to a man wearing a sympathetic smile. His clothes were filthy like everything and everyone else in this cell. The man had large blue eyes that popped out of his pale face. More copper hair poofed up on his head, giving the man's slender build a few extra centimeters. He seemed familiar, but Braxton was too tired to try and puzzle it out at that moment.

The man opened the carton and held it up to Braxton's lips.

With no other choice, Braxton drank.

"Thanks, mate," he said once the carton was empty.

The sugar and protein helped a little. He no longer felt like he was on death's doorstep.

"Any time." The man sat down next to Braxton. "I've always been a fan of yours. Er, your cooking, I mean," he added quickly. "Not you. I mean, not that there's anything wrong with you, looks-wise. At all." He smacked his palm to his forehead. "I didn't mean it like that. Well, I could have, but I know you·don't…I mean…." He groaned and hid his face in his arms. "Excuse me while I go die."

Braxton chuckled, which came out as more of a pained wheeze. "It's okay, and I appreciate the compliment. My ego could use it right now. It's nice to meet you—" He trailed off, waiting for a name.

The man peeked out from his arms. He was still blushing hard enough that the tips of his ears had turned red.

"Reuben," he said, giving Braxton a hesitant smile.

"Wait a second," Braxton said, recalling where he'd seen this man before. The hair should have been a giveaway, but the prison jumpsuits and grime made them all more or less indecipherable. "You're that Gourmand who kept calling Rosemary *mom*."

Reuben's hand flew to his left wrist, which Braxton just noticed had a bracelet poking out from under his drab uniform sleeve. A charm bracelet. Just like Rosemary's necklace.

"You really are her son," Braxton said in amazement. "But then, why—"

"Didn't my own mother recognize me?" Reuben asked.

He sounded a lot less bitter than Braxton would have in the other man's position.

Reuben drew up his knees and laced his fingers around them. "Well, that's been years in the making. I don't know how much you know about the superfood, but my mother was forcibly recruited to work on it from the beginning. It…did things to her mind." Reuben touched one of the charms on his bracelet, smiling sadly. "The same thing happened to my father, before the superfood finally killed him."

"You seem like a good person," Braxton said. "And my girlfriend really likes Rosemary. If you don't mind my asking, how the hell did your family become mixed up with the Gourmands?"

In Braxton's experience, decent people and the Gourmands didn't mesh.

"My father was asked to become a Gourmand because he was involved with the original superfood recipe," Reuben explained. "Once he started working with Benedict, the two of them realized they wanted the superfood for totally different reasons." He laughed darkly. "My father came up with the superfood recipe because he believed culinary magic was meant to be shared, and he wanted a way to give a little bit of it to every Vanilla in the entire world. Benedict, of course, wanted to use the superfood to control magic and annihilate any threat to our secret. So…that got awkward."

"Ah." Braxton could only imagine.

"My father threatened to tell the entire culinary magic community and let them decide what was right," Reuben continued. "To keep him quiet, Benedict basically made him and my mom guinea pigs for the superfood." He sniffed and looked down at the floor. "And I stayed because it was the only way to make sure the Gourmands didn't kill my mom."

Before Braxton could come up with something appropriate to say, they were both jostled by inmates fighting over what appeared to be half a ham sandwich.

Bits of bread and meat flew into the air. There was a pileup on the ground as chefs threw themselves on what amounted to a few bites of dirty sandwich. Braxton looked away, disgusted by what they'd been reduced to in so short a time.

Summoned by the noise, Hunters appeared in the hallway outside their cell. The Hunters began beating their chains against the bars, forcing the chefs standing at the front of the cell to fall back. Braxton and Reuben were squeezed close enough that their shoulders ground together.

"Shut up, you devils!" one of the Hunters shouted. "Cane has a few words to say." He clanked his chains across the bars again, even though everyone had gone mostly quiet in anticipation of whatever was coming next.

The dozen-or-so Hunters parted to make room for Cane to approach the front of the cell. The man was even taller close up than he'd seemed at a distance. He also had dried skin hanging from his unnaturally-pale lips, which struck Braxton as obscenely gross. The people in this cell had an excuse for being unkempt. Their oppressors did not.

"We've determined the public trial and subsequent execution for any found guilty of food witchery will be held tomorrow morning," Cane said.

The sour stink of fear permeated the air as the prisoners began muttering to each other.

Braxton, for his part, was too weak to feel much of anything. His magic was barely a flicker inside him, and his body was useless. Part of him had known from the moment he threw himself at those soldiers that it would be the end for him, and he'd been okay with it.

Maybe even a little relieved.

"I have nothing against any of you personally," Cane continued, using a mollifying tone. "I simply don't want to see any more people die because of the corruption that lives inside you." He turned to walk away.

"Wait!" A skinny chef grasped the cell bars with his dirt-encrusted fingers as he tried to reach out to Cane. "If I can give you the most powerful culinary magician in the entire world, will you let me live?"

That got the Hunters' attention.

"How are you going to do that?" Cane asked. He gave the man a thin-lipped smile.

"I'm gonna make her boyfriend tell you where to find her." He turned and pointed at Braxton.

A red haze of rage shimmered across Braxton's vision.

"His girlfriend is the strongest of all of us." the chef continued, basking in the fact that he had everyone's attention. "If you kill her, that would be a great victory for the Hunters."

"Yeah, it would be," Braxton said through clenched teeth. "Too bad you've got a far better chance of being executed tomorrow than finding her." He looked past the skinny chef and met Cane's milky gaze. "Do whatever you want with me. I'll never tell you where to find her."

The skinny chef clutched at the bars, trying to keep Cane's attention. "There's a recipe. Half-moon cookie. It'll let me see into his memories." He pointed at Braxton. "I'll look into his mind and see where she is. All I need is twenty minutes in the kitchen."

Braxton's blood turned to ice.

"We are Hunters," Cane said, giving the skinny chef a disdainful look. "We protect the world from food magic. We do not condone it."

"Yeah, but think about it this way," the skinny chef wheedled. He spoke fast, knowing his life depended on what he said next. "It's only a little bit of magic, and it'll let you destroy a whole lot more."

Cane couldn't possibly agree to this. It would undermine everything he stood for.

"Yes," Cane said, with a sage nod. "Yes, that does make sense."

"I can oversee the cooking, Sir," Nurse Ratched said, appearing from between two Hunters like a wraith. She straightened the hem of her already-straight white scrub top. "I'm familiar with the process, as distasteful as it is." She wrinkled her nose as though the simple mention of magic was odorous.

One of the prisoners coughed. It sounded like "Hypocrites." A few other prisoners snickered.

"Very well," Cane said, nodding to one of his Hunters, who unlocked the cell door. "You will make this recipe, and then we will discover where this most dangerous of food witches is residing. It will be a great victory."

The Hunters ushered the skinny chef into the hallway. The door was locked again behind him.

"Reuben," Braxton said in a low, urgent voice as soon as the Hunters had disappeared around the corner. "I need you to do something for me."

"'Course," Reuben said.

"I need you to kill me."

"W-what?" Reuben stammered.

"Break my neck," Braxton said. "It'll be easy given how weak my body is. Just give it a good twist."

"I'm not going to kill you," Reuben said with an uneasy laugh.

"Please," Braxton said, his voice rising in his desperation. "I can't let them look into my memories. If they do, they'll know where to find Kenzie."

"There has to be another way," Reuben hedged.

"There bloody isn't!"

"I'm a vegetarian," Reuben whispered. "I'd never even hurt an animal."

Jesus fucking Christ.

"If you don't do this, they're going to kill my sister and the woman I love," Braxton pleaded. "If anything happens to them, I couldn't live with myself. And your mother is with them." He should have led with that, he realized, as Reuben's eyes bugged. He pressed his advantage. "If those Hunters find Sofia and Kenzie, they'll find your mum."

"I—" Reuben stammered.

"Do it now, before they come back," Braxton insisted.

Reuben knelt. He swallowed. With shaking hands, he reached up and grasped the sides of Braxton's face.

"Thank you," Braxton said, giving him a little nod to let him know this was all good. "Seriously, mate."

Reuben's harsh breathing filled Braxton's ears.

"I—" Reuben licked his lips.

"You can do this," Braxon encouraged. "For our families."

Reuben gave him a jerky nod. He tightened his grip on Braxton's neck. Braxton let his eyelids flutter shut.

I'll see you soon, Aid, he thought. He drew in his final breath.

CHAPTER 25

GRAHAM

Graham found Sofia on her hands and knees. She was trying to drag herself out of a patch of fully-matured magical mint.

"D-don't!" Sofia gasped, holding out a shaking hand to stop him. "C-cold."

There was no magical mint in the Reaper's garden, so Graham didn't know anything about the plant.

He edged around the patch of luminous green mint until he was crouching beside Sofia. An icy wind was radiating off her skin.

Sofia's lips had turned an alarming shade of blue. Her teeth were chattering so hard her entire body was convulsing.

"Put your arms around me," he ordered.

She did, and Graham lifted her out of the mint without touching any of the leaves himself. He laid her carefully on the bare rock and settled her head against his leg.

"You're freezing," he murmured.

"D-duh," she chattered.

Graham chuckled. She couldn't be too bad off if she was still sassing him.

He draped his jacket over her like a blanket and tried to rub feeling back into her arms.

As the seconds ticked by, her shivering got worse rather than better. The magic coursing through her system was growing like a virus.

"C-cold." The word came out of Sofia as a whimper. "S-so cold."

In that moment, Graham would have given his right arm to draw the pain out of her and into himself. He pressed one palm to her cheek and closed his eyes, trying to set aside his growing fear so he could figure out how to help her.

As soon as he concentrated on the magic rather than Sofia's discomfort, he could sense everything more clearly. The magic unfolded like a movie script behind his closed lids. He could see that the mint had entered her body through her pantleg and was now winding its way through her. It was clinging to her magic and using it as a conduit to attack every source of warmth in her body.

Graham gently moved her head off his leg so he could crawl down by her ankle. He took hold of her pantleg and tore the fabric, taking care not to touch the material any more than he needed to.

He started to rub her bare ankle, trying to coax some warmth back into her icy skin.

It wasn't working. Instead of growing fainter, the magic was attracted by the friction, using the added warmth to stimulate its expansion.

An idea occurred to Graham.

He remembered watching the Reaper slice open a rhubarb stalk to drain out excess magic. Maybe, if he did the same thing to Sofia….

No. Absolutely not.

The mere thought of slicing open Sofia's skin made Graham sick to his stomach. He had to get the magic out another way.

Graham lay down next to Sofia and leaned close enough for their foreheads to touch. It felt like pressing his face against a sheet of ice. He could sense the magic more clearly this way, but it wasn't enough. The magic was content inside her. It didn't want to leave.

He cringed, knowing what he was about to say and exactly how she would react.

"I'm going to kiss you, okay?" he said. If he was right, he'd be able to draw the magic out of her and into himself.

"N-no," she said, weakly twisting her face away. "I don't want you. Sloppy s-seconds…." She trailed off as shivers wracked her body.

"The alternative is slashing open your ankle with a jagged rock to drain out the magic," he said, more harshly than he'd meant. "Would that really be your preference?"

"Y-yes," she said through chattering teeth.

Graham steeled himself against the blow to his heart.

"Well, it's not mine," he replied. "Close your eyes and pretend I'm someone else if that helps."

He was surprised by the bitterness in his voice and mentally told himself to knock it off. Right now, his hurt feelings were not the priority.

Sofia's body had gone limp. Her breathing was shallow, and her pulse was too slow.

Graham cursed. Feeling like a perv, he touched his lips to hers.

Almost at once, the magic surged out of her and into him. He'd been prepared for cold, but this was something else entirely. His head started to pound. Icicles streaked through his veins.

Sofia gasped. Graham was vaguely aware of color returning to her lips and cheeks. His own limbs began to seize up.

"Oh God, Graham," Sofia said. "What did you do?"

She sounded far away, even though he could feel her hands on him.

He reached for her but missed. His arm thumped lifelessly to the ground, but he felt nothing. He didn't even feel cold anymore.

Hypothermia, he thought dimly.

He had to get rid of this magic. He flailed around, the mint making him clumsy. His breathing was a harsh rattle in his chest. Everything hurt.

He tried several times to grasp a sharp rock before he managed to close his fist around the stone. Ignoring the jabs of icy pain that pricked him with every movement, he leaned forward and raked the sharp side of the rock across his ankle, right in the place where the magic had entered Sofia.

"Graham, what the fuck?" Sofia shrieked.

Graham tried to respond, but he was too cold to make his mouth work.

He'd expected to feel relief as the magic began trickling out. Instead, the numbness was replaced by bone-jarring shudders.

He felt Sofia doing something to his ankle, although he was too overcome by the cold to pay much attention. He did start paying attention when Sofia began undressing him.

"W-what are you doing?" he asked.

Sofia said something about body heat. Between the ice stabbing through his limbs and the fact that she was yanking off his pants, he couldn't process the rest of her words.

His whole body was convulsing. He probably would have given himself a concussion from his head flopping around on the hard ground, except Sofia slid one of her arms beneath his neck.

She was cradling his head against her chest. Her very bare chest.

Graham didn't have a chance to work his sluggish brain around this new development before Sofia was weaving her body around his. They were both naked.

Graham knew he was supposed to be confused by this turn of events, but it felt too incredible. She was soft in all the right places, and warm. The actual temperature of her skin wasn't much better than his, but that didn't stop him from using every ounce of his remaining energy to get closer to her. As close as possible.

"Wow." Sofia cleared her throat. "You're even more attractive than my magic guessed. Didn't think that was possible."

"W-what?"

"Nothing." Sofia twined her legs with his. "Tomorrow, we're going to pretend this never happened. Deal?"

Graham's body chose that particular moment to take note of the gorgeous woman wound around him. All the blood in his body rushed straight to his dick. He tried to will away his obvious and growing desire for her, but the entire situation was beyond his control.

"Sofia," he murmured, trying to wrap his arms around her but failing to exert any degree of control over his limbs. He wanted to kiss her more than he wanted his next breath.

Damnit. He was naked with the woman of his dreams, and he was too numb to do anything about it.

"Shut up," she said, rubbing sensation back into his arms. Her long hair hung over his torso like a blanket.

"You can tell Clementine it was a life-or-death situation," she said.

Graham's brain was still half-frozen, so it took him several beats to understand what she was saying.

"I'm not going to tell Clementine anything about this."

So what if Sofia was only doing it to save his life? It wouldn't stop him from hoarding the memory. He wasn't going to share it with Clementine or anyone else.

"Seriously?" Sofia said. She sounded angry, although Graham couldn't work out why. He was feeling sleepy and more content than he could ever remember being.

"Some boyfriend you are," Sofia grumbled. "Poor Clementine."

It sent needles shooting through every inch of Graham, but he forced himself to roll to the side so he was facing Sofia. He ignored the fact that her perfect chest was pressed against his own and cupped her face in his hand. She shivered but didn't pull away.

"Sofia," he said. "Clementine and I aren't together."

"But—" Sofia's brow furrowed. "You kissed her."

Graham's stomach dropped. Had she seen that disastrous misunderstanding?

All at once, a lot of Sofia's strange behaviors since she'd shown back up made more sense.

He leaned forward and kissed her so softly it was barely more than a touch of lips.

"I didn't want that," he said. "And that's what I told Clementine."

"Oh."

They lay there, holding each other as they both tried to gather their thoughts. Sofia was the first to break the silence.

"I'm sorry for what I did to you, Graham."

For once, there was no hint of snark or haughtiness in her voice. Graham could feel the way her heart raced against his chest and knew what those words cost her. He tightened his hold on her.

"I saw the case file and those pictures of your parents, and I didn't stop to ask any of the right questions," Sofia continued. "I should have known you wouldn't do something like that without a damn good reason. So, yeah. I'm…sorry."

Because she'd been so honest with him, Graham thought it only fair to return the favor. Regardless of the consequences.

"You're the only person I've ever wanted to be with," he admitted. "You're it for me, Sofia."

She was quiet for so long Graham thought maybe she'd fallen asleep. He let his own heavy eyelids fall shut and enjoyed the way their bodies molded together. His mind drifted pleasantly as he waited for unconsciousness to claim him.

"Graham?" a soft voice said, piercing through his hypothermic fog.

"Yes, Sofia?"

"I'm going to kiss you, now."

And then, she did.

CHAPTER 26

KENZIE

Kenzie slurped her coffee—her fourth…maybe fifth cup of the day. After a certain point, it was anyone's guess, really.

A radio her dad had found sat on the counter, and upbeat music filled the kitchen. Kenzie's dad hummed to himself as he stripped thyme leaves from their stem. He caught Kenzie watching him and smiled at her from across the kitchen. Kiwi was munching on a raspberry as he perched on top of Rosemary's head, which seemed to be his preferred vantage point these days.

The heartwarming scene was everything Kenzie had been missing for the last five years…minus the reason they were cooking.

Cane and Nurse Ratched had Braxton, along with all the other culinary magicians they'd captured from that failure of a war council.

"He's going to be fine, hon," her dad said, reading the worry she was obviously doing a terrible job of hiding.

"How can you be sure?" Kenzie asked, measuring out a teaspoon of vanilla extract and adding it to her batter.

"Because," her dad replied. "He's got you coming to save him."

Kenzie stared down into her bowl, trying to remember what she was supposed to do next.

"Don't sweat it, Snow White," Zack said, coming up behind her and swiping his finger through her batter. "I've already broken out of Rikers once. How hard could it be to get in?"

"Did you just call me Snow White?" Kenzie elbowed him. "And get your filthy paws out of my batter."

"Skin white as snow," Zack said in a deep, guttural voice that actually sounded like a Disney voiceover. "Lips red as blood. Hair black as ebony."

"What about the tattoo sleeves?" Kenzie asked, gesturing to her ink. "And it's not just the getting into Rikers part I'm concerned about. Need I remind you we also have to get back out?"

"We do?" Zack asked, feigning surprise.

Kenzie cracked a grin. Who knew a relative of Rick's could be so decent…multiple arrests and petty crimes aside.

"How are you and Rick from the same family?" she asked.

"Easily," Zack replied. "Rick got most of the magic, while I got the looks and personality." He winked at Kenzie.

"Too bad neither of you were blessed with brains," Chef Levy grumbled, striding into the kitchen. She was wearing combat boots and had a rifle slung over her shoulder.

Aralia was right behind her. She had her bow and arrows, as well as two daggers tucked into her braided leather belt. She looked like a Viking princess about to go to war.

"What time is it?" Kenzie asked, wondering if night had turned to morning without her noticing. Without any windows, or anything remotely resembling sufficient sleep, she didn't know which end was up.

"Still early," Aralia reassured her. "Chef and I have been doing recon on Rick."

"And?" Kenzie asked.

"All we know so far is that he and most of the Gourmands made it out of the ballroom without getting captured," Chef Levy said.

There really was no justice in the world.

"While the rest of you are doing your little jail break routine, I'll see if I can find out where he's holing up," Chef Levy said.

Little jail break routine? Kenzie was offended.

"Once we get rid of him," Chef Levy continued, "you'll need to be ready to take down the Gourmands."

She didn't look at Kenzie, even though the statement was clearly meant for her. Chef Levy was busy dipping her index finger in Kenzie's translucent cake batter and frowning at it.

What was this…tasting Kenzie's shit without her consent day?

Kenzie swatted Chef Levy's finger away. She poured her batter into a springform pan and slid her cake into the oven.

"It's my fault if I forget the salt," Rosemary sang in her off-key voice. "Too much pepper, and I'll become a leperrrrrrr." With one hand, she stroked her charm necklace. Her other hand clutched at the insulated lunch tote she'd been carrying around since the Times Square massacre.

"Rosemary," Kenzie said, using a soothing tone and avoiding any sudden movements. "How about you give me that lunch bag, and then you can—"

The second Kenzie's fingertips made contact with the shoulder strap, Rosemary hissed and snatched the lunch bag away.

Alrighty, then.

Kenzie was saved from any more weirdness with Rosemary by a commotion in the hotel lobby. There was a dull hum of voices, followed by footsteps.

Aralia, who had been mid-staring contest with Kiwi, let out a deafening squeal as Sofia and Graham entered the dining room. Sofia barely made it out of the way before Aralia launched herself at Graham.

It was a good thing Graham was a big dude, otherwise he would have been flattened like a pancake. Fortunately, he caught Aralia easily and twirled her in a circle that took out several of Polly's framed portraits.

Aralia clung to Graham and gave him what was undoubtedly the realest smile Kenzie had ever seen on Aralia's face. There was no hint of malice or threat—just pure joy. It made Kenzie ache for Sofia, who was watching their display of sibling affection with obvious distress.

Kenzie beckoned to her.

"We're almost ready," Kenzie said, wanting to give Sofia all the confidence Kenzie herself wasn't feeling. "I'm going to get all of us into Rikers. Zack said he can open the cell, and—"

"Zack?" Sofia's jaw unhinged. "Zack's here?"

"Blondie!" Zack exclaimed, wiping his hands on his jeans and skipping over to Sofia.

"The Three Musketeers are reunited!" Zack dragged Sofia over to Kenzie's dad.

"How are you, my dear?" Kenzie's dad asked Sofia, as Zack initiated a three-way hug.

"I thought you were running off to New Jersey," Sofia said.

"What can I say?" Zack grinned at her. "Turns out I like to be in the middle of the action."

Kenzie's dad gave him an affectionate clap on the back.

The three of them chatted for a few minutes, while Kenzie marveled over the fact that a McKaid, an Ashner, and a Santiori were huddled together like, well, the Three Musketeers.

Aralia and Graham joined the party in the kitchen. While Aralia scampered around putting together breakfast for Graham, he watched Sofia with undisguised longing. Kenzie felt bad for the guy…at least until she caught Sofia sneaking her own glances at him.

"Where's Raina and Baby Hiroto?" Kenzie asked Sofia, realizing she hadn't seen them come in.

"Raina decided to stay at the Reaper's," Sofia said with a shrug. "She likes digging around in the dirt for some inexplicable reason, and Clementine has practically adopted the kid. So, they're as happy as they could be given the situation."

Kenzie's stomach gave a painful squeeze at the reminder of what Raina and Hiroto had lost.

"Raina's tough," Sofia said, before turning away. "She'll get through this."

Kenzie's internal timer told her that her cake was done. She opened the oven and carefully removed her jiggling, translucent water cake.

She'd gotten the idea from a fad that had run rampant through social media a bunch of years back. Personally, Kenzie had never understood the appeal of a cake that looked and tasted like a giant, vanilla-infused raindrop. Especially when it still managed to pack a caloric punch. But the cake happened to pair well with magic that would get them into Rikers with the least amount of fuss.

Kenzie slid the gelatinous cake into a glass container and covered it with a lid.

"Rosemary," Kenzie began, when she noticed the woman putting on her shoes and acting like she was going somewhere. "You're going to stay here with my dad, remember?"

It was too risky for Rosemary to go anywhere near the Hunters. If they got a hold of the superfood recipe…. Well, the consequences didn't bear thinking about. And Rosemary seemed to trust Kenzie's dad more than anyone else in their group. He would be able to make sure she didn't wander out of the food bank alone.

Her dad had reluctantly agreed that, since he wasn't a culinary magician, it would be safer for all of them if he stayed behind. Not that Kenzie would have let him come either way. She'd just gotten her dad back. There was no way in Hell she was letting him go near Rikers again. Ever.

"Rosemary is going with you," Rosemary stated.

"Rosemary," Kenzie began.

"Rosemary is going," Rosemary insisted.

She was stroking her charm necklace the way she did whenever she was agitated. She shouldered her lunch bag and marched to the door.

Kenzie threw up her hands in surrender.

"It'll be fine," Sofia said in a rare show of optimism. She held up a lumpy burlap sack. "Graham and I have this whole thing covered, anyway. The rest of you are just backup."

"Um…."

"Shall I procure us a car, my lords and ladies?" Zack asked, whipping his screwdriver out of his pocket and blowing on it the way a gangster might blow on the tip of his gun.

Two minutes later, Zack was busy hotwiring some poor schmuck's minivan. Kenzie said a quick goodbye to her father, who was doing an admirable job of hiding how displeased he was that she was going to Rikers. Rosemary, Sofia, Graham, Aralia, and Zack piled into the minivan. Kenzie would have felt worse about stealing it, except that it was illegally parked in a handicapped space. So, maybe justice had to be manufactured rather than coming ready-made.

At least, she was pretty sure she'd gotten a fortune cookie to that effect one time.

While Zack and Sofia argued about the radio station, and Aralia complained about carbon emissions, Kenzie sliced into her water cake.

She picked up a piece and took a bite. Vanilla-infused sweetness hit her tongue. She took the rest of her slice and ground it into the van's dirty floor mat. Then, she passed the remaining cake to the others.

As soon as everyone, including the car, had gotten some of the cake, Kenzie did her thing. The tendrils of magic were ready and waiting for her. Unlike the whole debacle in Times Square when she'd absorbed everyone else's magic inside her, this recipe came easily. The magic was almost eager as it wrapped around the car and everyone inside.

They were stopped next to a black-glass building, which reflected the minivan…at least, until the magic took hold. The vehicle shimmered and then disappeared from view.

"Whoa," Sofia said.

"Dude," Zack said.

"Not bad, Number Eight," Aralia said, reaching out and squeezing Kenzie's boob. "Not bad."

Kenzie slapped at her. Or tried to. Kenzie could smell Aralia's citronella soap but couldn't see her. When she looked down at herself, Kenzie saw only the dirty pavement of the road.

Weird.

"Now, this is what I call travelling incognito," Zack's disembodied voice announced.

"Drive carefully," Sofia ordered. "Just because no one can see us, it doesn't mean you can't still get us all killed."

"Rosemary and thyme and basil and coriander and caraway and dill," Rosemary sang.

And with that, they were off.

Hang on, Braxton, Kenzie thought. *We're coming for you.*

CHAPTER 27

BRAXTON

Braxton drew in his final breath and waited.

He thought about Aidan. He pictured Kenzie's face. He imagined the sound of her voice, hoping it would be enough to drown out the snapping of his neck.

Her voice was so clear. Damn, he had no idea his imagination was so vivid. He could hear her talking, and Sofia responding, and—

Braxton's eyes flew open.

Holy shit. Kenzie and Sofia were here.

"Wait," he gasped, just as Reuben started to twist his neck. Reuben froze.

"Brax?" Sofia called in a hushed voice.

Reuben's hands fell away from Braxton's neck. They were both shaking. Braxton strained to sit up further, but he couldn't see anything from his position in the corner of the cell.

"Sofe? Kenz?"

"Braxton!" Kenzie said. "Are you okay?"

More or less….

"What the hell are you two doing here?" He sounded angry.

Fuck, he was angry. Every time he tried to protect these two, they found a way to endanger themselves even more.

A space had opened up between the prisoners, giving Braxton a view to the front of the cell. Still, he couldn't see Kenzie or his sister.

"Get us out of here!" a woman with her face pressed to the bars begged. She whipped her head back and forth, trying to see whoever Braxton was talking to.

"Where are the Hunters?" Sofia asked, her voice all business.

"They took one of the prisoners to the kitchen," Braxton replied. "We should have at least fifteen minutes before they're back."

"Plenty of time," a different, male voice said. Braxton wasn't sure, but he thought it was Rick's cousin who had helped them escape from the Gourmand dinner.

"Alrighty, then," Kenzie said. "I'm letting this magic go."

There was a slight shimmer to the air, and then the most beautiful sight Braxton had ever seen materialized outside the cell. Kenzie was there, surrounded by Sofia, Graham, and Zack.

"I could seriously kill you for coming here," Braxton growled.

"Eh, don't blame Blondie," Zack said, fiddling around at the cell door with his screwdriver. "We were both getting a little nostalgic for this place." Sofia rolled her eyes.

"Oh yeah," Zack said to the door. "You're my bitch now."

The lock clicked, and the door sprang open.

The prisoners surged forward.

"Whoa, whoa, whoa," Sofia said. "You are *not* going to race out of here like a herd of wild beasts and alert every Hunter in the place that you're loose. Either be quiet and civilized, or I'll lock you back in there myself."

"Your sister's a little scary," Reuben whispered.

"Tell me about it," Braxton replied.

Despite the fact that Sofia was one person against a hundred desperate, starving chefs, the prisoners filed out of the cell one at a time. Then, they turned to her, waiting for instructions. Braxton would have laughed if he had the energy to spare. Instead, he tipped his head back against the cell and waited for the inevitable moment when his sister and girlfriend caught sight of him.

"Ohmygod, Braxton," Kenzie gasped. She crouched in front of him and started prodding various parts of his body as she clucked in dismay. "Did you get shot?!"

"He's in more acute danger from his broken ribs," Reuben unhelpfully supplied.

"Broken ribs?" Kenzie squeaked. "Plural?"

Braxton glared at Reuben through his one good eye.

Thanks, mate. Thanks very much.

"Kenz, this is Reuben," Braxton said. "Rosemary's son."

"Oh, nice to meet you, Rolex," Kenzie said distractedly. She was still busy assessing Braxton's ruined body and didn't so much as spare Reuben a glance. This time, Braxton did manage a chuckle.

"Rosemary's here," Sofia told Reuben, giving Braxton a worried look of her own. "She's outside keeping a lookout with Aralia."

"Really?" Reuben asked, his expression a mixture of anticipation and trepidation.

"Okay," Kenzie said, offering Braxton a wobbly smile. "Let's get you out of here." She reached down a hand to pull him up.

Braxton shook his head. "Baby," he said softly. "I appreciate you coming to rescue me, but I'm not going anywhere."

He couldn't stand, let alone walk out of here.

"Can you get an arm around my neck?"

The gruff question came from Graham. Braxton hadn't even notice him come into the cell, since all of his focus was on Kenzie.

Braxton looked at Graham. The bloke was big, but there was no way he was strong enough to—

"Are you bloody joking?" Braxton grunted as Graham lifted him off the ground like he was a child. "This is goddamn embarrassing."

Sofia took one look at Braxton, cradled in Graham's arms, and let out an indecent snort. She pulled her phone out of her pocket and snapped off several pictures.

"I'm going to get you back for this," Braxton assured her. He had a recipe for magical molasses that wouldn't wash out of her hair for months…. Or possibly a recipe for facial hair growth enhancement….

"Let's get moving," Graham said, his voice rumbling through Braxton.

Braxton had always been confident in his masculinity and level of fitness. This whole experience had him questioning both.

"Um," Braxton said. "I'm guessing this would be a bad time to say sorry for being such a dick to you?"

Graham gave him a half-smile. "Apology accepted."

Reuben, who was holding onto the cell bars, took a few hobbling steps and let out a small moan.

"What's wrong with you?" Sofia, Ms. Sensitivity, demanded.

"My ankle," Reuben muttered. "I sprained it back in the ballroom."

"Come on, angel," Zack said in a voice that was devoid of any mockery. "Lean on me."

He slid Reuben's arm around his neck.

At least Reuben had the dignity of being able to sort of walk on his own two feet. Braxton, meanwhile, couldn't have been more useless. He was going to get all of them killed.

"Alright, everyone," Sofia said in a voice that brooked no arguments. "Stay behind me. And keep quiet. If any of the Hunters come, don't panic. Let me deal with them."

Braxton wanted to ask her what she was going to do against a hundred crazed zealots with chains and truncheons—even his sister had her limitations—but the simple act of holding his head up was taking more energy than he had to spare. And fainting in Graham's arms was a line he refused to cross.

"I really appreciate you helping me," Reuben told Zack shyly. "I'm sorry to be a burden."

"Couldn't be less of a burden if you tried, angel," Zack replied. "You're light as a feather."

Braxton glanced over Graham's shoulder to see Reuben's face turn as red as a boiled lobster. He was smiling at Zack, though. And Zack was smiling back. At least they were enjoying themselves.

Braxton turned slightly to Graham—not too much, though, otherwise they'd practically be making out. "I hope you're not going to take it personally that I'm not flirting with you."

Graham chuckled. "Would it make you feel better," he said, "if I told you the only McKaid I want to hit on is your sister?"

"Given the circumstances," Braxton replied gravely, "absolutely."

Graham laughed again.

"You're alright, mate," Braxton grudgingly acknowledged.

"Aww, you're getting along," Kenzie said, sounding delighted. "So freaking precious."

Then, just to add insult to injury, she gave Braxton a patronizing pat on his arse.

"Careful, baby," Braxton warned. "I'll get my strength back eventually, and then you'll be in for some payback."

Kenzie fanned her face. "Did it just get hot in here?"

"I'm nauseous," Sofia announced.

The hallways were strangely empty as they wound their way through the jail. Sofia and Zack led the way, seeming to know exactly where they were going. When they passed through a hallway that was covered in scorch marks and burned almost beyond recognition, Sofia and Zack exchanged a fist-bump.

"This feels wrong," Graham said, his voice once again reverberating right through Braxton. "Someone should have tried to stop us."

Braxton agreed. They hadn't exactly been as quiet as mice, and yet not a single person had come to investigate. The Hunters would have to be deaf and blind not to know something was up.

"Don't look a gift horse in the mouth," one of the other prisoners advised.

Still, they all stopped talking and picked up their pace. Between Kenzie's magic, and Zack's screwdriver, they made it out to the parking lot where they were rendezvousing with Aralia and Rosemary. Everything was going according to plan, which somehow only served to increase Braxton's sense of foreboding. It didn't help that he could feel tension radiating through Graham's body.

And that was a thought he'd never expected to have….

His anxiety eased somewhat when he saw Aralia and Rosemary, waiting quietly in a shady patch between two buildings.

"All quiet on the East River front," Aralia announced.

Reuben hobbled forward a few steps and gave Rosemary a tentative wave.

"Mom?" Reuben said, his voice breaking on the word. "Do you—" He swallowed. "Do you remember me?"

"Rosemary and thyme and basil and coriander and caraway and dill," Rosemary whispered. She touched her necklace with quick, manic strokes of her finger.

Zack helped Reuben limp to Rosemary and then drew back, giving the two of them some space.

"Look," Reuben said. He pulled back his sleeve to show off the matching charm bracelet he wore.

For several seconds, Rosemary didn't react. Her hand stilled on her necklace.

Braxton found himself holding his breath, wondering whether Rosemary was too far gone to recognize her own son.

"Reuben?" she said.

"Mom." He took two steps forward and enfolded Rosemary in a careful hug.

After a brief pause, Rosemary wrapped her wiry arms around her son.

"Reuben," she cried. "Reuben. Reuben. Reuben."

"I'm here, Mom." He laid his head down on his mother's shoulder. "I'm here."

Braxton swallowed around the lump in his throat.

"Reuben," Rosemary said again, reaching up to run her hands through her son's hair.

"Yeah," he said, laughing and crying at the same time. "We're free. We're going to be together now."

"Together," Rosemary repeated. She lifted Reuben's wrist and kissed his bracelet.

"She and I made these for each other," Reuben explained, blushing furiously. "Right before my dad became a Gourmand. It's kind of our last happy family memory."

"My Reuben," Rosemary said, adjusting the strap of her lunch bag on her shoulder. "No one will take you away. Never again."

"That's right," Reuben said patiently. "We've got friends to help protect us, now."

Rosemary relaxed and smiled at her son.

"Damn right," Zack said. "And as your friend and protector, I'm going to suggest we make like a bread truck and haul our buns out of here. I've got a feeling we're running short on time."

"We've got the busses ready to go," Aralia said, gesturing to four New York City Corrections busses that were, indeed, already running.

"I can't believe I almost got killed for this magical mint, and now we're not even going to get to use it," Sofia complained.

"It wasn't all bad," Graham said.

Something passed between them that Braxton was perfectly happy not to understand.

The prisoners quickly loaded themselves onto the four busses. Graham managed to carry Braxton onto the first bus with a shocking amount of grace.

"Thanks, mate," Braxton said gruffly as he tried to disentangle his screaming limbs from Graham.

"Don't mention it," Graham replied.

"And we're outta here," Zack announced, hopping into the driver's seat and revving the engine. "How many people have broken out of Rikers twice, you think?"

"Two," replied Sofia from the seat behind Braxton's.

With a mad cackle, Zack hit the accelerator.

Braxton looked behind him once, just to make sure the other three busses in their convoy were on the move. Then, he let his head loll back against the vinyl headrest.

"I'm going to cook you a magical feast when we get back, okay?" Kenzie said, scooting across the seat and gently rubbing Braxton's shoulders. "I have all these ideas for recipes that'll help rebuild your bones and muscles. And I think I have a plan for getting rid of that bullet without any pain, too. You'll be good as new in a jiffy."

Braxton leaned against Kenzie and pressed his nose into her apple-scented ponytail. "Have I told you lately that I love you?"

Braxton felt Kenzie's smile against his neck.

"Never going to get sick of hearing it," she replied.

There was a squeal of breaks, and then Braxton's head smashed into the seat in front of them. If Kenzie hadn't grabbed his shirt, he would have been on the floor.

"You drive like my sister," Braxton complained as he and Kenzie sorted themselves out.

Because of Braxton's useless body, it took him longer to get vertical and see the reason why everyone else was gasping and cursing.

The Rikers Island Bridge…the only way out of this cursed place…was completely blocked off. Two rows of police cruisers spanned the entire width of the bridge. There were at least two-dozen armed police officers standing next to their vehicles with their weapons raised. Soldiers dressed in military fatigues and armed with machine guns were lined up behind the cops.

Hundreds of Hunters—far more than Braxton had seen inside the jail— were also standing on the bridge. Each of them was holding a weapon of some kind. And there, right in their midst, was Cane and Nurse fucking Ratched.

A helicopter hovered overhead. In case all the rest hadn't been overkill enough.

"Holy fucking shit," one of the other prisoners said.

That about summed things up.

Cane raised a megaphone to his lips.

"The demons are strong in you, food witches," he called out. "Prepare to die."

CHAPTER 28

SOFIA

I've got two words for you," Sofia said to Cane, even though there was no way he could hear her since their bus was parked a good forty meters from the bridge. "You. Wish."

"Why do you look so excited right now?" Braxton asked, giving her a wary look.

"I'm not excited," she replied, plunging her hand into the burlap sack she'd carried all the way from Maine. "I'm bloody thrilled."

Sofia unloaded twelve paintball guns from the bag. She and Graham had taken an hour-long detour on their way back from the Reaper's to procure the weapons, but it had been so worth it.

"You can't be serious, Sofe," Braxton said incredulously. "You realize the people out there have actual guns?"

"Oh, I'm aware." To Aralia, she said, "On that note, are you ready?"

"Born ready," Aralia replied.

Aralia reached into her cleavage and pulled out a small container. She uncapped the lid and tipped a glistening piece of gray rock candy into her mouth. She crunched down on the candy.

Aralia's face reddened as magic shot out of her and wrapped around all four busses. There was a crackling sound, and then the busses' white paint exterior transformed. The vehicles' outer surface now seemed to be made of rock candy.

"Nifty," Zack said, sliding down his rock candy-covered window and rapping on the bus's exterior. His fist made a thudding sound against the thick rock shield. "Is it bullet-proof?"

"Fucking duh," Aralia replied, panting a little as she controlled the magic.

"Drive as close to the bridge as you can get," Sofia ordered Zack. "Our range isn't that good." She patted one of the paintball guns.

"'Til we see the whites of their eyes?" Zack asked, revving the engine.

Whatever.

Sofia turned her attention to the task at hand. She snapped on a pair of gardening gloves that would protect her skin, as long as she didn't handle the magical mint for too long.

After harvesting the mint and managing to drag their frozen arses back to the garden, the Reaper had deigned to teach them how to avoid turning themselves into human ice cubes. Now, she and Graham were practically experts on the ingredient.

These Hunters were in for one hell of a surprise.

Sofia opened one of the gallon bags that she and Graham had filled with spherical ice cubes. Each cube was the exact size and shape of a paintball bullet and had a piece of magical mint leaf frozen inside.

The mint was so cold they hadn't needed to worry about the cubes melting, even without insulated bags or ice packs. As soon as Sofia took out one of the cubes, frigid air whooshed through the entire bus.

"Getting a bit nipply in here," Zack observed.

Muffled screams filled the bus as real bullets pinged and ricocheted off the bus's rock candy-protected exterior. Everyone calmed down as soon as they realized nothing could penetrate the bus as long as they had Aralia's magic protecting it. For now, they were safe.

"Take that, you Hunter motherfuckers!" someone shouted.

Their bus was close enough to the bridge's entrance that they could, indeed, see the whites of the Hunters' eyes. More unsuccessful gunfire peppered the bus's exterior.

"You ready for this?" Sofia asked Graham.

"Mhm." Graham hovered his hands over the bag of ice cubes and closed his eyes.

Sofia was counting on his magic to make sure the mint didn't kill anyone inside the bus before it reached its actual targets.

She quickly loaded the bullets into the paintball guns, while Graham made sure that the mint cubes didn't immediately burn right through the plastic weapons.

Sofia took one of the guns for herself and passed around the others. She lowered her window just enough to fit the gun's plastic nozzle out of the opening.

"Alright," she muttered. "Let's see if the blokes who sold us these were telling the truth about the high-pressure tank."

"Don't forget about their sweet propulsion distance," Graham said, opening one eye and grinning at her.

"On three," Sofia called, aiming her gun.

Plastic nozzles lined up at every window.

"Three!"

Plastic triggers were pulled. Ice bullets ejected.

All hell broke loose.

The entire front row of Hunters on the bridge began to scream. Weapons shattered from the force of the cold. Bits of frozen metal pierced right through their clothes. The men clawed at their skin as droplets of mint-infused crystal shards began to spread across their bodies. Some of them fell to the pavement, already too numb to so much as twitch.

"Aralia," Graham said. "How powerful is your rock candy?" He pointed up at the helicopter, which was moving in. An enormous, definitely-not-plastic gun was pointing out of its open door at the group of busses.

Sofia tried to open her window more, but the rough candied rock exterior made it grind to a halt halfway down.

Graham, seeing her dilemma, said, "Shield your face." Then, with a sharp jab of his elbow, he broke right through the rock candy window.

"Cover me," Sofia said, grasping one of the ice cubes in her gloved hand and taking aim.

She threw her cube at the helicopter. The heat-seeking magic in the mint leaf got the cube further than she would have managed on her own. Regardless, it was a pretty excellent throw.

A horrible, ear-piercing screeching sound filled the air. The cops and soldiers on the bridge stopped firing as everyone looked up. As they watched, a thin sheet of ice encased the chopper's exterior.

"Wow," Graham said. "Good arm."

"Graham used to play baseball," Aralia announced. "So that's basically foreplay for him."

"Can we not talk about our siblings' foreplay?" Braxton grumbled. He didn't really seem mad, though.

The helicopter's rotors came to a grinding halt. The bird lilted dangerously to the side, and then it started a nosedive into the East River.

"Holy cannoli," Kenzie said, pausing in her paintball gun frenzy.

"You really are something else, Sofe," Braxton said.

"I can't take all the credit," she replied, nudging Graham with her shoulder.

Graham leaned in and pressed a shy kiss to her cheek. That subtle brush of his lips set a horde of butterflies aflutter in her stomach.

"Oh, fucking fuck," Zack said, reminding Sofia that they were in the midst of a veritable warzone.

Blood streaked across one of the bus's back windows as a chef slumped in his seat. His paintball gun fell to the floor with a clatter. Graham leapt over the seat and bent down to hover his hand over the trickle of water that was oozing out of the cracked paintball gun.

"Window!" Aralia screeched. She picked up the dead chef's paintball gun and started firing it out of Sofia's broken window, which was gaping wide open and calling to their enemies like a siren song.

Meanwhile, they were reaching the dregs of their mint bullets. For as many people as they'd taken down, the bridge was still crawling with their enemies.

And there were three busses behind them full of people who had nothing to defend themselves.

"How many ice bullets do you have left?" Graham asked, frowning as he gazed out of their broken window.

"Two," Sofia replied.

They looked at each other.

Sofia took in their bus's ravaged interior. Seven people were already dead, hit by stray bullets that had snuck in through open windows. Some of the chefs were crying quietly in their seats. Others were staring morosely at their bloodied companions as they waited for the end.

Kenzie, her empty paintball gun abandoned on the seat next to her, was leaning into Braxton. Their hands were clasped as they spoke quietly to each other.

Aralia had pulled two daggers out of her belt and was twirling them around as she talked about last stands.

Sofia's heart plummeted. It didn't matter how talented Aralia was with those daggers; their enemies had guns. Sofia could see the Hunters on the bridge gathering themselves and reforming their lines. In another thirty seconds, they were going to realize that no more of the deadly mint bullets were coming their way. Then, everyone on Sofia's side would be fucked.

Zack took a startled Reuben's face in both hands and kissed the hell out of him. After a moment of stunned hesitation, Reuben kissed him back with equal enthusiasm.

"Sofia," Graham said, his smoky voice drawing her attention away from the happy couple. He bent close enough for Sofia to see the light dusting of freckles on the bridge of his nose and cheeks. Unable to help herself, she traced the freckles with her fingertip. His whiskey eyes held her spellbound. "I want you to know—"

"You are under arrest for food witchery and escaping from prison," Cane's voice, amplified through a megaphone, called out.

The Hunters began marching forward. Their hands were full of chains and handcuffs. They were backed up by row upon row of soldiers standing on the bridge, all of whom were holding machine guns.

"Rosemary and Kenzie," Aralia said. Her expression was deadly serious. "If the Hunters get them and figure out how to get access to the anti-superfood, then all of culinary magic is done for."

"Don't even fucking think about it," Braxton snarled.

Sofia's throat tightened as the meaning of Aralia's words sank in.

"She's my mother," Reuben said, standing up. "I'm not going to let you kill her, just because it would make things more convenient."

"Rosemary and thyme and basil and coriander and caraway and dill," Rosemary sang.

"You can come out of your own free will," Cane called. "Or we can take you by force."

All four busses were surrounded by Hunters.

"Flour power," Rosemary sang. "Feel the cornmeal." She pulled the lunch bag off her shoulder and began unzipping it with methodical slowness.

Aralia lifted her daggers over her head. Reuben moved in front of Rosemary. Zack took up a protective stance in front of Reuben.

Rosemary didn't pay attention to anything except her lunch bag and her superfood song. She seemed to be the only one who wasn't concerned about the threats on her life coming both from inside and outside the bus.

"It's my fault if I forget the salt," Rosemary sang. "Too much pepper, and I'll become a leperrrrrrr."

Rosemary tipped the contents of the lunch bag into her mouth. Her throat worked as she swallowed.

Ruby-red syrup dribbled down her chin.

"Cranberries. Nice and red, or you'll be dead. All hale the holy kale. Nev—er forget the jalapeño pepp—er!"

"Rosemary, stop," Kenzie said. "You're taking too much."

"Mom, what are you doing?!"

Rosemary ignored them both. Her throat bobbed as she swallowed again and again.

"Someone stop her," Kenzie said, getting up from her seat and scrambling toward Rosemary. "A couple of drops of that stuff is too much."

Reuben and Zack got to her first, but Rosemary danced out of reach. She tapped the bottom of her lunch bag to get all the liquid into her mouth.

By the time the men wrestled the bag away from her, it was too late. The lunch bag fell to the floor, but not even a drop spilled out.

For several seconds, everyone waited for whatever was going to happen next.

Rosemary took a few tottering steps toward the front of the bus. All at once, tendrils of magic began to shimmer into existence.

More and more appeared until the air was saturated. The wisps zinged around the bus as the temperature began to rise. And rise. A high-pitched squeal filled the air.

Sofia's heart was racing. Sweat began pouring down her neck and back. Beside her, Graham's every muscle had gone taut as a bowstring. Sofia felt like the bus had become a vacuum, and they were all being squeezed.

"I can't stop it," Kenzie gasped, her voice barely audible even though she was sitting across the aisle from Sofia. "It's too powerful."

Aralia was gripping the seat in front of her and cursing at the top of her lungs. Zack and Reuben were clinging to each other. Braxton was slumped against Kenzie and seemed barely conscious.

The magic congealed. It clustered into a tight knot of unimaginable power. It pulsed and crackled as it hovered below the bus's ceiling. Then, it zoomed into Rosemary.

Rosemary jerked back with an "Oof!"

She hit the side of the bus with enough force to rock the entire vehicle. Rosemary didn't seem hurt, though. In fact, a manic kind of energy surrounded her. She bounced on the balls of her feet and quivered in anticipation.

In anticipation of what…Sofia didn't know.

A ruby light pulsed in Rosemary's irises and radiated from her skin. Even the roots of her hair seemed more red than their natural rust-orange.

"Mom," Reuben said in a breathless voice. "Are you okay?"

Rosemary didn't say anything. Instead, she opened her right hand that had been curled into a fist. Her charm necklace, which Sofia just noticed was no longer around Rosemary's neck, was crumpled into a ball on her glowing palm.

Rosemary pressed her necklace into Reuben's hand. She closed Reuben's fingers around the necklace, brought his hand to her lips, and kissed it.

"Mom," Reuben said again, but she just smiled and shook her head. Then, she turned to Sofia.

"Give me," she said, gesturing to the paintball gun in her lap.

Sofia hesitated. She only had two bullets left, and she'd been saving them for their last stand.

Rosemary didn't bother with an answer. She gave the gun a yank and, before Sofia could warn her against it, ejected one of the two bullets from the gun.

"Don't!" Sofia said, but it was too late.

A shudder went through Rosemary as the ice cube fell onto her bare palm.

The superfood must be protecting her, because Rosemary didn't immediately turn into a block of ice. Instead, the red tinge to her eyes and skin flared brighter. Heat wafted off Rosemary, along with the scent of mint.

"Mom, what's happening?" Reuben demanded.

Rosemary didn't answer. Droplets of mint water dripped through her clenched fingers as she walked down the bus's aisle. She hit the button to open the door. She hopped down all three steps and onto the pavement. The door slid shut behind her.

"No. Mom. What are you doing?!" Reuben tried to open the door, but it seemed stuck. Zack started kicking at the glass to no avail.

Threads of magic shot out of Rosemary and cocooned the bus in a red web. Whatever she'd done was making the door impossible to open. All the windows had sealed themselves back up, too. Even the window Graham had broken was covered in an impenetrable web of red magic.

"Mom!" Reuben shouted, pounding on the door. It didn't budge.

There was nothing they could do. They all gathered around the windows and watched as Rosemary barreled right through the Hunters.

The men in white fell back, crying out and clutching at themselves as though they'd been burned. The soldiers on the bridge raised their guns.

Zack pulled Reuben to him so Reuben's face was buried against his chest. Sofia curled her fingers into Graham's sleeve as she waited for Rosemary to collapse on the pavement.

More than a hundred weapons centered on Rosemary. Gunfire filled the air.

Rosemary didn't fall. She didn't even falter.

Her skin flared bright red, and then mint-green flames began erupting from the palm she'd been using to hold the ice cube bullet. The green flames spread until they were encompassing Rosemary's entire body. She was wreathed in green fire.

Sofia had never seen anything like it. It was horrible and…beautiful.

The soldiers and Hunters were coming at Rosemary with every weapon they had, but it didn't matter. Nothing penetrated the green fire.

The flames rose higher and turned a darker shade of green as they multiplied, until it was no longer possible to see Rosemary at their center.

The thick-skulled idiots on the bridge began to realize their bullets were useless against Rosemary. They started to retreat.

Too late.

The green flames touched the nearest soldiers.

Their clothes didn't catch the way they might if it had been a normal fire. Instead, the men flared mint-green as a thick layer of ice encased their entire bodies. The change was nearly instantaneous. One second, the soldiers were firing their weapons at Rosemary, the next, they were frozen solid in a block of translucent green ice.

Rosemary was turning the soldiers on the bridge into human popsicles. They were frozen solid…at least until Rosemary came within touching distance.

She struck out with her superfood-red fist, which was wreathed in green flames. As soon as she made contact with one block of ice after another, the soldiers exploded.

Frozen molecules of mint and flesh burst outward like shards of glass.

Once the other soldiers got a preview of their future, they threw down their weapons and started to run. They fled toward the other end of the bridge as fast as their cowardly legs would carry them. The ones who couldn't make it in time hurled themselves off the bridge rather than succumb to the same fate as their comrades.

Sofia expected Rosemary to chase the fleeing soldiers. Instead, she stopped when she reached the center of the bridge.

At first, Sofia thought Rosemary had collapsed. Maybe all those bullets had gotten through the fire, after all.

But as Sofia watched, she could tell Rosemary's body was still intact beneath the flames. There was no blood, and Rosemary wasn't behaving like she was in pain. She crouched down on her knees. Raising her flaming fists in the air, she brought them both down on the pavement.

Sofia felt the ground shudder, even with the distance separating her from Rosemary. She could see cracks travelling down the asphalt and filling with green flames.

Rosemary's fists came down a second time, and that was all it took. The bridge began to collapse. Chunks of cement and metal fell down to the water below.

Rosemary's body, still engulfed in green flames, sank right though the bridge.

Rosemary hit the river. A green fireball exploded out of the water. It was so bright Sofia was temporarily blinded.

The water frothed and burned mint-green as the nearly mile-long bridge continued to crumble into the East River. Green flames floated on top of the water like an oil slick, devouring everyone who wasn't already dead from the fall.

It seemed to take forever and no time at all for the bridge to stop collapsing and for the people to stop falling.

Sofia jumped when the bus's door, which had been sealed shut, swung open. The red glow surrounding the bus disappeared, along with the magical heat that still lingered.

That was how Sofia knew Rosemary was dead.

CHAPTER 29

KENZIE

The bus door was open, but no one moved. The only sound was Reuben's muffled sobs and Zack's hushed voice as he tried to offer words of comfort.

"I'm not trying to be callous here," Aralia said none-too-gently, "but we have four busses full of people, and our only way off the island was just shot to shit."

"I have an idea," Sofia said, releasing a shuddering breath and unwinding her arm from Graham's. "Come on."

Now that Rosemary was…gone…whatever the superfood had done to keep them all trapped on the bus had disappeared.

A little shiver took hold of Kenzie as she passed through the remnants of magic surrounding the bus. She had never in her life felt so much raw, untamed magic. It had terrified her, all the more because she couldn't control it.

"Come on," Sofia said, taking charge and ushering everyone off the bus.

Graham slung one of Braxton's arms across his neck. Aralia ducked under his other arm. Together, Graham and Aralia partially-helped, and mostly-dragged, Braxton off the bus.

Sofia led the way to the chewed-up edge of the Rikers Island Bridge. Wires and cables protruded from the concrete, looking to Kenzie like bones and torn sinews.

The flames on the river had died down, and the water was its normal murky-blueish shade again. A few bodies bobbed on the surface, but their corpses were too blackened to be able to identify if any of them were Rosemary.

Kenzie remembered the joy on Reuben's face when his mother had recognized him. He'd had mere minutes with her before he'd lost her.

It made Kenzie want to scream. She wanted to rage and throw things. She wanted to strangle Cane, Nurse Ratched, and the rest of those Hunters.

There was a dull *plop* as Sofia dropped her last ice cube bullet off the bridge and into the water.

A beat passed. Then, Kenzie heard a crackling sound. As she stared down at the water, the choppy surface began to flatten out into a single sheet of ice.

"Holy crap," she whispered.

A single magical mint leaf had just frozen the entire East River.

"Anyone have any ice skates?" Zack asked, smiling weakly before wrapping an arm around Reuben's hunched shoulders and squeezing.

"I'd kill to go ice fishing right now," Aralia said with feigned enthusiasm.

"I don't think you want to eat anything that comes out of the East River," Kenzie pointed out. "Unless you feel like growing a third arm or something."

Their attempts at humor were lackluster at best, but it was all they had to offer Reuben.

"Ice fishing is fantastic," Aralia forged on. She slowed her pace until she was keeping stride with Reuben. "I could teach you sometime, if you want."

Reuben offered her a dull nod before trudging on.

Kenzie could only imagine the sorry picture they made as no fewer than a hundred bedraggled former prisoners scrambled down the steeply-sloping pavement, formerly known as the Rikers Island Bridge. From there, they slipped and slid their way across the now-frozen East River.

The only benefit working in their favor was that the Hunters and soldiers who survived the bridge collapse had turned tail and made themselves scarce. For the moment, at least, Kenzie's people were enemy-free.

It was close to a mile to the other side of the river, but it somehow felt much longer. The weight of Rosemary's loss hung heavily over all of them. Kenzie hadn't known her for long, but they'd survived Cutthroat Cuisine together. Kenzie silently swore to Reuben, and herself, that they would get the revenge Rosemary deserved.

By the time they finally reached the other side of the frozen river, Kenzie wanted to kiss the pavement. Braxton looked paler than Kenzie had ever seen him. He couldn't even hold up his head.

At least they were only a block from the subway. They'd be back at the food bank in half an hour. A magic dinner, shower, sleep, and maybe some sexy time would go a long way toward healing Braxton.

Kenzie was so anxious to get back and initiate Plan Restore Braxton to his Former Glory that it took her brain several precious seconds to register the wave of red that was coming down the street toward them. And the sneering man leading the charge.

Rick and the Gourmands were heading straight for them.

Kenzie glanced from side to side, looking for an easy escape. No such luck. They were bracketed by buildings on both sides, and the river was behind them.

Crap. They so did not need this right now.

The Gourmands stopped halfway down the block. Rick took a few steps forward so he could draw full attention to his smug self.

He was wearing a suit that probably cost more than Kenzie had made during her entire tenure at *Good Ol' Apple Pie*. The thick gloves he was wearing seemed to be a new addition to his ensemble.

Rick was tossing something high in the air and catching it. Kenzie kind of admired his dexterity. But mostly she was annoyed that he was blocking her path.

"You're in our way, Dick," Kenzie called.

"I'll warn you I'm in no mood for your fuckery," Aralia added. "Either get out of my way or there's going to be blood. Specifically, yours."

Rick jutted his pointy chin. The Gourmands moved with alarming synchronicity, creating a narrow path for Kenzie's people to pass between them.

As if.

"You think we were born yesterday?" Kenzie said, not trusting a one of them as far as she could throw them.

"I'm not in the business of harming culinary magicians," Rick said. "In fact," his beady eyes raked over their downtrodden group. "Any of you who wish to come with me will be put under the Gourmands' protection. Effective immediately."

"I can protect you, too," Kenzie piped up before stopping to consider whether or not it was a promise she could keep. But screw it. Anything Rick could do, she could do better. "Rick is just a murderer and an imposter."

"Who are you going to trust?" Rick asked, addressing the crowd of prisoners at Kenzie's back. "Someone who didn't know shit about our world a month ago, or a leader whose family has been at the forefront of our community for generations?"

"Nepotism isn't sexy," Aralia informed Rick.

"Neither is murdering culinary magicians for sport," Rick said, smiling evilly at Kenzie. "Go ahead and tell them. Tell them how you used your culinarian magic to put on a show for the Gourmands."

"I didn't—" Kenzie began, but Rick just talked over her.

"After all this talk about how powerful you are, I haven't seen you save a single life. You've taken plenty, though. Haven't you, Champ?"

Kenzie couldn't hide her flinch at the sound of the name she'd gone by during Cutthroat Cuisine.

"Or was it the Thief?" Rick persisted. "That was what they started calling you after the second time you stole another chef's magic and used it to kill them, wasn't it? Or was it after the third time you did that? I forget."

Brute. Scarlet. Toxic…. Her Cutthroat Cuisine victims passed across her vision in a horrifying blur.

"I didn't have a choice," Kenzie murmured.

She sounded like a child. A scared, little child.

"I'm sure you didn't," Rick said. He took several steps closer to address the people standing behind Kenzie and absorbing every word of this conversation. "And I bet that's exactly what she's going to say after she gets each and every one of you killed, too."

Kenzie had no response to that.

She could feel the mood shifting behind her. Without even needing to look, she knew what everyone would decide. And she couldn't even blame them.

Rick had a horde of Gourmands at his beck and call. All Kenzie could offer was a ragtag band of outlaws.

Sure enough, the prisoners began to skulk over to Rick's side of the street. Some of them slid guilty looks Kenzie's way. Most of them didn't look at her at all.

"Big mistake, suckers," Aralia told the prisoners.

"You planning to kill the rest of us?" Sofia asked Rick, her posture stiff and her fists curled like she was ready to take down every one of the Gourmands with her bare hands. If anyone could manage such a feat, it was Sofia.

"Like I said, I don't kill culinary magicians unless I have to." Rick made a sweeping gesture with one gloved hand. His other hand, the one that was holding whatever he'd been tossing around before, was now hidden behind his back.

"Besides," Rick continued. "The last thing I want is for us to be fighting among ourselves when we should all be focused on our true enemy."

"If you're fucking with us right now," Aralia said, "I'll rip your dick off."

Rick just waited.

After a pause laden with tension, Aralia led the way forward.

"Aralia, hang on," Graham said, waiting just long enough to make sure Braxton was steady on his feet before running after his sister. Shockingly, none of the Gourmands moved to restrain them. Graham and Aralia passed through unhassled.

"Go on, beautiful," Rick said, gesturing to Sofia.

"I'm not going anywhere without Braxton," Sofia said, planting her feet.

"Sadly, he won't be leaving," Rick said. "You either, Culinarian."

"Gee," Kenzie said, stalling for time. Her gaze bounced around the street as she searched for a way out. "Why am I not surprised?"

"I said I didn't kill culinary magicians unless I have to," Rick said, looking inordinately pleased with himself. "Repeated attempts on my life constitutes a definite need to kill both of you. No one's going to argue with that."

The Gourmands fanned out so they blocked off both ends of the street. Sunflower seed shells littered the pavement around them. Kenzie caught a whiff of the burnt sugar smell of synthetic ingredients.

"Rick, you bastard," Braxton said. "This is between us. Let Kenzie and my sister go."

"Don't think I will," Rick replied smugly. "Your sister had her chance. And your Culinarian girlfriend was never going to make it out of here."

"Rick, please—" Braxton said, his voice cracking.

"I've been waiting for this moment for so long," Rick said with a sigh. He tossed the object in his gloved hand again. He opened his palm and held it out, giving them a better view.

Now that she was closer, Kenzie saw that he was holding a green prickly pear cactus fruit. Magic wafted off it.

"Magical prickly pear cactus," Rick said, confirming what Kenzie could see for herself. "See these little glochids?" he asked, pointing to the spots on the fruit's green flesh. "They hurt like a motherfucker when the nonmagical varieties get into your skin." He tossed the fruit in the air and caught it again. "Can you imagine how bad it feels when it's a *magical* prickly pear?"

Kenzie knew Rick wasn't kidding about the nonmagical variety. The teeny hairlike thorns were almost impossible to see and were like splinters on steroids. They sucked, to put it mildly.

That explained Rick's gloves. Now that Kenzie was looking more closely, she saw that his gloves were the super heavy-duty kind that not even metal could pierce.

"Tell you what, McKaid." Rick smirked. "I'm feeling in a generous mood. So I'll put you out of your misery first."

Kenzie saw everything as though it were happening in slow motion.

She saw Rick pull back his arm and aim at Braxton's chest. She even saw Rick's tongue poking out of the corner of his mouth as he concentrated.

She saw him throw the prickly pear fruit.

Braxton stood on his own two feet, waiting for the inevitability of the deadly fruit striking him.

I don't freaking think so.

There was no time to reach for the magic or try anything fancy. So, Kenzie did the only thing she could. She dove.

There was a hard thump as the fruit hit her smack-dab in the center of her chest, right where it was meant to hit Braxton. Pain exploded.

Kenzie looked down at her sternum, which felt like it was on fire. She gasped. It came out as a gurgling, sucking sound.

The prickly pear was embedded in her chest.

Magic pulsed around the fruit. Blood gushed. Bits of bone and other innards clung to the prickly pear as it burrowed deeper and deeper inside her.

The pain was unbearable. Kenzie tried to reaching inside herself to pull the cactus out, but every movement was excruciating. She couldn't even summon a scream.

She stood there, silent, as she stared down at her chest and watched the fruit eat its way through her.

Kenzie saw her own heart. That wasn't a metaphor. It was there, pulsing next to the prickly pear fruit. Then, the fruit was burrowing into her heart.

Blood began to gush from the ruined organ.

Kenzie heard Braxton shouting, but for some reason, the last words that went through her mind weren't whatever he was trying to say. They were words her father had repeated a number of times when she was growing up.

Making a sacrifice for a person you love is the greatest gift you can ever give.

And she loved Braxton. With every molecule of her shredded, shattered heart.

It was her last thought before her world went dark.

CHAPTER 30

SOFIA

Everything was a blur. Somehow, Graham had fought his way back through the Gourmands and positioned himself in front of Sofia. There wasn't time to do anything else before Rick pulled his arm back and threw.

Several meters separated Sofia from Braxton and Kenzie. She tried to get to her brother, but Graham held her back. Sofia was powerless to do anything except watch as the prickly pear fruit came straight at Braxton.

Sofia screamed.

Instead of striking its intended target, a blur came out of nowhere.

Kenzie leapt in front of Braxton at the last second. The magical fruit struck her in the chest. It clung to her and immediately began worming its way into her body.

Braxton was right there, reaching into Kenzie's open chest cavity to try and pull the magic fruit out, but it was too late.

There was a loud sucking sound, and then Kenzie's heart...exploded. Tiny pieces of bloody muscle flew through the air. Red bits covered Braxton's face and caught in his hair.

Kenzie's body collapsed onto the pavement.

"No!" Braxton clutched her to him. "Kenzie!"

Sofia's scream cut off as the sound of gunfire split the air.

Where was it even coming from?

She whipped her head around, yelping when bullets peppered a nearby building. Graham grabbed her arm and pulled her against him, curving his body protectively around hers.

Everything was happening so fast Sofia could barely process any of it. Ducking under Graham's arm, she caught sight of the shooter.

Chef Levy was perched on the roof of a nearby building and was firing down at the Gourmands. Several of them fell, but not the one who most needed to die.

Rick used his own people for cover as he darted back down the street and threw himself into a waiting SUV. The vehicle took off, leaving tire tracks and a cloud of exhaust fumes in its wake.

Chef Levy raced across rooftops as she tried to track the SUV, even though it was a pointless venture. Chef Levy would never catch Rick. Even if she did, the damage had been done. Kenzie was lying in the middle of the street in a pool of her own blood. Dead.

The remaining Gourmands fled the scene in a whirl of scarlet robes and a scattering of sunflower seed shells.

The prisoners who had been so quick to turn traitor after they'd been rescued began to back away. None of them seemed to know what to do now that their fearless leader had abandoned them. And Sofia would plunge a dagger into her own heart before she helped one of them ever again.

Graham moved out of his protective stance now that the threat had abated. He stood behind Sofia, wrapping his arms around her chest and tucking her against him. They stood locked together as they watched the nightmarish tableau that was playing out in front of them.

Braxton was on his hands and knees beside Kenzie's body, his head bowed like he was praying. His shoulders were shaking. A tortured sob tore free from his throat.

"Kenzie," Braxton groaned.

With just that one word, a staggering realization sent Sofia's head reeling.

Braxton wasn't going to survive this. Losing Aidan had destroyed a part of him, but even when they'd watched Aidan's coffin being lowered into the ground, Sofia had known Braxton would eventually be okay. That wasn't the case this time.

"Don't leave me," Braxton was begging Kenzie, even though she was already gone. "Please, baby. Don't leave me. Please—" His words devolved into sobs that made his entire body convulse. He leaned down until his forehead was pressed to Kenzie's stomach.

Sofia felt wetness on her face and heard a horrible rasping sound. She realized it was coming from her when she felt Graham's arms tighten around her.

Nothing could bring Braxton back from this. Even if his heart continued to pump and magic healed his melted muscles, he'd be destroyed.

Kenzie had given her life to save him, but it didn't matter.

There was no blood or gore, but Braxton was as gone as Kenzie. His body just didn't know it yet.

CHAPTER 31

BRAXTON

Please," Braxton begged Kenzie, even though he knew she was beyond hearing him. "Don't leave me."

He tried to breathe her in, but all he smelled was the sickly-sweet stench of blood. The tart apple smell that was all Kenzie had faded.

Just like the rest of her.

He laid his head down on her stomach and let the world fade around him. He might never have moved again, except he was overwhelmed with the urge to kiss her goodbye.

Ignoring his protesting body, Braxton shifted so his lips hovered over hers. He kissed one of her closed eyelids. Then the other.

His nose brushed against hers as he carefully tucked a strand of black hair behind her ear. It was crusted with dried blood.

Choking back a sob, Braxton leaned in until his lips touched hers.

He expected her mouth to be stiff and cool, like hardening wax. But her lips were still warm. He could have sworn they twitched beneath his, almost like she was trying to kiss him back.

It must have been some cruel trick of the magic that was making her skin feel…alive.

Braxton leaned in for another kiss…just one more…when he heard it.

Da-dum. Da-dum.

That sounded like—

It was his own heartbeat. It had to be. His desperation and grief were making him hope for impossible things.

Braxton leaned back, forcing himself to look at Kenzie's ruined chest. Maybe if his eyes were presented with irrefutable evidence, his brain could accept the truth.

The hole in Kenzie's chest was still there, but there was movement coming from inside. Leaning closer, he followed the *da-dum* sound that was almost definitely coming from her chest rather than his broken psyche.

Her heart, which Braxton could have sworn he'd seen explode with his own eyes, was inside Kenzie's body. It was whole and jiggling around as it pumped.

Da-dum. Da-dum. Da-dum.

It wasn't possible for someone's heart to literally explode and then reform itself. And yet, here Kenzie's heart was, beating away.

And unless he really was hallucinating, the gaping hole in her chest was becoming smaller.

There was a little *pop* as the prickly pear fruit wriggled out of Kenzie's heart and sailed out of her chest cavity. It plunked down onto the pavement and rolled, leaving a bloody streak in its wake.

"Brax?" Sofia said from somewhere behind him.

Braxton couldn't tear his eyes off Kenzie to so much as acknowledge his sister. Something was happening.

With every second that passed, the hole in Kenzie's chest shrank. The torn, bloody hole in her shirt stayed shredded, but bone and skin were knitting back together. Kenzie's eyes stayed closed and she didn't make a sound as her body…healed itself.

"Holy shit," Sofia was saying as she grabbed his shoulder and shook him. "Holy shit, Brax. Are you *seeing* this?!"

Braxton couldn't respond. His heart, which he'd been certain had stopped beating at the same moment as Kenzie's, was lodged in his throat. His gaze was fixed on his girlfriend's eyelids, which had started to flutter. Then, they opened.

Braxton found himself staring into gunmetal-gray irises that were full of surprise and love and…life.

Kenzie was alive.

"Wow," Kenzie gasped. She sat up and rubbed her chest. "That *sucked*."

Braxton still couldn't speak. He couldn't move, and it had nothing to do with his ruined body. He had just watched Kenzie die and come back to life.

He was petrified that if he so much as blinked, this impossible turn of events would reverse course and he'd look down to find her dead again.

Braxton didn't believe in God or miracles or life after death. There was simply no rational explanation for what all of his senses were telling him was reality.

Kenzie smacked her lips together. "Did you feed me strawberries?"

"What?" Braxton croaked.

"Strawberries," Kenzie repeated, blinking up at him. "I taste strawberries." Her tongue darted out to trace her lips. "Mmm. And white chocolate." She cocked her head at him. "What did you give me?"

He just shook his head.

"This is bloody impossible," Braxton rasped.

"No, it isn't." He felt Sofia's nails dig into his shoulder. "Brax. Holy shit."

The urgency in his sister's voice had him tearing his gaze off Kenzie for just long enough to take in his sister's incredulous expression.

"The wish truffle," Sofia said. She snapped her fingers in Braxton's face when he continued to stare dumbly at her. "What was your exact wish?"

"Uhh…." The gears in Braxton's brain were slow to grind.

Wish truffle…exact wish….

Braxton thought back to those chaotic moments after Kenzie won Hex Kitchen. She'd leaned in to kiss him, and then she'd thrust the wish truffle into his mouth. She'd told him to use the wish to save his family, but all he'd been able to think about was the fact that she'd been dying of poison.

Oh. *Oh.*

"I…I wished…." He looked down at Kenzie, who was staring back at him with pure wonder in her eyes. "I wished that you'd live an incredibly long and healthy life."

Kenzie reached up and cupped his jaw. "I'd be dead right now if it wasn't for you," she murmured.

"And Braxton would be dead if it wasn't for you," Sofia told Kenzie. "You know, I'm starting to see why my brother loves you."

Sofia engulfed a laughing Kenzie in a hug. Meanwhile, Braxton tried to remember how to breathe.

CHAPTER 32

GRAHAM

After watching Kenzie die and come back to life, Graham trailed Sofia like he was her shadow. He couldn't help himself. All he wanted to do was climb into a bed with Sofia someplace safe and hold her for a week straight.

"She just—brought herself back to life," an awed voice said.

Graham turned, realizing that their little group wasn't alone. They were surrounded by the prisoners they'd freed from Rikers—the same ones who had abandoned them for Rick and the Gourmands. Since Chef Levy had chased away the Gourmands, the prisoners were again left to fend for themselves.

"She really is a Culinarian," another prisoner said, pressing her hand to her heart. "I didn't believe it until this moment."

"I'm sorry," cried a third. "I never would have picked Rick over you if I'd known. Please forgive me!"

No one pointed out that they had known, since Kenzie had told them; they just hadn't believed her.

All around them, the prisoners were expressing their astonishment over what Kenzie had done. Then, someone knelt down at Kenzie's feet.

"I'll never be disloyal to you again," the man swore, bowing his head in a submissive gesture. "I'll cook, fight, and even die for you. Anything."

The other prisoners hurriedly echoed the sentiment.

"Oh, um, that's not necessary," Kenzie said.

No one listened to her. Within seconds, every single one of the prisoners was on their knees before her, like she was some kind of culinary magic royalty.

"We're yours to command," one of the prisoners said, his head still bowed in reverence. "Tell us how we can serve you."

"I don't know about serving me," Kenzie began awkwardly. "But if you want to help, there is something you can do...."

* * *

It was fortunate the food bank was large enough to accommodate their newly-expanded company.

The ex-prisoners began prepping various dishes for the task Kenzie had assigned them. Kenzie and Sofia were busy cooking up a storm to help restore Braxton's health. Graham sat at a table with Aralia. He shelled peas for one of Kenzie's recipes while he caught up with his sister.

He stopped mid-sentence when Sofia let out a yelp followed by a curse. Graham jumped up, spilling his bowl of peas all over the floor.

"Damn," Sofia said, wrapping a towel around her finger. "Forgot how sharp knives were outside of jail."

Graham, his heart racing and his legs gelatin-like, sat back down. Aralia flicked a stray pea at him.

"I might be a little on edge," he told his sister, giving her a sheepish look.

Watching what happened to Kenzie—and more specifically, Braxton's reaction to it—had gotten into Graham's head. The whole time, he had imagined Sofia or Aralia lying on the ground. He shuddered.

Aralia flicked a pea all the way across the room and hit Sofia square in the forehead. Sofia retaliated by giving Aralia the finger.

Aralia chuckled before turning back to Graham. "You know," she said, "I almost killed Sofia after she brought you down to Tennessee and set the cops on your ass."

"I'm very glad you didn't," Graham replied.

In the other room, Sofia laughed at something Kenzie said. It made her whole face light up.

Aralia noticed Graham's attention.

"Oh yes," she said. "Those two have been thick as thieves ever since Sofia convinced Kenzie to make her a culinary magician."

Ah. So that was the explanation for how Sofia had all that magic inside her. Graham had been wondering where she got it.

"Being a culinary magician suits her," Graham said, watching the way Sofia owned the kitchen with the same confident ease she did everything she attempted. "Must have been a nice consolation prize after Rick stole her magical ingredients."

"Mm." Aralia had a pensive look on her face as she squinted in Sofia's direction. "At first, I thought losing those ingredients was her motivation for becoming a culinary magician." She drew imaginary circles on the tabletop with her finger. "When I realized that wasn't the reason, I thought maybe she did it for Braxton. To save him from the deal he made with me."

Graham pinned his sister with a hard stare. "I thought I told you to let him out of that bargain."

"Yeah, well, I changed my mind after Sofia betrayed you," she said with a dismissive wave of her hand. "I might have gotten slightly hysterical when I found out what she'd done."

Graham felt his lips twitch at that. A slightly hysterical Aralia was like a slightly deadly A-bomb.

"Anyhoo," Aralia continued. "I thought Sofia's reasoning for becoming a culinary magician was for her brother's sake, but then I found out what she did for you in the jail—"

"Hold on," Graham said, stopping Aralia before she sent another pea flying. "What did she do for me?"

Aralia's mouth fell open. "She didn't tell you?"

Graham shook his head.

A little smile curved Aralia's lips. "She faked your death."

"What?" Graham asked when he finally managed to unhinge his jaw.

"You're dead," Aralia repeated. "At least, according to your Rikers Island prison file. Deceased as of May 2 and cremated in the Rikers Island morgue." She gripped his arm and gave him a little shake. "No one is looking for you anymore, Graham. You don't have to worry about going out in public." She shook him again. "You're free."

Free.

The thought of being able to walk down the street…into a restaurant…through a park…without fear of being recognized….

He wouldn't have to hide his face or duck around the nearest corner every time law enforcement showed up. For the first time in eight years, he could have the gift of a normal life.

"Might be a good idea to change your last name," Aralia was saying. "Sofia seems like the type who would want you to take her name, anyway, though."

Graham just laughed. His head was spinning. He couldn't believe he was really, truly free. And Sofia was the one who had made that happen for him.

"Why didn't she tell me?" he asked, his thoughts still flying in a thousand different directions.

"Oh, probably because she didn't want you feeling gratitude or thinking you owed her." Aralia rolled her eyes. "It's a McKaid thing."

Graham looked up at that moment and found Sofia was staring back at him. There was no way she could have heard their conversation, but there was a knowing look in her eyes that told him she understood what he and Aralia had just been talking about. She gave him a short nod and turned away.

A tiny but fierce tornado, otherwise known as Elyannah Levy, swept into the dining room. She looked as frazzled and furious as Graham had ever seen her.

"Rick got away," she said, tossing her hopefully-unloaded rifle onto the floor and stomping into the kitchen. She bypassed the mug of coffee Kenzie offered and rummaged around in the freezer. She emerged with a handle of vodka.

"I followed the Gourmands to NoHo. They've got an entire residential tower protected by culinary magic. No one's getting in without him knowing about it." She took a swig of vodka. "And Hunters aside, the rest of the Vanilla population is getting anxious about their safety. It won't be long before the military starts rounding us up."

Kenzie was the one who broke their uneasy silence.

"Let's focus on one problem at a time," she said, waving a ladle as she spoke and flinging droplets of chicken soup through the air. "There's nothing we can do about the Vanillas at the moment, and we can deal with Rick and the Gourmands later."

"That so?" Chef Levy raised an eyebrow.

"Yep," Kenzie replied. "At this very moment, Rikers Island is sitting empty and abandoned. And we're going to fill it. With the Hunters."

The dining room erupted into cheers.

Graham was about to join in, when he felt the brush of a warm hand on his back. He turned to find Sofia at his side. His heart leapt, until he saw the expression on her face.

"What's wrong?" he demanded, hardly able to hear his own voice over the shouting and sound of fists thumping against the tables.

In answer, Sofia held her phone out to him.

"Hello?" Graham strained to hear the person on the other end.

"Graham?" a small voice asked.

"Clementine?" he said.

"Graham, ohmygod," Clementine cried. "I don't know what to do. You have to come back right away. Please hurry."

"Just slow down," he told her. "Tell me what's going on."

"Reaper Lee is dying."

CHAPTER 33

KENZIE

Kenzie was pretty sure she'd died for a few minutes earlier. That was a thing that happened. Predictably, her dad and Braxton were both sticking to her like caffeine on cappuccino. Not that she could exactly blame them.

She still hadn't quite come to terms with what Braxton's wish had done for her, and what that might mean for her going forward. Right now, though, she had a city to save.

Kenzie stood on the edge of the East River. It had mostly-thawed, although chunks of ice still bobbed in the water. The bridge itself was still in shambles. Aside from warning signs and concrete roadblocks, no moves had been made to begin repairs.

Gotta love New York.

Sofia, Braxton, and Chef Levy waited beside her.

"You doing okay?" Kenzie whispered to Braxton.

"Never better," he replied with a tired smile.

"You should have stayed behind," Chef Levy complained. "You're too weak to do any magic."

"And miss all the fun?" Braxton replied. "No thanks."

All of Braxton's broken bones and torn muscles were healed, thanks to a magical healing cookbook that Sofia had found in the food bank's kitchen. Kenzie and Sofia had made every single recipe in the book, and after a night's rest, Braxton was back to his old self. Physically, at least. He still looked exhausted. And a little bit haunted.

She wished they had a day…a night…a few hours…just to be together.

"You waiting for an invitation, Ashner?" Chef Levy demanded.

Sigh….

"On it, Chef."

Kenzie popped a piece of cotton candy in her mouth and let the sugary fluff dissolve on her tongue. The magic fell into place almost at once. Kenzie tilted her face skyward and breathed out a puff of air.

A few seconds later, words appeared in the sky.

Come and get us, Hunters. Rikers Island Bridge.

Kenzie didn't have to wait long to see whether the Hunters would take her bait. Not even five minutes later, a convoy of white vehicles of various makes and models appeared at the other end of the street.

"I hope you know what you're doing, Ashner," Chef Levy said.

That makes two of us.

"Uh, yeah," Kenzie said, convincing no one. "Did you get the thing I asked for?"

Chef Levy scowled. "You know how many favors I had to call in to get it done?"

"So that's a yes?" Kenzie asked, gnawing on the inside of her cheek.

Chef Levy humphed.

Beside her, Sofia crumpled up a sheet of magical rice paper and put it in her mouth. Strands of magic flared out around her.

Kenzie said a little prayer that she wasn't about to get all of them killed.

The Hunters piled out of their vehicles. They had come without their military escort, but they were armed to the teeth with every kind of deadly weapon imaginable.

There were so many of them.

Kenzie's insides turned over in dread. Back in the food bank, this had seemed like such a good idea in theory. Here, in practice, it looked a lot like suicide.

Cane, with Nurse Ratched at his side, was the first to reach Kenzie's small group.

"You food witches are finished," Cane said, his milky eyes fixating on Kenzie. "You'll never kill another one of our kind again."

"Your daughter died of food poisoning, you imbecile," Sofia jumped in, ignoring the warning look Chef Levy gave her. "And we wouldn't be trying to kill the rest of you if you weren't murdering us, first."

Cane's pale face turned an unflattering shade of mauve.

"Arrest them," he hissed. "If they don't come quietly, kill them."

The Hunters surged forward.

Kenzie tensed.

"Oy!"

Half a block away, Aralia stepped out from behind a thick stretch of trees. Kenzie passed the most nerve-wracking few seconds of her life while she waited and hoped. Would anyone else come?

She let out a relieved breath when she caught movement in the trees.

Dozens of culinary magicians appeared behind Aralia. Spidery webs of magic danced above their heads as they ingested whatever they'd brought with them to the fight.

Dozens turned into hundreds. All of the culinary magicians Kenzie had helped free from jail were here…plus others. Their friends and families had come, too. And they outnumbered the Hunters by at least three-to-one.

Hell yeah.

"What the—" Nurse Ratched whispered.

"What are you waiting for?" Cane roared. "Kill them. Kill them all!"

"I wouldn't try anything, if I were you," Kenzie hurriedly told the Hunters. "Have you ever seen a magical flapjack created by hundreds of culinary magicians working together?"

A few of the Hunters gulped and shook their heads.

"I wouldn't want to be on the receiving end of that," Sofia added helpfully. "*Splat.*" She clapped both of her hands together dramatically.

Kenzie saw the color drain from the Hunters' faces. Some of them dropped their weapons and raised their hands in surrender. Others seemed like they were too scared to move at all.

Kenzie wasn't sure whether she should be offended or flattered.

Aralia and the three-hundred-or-so-chefs who had shown up to fight for their side started forward.

"Hold your fire," Chef Levy ordered, motioning for them to keep their distance.

"We don't want any violence," Kenzie told Cane. "But you are going to answer for all of the culinary magicians you murdered."

Cane's response was drowned out by a deafening horn blast. An enormous barge drifting down the river drew up next to the ruined bridge.

Thank you, Kenzie mouthed at Chef Levy.

Chef Levy did something with her lips that might have been a smile.

"These food witches are the devil," Cane said, his voice growing hoarse with desperation. He gave one of his fellow Hunters a shove, making the chain grasped in the other man's hands rattle. "You have to kill them before they kill us. Do it now!"

"You have two choices," Kenzie told the Hunters. She shifted from foot to foot as adrenaline coursed through her. "You can get on this boat and let it take you to Rikers, where you'll serve out fair jail sentences—" She paused and took in Nurse Ratched's stricken expression.

Normally, she didn't relish other people's pain, but for Nurse Ratched, she was willing to make an exception.

"—Or," Kenzie continued, "we'll use our food witch magic on you."

She was tempted to add a ghostly "*Woooo*" and accompanying finger wave but decided against it. Taking the high road could be such a drag.

Ignoring their fearless leader's shouts, the Hunters began filing onto the barge. No fuss, no muss.

Kenzie's army—yeah, she totally had an army—stood by and gave the Hunters menacing stares. It was about that time when the cops showed up.

"Thank God you're here," Cane said, pointing a bone-white finger at Kenzie as he tried to take control of the situation. "Arrests need to be made."

Poor man really hadn't caught on to this whole peaceful surrender thing.

The police looked from the Hunters to the culinary magicians, assessing the situation. When their gazes landed on the mob of culinary magicians, Kenzie saw fear in their eyes, plain as day.

The cops were afraid of magic.

Some of the police were reaching for their weapons. Most were keeping their eyes on the ground like they would rather be responding to any other call at that moment.

"What's going on here?" a policewoman with an *awesome* New York accent asked, stepping in front of the others and making a valiant attempt to sound brave.

"What's going on here," Sofia said coolly, "is that we've collected 263 wanted criminals for you." She passed the policewoman a stack of printouts that contained the Hunters' names and photo IDs. "You're welcome."

"Liar!" Cane thundered. "These are the food witches. Arrest them, officer. Arrest them, now!"

"Cross-check these printouts against your records," Sofia ordered the cops.

The officers returned to their cruisers, conferring among themselves. Kenzie took it as a good sign when they started going through the printed sheets and comparing them to images on their devices.

"How did you get all of these criminals here at once?" one of the cops asked when the group of them returned. They were regarding Kenzie and her friends with newfound respect. "We've been looking for some of these guys for decades."

"Just doing our civic duty," Kenzie said sweetly as a policeman slapped a pair of handcuffs on Cane and escorted him onto the barge.

"But they're food witches," Cane spluttered, ineffectually trying to wriggle free from his cuffs. "You should be arresting *them!*"

"Don't feel too bad," Aralia said, keeping pace with the cop who was escorting Cane onto the boat. "On the bright side, you'll have Rikers all to yourselves." She gave Cane's cheek a patronizing pat. "Bad news is that you might be a little low on food and cleaning staff, what with the broken bridge and all. I wouldn't expect the mayor to make you murderers a priority."

Whatever Cane might have said in response was drowned out by Nurse Ratched. The evil nurse was fighting tooth and nail to escape from a policeman who was restraining her. It wasn't going well for Nurse Ratched, especially once the cop got her cuffed.

"Do something," Nurse Ratched begged as she was paraded past Kenzie's group. "I'm a culinary magician. I'm like you. I don't belong with them!"

"Oh yeah," Kenzie scoffed bitterly. "As I recall, you were singing a different tune when these assholes were murdering our people left and right. In fact, if memory serves, you were helping them."

Nurse Ratched's pathetic pout turned into a sneer. She stared down her nose at Kenzie. "Don't act all high and mighty around me, Miss Culinarian. I saw what you did in Cutthroat Cuisine."

Kenzie couldn't stop herself from flinching like she'd been physically struck.

"Shut your motherfucking mouth," Braxton growled, putting a protective arm around Kenzie.

Like a shark smelling blood, Nurse Ratched had seen her advantage and was closing in for the kill. She also had nothing left to lose.

"You killed those other competitors without a second thought," Nurse Ratched told Kenzie. "You're no different from me. You did what you had to do to survive, just like I am. If I have to be punished, then so do you."

"Enough of this," Sofia announced. She went over to one of the culinary magicians standing with Aralia. The man was holding what appeared to be a pitcher full of magical fruit punch.

"Can I borrow this?" Sofia asked.

"The magic isn't ready," the chef protested as Sofia took the bowl without waiting for permission.

Sofia marched right past the law enforcement personnel and faced off against Nurse Ratched.

"I'm tired of you ragging on Kenzie," Sofia informed the woman. Then, without further ado, Sofia dumped the fruit punch all over Nurse's Ratched's pristine white sneakers.

Nurse Ratched's enraged bellow was music to Kenzie's ears. As was the squishy, squelching sound her sneakers made as she hopped around in place and tried unsuccessfully to blot out the fuchsia stain on her pantlegs.

"You'll be sorry!" Nurse Ratched shrieked. "You'll see."

She was still screaming threats when she was dragged onto the barge with the other prisoners.

"You're officially my hero," Kenzie informed Sofia, sighing contentedly.

"Sofe," Braxton said, giving his sister a contemplative look. "What exactly did your rice paper do?"

"Oh, not much." Sofia raised an eyebrow. "Except it might have magically tied those Hunters' identities to all sorts of unsolved crimes. And digitally logged the evidence, of course." She grinned at her brother.

"Brilliant," Braxton said, shaking his head in amazement. "Wait. Did you get that idea from—"

"Aidan," Sofia finished. She turned to Kenzie and explained, "Our brother made a rice paper recipe when we were kids that adjusted our grades in the electronic system. It was my inspiration for this dish."

Braxton laughed. "That's amazing, Sofe."

"Well," Sofia replied. "I had a little help."

She held out her hand to Kenzie for a high-five.

The barge gave a blast of its horn and started pulling away from the water's edge.

Kenzie leaned over the railing of the broken bridge. She watched the barge transport the Hunters across the river to Rikers, where they wouldn't be able to harm anyone ever again.

* * *

Back in the food bank's kitchen, it was no rest for the weary. The Hunters were no longer a problem, but that still left them with the real threat: Rick and the Gourmands.

Which was why Kenzie needed a baller recipe.

"It's gotta be something that will convince Rick to come out of hiding before he's ready," Aralia said.

"Ideally something that will negate the Gourmands' sunflower seeds, too," Chef Levy added. "As well as any other magical ingredients they have at their disposal."

"Easy peasy," Kenzie grumbled.

As she'd learned in Times Square, she couldn't steal all of the Gourmands' magic without the risk of burning herself out. And even if she tried, Rick's people would kill her before she managed to do any real damage to them.

Since Kenzie couldn't go to him, that meant she needed to bring Rick to her.

She needed a way to get Rick out of his comfy, magically-protected residential tower. Maybe they could talk the city's rat population into storming the place, or….

Kenzie searched the kitchen for inspiration. Her gaze landed on Kiwi's habitat, which reminded her that it was his dinner time. As she started gathering his wriggling waxworms and crickets, an idea occurred to her.

"This will definitely get the Gourmands' attention," she told her chameleon, who was none-too-pleased that his dinnertime was about to be pushed back by Kenzie's eureka moment.

"Sorry," Kenzie told the poor cricket who had the misfortune of becoming the subject of her magical experiment. Its back legs twitched, and the insect made an escape attempt before Kenzie cupped her hands around it and deposited it safely back onto the plate.

"Um, Kenz, what are you doing?" Braxton asked.

"Shh," she replied.

One of the first times she'd ever knowingly performed culinary magic, she'd done something to Kiwi's raspberry-and-waxworm salad that had resulted in her lazy little pet dancing the Macarena. Hell if she knew what.

The magic she was attempting now was a bit more complicated. And the cricket was a lot wilier than those waxworms had been.

Kenzie had to quickly pull together her magic as the cricket hopped around the plate. Nothing she was doing would hurt it, but the creature seemed determined to avoid Kenzie's magic. Go figure.

Kenzie had to infuse greater degrees of magic into the dish to make up for the fact that the critter kept moving. There was added complexity because she needed the magic, when it initiated, to be intense. She kept adding more and more power in the hopes that it would be enough. After all, it was going to take one big-ass cricket to scare Rick and the Gourmands out of their lair.

Kenzie lost herself to the task, falling into an almost trance-like state. She was almost finished when—

Oh no. Ohhhhh no.

"I tried to stop him," Braxton said, giving Kenzie an apologetic look.

Kiwi, the little hellion, had apparently decided that he was done waiting for his dinner delivery and had taken matters into his own claws.

"Kiwi," Kenzie gasped.

Too late.

Kiwi's long tongue retracted back into his mouth as he crunched down on his snack. The very same cricket that Kenzie had spent the last hour magically enhancing so it would grow.

"What did you do to that cricket, Ashner?" Chef Levy asked.

More importantly, what was going to happen to Kiwi, now that he'd eaten the cricket?

Kenzie didn't have long to wait and agonize.

"Dude," Zack observed.

"Number Eight," Aralia said. "This is the coolest thing I've ever seen."

One of the ex-prisoners screamed. Someone else fainted.

"Should we, like, hide?" Sofia asked calmly.

Kiwi was growing. And growing. And growing.

He kept it up until he was about as large as a horse. But with his reptilian good looks, he appeared to be more of a mid-sized dinosaur.

Kenzie blinked. She was comparing her pet to the size of a dinosaur. A freaking dinosaur.

How was this her life right now?

Kiwi opened his mouth and unraveled the longest tongue Kenzie had ever seen.

"Holy shit," Braxton said.

"I'm going to make him a saddle and bridle," Aralia announced. "He's going to be my war steed when we go to battle against the Gourmands. Rick's going to shit himself."

"You can't ride him," Sofia said. "He's feral. He'll probably eat you."

"Not if I train him," Aralia replied, sounding miffed.

The two of them argued as they skirted around Kiwi, whose freakishly-enlarged bulbous eyeballs followed their every movement in a way that made Kenzie more than a tad nervous.

"You need to get your shit straightened out," Chef Levy said, pinning Kenzie with an accusing stare.

"Gee, why didn't I think of that," Kenzie huffed. And puffed. And tried with all her might to undo her magic.

It was no use. Kenzie could feel how embers of her cricket-enlarging magic had mutated and stuck to Kiwi. She just couldn't control it.

Super. Super freaking duper.

"You should go see the Reaper," Sofia suggested. "Graham says he's still pretty out of it, but he's getting better. If there's anyone who might be able to tell you how to fix this, it's Qiang Lee."

"I think that's a good idea," Braxton said, rubbing Kenzie's shoulders, which had gotten all knotted with tension for some inexplicable reason. "And maybe the Reaper will have an idea about how to lure Rick and the Gourmands out in a way that won't be so…dangerous." He gave Kiwi the side-eye. Kiwi side-eyed him right back. With those orbed eyes magnified to a hundred times their original size, it was pants-wettingly terrifying.

"Yeah," Kenzie said, nodding her head in a frantic way that matched the frantic stutter of her pulse. "Yeah. Let's go see the Reaper."

But first, she needed to figure out where in New York City she could buy enough crickets to feed a horse-sized chameleon.

CHAPTER 34

GRAHAM

Graham accepted a warm mug of tea from Clementine. The liquid was scalding, but as soon as it hit his tongue, strength started flowing back into his exhausted limbs.

"You saved Reaper Lee's life," she said, her eyes glittering with unshed tears. "I've never seen anything grow that fast. You're amazing."

"It's not going to last," Graham said, taking another gulp of tea. The room stopped spinning and his headache was already beginning to fade. "The magic in that parsley isn't nearly strong enough to undo whatever is happening to the Reaper."

"I know," Clementine said.

What's wrong with him, Clementine?" Graham asked, taking another sip of tea to soothe his aching throat.

"Alzheimer's," Clementine whispered. "Reaper Lee has been fighting his memory loss with magic for years, but that's causing other parts of his body to shut down. That's why he keeps getting nose bleeds and collapsing and—" She turned her head away, taking a few seconds to compose herself. "And it's why the disease is killing him faster."

Graham's mouth opened and closed. He waited for horror that never came. Because some part of him had already known.

"The apples from that tree are the only thing that can save him," Clementine continued.

Graham had, on some level, known that too.

"Reaper Lee bred that variety of magical apples himself," Clementine continued. "He's been working on it since his diagnosis. But the sicker he gets, the weaker his magic becomes, and the tree—"

She didn't need to finish for Graham to understand. The tree was connected to the Reaper's magic. And the Reaper was dying.

"Why didn't you tell me any of this sooner?" Graham asked, too tired to be angry.

"Reaper Lee wouldn't let me," Clementine said, her chin trembling. "He said if you tried too hard to heal the tree, you'd burn yourself out and die." She latched onto his arm with both of her small hands. "You won't do that, will you?"

"Don't worry," Graham said, gently unwinding his arm from her grip. "I'm not going to burn myself out."

But I am going to heal that tree.

* * *

Graham was intensely grateful that Raina had stayed to help out around the garden. She'd quickly taken over all of the normal garden chores, moving from task to task with a gurgling Hiroto strapped to her chest in a makeshift sling. That left Graham free to devote his time to the apple tree.

Not that it had done much good thus far.

He knelt down and pressed his hands to the base of the tree. A little thrill went through him as his energy connected with the tree's magic, weak as it was. He could feel loose sparks of power firing in each of the three apples still hanging from the leafless branches. The rest of the apples lay scattered and rotting on the ground.

Graham patiently began to untangle the magic in the tree's core one strand at a time, mending the broken ones as he went. He was just getting into a rhythm when he discovered all the repairs he'd made had reversed themselves. The rot was back. It was like Graham had done nothing at all.

Graham sat back on his heels and swore.

It was like he'd just spent hours screaming into a void. He felt completely hollowed out, and for what?

A few reminiscent strands of his magic floated on top of the soil before they were sucked down and lost.

Graham let the weight of his failure drag at him until he was crouched on the soft ground. He stared at the setting sun without appreciating the vibrant colors.

It had been mid-morning when he'd begun his pointless task.

"Hi," Raina said, startling him.

Graham looked up to see her standing over him.

Raina's clothes were covered in dirt, her hands were bleeding from the various thorns she'd encountered during her weeding escapades, and yet, she was smiling. There was a brightness to her that Graham hadn't seen before.

"Gardening suits you," Graham observed. "You look well."

Hiroto was happily dangling from his makeshift sling. He was drooling as he gummed a nonmagical strawberry clutched in both of his chubby fists. His flannel onesie had a picture of a bowl of soup and chopsticks. Beneath it were the words *Miso cute.*

"I know, right?" Raina wiped her muddy hands on her dirt-stained shirt. "This is the first time I've gotten out of my own head in days." She closed her eyes and breathed the garden in. "There's something about this place."

"There is," he agreed.

She cocked her head. "I feel almost like I—"

"Belong here," they both said together, and laughed.

They turned at the sound of footsteps.

Graham's heart lurched and then stopped altogether as Sofia strode into the garden.

Her blonde hair hung in loose waves down her back. She was wearing a dress that cut off at her mid-thigh and bared miles' worth of the most incredible legs in the history of humankind.

"Close your mouth," Raina whispered, nudging Graham. "Isn't it enough I have one drooling man in my life?"

Graham couldn't help himself. Every time he saw Sofia, he lost his mind a little bit. But seeing her here, in this place he had started thinking of as home, was almost more than he could bear.

"Hi," Graham said lamely, holding his arms at his sides to keep them from accidentally mauling her.

In spite of everything they'd been through together, he wasn't sure where they stood.

"Hi," she said back, giving him an unreadable expression.

Say something, you moron.

"I missed you," he blurted out.

The briefest hint of a smile flickered across Sofia's face.

"I think it's time for Hiroto's snack," Raina said in an overly-cheery voice. She gave Graham an exaggerated wink and mouthed *Go get her* before leaving Graham and Sofia alone.

"Remember a while back when you said you wanted to date me?" Sofia asked. She was busy picking nonexistent dirt from under her nail.

When Graham tipped her chin up to read her expression, he saw that Sofia's cheeks had turned bright pink.

"I remember," he said, a little thrown by the topic but more than happy to go with it. He gave in to the urge to lean in and brush his thumb over her flushed cheekbone.

"Well." She cleared her throat. "I wasn't ready to have that conversation, then. But I am, now. I want you to ask me again."

Graham bit the inside of his cheek to keep from grinning like a fool. He didn't want Sofia to think he was laughing at her, when the reality was that he was delirious with hope.

Instead of saying anything, he slid his hand around the back of her neck and brought her face up to his.

He meant for the kiss to start out as a soft brush of lips, but as soon as he felt the warm satin of her tongue, all thoughts of going slow left him.

For how much time he'd spent remembering the way it felt to kiss her, his memory had been pathetically inadequate. She was impatient and demanding and perfect. He could kiss her forever and it wouldn't be enough.

"Be with me," he gasped when they broke apart. "I mean, I want you to be with me. I want you to date me."

He was babbling, but Sofia looked as dazed as he felt. Her green eyes were glassy and her coral lips were swollen.

"I want that, too," Sofia said. She hooked her fingers into his collar and pulled him back for more.

"Ohmygod," a voice exclaimed. "Did you bring us a pony?!"

It took Graham's foggy brain several seconds to register that the voice belonged to Clemetine.

Graham gave Sofia a questioning look.

Sofia rolled her pretty eyes. Taking his hand, she led him over to the source of the commotion.

Sure enough, a horse trailer was backing into the garden. Aralia parked the truck and hopped out. Kenzie, Braxton, and Kenzie's father were next.

"What's this?" Graham asked.

"Oh, nothing too crazy," Sofia said evasively.

"Graham," Aralia called, "get a load of this."

Graham's trepidation skyrocketed as Aralia unlocked the back of the trailer. Whenever his sister got this excited, it usually meant something horrific and potentially civilization-ending was nigh.

"Ho-ly shi—take mushroom," Raina said.

What the hell?

Something out of *Jurassic Park* was backing out of the horse trailer.

Graham was overcome by a sudden, fierce urge to grab Sofia and hightail it out of there. He wasn't even ashamed that his life was flashing before his eyes.

"Aralia, get away from that thing," Graham ordered, barely able to hear himself over the sound of his pounding heart.

"Don't be such a worry wart," his sister replied. She began making kissy noises at the beast as she coaxed it off the trailer.

Graham nearly died.

The creature—which Aralia and Kenzie were calling *Kiwi*—yawned. There was a commotion when it tried to climb Reaper Lee's prized Italian Cypress and, predictably, uprooted the entire tree.

Graham stood by and prayed that no one got accidentally flattened by either the tree or Kiwi.

Aralia and Kenzie tried to reason, and then wrangle, the beast off the now-ruined tree. The whole fiasco came to an anticlimactic conclusion when the-dragon-named-Kiwi turned his scaly skin the same evergreen color as the tree and fell asleep on top of its leafy remains.

"Whew." Kenzie wiped her face on her sleeve. "So, this is awkward." She stared at the tree's remains.

"Reaper Lee is going to *kill* you," Clementine said with a little giggle that somewhat diminished the threat's severity.

"If I were hypothetically going to start digging up this garden for worms and such for this soon-to-be-rideable chameleon," Aralia said, "where would I do the least amount of damage?" Her words trailed off as she caught sight of Graham and Sofia.

Graham hadn't even realized that he was holding Sofia like—like there was a chameleon on the loose that was big enough to devour the woman he'd been dating for all of about two seconds. He forced himself to ease his grip on Sofia before he cut off her circulation.

Aralia's shrewd gaze narrowed. "Aw, hell. You shared *emotions*." She tipped her head back and groaned. "Now I'm *never* going to be rid of the McKaids."

Braxton chuckled and slung an arm over Aralia's shoulders. "Looks like you're stuck with us, Aralia." His humor faded a little as he turned his attention to Graham.

"I'm sorry we got off to a rocky start." Braxton held out his hand. "Can we try again?"

"Of course," Graham said, shaking Braxton's hand.

Braxton nodded. Instead of letting go, he tightened his grip and pulled Graham closer. "But if you ever hurt Sofia, I'll kick your arse."

Sofia gave her brother a little shove. "If Graham ever hurts me, *I'll* kick his arse."

"And if anyone hurts Graham," Aralia said pleasantly. "I'll disembowel them and feed their entrails to the vultures."

Graham wasn't sure his heart could stand being so full.

"I'm not going to hurt you," he promised Sofia.

There was nothing he wouldn't do to make her happy.

And then, uncaring that his sister and her brother were standing feet away, Graham pulled Sofia against him and kissed her.

* * *

"So are you telling me," Braxton said slowly, "that the Reaper will only help Kenzie with her magic if you can heal this impossible-to-heal magical apple tree?"

"Not necessarily," Graham hedged. "I'm just saying that Reaper Lee…isn't at his best right now." That was an understatement, but Graham wasn't going to go into details about how frail Qiang actually was. "I'm just saying he'll be in a better position to help fix the chameleon if I can get this tree working properly."

As for their problem with Rick and the Gourmands, there was no chance the Reaper would want to get involved with that on any level. Graham figured he'd let Qiang break that news to everyone himself, though.

"Why are you so intent on fixing this tree, anyway?" Sofia asked. She nudged its base with her shoe. A few flakes of black bark fluttered to the ground.

"The Reaper has Alzheimer's," Graham explained. He felt badly about exposing Qiang's secret in front of all these people, but he couldn't bring himself to lie to Sofia.

"You mean these apples effect memories?" Sofia asked, her beautiful eyes alight with interest.

Graham shrugged. "I assume so."

"Not exactly," Clementine said. "Whoever eats the apples can alter people's minds."

"Holy crap," Kenzie said.

"At least, that's the way the magic is supposed to work," Clementine said. "I don't think Reaper Lee ever got the magic strong enough."

"Hmm," Sofia said, tilting her head and studying the tree. "That changes things."

"What do you mean?" Graham asked her.

"Apples that can alter people's minds?" She gave him an incredulous look. "Think about it, Graham. If we can fix this tree, then we can solve our problem of the Vanillas being terrified of us. We can take away their memories of culinary magic. Then, we won't have to worry about them coming after us anymore."

"You can't just take away billions of people's memories like that." Kenzie snapped her finger. "Haven't you ever heard of, like, ethics?"

"We're not taking away all their memories," Sofia huffed. "Just the ones that could result in a culinary magic genocide. I don't think any of our people would mind trading a few Vanilla memories in exchange for a future free from persecution."

The revelation left Graham speechless. Sofia was right. This tree had the potential to undo the damage Rick had caused by so thoughtlessly exposing their world to the Vanillas.

Too bad you're going to disappoint her, Graham's father taunted. *Too bad you're going to let your mentor* die....

Graham curled his hands into fists.

"Great idea, Sofe," Braxton said. "Except for the part where Graham and the Reaper can't get the tree to work."

"Maybe I can help," Kenzie offered, taking pity on Graham. "My Culinarian magic has to be useful for something besides enlarging hapless chameleons."

"Normal culinary magicians can't do shit with magical ingredients," Aralia informed Kenzie.

"Normal being the operative word," Sofia replied. "Kenzie isn't normal."

"Hah," Kenzie said. "I'll take that as a compliment."

"Reaper Lee always says strong magic attracts more strong magic," Clementine said. "Maybe your magic—" She gestured between Graham and Kenzie. "—brought you together for this purpose."

"I guess we could give it a try," Graham said without confidence.

If he and Reaper Lee hadn't been able to alter the tree's magic, he didn't see why someone without cultivator magic should be able to. Still, what did they have to lose?

"Tell me what to do," Kenzie said, going over to the tree and pressing her hand to the trunk.

"Um," Graham began.

"Never mind," Kenzie said. "I can feel the magic, and, oh wow. That's messed up."

Graham joined her, sensing the way her presence was stirring up the tree's inherent power.

"It's reacting to you," Graham said, throwing his own magical muscle behind Kenzie's, hoping to create a wedge that would stop the rot from spreading. If Kenzie's magic was powerful enough, maybe together, they could begin pushing the decay back.

"Come on, you obstinate little fucker," Kenzie muttered as the blight oozed around their healing magic.

Together, they were strong enough to do this. Graham could feel it. If they could just infuse a little more power—

There.

The rot thrust away from the tree's core as Kenzie and Graham's magic locked together. The center of the tree flared bright.

In his mind's eye, Graham could see branches laden down with ruby apples bursting with flavor and magic. He could see an entire orchard of the trees.

Kenzie cried out.

The pulsing light of their combined magic shuddered and receded. The decay, which had been breaking apart into oily fragments, congealed once again. It began its slide back toward the tree's center.

"I'm sorry," Kenzie gasped. "I can't. It's too much."

Kenzie was on her knees, leaning against Braxton, who was holding her upright. She curled her fist to her chest. "It felt like the tree was trying to rip the core of my magic right out of me." She let out a hollow little laugh. "It's like when you read about a drowning person climbing on top of the person who's trying to save them."

"Your magic is a part of you, Kenz," Braxton said, brushing her hair away from her sweat-dampened face. "Probably even more so for you than the rest of us."

Braxton was right. And that meant it didn't matter how many times Kenzie tried to help fend off the disease eating away at the apple tree. As soon as she pulled her magic back to herself, the rot would return.

"In that case," Sofia said, "let me try."

When Graham looked at her, she was busy studying a patch of magenta moss on the ground.

"My magic isn't a part of me," Sofia said, still staring at the ground. "Not really. Not like it is for the rest of you."

Before anyone could argue, Sofia went over to the tree and put both of her palms on the trunk.

"Show me what to do," she ordered Graham.

He stood behind her, placing both of his hands on top of hers. He felt her small intake of breath as his chest settled against her back. She was so warm.

"What do I do?" Sofia asked again. She turned her head to the side, bringing their faces within inches of each other.

Graham couldn't help himself. He leaned in and kissed her.

"You have to let some of your magic out," Graham said, speaking against Sofia's ear. "I'll take care of the rest."

"I don't—" Sofia began, before stopping herself.

Graham could already feel the magic beginning to leave Sofia's body. At first, it came out of her in gentle wisps that were easily absorbed into the tree's core.

The more magic Sofia released, the greedier the tree became. It slurped the magic from her until Graham found he was no longer directing the magic into the tree and was actively trying to slow the process.

Sofia's whole body went rigid against him.

"Stop," Graham ordered. "Sofia, stop. That's enough."

Too much magic was slipping out of her too quickly. At this rate, she was going to pass out. Or worse.

"It won't let me give some of my magic," she panted. "It's all or nothing."

The answer was simple.

"Nothing, then." His hands tightened reflexively around hers. He needed to help her…to protect her.

"Fight it," he commanded.

In that second, he didn't give a damn about the tree. He couldn't even remember why he was supposed to care about it. All that mattered was Sofia.

Sofia's body trembled. On an inhale that seemed to rattle her bones, Sofia took hold of her magic. For several weighted seconds, she and the tree were in limbo. The magic hovered perfectly-balanced between them.

"Oh God," Sofia whispered. "Graham."

When she looked at him, her eyes were full of too many emotions for him to comprehend.

"Um, Sofia?" Kenzie's voice said from somewhere nearby.

Graham had forgotten there was anyone else in the world except for him and Sofia.

"I know," Sofia said, letting out a shuddering breath. "I can feel it."

"Feel what?" Graham and Braxton both demanded.

Graham's heart was in his throat.

Kenzie was the one who answered. "The magic I give as a Culinarian is different from the kind you're born with. Losing all of her magic won't hurt Sofia the way it would for any of us who were born with it, because the magic isn't woven into the fabric of her being, like it is for us." Kenzie swallowed. Against Graham, Sofia's body tensed even further. "But if you go through with this—" Kenzie motioned between Sofia and the tree.

"—you won't be able to give me magic again, will you?" Sofia finished in a near-whisper.

Kenzie nodded.

"I can sense it," Sofia said in a hollow voice that made Graham feel even more helpless. "It's like that part of me is closing off with every bit of magic that leaves me." She turned to Graham. "What do I do?"

The terror in her voice gutted him.

All Sofia had ever wanted was to be a culinary magician. She'd only recently gotten her dream, and now she was being faced with the possibility of losing it. Forever.

The tree was burning hot beneath their joined hands.

Sofia could save it. She could grow the apples that would restore the Reaper's life and take away the Vanillas' memories of culinary magic. But to do so, her power would have to live on…inside the tree.

"It's your choice," Graham said, holding her as the magic hung suspended around them.

Sofia breathed in deeply. And let go of her magic.

CHAPTER 35

BRAXTON

I don't like it, McKaid," Chef Levy growled into the phone.

Braxton was pacing around the Reaper's hut as he held Sofia's small burner phone to his ear. It was eight o'clock at night, but all the plants growing outside were bright enough that he hadn't needed to turn on any lamps.

"I don't like it either, Chef," Braxton replied. "I'm just not sure what we're supposed to do about it."

Chef Levy, Zack, Reuben, and the rest of the culinary magicians who had joined their cause had stayed behind in Manhattan. They'd been unsuccessfully canvassing the city for any information about Rick's next move. The problem, as Chef Levy had just explained, was that Rick and the Gourmands had disappeared.

"Hundreds of people don't suddenly vanish," Chef Levy said. "They're planning something."

Braxton heard the thump of her fist on the other end of the line.

"No arguments here, Chef," Braxton said.

"I'm not letting the Gourmands keep getting away with murder," she fumed. "They took everything from me, and I won't rest until I've obliterated their entire organization."

At this rate, steam was going to start coming through the phone.

Braxton rubbed his head, which was beginning to ache.

"Have you talked to the Reaper yet?" Chef Levy demanded. "Maybe he's got something in his garden that can help us track down the Gourmands and destroy them with minimal bloodshed."

"Kenzie's talking to him right now," Braxton said with all the patience he could muster. "I'll call you back as soon as we know something."

After Braxton ended the call, he stared out the open window while he tried to gather his thoughts. Graham and Sofia were still working on the apple tree. Kenzie and the Reaper were deep in conversation. Everyone else was gathered on the lawn for an impromptu picnic dinner.

From the open window, Braxton could hear Aralia's loud voice, followed by Clementine's high-pitched laugh.

"Go join them, son," Walter said, startling Braxton.

He'd forgotten the other man was even in the hut.

"You're looking a little peaked," Walter added.

Walter tossed a handful of fragrant spring onions into his pan of fried rice. He fluffed the rice with a fork, filling the hut with the heady aromas of sesame oil and rice wine vinegar.

Braxton was about to do as he was told, when the hut's door swung open.

Raina, one arm curled around her sleeping baby, stepped into the hut.

For several long, uncomfortable seconds, Braxton and Raina just stared at each other.

"Um," Braxton began, and then stopped. He really had no idea what to say to her. The two of them had managed to avoid each other since Times Square. This wasn't a conversation Braxton was prepared to have.

"I'm sorry," they both said at the same time.

They shared an awkward chuckle.

"If I could take back everything that happened," Braxton told her. "Believe me, I would."

"I know what happened to Philippe wasn't your fault," Raina said. She adjusted Baby Hiroto in her arms. "And I understand why you were so angry at him. I don't blame you for any of it, Braxton."

Braxton shook his head vigorously enough that his vision wobbled. "I was an arse to Philippe, and that's something I'll never be able to take back. I'm so damn sorry, Raina."

Raina stood up on tiptoes and kissed Braxton's cheek. "You're forgiven," she said simply. "Philippe—" She looked away while she composed herself. "Philippe wanted to do the right thing." She raised her sleeping son and pressed a gentle kiss to his forehead.

"He was a good man," Braxton said, his throat feeling like it was lined with gravel. "I wish—I wish I could have told him."

"He knew," Raina whispered. She swiped at the tears falling down her cheeks. She gave Braxton a wobbly smile and moved past him.

Braxton just stood there, knowing he didn't deserve half of the kindness Raina had shown him.

Laughter floated through the open window. Braxton stared outside, but instead of a full picnic blanket, all he could see were empty spaces that should be taken up by the people they'd lost.

I miss you, Aid, he thought. *So fucking much.*

Aidan didn't talk back.

A heavy weight of exhaustion descended on Braxton.

"Let's take a walk, son," Walter suggested.

Having small talk with his girlfriend's father was the last thing he wanted to do at that moment. He needed to be alone. To breathe.

Walter's hand clamped down on Braxton's shoulder, steering him out of the hut and giving him little choice in the matter.

They walked in silence until they could no longer see or hear the others. Braxton followed the other man onto a secluded path lined by trees.

"Life is for the living, son," Walter said, stopping and turning to face Braxton. "You need to let go of your regrets."

"Just like that?" Braxton said with a skeptical eyebrow raise.

Walter gave him a kind smile. "Not saying it'll be easy."

As he stared into the darkness, Braxton was reminded of something Philippe had told him before he died. Philippe had said he wanted to live the life that would have done Hiroto proud.

Of all the times Braxton had done something in Aidan's memory, so few of his actions had been consistent with the kind of a life that would have made Aidan truly proud.

Aidan had done everything—cooking especially—for the sheer joy of it.

Walter was right. Life was for the living. Braxton needed to—

"I told you I could find it," someone whispered.

Braxton whipped around, searching for the source of the voice. He peered into the darkness, but they'd walked far enough that the lights of the Reaper's magical plants were barely visible. He couldn't see anyone besides him and Walter.

But that definitely hadn't been Walter's voice.

"Yeah, you found it alright," someone else drawled.

Icy needles speared through Braxton's chest. It couldn't be.

This garden didn't exist on any maps and was impossible to find unless you knew exactly where to go.

"Who is that?" Walter whispered.

Braxton didn't answer.

There was a rustling through the underbrush. Braxton saw the flash of Gourmand-crimson cloaks through the trees.

"Oh McKaid," that same voice taunted. "You in there, McKaid? Come out, come out, wherever you are."

"I get to kill the Culinarian wench," a female voice said.

Braxton reared back as two faces poked through the thick shrubs.

Rick Santiori and Nurse Ratched.

"Go," Braxton said, pushing Walter. "Run."

Walter made it two steps before a Gourmand caught him. Braxton found his own arms being wrenched behind his back. A rope was tied around his wrists tightly enough that he immediately felt the loss of blood flow. A foul wad of cloth was stuffed into his mouth.

"There's not going to be any need for you to talk," Rick said, stepping in front of Braxton. "All you need to do is come along and enjoy the show."

Rick gave the ropes around Braxton's wrists a fierce tug. And then, the fucker smiled.

CHAPTER 36

SOFIA

Sofia twitched a little when she felt Graham's big hands cover hers. With a simple touch, he infused her with warmth and a quiet strength.

Like mist coming off a lake, she let her magic rise out of her. It wasn't painful or difficult, because her magic had never really been attached to her.

Sofia watched the tendrils as they drifted out of her and into the apple tree.

Then, the magic disappeared. Or, that was how it seemed to Sofia. She knew it was inside the tree, but she could no longer sense it.

Graham's skin was shiny with perspiration, but she couldn't feel the heat of his magic anymore. And it wasn't just Graham. She couldn't sense the garden's magic.

So, that was it, then.

She was normal again. Powerless.

"Are you okay?" Graham asked.

"Yes," she replied, a little surprised to find it was the truth. She had given her culinary magic to the tree, but she didn't feel empty or bereft like she'd expected to. She felt…normal.

Sofia supposed she hadn't been a culinary magician long enough to be able to miss it. At least, that was what she was telling herself.

They both looked up as the black branches overhead began to wiggle. Sofia's heart sank when the last of the shriveled apples fell off their stems and plopped listlessly onto the ground.

Before Sofia could feel defeated, small red buds began appearing on the tree's branches.

Sofia blinked, wondering whether her sudden powerlessness and sheer exhaustion were making her hallucinate.

"Sofia," Graham whispered. "Are you seeing this?"

Okay, maybe she wasn't hallucinating.

As she watched, the buds transformed into teeny, perfectly-proportioned apples the size of Sofia's thumbnail. In another minute, they were the size of crabapples.

She didn't move for fear of interrupting whatever was happening with the tree.

Sofia still had her hands pressed to the tree trunk, and she could feel Graham's muscles trembling as he strained to make the apples grow. His breaths came in short, uneven pants.

Sofia had no idea how much time had passed when Graham staggered back. She threaded her arm through his, because he looked like he was on the verge of collapse. Together, they stared up at what Graham had done.

No. What *they'd* done.

The branches were bowed from the weight of the biggest, shiniest, reddest apples Sofia had ever seen. The tree still didn't have a single leaf on it, and the black branches made the ruby apples stand out in even starker relief.

"Incredible," Sofia whispered.

She was having trouble processing the fact that her magic had helped create this.

"Do you regret it?" Graham asked, studying her. "Giving away your magic in exchange for saving Reaper Lee and changing the Vanillas' memories?"

Sofia reached up and plucked one of the apples. Ruby light pulsed from the fruit.

"I was a productive member of society before I had magic." She released the breath she hadn't realized she'd been holding. "I'll be valuable again without it."

"Damn right you will." Graham took her face in his hands and kissed her.

When they broke apart, Sofia looked down at the apple resting on her palm. She knew wisps of magic were probably spinning around the fruit, but she couldn't sense them.

Sofia waited for that observation to make her feel regret or crushing loss. Instead, all she felt was an enormous sense of accomplishment. She might have given up her borrowed magic to help heal this tree, but in doing so, she was going to save the most powerful person in their world. She was going to make sure culinary magicians didn't face any more violence from the Vanilla population. If those two accomplishments weren't a good use of her magic, then she didn't know what was.

"Even though their magic will only work for a culinary magician," Graham said, nodding at the apple and giving her an apologetic look, "you should still be the first to taste one."

Hesitating for only a moment, Sofia raised the fruit to her lips and took a bite.

The apple was crisp and sweet. The juice that ran down her chin was ruby red and thick as honey.

"Well?" Graham asked, his face awash with concern.

Sofia finished chewing and swallowed the bite in her mouth. "That's—" She paused, searching for the words.

"It's bloody delicious."

Graham laughed. He lifted her up as though she were weightless. "You did it, Sofia."

"We did it," she corrected, unable to keep her own laughter from spilling out of her.

"Sofia." His whiskey irises smoldered as he held her so her face hovered above his. "I'm pretty sure I'm in love with you."

Sofia's heart somersaulted in her chest. "I think I might be in love with you too, Graham."

Graham's smile was so brilliant it stole her breath.

"In that case, can I take you somewhere more private and show you exactly how much I love you?" he asked.

Sofia hooked her ankles around Graham's waist. "I thought you'd never ask."

✴ ✴ ✴

There was grass in Sofia's hair. Rocks were digging into her bare back. She was pretty sure a family of ants was building their home under her ankle.

And she didn't give a damn.

She was tangled up with Graham. His strong arms were wrapped around her, and he was lavishing soft kisses on every part of her that he could reach. The night sky, salted with stars, stretched out endlessly above them.

"I didn't expect you to be a cuddler," Graham murmured. His voice was low and throaty, which sent a shiver dancing across Sofia's oversensitized skin.

"I'm not." She wiggled even closer, enjoying that she couldn't tell where her body ended and his began.

"Mmm." He reached down to squeeze her ass. "In that case, let's not cuddle a while longer."

Sofia laughed.

They were nestled in a little cove that was kilometers away from the Reaper's garden. It was surrounded by water on one side and cliffs on all the others, which meant they could be as loud as they wanted without being discovered by nosy siblings.

"Lucky we found this place," Sofia said, muffling a yawn against Graham's shoulder.

"Well." Graham chuckled sheepishly. "I might have made a mental note about this place when I came across it a while back. It seemed like it might be good for—"

"Graham Malyung." Sofia gave his chest a light smack. "You were planning for this, weren't you?"

"Not planning so much as fantasizing," Graham said, ducking his head to kiss her throat.

"And did I live up to your fantasies?" Sofia asked, tipping her head back to give him better access.

Graham stopped kissing her and gave her a look that was so serious Sofia had to stop herself from fidgeting.

"Fantasies can't hold a candle to the reality of you, Sofia," Graham said.

If those words had come out of anyone else, Sofia would have rolled her eyes and gagged. But Graham said them with such earnestness that she could do nothing except let the compliment wash over her nice and easy.

"My head is so quiet right now," Graham said, locking his arms around her and sighing in contentment. "I could sleep for the whole night."

"Yeah." Sofia rested her head on his chest. "Me too."

"No, you don't understand." Graham's thumb traced idle circles along her bare back. "For so long…my whole life, I think…my father told me I wasn't enough."

A hundred furious rebuttals rose to the tip of Sofia's tongue. Before she could vocalize any of them, Graham continued.

"Even after I killed him," he said, "I still heard his voice. I should hear it now, saying you're too good for me."

Sofia wanted to bring that man back to life and kill him again for making Graham feel that way. Since that wasn't an option, she smoothed her hand down Graham's chest.

"You're just right for me," she said. "You make me feel stronger even when I'm depending on your help. That's…new for me."

A crackle through the brush made both of them freeze.

"Who's there?" Graham called.

No answer.

There was another rustle followed by a sound that was unambiguous footsteps.

They both sat up and hurried to gather their discarded clothes.

"Brax, if that's you," Sofia called, "you might want to wait a sec unless you want to be scarred for life."

Sofia had just managed to pull Graham's shirt over her most important bits when Qiang Lee burst into the clearing. And collapsed.

Graham sprang forward and caught the old man. Sofia gasped.

Qiang's face was streaked with blood. His cloak was torn. His whole body was shaking violently.

"What happened?" Sofia demanded.

"Listen to me," Qiang rasped, curling bloody fingers around Graham's biceps. "You're me, now. Do you understand?"

He was raving. Delirious.

"You're going to be fine," Graham insisted. To Sofia, he said, "Get me something to use as a tourniquet. He's bleeding. Badly."

Sofia used her teeth to rip the bottom part of Graham's shirt. She unwound a long strip of cloth and flung it at Graham.

"What happened?" Sofia asked again. Panic was beginning to eat through her esophagus. "Where's everyone else?"

Qiang didn't answer her.

"The garden is yours," Qiang told Graham. "You're the next Reaper."

"Don't talk like that," Graham said as he started winding the makeshift bandage around Qiang's stomach. It was instantly soaked through with blood. "We fixed the apple tree. We can cure your Alzheimer's. Everything's going to be fine."

"I believe…I was wrong," Qiang murmured. Graham and Sofia both leaned closer to hear him. "She was right. I should have shared my ingredients instead of destroying them."

With a start, Sofia realized she was the *she* Qiang was talking about.

"I stayed isolated because I was afraid," Qiang said quietly as he clutched at Graham. "Now, everything is ruined. Everything."

"Reaper Lee—" Graham began, but Qiang seemed beyond hearing him.

"I never prevented the Gourmands' abuse of power." The Reaper's unfocused eyes stared past Graham and Sofia at something neither of them could see. "I only facilitated it."

"We need to get you back to the hut," Graham said, his voice breaking.

"Tell her," Qiang begged Graham. "Tell her I was wrong. Help her to share the ingredients. Use them to make things…better."

"I will," Graham choked. "We will."

"Yes." Qiang sighed. "The two of you together will do more than I ever could."

"That's not true," Graham said. "There's so much you have to teach me. Please, Reaper Lee. I need you."

Qiang released a long, shuddering sigh. His body relaxed against Graham.

"No," Graham whispered.

The Reaper's open, sightless eyes were fixed on Graham.

"No," Graham said again, louder this time.

"Graham," Sofia said, her voice unsteady. "We have to leave."

The Reaper was dead, and whoever had killed him was likely on their way to finish off the rest of them.

"We have to leave," Sofia repeated. Her voice sounded too loud in the stillness that had fallen. "Braxton and Aralia need us."

That got Graham moving.

While Sofia stood on trembling legs and finished getting dressed, Graham gently laid Qiang down on the ground and closed his eyes. He let Sofia haul him to his feet. She clasped his hand, which was sticky with Qiang's drying blood.

Together, they ran.

CHAPTER 37

KENZIE

Something was wrong. Kenzie's dad and Braxton had wandered off more than an hour ago, and they still weren't back.

Kiwi, who had been napping on top of his commandeered tree, opened his eyes and swiveled his head. That was when Kenzie sensed it. Magic.

"Aralia," Kenzie said.

"I feel it," Aralia replied, getting silently to her feet and fitting an arrow to her bow.

"What's wrong?" Raina asked, scooping Hiroto off the ground and clutching him to her breast.

Aralia spoke before Kenzie could say anything. "Are you powerful enough to make a magical sticky toffee pudding?" she asked Raina.

Raina nodded.

"Then lock yourself and the kid inside and do it," Aralia said. "If you make it right, it'll prevent anyone from getting inside the hut. Don't release the magic until I say so."

"I don't know where the Reaper keeps any of his ingredients," Raina said, her voice rising. "And I can't cook while I hold Hiroto."

"I'll help you," Clementine said in a soothing voice. "Come on."

The three of them barely had time to close themselves inside the hut before the woods around them came alive with sound.

"Where the fucking fuck is Graham?" Aralia muttered, squinting at the flicker of light visible beyond the trees.

Where was Braxton? And Kenzie's dad? And Sofia, and the Reaper?

Kenzie smelled the acrid tang of burnt sugar just before the forest lit up around them. Blue flames engulfed the trees that surrounded the garden, eating away at the wood at a speed that would be impossible for any normal fire.

Kiwi let out a terrified roar and reared up onto his hind legs. Aralia released one of her arrows. It sailed through the blue fire and was followed by a very human cry. Another arrow soon followed.

"Don't just stand there!" Aralia shouted at Kenzie. "Once this fire goes out, we'll be exposed."

Right. Plan, Ashner. You need a plan.

Kenzie started moving before she had a clear destination.

"Drop your weapons and lie down on the ground," someone shouted. "By order of the Gourmands."

"Blow me!" Aralia shouted back, releasing another arrow.

Oh, boy. Of all the people to be in charge of mediation conflict....

Kenzie stopped in her mad dash to nowhere as her attention snagged on a tomato plant. There were no magical tomatoes on the vine, but there were plenty of nonmagical ones.

Hmm....

She grabbed as many tomatoes as she could carry, giving special priority to ones that were overripe.

Kenzie skewered a few of the tomatoes on a stick she found lying on the ground. She thrust her makeshift kebab into the flames that were turning the surrounding trees into ash.

Almost at once, the fruit began to blacken. The sweet smell of roasted tomatoes permeated the chemical stink of the unnatural fire. It reminded Kenzie of her time in the Cutthroat Cuisine arena, when the Gourmands had pelted her with rotten tomatoes and ordered her to kill her opponent. For their entertainment.

Come on, Kenzie muttered to her magic, urging it into the tomatoes.

She finished her magical roasted tomatoes just in time. The flames turned to smoke.

Everything was tinged with a gray-blue haze, making it difficult for Kenzie to get an accurate head count of her enemies. Still, she didn't need a clear view to see that their little slice of woodland paradise was filled with Gourmands.

Gathered together like this, with their crimson robes undulating around them, it was staggeringly obvious just how many of them there were. There had to be hundreds of them.

It was a damn shame the majority of her people were back in Manhattan.

Doesn't matter now, she told herself.

She began pelting her magically-enhanced roasted tomatoes at the Gourmands. The tomatoes turned into molten balls of lava that exploded as soon as they got anywhere near their target. Good thing, too, since Kenzie's aim wasn't about to win her an Emmy…or whatever the sports equivalent was.

The Gourmands screamed and clawed at themselves as bits of tomato guts set their robes aflame.

"Yeah? How do you like it when someone's throwing tomatoes at you?" Kenzie shouted as she threw her magical missiles. "Payback's a bitch, huh?"

Kenzie only made it through her first few tomatoes before the Gourmands wised up. The nutty aroma of magical sunflower seeds hit the air. Then, the Gourmands were moving too fast for Kenzie's tomato-missiles to find their marks.

The Gourmands disappeared in a swirl of red fabric.

"Cowards!" Kenzie shrieked.

The word was barely out of her mouth before the Gourmands returned. They fired back with kernels of magical popcorn that exploded with the force of grenades. Kenzie hurled herself behind a boulder and covered her head.

"Keep 'em busy," Aralia called as she sprinted past.

"How?" Kenzie asked.

"You're a goddamn Culinarian!" Aralia yelled. "Do what you do!"

Huh. The girl had a point.

"Where are you going?" Kenzie demanded.

There was no answer. Typical.

"Alright." Kenzie managed to avoid another magical popcorn-related explosion. "Enough of this."

Kenzie cast her power out like a net. It drifted up and out, capturing every wisp of magic floating through the air. She dragged her imaginary net through the air, collecting all the ingredients' magic.

The magical popcorn stopped exploding. The Gourmands stopped zipping around at an inhuman speed as their sunflower seeds became inert.

"That's better," Kenzie said.

She took a step back as all the magic she'd captured in her imaginary net slammed into her. Kenzie could feel that familiar magic-drunk sensation overtaking her.

She knew if she didn't ease up, she'd end up with a repeat of her Times Square debacle.

Earlier, when she'd been talking with the Reaper about her magical misfire with Kiwi, he'd explained to her that all magic had its limits. Even hers.

Since Kenzie had no desire to magically implode and pass out in a field of her enemies, she eased off the magic-stealing before she went too far.

Her enemies didn't give her time to adjust to the magic zipping through her veins. They simply changed their tactic.

Those red-robed bastards started pulling nonmagical but very, very deadly guns out from under their cloaks.

Uh-oh.

Kenzie was trying to formulate a Plan B…and quickly…when the ground began to shake.

Kiwi, with Aralia sitting astride his back, came galloping into the garden.

Kiwi had changed his scaly skin to black, which made him blend into the hazy smoke swirling all around. He looked like a war steed straight out of Hell. Aralia held a dagger in each hand, and she seemed to be steering Kiwi with her legs. Either that, or Kenzie's pet had some innate battle sense that Kenzie had been wholly unaware of.

The Gourmands turned their guns away from Kenzie and onto her chameleon.

Kenzie screamed as the Gourmands opened fire.

There were metallic *pings* and sparks of light as bullets hit Kiwi…and bounced right off his scaly hide. Clearly, whatever had made Kiwi big as a dinosaur had also made him tough as nails.

Go, Kiwi. You rockstar, you.

Kiwi barreled right through the Gourmands. The ones that weren't immediately flattened by giant reptile claws got cut down by Aralia's blades.

"Damn," Kenzie said as the pair blew past. "I'm so glad you're on my side."

Aralia flashed Kenzie a smile that was all teeth. "You know it, Number Eight."

Then, with a whoop, Aralia was off again.

Defenseless and completely out of ideas, Kenzie settled in to watch Kiwi and Aralia kick butt. She was looking for a safe place to sit down, when someone burst out of the smoke and almost landed on top of her. Kenzie was ready to use her nails to claw his face off…knee him in the balls…whatever it took…when she caught sight of his face.

"Graham?! Oh, thank God!"

Sofia was right behind him, her frantic gaze searching the area. The garden probably looked completely unrecognizable to both of them. What had once been orderly rows of beautiful plants had become a battlefield.

"Where's Braxton?" Sofia demanded.

"What do you mean?" Kenzie asked, panic lighting up her insides. "I thought he and my dad were with you."

"Duck!" Aralia shouted.

They all hit the deck as another round of gunfire peppered the air. Kiwi appeared out of nowhere, providing a living barricade that protected Kenzie and the others from the bullets. Then, he was gone again. He and Aralia left a line of headless bodies in their wake.

"I have an idea," Graham said. He turned to Kenzie. "Can you lend me some of your magic?"

Kenzie grinned in relief. "As it happens, I have some extra to spare."

"Aralia," Sofia called. "Help me give these two some cover."

The next several minutes were a complete blur. Kenzie filtered her stolen magic into Graham, and Graham passed it into the plants surrounding them. After that, the real fun began.

"Oh my God!" one of the Gourmands shouted. "Run!"

A tangle of Venus fly traps came to life before Kenzie's eyes. Their interlocking plant teeth elongated and made clicking sounds as the vines picked themselves off the ground and started to chase the Gourmands.

The Venus fly traps were small but vicious. They bit and tore at the Gourmands' ankles, leaving trails of blood behind the men and women who couldn't run fast enough to escape them.

The garden was even less impressed by the Gourmands' bullets than Kiwi.

Enormous watermelons started sailing out of their patch and smashing into nearby Gourmands. A tangle of yellow Buddha's hand citron began to elongate. Their carrot-like protrusions extended and turned rubbery as they slapped at the Gourmands' faces.

Tree roots rose from the ground to trip them. Vines appeared out of nowhere to blind the Gourmands or wrap them in straightjackets made of thorns. Lemons and limes squirted acerbic juice directly into their enemies' eyes. Horned melons raked across the Gourmands' faces and embedding themselves in their flesh. Enormous jack fruits thunked down on the Gourmands' heads, felling them mid-step.

Kenzie was so busy watching the garden kick ass that she forgot to watch her own ass.

"Kenzie, move!" Raina shouted. The hut door opened, and a variety stone crockery came flying out before the door slammed shut again. The pottery smashed into a handful of Gourmands who were sneaking up behind Kenzie.

Between the flying crockery, Team Kiwi and Aralia, and Graham's control over the garden, Kenzie had enough time to make another batch of her roasted lava tomatoes.

"We're winning!" Clementine gleefully yelled from inside the hut.

Yeah, they were.

"You really aren't."

Kenzie spun around as the owner of that voice emerged through the smoke.

Nurse fucking Ratched.

"How did you get off Rikers?" Sofia demanded.

Good freaking question. Kenzie had seen Nurse Ratched on the Rikers-bound barge with the rest of the Hunters. There was no way she could have escaped….

"The Hunters made the mistake of forgetting that I'm a culinary magician." Nurse Ratched smirked. "All it took was an hour in that disgusting prison kitchen for me to make them a last meal they wouldn't forget."

"You killed the Hunters?" Kenzie gaped. "All of them?"

"Not *all* of them." The sadistic nurse smiled to herself. "Didn't even need magic. Just some good old fentanyl." She lifted one foot off the ground and brushed an imaginary speck of dirt from her new, once-again-pristine white sneaker. "After that, getting off the Island and finding you was simple. I have quite a knack for tracking recipes." She cocked her head at Kenzie. "And I grew very familiar with your magical footprint during our time together in Cutthroat Cuisine."

Kenzie searched around for a blunt object to bash against the nurse's head. That was when she saw one of her magical tomatoes on the ground. *Perfect.* This was one soon-to-be corpse that Kenzie wasn't about to mourn.

"Ah, ah, ah," someone else said. "I wouldn't do that if I were you."

Rick, his haughty expression on full display, oozed into place beside Nurse Ratched.

"Oh hey, Dick," Kenzie said. "And yeah, I really will." She balanced her tomato on the edge of a stick and prepared to fling it. Maybe, if she got the angle just right, she could take out both of them….

"Out of curiosity," Rick said, his lip curling in malice. "How did you survive my magical prickly pear?"

"Culinarian. Remember?" Kenzie returned Rick's smirk with one of her own. The twerp didn't need to know the real reason for her miraculous recovery had nothing to do with her own magic. A girl had to have a few secrets.

"Powerful," Rick murmured. "Celestial, almost. I happen to have a bit of that myself, these days."

Rick snapped his fingers at one of the Gourmands, who stepped forward and lifted the cover off a plastic tray, revealing a large antipasto platter.

Kenzie was assaulted with such a heavy dose of synthetic magic that it was an effort to stay standing. While she tried to gather her scattered nerves, Rick began to gobble up the food as fast as he could stuff it into his mouth.

Marinated artichokes, mushrooms, and black olives disappeared from the platter. Rick gobbled down thin slices of prosciutto, followed by cubes of pepperoni and salami that he swallowed whole.

Curls of parmesan, creamy balls of mozzarella, and dollops of goat cheese disappeared. Rick's throat made a glugging noise as he drank down olive oil and balsamic from a little container on the tray.

The Gourmands kept their guns trained on Kenzie and her friends to make sure no one interfered with Rick's gorging.

The hideous feast concluded when Rick swallowed down a handful of dried fruit. He massaged his swollen stomach. The burnt sugar smell of synthetic ingredients stung Kenzie's nose.

"Enjoy that, Rick?" Sofia asked, disgust plain in her voice.

Rick didn't respond. He was too busy staring down at himself.

His body began to transform. Bones creaked. Muscles swelled.

Rick was growing.

Not good. This was seriously not good....

His bony shoulders turned into massive boulder-like protrusions that strained against the sleeves of his suit jacket. His skinny stomach transformed to eight-pack abs that were visible even through his dress shirt. There was a ripping sound, and Kenzie realized it was the sound of seams splitting.

Rick's suit, which had previously made him look like a little kid playing dress-up, was now stretched so tight it barely fit.

Craning her neck to look up at him, Kenzie was now the one who felt like a little kid.

Rick looked like he could tear off his ragged suit and go charging into a battle. For giants.

"That's better," Rick said.

Even his voice sounded different—deeper and less petulant.

The man standing in front of them wasn't a wannabe leader. He was a warrior.

A fierce, unnatural power radiated off Rick.

Kenzie had to take it away from him.

She started to haul on the strands of his magic, trying to unwind them the way she had before. Nothing happened.

The magic stubbornly clung to him.

As though he could sense what she was doing, Rick turned to Kenzie and smiled.

"Figured you'd try to do that," he said with a dark chuckle. "Thing is." He leaned in close enough for Kenzie to smell the pepperoni on his breath. "With all these synthetic ingredients in my system, I'm as powerful as you."

Dread pooled in Kenzie's stomach.

"You can try to take away my magic all you want," Rick gloated. "I'm too strong."

That meant Kenzie had no defense against him.

With a casual flick of his wrist, Rick knocked the tomato Kenzie still had poised to launch right out of her grip.

The tomato flew several feet away. It landed on a nearby hydrangea bush, which instantly began to melt.

"Oops," Rick said, giving Kenzie an evil little smirk.

The Gourmands gathered around Rick. Kenzie could almost feel their sense of victory. Kenzie tried not to let any of them see her growing terror.

She was supposedly the most powerful culinary magician in the world, but she couldn't protect her friends now.

"My father was a real asshole, but I learned a lot from him over the years," Rick said conversationally. "One of the lessons Papà taught me was to see every unexpected development as an opportunity." He raised an eyebrow at Kenzie. "I'll admit, I didn't expect you to be a Culinarian. So, when you revealed that little tidbit, I was forced to adapt."

"Ahem."

Rick frowned at Nurse Ratched, who was clearing her throat and tugging on his sleeve, like an obnoxious kid trying to get her parent's attention.

"I'm sorry for the interruption, Mr. Santiori," Nurse Ratched said, not sounding sorry at all. "But you and I had a deal. I believe you said that if I found her, you'd let me kill the Culinarian."

"Yes, Lynn," Rick replied, with more than a touch of saccharine politeness. "Later."

Nurse Ratched's face turned as red as the Gourmand's robes.

"I'm tired of waiting," she announced. She reached into her pocket.

There was a flash of metal as Nurse Ratched brandished a knife. Her murderous gaze fixed on Kenzie.

"I'm going to—"

Nurse Ratched never got to finish her sentence. Something enormous and purple whipped out and wound around Nurse Ratched's neck. The knife fell out of her hand and hit the ground with a dull thud.

Kenzie was in full fight-or-flight mode, so it took her several seconds to realize she wasn't about to die. As her pulse skittered and tripped over itself, her adrenaline-fueled brain managed to identify the purple noose that was wrapped around Nurse Ratched's neck.

It was Kiwi's tongue.

Nurse Ratched's eyes bulged as she clawed at Kiwi's tongue. Her face turned almost as purple as the drooly noose around her neck. She managed a single, gurgly plea before Kiwi yanked his tongue back the same way he did whenever he was lapping up a tasty mealworm.

There were several screams from the Gourmands. Kenzie didn't so much as blink as Nurse Ratched's head disappeared inside Kiwi's mouth. There was a loud *crunch*.

Blood spurted. Bones flew.

Nurse Ratched's white sneakers were the last part to go down Kiwi's gullet.

Kiwi let out a loud belch and rolled his bulbous eyes as he hunched down on his giant forelegs.

"Who's a good Kiwi?" Aralia cooed into the horrified silence that followed.

Rick hissed. "No matter. Your beast can't eat them all." He nodded to the Gourmands, who had made a ten-person-deep ring around Kenzie et. al. Even with Kiwi among them, their group didn't hold a candle to Rick's forces.

Shit shit shit.

"So ends the last Culinarian," Rick said, wiping away a fake tear. "A bit of an ignominious end, wouldn't you say?"

"Not so fast, Santiori."

The authority in that voice made everyone hesitate.

Chef Levy, flanked by Zack and Reuben, shoved their way into the circle.

When the Gourmands raised their guns, Rick shook his head and beckoned the newcomers forward.

"Hiya, cousin," Zack said, twirling his screwdriver between his fingers as he eyed Rick. His expression wasn't friendly.

"Come to die with your new friends?" Rick sneered. "You always did belong with the strays."

"If Zack belongs with us," Reuben said bravely, "then, by definition, he isn't a stray."

"Aww, an academic." Rick gave Reuben a look of mock sympathy. "You seriously desperate enough to get with my cousin?"

"Here's the deal, Santiori," Chef Levy said, clearly uninterested in wasting time trading minor insults. "We've got you surrounded."

Rick guffawed. "You and what army?"

Chef Levy smiled. "This army."

Kenzie silently cursed her shortness, because she couldn't see what was happening beyond the ring of Gourmands. At least, she couldn't until Aralia reached down a hand and said, "Get on up here, Number Eight" and hauled her onto Kiwi's back behind her.

That did the trick. From atop her chameleon's massive, scaled back, Kenzie tried to make sense of what her eyes were telling her. The army Chef Levy had brought…their army…had to be ten times' the size of the Gourmands. Everyone was holding some kind of magical food.

"Holy crap."

That astute observation wasn't meant to be said out loud, but Kenzie's powers of self-monitoring had seemingly left the building.

The hundred-or-so prisoners they'd rescued off Rikers were here, but where had all these other people come from? There had to be a thousand culinary magicians, surrounding the enemies who were surrounding Kenzie.

"How in the world did you organize all of this so quickly?" Sofia asked in an awed voice, since everyone else seemed beyond words.

"I didn't," Chef Levy replied. She gestured to a woman in the center of the crowd, who had her arms raised and was jumping up and down. "Hey, McKaids!" she shouted in an Aussie accent. "Where you at?"

"Natalie?" Sofia asked with a huff of disbelieving laughter. "What in the world are you doing here?"

"You really think your brother scared me off so easily?" she called back. "He told me to get the hell out of dodge. So, I went and got you an army. Where is the cranky bastard, anyway?"

Good freaking question. With everything that had been happening, Kenzie hadn't had time to sufficiently panic about the whereabouts of Braxton and her dad. Now, with a temporary reprieve from imminent death, anxiety spiked right back up.

"We love you, Sofia!" a different woman in a white chef's hat shouted. "We've got your six!"

The air began to fill with the sentiment which, even amid her worry over Braxton and her dad, was too beautiful for Kenzie to ignore.

"You see this, Santiori?" Chef Levy said, motioning to the army of chefs, who were loudly declaring their loyalty to the McKaids. "As it happens, friendship may be a stronger form of currency than your bullshit."

For once, Rick didn't have a comeback.

Hah. Take that, Dick.

Kenzie turned to the man himself, not wanting to miss a single lip curl as he watched his carefully-curated plans fall to ruin. When Kenzie looked at Rick, she saw irritation on his face, but not the soul-crushing defeat she'd been hoping for.

"Very good," Rick said, giving them a slow clap. "But you might want to hold off on your victory dance for just one more minute." He raised his hand in the air and made a *come hither* motion.

Kenzie didn't manage to completely stifle her cry her when a group of Gourmands marched into the center of their circle. There were six Gourmands—three guarding each prisoner.

Braxton and Kenzie's dad were shoved onto their knees at Rick's feet. Kenzie's dad looked grim. Braxton's eyes were full of fury.

Both men had their arms tied roughly behind their backs. Gags were stuffed in their mouths. There was a deep gash along Braxton's cheekbone.

"Rick, you son-of-a-bitch!" Kenzie shouted. She started to scramble off Kiwi's back, but Rick wasn't finished.

More Gourmands were bringing Raina, Clementine, and Baby Hiroto into the circle and forcing them down with the rest of the prisoners. Hiroto was crying, but the sound was muffled because he was gagged, too. Raina was fighting like a wildcat against the Gourmands who held her, until one of them slapped her across the face. Raina fell limply onto the grass.

Kenzie saw red.

"I've gotta hand it to you," Zack told Rick, disgust etched into every one of his taut muscles. "You're even more depraved than I ever gave you credit for."

"Why thank you, cousin," Rick replied.

Rick directed his next words to Kenzie. "Lots of people are going to die today, and these ones—" He dug the toe of his shoe into Braxton's knee. "—will be the first to go."

This couldn't be happening. Kenzie had to think. She had to do something.

But no matter how hard she wracked her brain, she couldn't concentrate on anything besides the fact that the most important people in her world were bound and gagged and completely at Rick's mercy.

Kenzie was still frozen in panic when Aralia let out a battle cry and leapt off Kiwi's back. She held a dagger in each hand.

It seemed to Kenzie that time stopped. Aralia hovered in the air, her white-blonde braids floating around her head. Her knees were hiked up almost all the way to her shoulders in a feline crouch. Her teeth were bared. All of her momentum was directed at Rick.

Aralia's body gave an abrupt jerk in mid-air. Her eyes widened and her mouth formed into an O of surprise. Kenzie heard gunshots a moment later, as though there had been a sound delay. She heard Graham's agonized shout. Then, she saw blood streaming from two holes on the side of Aralia's neck.

Graham caught Aralia just before her body hit the ground. Her daggers slipped out of her grip, and for a bewildering moment, Kenzie couldn't understand why Aralia didn't pick them back up. Aralia never let her daggers get away from her.

Then, Graham was curled over Aralia as hoarse, broken sounds tore out of him. Sofia was covering her mouth with her hands. Kenzie clenched her jaw to stop the incessant chattering of her teeth.

Graham was holding Aralia against him and rocking her like she was a sleeping child. From her position on Kiwi's back, Kenzie could see the expression of shock still frozen on her dead friend's face.

Her friend.

Yeah. That's what she and Aralia had been. Maybe not in the traditional sense, but what were friends if not people who gave each other shit and then had each other's backs?

And Rick's people had killed her.

Kenzie's attention was drawn to Braxton, who had managed to knock down one of the Gourmands even with his arms tied behind his back. Five more tackled him. The gag muffled his words, but Kenzie understood what he was shouting over and over.

"Rick, you fucker."

Graham laid Aralia down with such tenderness it made Kenzie's vision blur. He stood up and faced Rick with murder in his eyes.

"Try me," Rick taunted. "You can join your slutty sister."

Graham surged forward.

"Don't you dare," Sofia said, her voice strung out as she put her hands on Graham's broad chest and tried to push him back.

All around them, people were readying their weapons—both magical and non…all deadly. This was about to be a bloodbath.

"Stop."

Kenzie had no idea whether anyone actually heard her or not. She only had eyes for Rick.

"We can do this without everyone dying," she told him, letting her hatred congeal and fester deep inside her.

"How are we going to do that?" Rick asked, a gleam of amusement twinkling in his eyes.

"By ending it the way it all started," Kenzie replied. "With a culinary magic competition. Between you and me. Here. Now."

Rick cocked his head at her, considering.

"You've got as much magic as I do now," Kenzie pressed, desperate for him to agree. "We're on even footing."

"You were never on even footing with me," Rick scoffed. "You've always been beneath me."

"Fine," Kenzie agreed. "Then, you shouldn't have any problem agreeing to compete against me.

"I won't cheat," she added, sensing his hesitation.

"Oh, I know you won't." Rick laughed. "Because if you try any funny business—" He made a show of glancing down at Braxton and Kenzie's dad. He didn't finish his sentence, but he didn't need to. His threat was more than clear.

"So, what do you say?" Kenzie asked. "You and me. A culinary magic battle to the death."

"You've got yourself a deal." A slow smile spread across Rick's lips. "I'm going to enjoy this."

CHAPTER 38

BRAXTON

It was déjà fucking vu.

At the end of Cutthroat Cuisine, Braxton had been standing outside a kitchen, unable to do anything except watch as Kenzie cooked to the death. As it turned out, that battle had actually been Rick disguised as Kenzie. But the point was, Braxton was once again relegated to the status of useless bystander while his girlfriend had to be the one to fight for all of them.

With how powerful Rick had become, Braxton doubted the wish truffle would be strong enough to protect Kenzie against whatever he was planning.

Braxton was ready to combust from all of his nerves and fury and grief.

Aralia was lying dead on the ground beside him. He and four others were tied up and useless. Natalie had organized an entire army to come and battle the Gourmands alongside them, and here he was, on his knees at Rick's feet with a wad of dirty cloth stuffed in his mouth.

And Kenzie was about to cook against Rick. Alone.

After what had gone down in the Cutthroat Cuisine finale, Braxton knew Kenzie wouldn't expect Rick to play fair. She would also have to know that if Rick did defeat her, he wouldn't simply allow everyone who had supported her to walk away unscathed.

Braxton didn't give a damn what happened to himself, but he did care about Sofia. He cared about all the people who had come here out of loyalty to his family.

Kenzie had been inside the Reaper's hut for the last half an hour. Rick had disappeared behind the throngs of his Gourmand horde.

Braxton was about ready to lose his mind.

"Time's up!" Chef Levy roared. "Ashner and Santiori, present your dishes!"

Chef Levy, who was now sitting astride Kiwi, had taken charge of refereeing this impromptu competition.

A harsh grating sound filled the air. Braxton struggled to his feet, which turned out to be a shockingly difficult endeavor with his arms tied behind his back and five Gourmands hovering around him. He whipped his head around, searching for the source of the noise. The mystery didn't last long.

What. The. Fuck.

Ten Gourmands were wheeling a device into the clearing that looked part-guillotine and part-giant rock slide.

"What is this?" Chef Levy demanded, since the gag in Braxton's mouth prevented him from saying anything at all.

"This," Rick said, gesturing to the device that was taller than two men stacked on top of each other, "is a human-sized mandoline slicer. It's made out of a combination of oyster, clam, and abalone shells. Magically enhanced, of course."

Braxton choked around his gag.

"That's horse shit, Santiori," Chef Levy snarled. "The agreement between you and Ashner was for each of you to cook a single magical dish. This—" She gave the mandoline a contemptuous look. "Isn't that."

"It absolutely is," Rick said with infuriating calm and a more infuriating smirk. "It's just a really, really large dish. And I wouldn't suggest trying to eat it."

Mandolines, even in their normal-sized, nonmagical forms, were known for being one of the more dangerous kitchen tools. They were used for thinly slicing vegetables, but if a chef's hand got too close to the blade, it was more than potatoes they ended up shaving. The blade on this 3-meter version looked beyond wicked.

The Gourmands dragged the mandoline close enough for Braxton to see the crushed-up clam and oyster shells that had been fused together in a single sheet-like slab. It was propped up at an angle like a slide.

Braxton's attention was drawn to the blade in the center of the mandoline. It caught the light and looked sharp enough to cut through stone.

Braxton cursed through his gag. He needed to get Kenzie away from that thing.

If only he wasn't so damn useless.

"Impressive, right?" Rick said, clearly enjoying the spectacle he was making. "You see, I had to come up with something that would work fast." His gaze, already bright with victory, fixed on Braxton. "You didn't think I'd give her magic a chance to heal her again, did you?"

Rick laughed at whatever expression crossed Braxton's face.

"This mandoline will destroy her body beyond the point she'll be able to heal herself," Rick said. "No amount of magic can save her now."

No. This wasn't happening. Braxton had to do something.

But what the fuck could he do? How was he going to protect Kenzie when he was bound and gagged and kneeling at Rick's feet?

Beside Braxton, Walter made a tortured sound.

"Look on the bright side, McKaid," Rick gloated. "After this, there's gonna be so much more of your girlfriend to love. Like, a thousand more pieces of her."

Braxton surged forward. He was going to kill Rick or die trying—

Rick sent him sprawling back onto the ground with a kick to his stomach.

"There will be plenty of time for that, McKaid," Rick said. "Not to worry."

At that moment, the Reaper's door opened. Kenzie stepped onto the sagging porch. She was holding a cake tray, although from Braxton's position splayed on the ground, he couldn't see exactly what kind of cake she'd made. He could see she'd tied back her hair in a high ponytail in the style she wore when she did her most serious cooking. There was a smudge of cocoa powder on her cheek. She was so beautiful it was almost painful to look at her.

She glanced at the mandoline and raised an eyebrow. That was as much of a reaction as she gave Rick before striding down the porch steps and marching over to them.

Kenzie looked so confident. In that moment, Braxton was struck by a memory of her during their first round at Hex Kitchen. Kenzie had been so overwhelmed by the crowd and the task before them that she'd almost had a panic attack right there in the dome.

That Kenzie was long gone. The version of her standing in front of him now was poised, determined, and merciless. Braxton couldn't have torn his gaze away from her if his life depended on it.

Kenzie was chewing hard on something that was making one of her cheeks bulge adorably.

"What the fuck is that?" Rick sneered, motioning at the odd concoction perched on top of her cake tray.

"I have to agree," Chef Levy said with a disdainful sniff. "You forget you're a gourmet chef, Ashner?"

"It's a graveyard cake." Kenzie spared her father a glance that held a hint of mirth. "Obvi."

Walter managed a smile in spite of his gag.

The cake did, in fact, look like a graveyard. The chocolate-frosted cake was topped with dark-chocolate cookie crumbles that were reminiscent of dirt. Gummy worm heads poked out of the cookie-crumb dirt. Kenzie had made ghosts out of marshmallows and dollops of whipped cream. Shortbread cookies stuck out of the cake like tombstones. White chocolate bones littered the edible graveyard. Chocolate-covered stick pretzels stabbed into the cake's perimeter looked remarkably like a wrought-iron fence.

A cloud of magic hovered over the cake.

"Well, it doesn't matter," Chef Levy said, still regarding the cake with a sour expression. "Rick already cheated."

"Oh, I don't mind," Kenzie said with far more cheeriness than the occasion warranted. "I expected Dick to pull something shady. It's cool."

Braxton tried to get her attention, making incoherent noises around his gag. He shifted his weight. Blood surged through his veins as he readied himself to throw his entire weight at Rick.

"No!" Kenzie said sharply. "No one interfere."

In a quieter voice that could only be heard by the people closest to her, Kenzie added, "the Gourmands will only fall into line if I beat Rick legitimately. The goal is to avoid a massacre, here."

Right now, all Braxton cared about was making sure Kenzie avoided the mandoline.

Kenzie chomped down on whatever she'd been chewing a few more times. Then, she opened her mouth.

There was a wad of gum balanced on the tip of her tongue. The gum formed into a pink bubble that began to grow almost instantaneously. It swelled into a wobbly dome that was soon large enough to encompass their group of prisoners, Kiwi, and the Gourmands nearest to them. The bubble gum dome molded around the people Kenzie clearly wanted to include, and pushed the rest outside the pink, translucent shield.

Braxton let out a muffled groan when the bubble stopped growing. The mandoline was inside with them.

"Holy shit, that's amazing!" Natalie's voice shouted from outside the bubble. Her voice had a tinny, faraway quality.

More shouts of encouragement joined Natalie's, along with jeers from the Gourmands. All of their voices sounded muffled. It was as if the people inside the bubble gum dome were separated from everyone else by a layer of water. They could see and hear each other, but everything was muted. And when the Gourmands tried to bash their way inside, they ricocheted right off the dome's exterior.

"Now we won't be bothered by the peanut gallery," Kenzie said. She poked the translucent pink wall, which wobbled but didn't break. "I got this idea from a recipe your mom made one time," she told Reuben. "She used magical bubble tea to save my life. So, we owe her for this one, too."

Reuben tapped his fist to his chest and nodded in acknowledgement.

"Fine then," Rick said, his amused smirk no longer in place. "Let's do this." He rolled up his sleeves and raised both of his arms up toward the mandoline. Magic crackled through the air.

"Kenzie Ashner," Rick called in a clear voice, still facing the mandoline.

As soon as he'd finished speaking her name, a fierce wind appeared out of nowhere. Braxton's hair slapped against his forehead hard enough to sting.

The wind blew faster and faster, until it congealed into a vortex. A vortex that centered around Kenzie.

Fury knifed through Braxton as the swirling eddy lifted Kenzie off the ground.

Braxton's anger morphed into terror when he realized what was happening. Wind and magic spun around Kenzie, making it impossible for her to break free. It was as though she were caught in the center of a cyclone…. A cyclone that was heading straight toward the mandoline.

It was going to bring her right into the blade.

Braxton barely noticed when the cake Kenzie had been holding slid off the plate and hit the grass. Clumps of chocolatey cake and marshmallow ghosts littered the ground.

Kenzie was yelling something, but her words were lost in the churning wind that had her trapped.

Braxton was frantic. Slick heat coated his wrists as he fought against the ropes that bound him. He head-butted a Gourmand, hearing the crack of their skulls but feeling nothing.

Kenzie was airborne when she shouted a single word.

"Wait!"

The swirling wind still held Kenzie captive, but it calmed enough that Rick's next words were clearly audible.

"You gonna beg me?" Rick gave her a smug smile. "Go ahead."

"Sorry to disappoint," Kenzie replied. "But I'm not really the begging type."

Before Rick could fully start up the vortex again, Kenzie raised her index finger to her lips. Braxton noticed the tip of her finger was coated in frosting. Chocolate frosting. From her ruined graveyard cake.

Kenzie put her finger in her mouth and sucked.

All at once, the vortex fell away. Kenzie landed neatly on her feet.

A cold, foul breeze that had nothing to do with Rick's magic swept through the bubble gum dome. Braxton heard a crackle. He felt the brush of ice crystals against his arms. When he gave his abused wrists a sharp jerk, the rope that had bound them came apart with a satisfying *snap*. Braxton lost no time in pulling out his gag before going to work on releasing the other prisoners.

By the time they were all freed and a wailing Baby Hiroto was back in his mother's arms, a real wrought-iron fence had sprung out of the ground inside the bubble gum dome. The grass had transformed into mud. Worms and spiders were squirming across the surface, and all of the insects were making a beeline for Rick. They crawled over his polished shoes and up his pantlegs. Rick wriggled around, trying to kick the insects off him. He screamed expletives until something else made him forget all about the bugs.

Ghosts were rising out of the ground.

The ghosts were translucent but in full color. Every detail was so clear they looked almost real. The ghosts were also damn familiar.

There was Aralia, her white hair resplendent and her bow hooked over her back. Philippe stood beside her, his clothes as disheveled as ever. His eyes, which had always held a humorous twinkle in life, had been replaced with milky orbs that fixated on Rick. It was the one characteristic that all the ghosts shared, Braxton realized.

More ghosts swirled around Rick. There was Hiroto—not the baby, but Braxton's friend who was murdered during Hex Kitchen. Braxton recognized Jacob, a man who had been killed by Rick's thugs after being interrogated about the Gourmands' synthetic ingredients.

There were also plenty of people Braxton didn't recognize. Some were dressed in suits. Others were just kids.

These were people that Kenzie couldn't possibly have met, and yet, her magic had somehow conjured them. That was when Braxton understood that he was looking at the ghosts of all the people Rick had killed.

A sharp pang clawed through Braxton's insides at the sight of Mum, so lifelike and yet not at all like herself, as she rose from the ground. She didn't so much as acknowledge Braxton or Sofia as she floated over to join the others.

"Get away!" Rick swatted angrily at the ghosts.

The incorporeal beings burst apart against Rick before reforming and coming at him again.

Rick was shivering, although it was unclear whether it was from the drastic temperature drop or from what was happening to his body.

Rick was beginning to shrink.

The height and muscles Rick had acquired from his magical antipasto were wearing off. Once again, he was swallowed up in his too-large suit, which was now full of holes from all the ruptured seams caused by his temporary growth spurt.

Standing there in his ragged suit, with the massive ghosts surrounding him, Rick looked…fragile.

The ghosts made swishing sounds as they whirled around Rick. They didn't speak, and as far as Braxton could tell, they couldn't actually cause Rick bodily injury. But they were scaring the hell out of him. For now, that was enough.

"Fuck you!" Rick shouted, kicking at the ghosts. "Leave me alone!"

When the ghosts didn't obey, Rick turned to the Gourmands standing inside the bubble gum dome.

"Don't just stand there," he roared. "Help me!"

The Gourmands responded by sinking to their knees and throwing up their hands in surrender.

Without warning, the ghosts stopped swishing around Rick. They all hovered directly in front of him. An eerie silence filled the bubble gum dome, punctuated only by Rick's harsh panting.

"And now for the pièce de resistance," Kenzie murmured.

White smoke began to swirl over the muddy ground. Another ghost began to form. It got bigger and bigger, until it dwarfed all the other ghosts. It got so big that even Kiwi began to seem small in comparison. The ghost barely fit inside the bubble gum dome by the time it finished growing and started to take on human characteristics.

White, transparent lines turned to full color. Details filled in and became familiar.

The ghost, wearing his traditional three-piece suit and holding a translucent cigar in his phantom fingers, spun in a slow circle as smoke continued to billow around him.

Braxton found himself staring into the sightless, milky gaze of Veneziano Santiori's ghost.

"Papà," Rick whispered. His face had gone almost as pale as the apparition that loomed over him.

Veneziano's ghost raised his hand as though to strike his son. Rick screamed.

Veneziano's ghost smashed against Rick. Ice crystals burst into the air as Rick shrieked and covered his head. The ghost dissipated and reformed before driving back over Rick. Frigid air gusted through the dome, making goosebumps rise on Braxton's skin.

Rick fell to his knees, cowering in the mud as Veneziano came at him again.

"Please," Rick begged. "Please, make it stop. I'll do anything. Please!"

He was crying, Braxton realized. Rick Santiori was crying and begging Kenzie to end his misery.

Kenzie's sneakers made squelching noises as she walked through the mud and stopped in front of Rick. Lank strands of his hair were plastered to his tear- and mud-streaked face as he looked up at her.

"I could kill you, you know," she said.

Rick was crying so hard that his bony shoulders were convulsing.

"I'm not going to, though," Kenzie continued. She snapped her fingers, and just like that, her magic unraveled. The ghosts vanished. The wrought-iron fence and insects sank back into mud, which was quickly replaced by green grass. The wintery wind vanished, and the air felt like spring again.

"Th-thank you," Rick babbled, still weeping and clawing at the ground.

"Don't thank me," Kenzie said, her voice cold and inflectionless. "I said I wasn't going to kill you. That doesn't mean you're going to live." She backed up and turned in a slow circle, locking gazes with Braxton and the rest of their friends inside the bubble gum dome. "Rick murdered people you love. It's only fair that you get to be the ones to finish him."

Kenzie gave Braxton a small nod before stepping back until she was leaning against Kiwi's foreleg. Chef Levy said something to the effect of "Atta girl, Ashner." After that, Braxton was aware of nothing except Rick.

Braxton and Sofia moved in tandem. Graham, Clementine, and Raina followed. Zack was right behind them. Together, they encircled Rick, who was still on his knees.

The expressions on each of their faces told Braxton that everyone in this circle had been hungering for this moment as much as much as he.

Braxton didn't have any magical food or even a weapon, but he had no need of anything beyond his own two hands. Rick wasn't putting up a fight. He wasn't even trying to get away. He curled in on himself on the ground and wept.

"This isn't quite how I imagined this moment going down," Zack said scratching his jaw as he regarded his cousin. "And believe me, I imagined this moment quite a few times over the years."

"Same for me," Sofia said, staring down at Rick with pure, unadulterated revulsion.

Graham, Clementine, and Raina didn't say anything. When Braxton looked at them, he saw unmistakable pity on each of their faces. Braxton turned to his sister and knew she was sharing his thoughts.

He heaved a heavy sigh.

"I can't believe I'm about to say this," Braxton said to the group. "But this piece of shit isn't worth the blood on our hands."

Clementine murmured her agreement. Everyone else stayed silent.

"And—" Braxton heaved out another sigh. "The people we're trying to avenge—" He looked at Sofia, but his mind was on the conversation he'd had with Walter earlier in the night. "—wouldn't want us to murder for their sakes."

Braxton gave Graham a half-smile. "Well, Aralia probably would…. But the others wouldn't."

"So then, what should we do with him?" Raina asked, cuddling Baby Hiroto closer to her chest. "If we let him go, he'll just terrorize more people and stab us in the backs the first chance he gets."

"Not if Kenzie takes away his magic and we lock him up in Rikers along with whatever's left of the Hunters," Sofia said.

Damn. Braxton's sister really was an evil genius. He loved it.

"I can do that," Kenzie said, coming forward. "The magic he got from those synthetic ingredients is gone, so he isn't strong enough to resist me anymore."

"Are we all agreed?" Braxton asked.

Everyone nodded.

Braxton was almost surprised he didn't feel so much as a twinge of disappointment at being denied the vengeance he'd craved for so long. This punishment might actually be better. For someone who valued power above all else, Rick wasn't going to enjoy living the rest of his life without it.

Right move, bro, Aidan's voice said inside Braxton's mind.

"Get up," Braxton told Rick.

Rick did as he was told, his shoulders bowed and his face downcast. His movements were sluggish…until they weren't.

Rick lunged.

Everything happened very fast. Braxton moved in front of Kenzie, certain she was the target of Rick's wrath. Graham and Sofia went for each other. Clementine and Zack protected Raina and the baby.

Rick didn't collide with any of them. Instead, he hurled himself at the mandoline.

"Rick Santiori!" Rick shouted.

The vortex spun to life around him. Rick arrowed his arms above his head like he was a diver about to go into the pool. The swirling mass of air drew him straight into the mandoline's blade.

A sheer, metallic whine filled the dome. Rick's scream was abruptly cut off as blood flew through the air like raindrops. Kenzie turned her face into Braxton's shirt as round slivers of flesh and bone shot out of the mandoline.

In seconds, a neat pile of human slices was all that remained of Rick Santiori.

CHAPTER 39

GRAHAM

Graham felt almost as numb as he had the first time he encountered magical mint. He mechanically began clearing away debris from a blackberry bush that wasn't completely annihilated. He disentangled a charred branch from the thicket. He didn't even feel the thorns as they pierced his flesh.

The Reaper's garden—Graham's garden, now—was in ruins. Aralia was dead.

It was cold comfort that the tree that should have saved Qiang Lee's life had survived the battle.

The same couldn't be said for all the other plants in the garden. Many of them had been trampled beyond repair by the hundreds of people who had come through the garden. Many more plants had been scorched to ashes by the Gourmands' fire.

Graham paused in his rote and mostly ineffectual actions when he felt a warm weight press against his back. Sofia draped her arms around his waist.

She didn't say anything or ask if he was okay. She was just there.

"Is it time?" Graham asked, reaching up to pick one of the apples.

Since the battle with the Gourmands was over, there was only one matter left to resolve. It would be up to Graham to use the apples to take away the Vanillas' memories of culinary magic.

"Not yet," Sofia said. "The others have been talking about it and think maybe we shouldn't take the Vanillas' memories, after all."

"What?"

Graham turned to face her.

"Since the Hunters' arrest and everyone finding out about them murdering kids, public opinion has shifted." Sofia lifted a shoulder. "It seems that, for the time being at least, we have a precarious truce. Chef Levy and some of the others think we should have a meeting to discuss whether or not we should take away their memories."

"But—" Graham shook his head, trying to process everything Sofia was telling him. "If we don't, then that'll mean you gave up your magic for nothing."

"I thought that at first, too." Sofia sat on the ground and pulled him down beside her. "Then I realized it didn't bother me." She linked her hand with his. "I meant what I said before. I made my peace with not having magic."

Graham buried his face against her shoulder. He breathed her in, needing to absorb a tiny fraction of her endless strength. They stayed like that for long enough that Graham's legs started to fall asleep.

"Does it ever go away?" he asked, his voice sounding as wrecked as if he'd spent the day screaming.

The question was vague, but Sofia didn't need to ask what he meant.

"No," she said simply. "That empty feeling in here—" She pressed her palm flat against his heart. "—never disappears. But you get used to living with it." He felt her shrug against him. "The pain gets less sharp over time, too. More bearable."

Graham closed his eyes and swallowed around the lump in his throat. When Sofia spoke again, her lips were right at his ear.

"That part will get easier with time, too," she said in a soft voice.

"What part?" he asked.

"The blaming yourself part. Torturing yourself with all the ways you might have been able to change what happened."

"Sofia." He reached around to pull her into his lap. "I—"

"Um, Graham?"

They both turned to Raina, who was standing a short distance away and holding a sleeping Hiroto. She gave them an apologetic look.

"Everyone keeps asking how they can help. Do you mind if I start putting people to work on cleaning this place up?"

"That'd be great," Graham said, grateful to have someone else take over the burden of decision-making. At least for a little while.

Clementine appeared next, hopping lightly over a pile of inert roots that were all that remained of a hundred-year-old crape myrtle tree. Her usual cheer was nowhere to be seen. Her eyes were red-rimmed, and the look she exchanged with Graham was full of grief and understanding.

"Chef Levy needs you to go to Reaper Lee's hut," Clementine told Graham. She turned to Raina, and her expression softened at the sight of the baby. "I'll take care of Hiroto while you're busy getting dirty." Clementine took the sleepy baby, whose onesie for the day had a fuzzy loaf of bread and the words *Over my bread body*. Baby Hiroto cooed happily and curled his fists into Clementine's shirt.

"See you later?" Graham asked Sofia.

"Of course." She gave his hand a quick squeeze and then let him go.

A few minutes later, Graham found himself crammed inside Reaper Lee's hut along with Chef Levy, several red-robed Gourmands, and Kenzie. At least Kenzie looked as uncomfortable as he felt. The two of them gravitated toward each other until they were standing side-by-side against the wall nearest the door.

"Just in case we need to make a quick getaway," Kenzie said out of the corner of her mouth, which helped relieve some of Graham's tension.

"Let's get down to business," Chef Levy told Graham and Kenzie. "You are the two most powerful members of the culinary magic world." She pointed to Kenzie. "You are in charge of the Gourmands by default; however, you—" She pinned Graham with her intimidating stare. "Are the Reaper. The Gourmands broke the accord they made with Qiang Lee and all of his predecessors. Therefore, you need to decide what happens with them."

Graham expected someone to challenge his new title or call him out for being a fraud. Instead, there was a rustle of robes as the Gourmands shifted nervously. None of them met Graham's eyes as he scanned the room.

"Where are the rest of the synthetic ingredients?" he asked, trying to buy himself a little time to gather his thoughts and figure out how he was supposed to handle this.

After an uncomfortably long pause, one of the Gourmands spoke up.

"There are no more ingredients, Reaper—" She paused, leaned her head toward one of the other Gourmands, who whispered to her, and then added, "—Malyung. Rick ate the last of them in his antipasto. Sir."

"Oh, okay." Graham felt his face heat as every pair of eyes locked on him, waiting for him to decide their fate.

With each second that passed, the tension in the hut thickened. The stench of sweat hung heavy on the air. Graham could even hear a few prayers being muttered in whispered voices.

He'd been the Reaper for all of about five minutes. How was he supposed to start passing judgment?

Chef Levy narrowed her gaze at him, making it clear that he needed to buck up and step up to the plate.

"In that case." Graham licked his lips. He tried to think of what Reaper Lee would say if he were here right now.

Get the hell out of my house, most likely.

Graham had to hide a little smile, and then suppress a stab of pain, at the memory of his mentor. Graham might not have known him for long, but he'd shared something with Qiang Lee that transcended time.

Graham recalled Qiang's final words…about how he regretted destroying his ingredients rather than sharing them. Graham thought about his promise to help Sofia distribute the ingredients to people who needed them.

All at once, he knew exactly what to say.

"As your penance," Graham told the Gourmands, "you will help restore this garden. And, once the ingredients are ready—" which, depending on the plant, would take anywhere from months to years, "—you will help harvest and distribute them to people who need them most.

"You will work for me until you've helped save two lives for every one life you've taken."

It would be immensely complicated to identify so many people in need, and match them up with ingredients that could solve their particular ailments. Luckily, Graham knew precisely the person to lead the initiative. After all, Sofia had already done it…albeit on a smaller scale. If anyone was up for the challenge of pairing ingredients to worthy recipients, it was her.

The thought brought a giddy smile to his lips that Graham was powerless to hold back.

"We'd be honored to help, Reaper Malyung," one of the Gourmands said in a tentative voice. "But I fear such an enterprise would keep us too busy to complete our usual Gourmand duties. With a new leader, our priority should be to assist with her transition."

"Oh, I'm good," Kenzie said with a casual wave of her hand. She offered the Gourmands a saccharine smile. "I'm sure I'll somehow muddle through without your invaluable opinions."

Graham swallowed down his laugh as the Gourmands tried to conceal their grimaces with varying degrees of success.

"That's that, then," Chef Levy said.

"Raina will give you your first assignments," Graham told the Gourmands as they filed to the door.

"You might want to take off those cloaks," Kenzie suggested, maybe taking slightly too much joy in the Gourmands' fall from grace. "I don't think gardening and velvet mix well."

CHAPTER 40

KENZIE

Kenzie was having a flashback. Middle school. Art class. A final presentation on the life and work of Frida Kahlo. The whole situation had been a disaster from start to finish because Kenzie's moronic eighth grade classmates had spent the entire time giggling over the artist's unibrow.

This was like the same thing, except no one was giggling, and no one had a unibrow. And instead of discussing Mexican artwork, they were talking about the future of culinary magic.

Oh, and rather than being the fidgety eighth grader hiding behind her poster board, Kenzie was the authority figure everyone was staring at in expectation of answers.

So, maybe not exactly same thing.

The thousand-or-so chefs who had come all the way to Maine in support of the McKaids were depending on Kenzie to set the tone for what came next. She couldn't let them down.

Gulp.

Since the Gourmands had shed their crimson robes, Kenzie had found herself as the sole—and extremely reluctant—person in charge.

Kenzie looked to her dad, whose *I believe in you* expression hadn't wavered since she was a kid. Somehow, it helped ease the panic that having a gagillion pairs of eyes fixed on her was stirring up.

Look confident, she ordered herself. She raised her chin and threw back her shoulders. *But not arrogant.* Her chin dipped down and her shoulders rolled forward a little.

Kenzie was getting the sense that she wasn't off to the best start….

"Ashner?" Chef Levy prompted.

Right.

"I guess the first issue we need to address is, um, the fact that I don't think I'm the right person to be in charge of…all of us."

Kenzie mentally added public speaking to her theoretical self-improvement list. It was a toss-up whether it would come in above or below weightlifting in terms of prioritizing. Kenzie freaking hated weightlifting.

"But you're the most powerful culinary magician in the world," someone in the crowd pointed out.

With the sun's angle, it was impossible for Kenzie to see who had spoken, but it sounded like Braxton's friend Natalie.

"I am for now," Kenzie said. "But I'm planning to change that."

Surprised murmurs rippled through the crowd. Kenzie intentionally didn't look at Braxton. She wasn't sure how he'd react to her decision, but now that she'd said it out loud, she felt a tremendous weight lift from her shoulders.

"What are you talking about, Ashner?" Chef Levy asked.

"I'm going to let my Culinarian magic go," Kenzie said. "I'll still be a culinary magician," she hastened to add. "I'm just getting rid of the parts that allow me to give and take away other people's magic."

Everyone had gone completely silent. Even the insects had stopped their incessant conversations.

"I'll be a regular culinary magician," Kenzie clarified, because awkward silences weren't her strong point.

"Have you lost your marbles?" Zack asked.

Not to my knowledge, but check back in later today….

"Why?' demanded Sofia.

"Because." Kenzie blew out a breath. "We got into this whole mess," she swept a hand out at the ruined garden, "because a few people controlled way too much magic. It gave them too much control over everyone else. I don't want that kind of power or responsibility. So, I'm letting it go."

And I might have accidentally misjudged my own power and turned my chameleon horse-sized....

Kenzie didn't say that tidbit out loud. If everyone else was too polite to bring up her faux paus, then she certainly wasn't going to remind them. Bygones, and all that.

When Kenzie finally worked up the nerve to glance in Braxton's direction to gauge his reaction, he was frowning at her. It wasn't an angry frown, though. It was his deep-thinking frown. What he was deep-thinking about, Kenzie couldn't begin to guess.

"That part of my magic and I never really saw eye to eye, anyway," Kenzie added. "It wasn't natural for me." And she got the sense that if she kept pushing it, she wouldn't like the results.

"Just like that?" someone in the crowd asked dubiously, drawing her attention back to her audience.

"Just like that," Kenzie replied.

Hah. She had no idea how she was going to release only the Culinarian part of her magic while retaining the rest.

"Since I'll soon be just another culinary magician," Kenzie forged on, "I think we should have a leader who actually knows how to lead. Someone who won't be intimidated or manipulated or corrupted. Someone who already has experience at judging." She paused. "Which is why I'm nominating Chef Levy."

It was a brilliant idea, in Kenzie's oh-so-humble opinion.

"Er," Chef Levy said.

It was the first time Kenzie had ever seen the woman look surprised. It was kind of exhilarating.

"I second that nomination," Braxton called in a clear voice.

"Let's give it up for Chef Levy," Sofia yelled.

"Woo!" Clementine cheered, pumping Hiroto's tiny fist in the air.

It didn't take long for applause to fill the garden, along with shouts of "Chef Levy!"

"Well." Chef Levy cleared her throat. "I suppose I'm not the worst person for the position." Her half-hearted scowl softened into a genuine smile. "Hanna would be in stiches if she could see me now."

"Hanna would be proud," Kenzie said with complete certainty, even though she didn't really know anything about Chef Levy's deceased girlfriend.

Chef Levy didn't reply, but as she took her place at the front of the crowd, Kenzie could have sworn the made-of-steel chef wiped away a tear.

As soon as was socially acceptable, Kenzie made her escape and went to go stand with the rest of her friends.

"I thought you were going to faint when you first got up there," Sofia observed, nudging Kenzie. "Glad you stayed conscious."

Braxton shook his head and smiled. "What my tactful sister means is that you were goddamn amazing up there." He moved a hand to Kenzie's back, subtly rubbing the knot of tension at the base of her spine.

"Isn't that what I said?" Sofia frowned at her brother.

"With the Gourmands no longer in charge of governing," Chef Levy said, planting her fists on her hips and getting right down to business, "I'll need a team of advisors to assist with lawmaking. Are there any objections to me appointing Kenzie Ashner, both McKaids, and the Reaper?"

The only objections were halfhearted grumbles from Kenzie, who had been hoping for some R&R time away from culinary magic politics.

"Let's give it up for our new government," Natalie called out.

Her shout was echoed by others. More people joined in, clapping and whistling their approval. The sound grew in volume until it was deafening.

The hairs on Kenzie's arms prickled in awareness of the fact that all these people were cheering for her. She felt like a total badass.

"Good," Chef Levy said, once everyone had finally quieted down. "Next essential order of business is the Vanillas. It's my understanding that Reaper Malyung has a means of taking away the Vanillas' memories of culinary magic." She paused and looked to Graham, who nodded. "However," she continued, "I don't think that's the right path forward. Forgetfulness isn't the only way of achieving peace, and I believe we could avoid a great deal of grief on all sides if we didn't have to hide."

Kenzie could feel the almost celebratory atmosphere of the crowd start to shift to apprehension.

"I haven't forgotten about the food witch nonsense," Chef Levy said, holding up a hand to stop the mutterings that had begun. "However, I think part of the reason for the past weeks' debacle was the botched way culinary magic was thrust on the Vanillas.

"We need to re-introduce magic in such a way that will demonstrate it isn't a threat, even to those who don't possess it."

"How the hell are we supposed to do that?" an angry voice shouted from the rear of the crowd.

"Uh, Chef," Reuben said, raising a tentative hand. "If you don't mind, I can field this one."

"Go ahead." Chef Levy nodded.

"My father was a Gourmand who argued for the benefits of sharing magic with the Vanillas," Reuben said in a clear voice that carried to the edges of the garden. "My parents developed a cohesive plan for educating the Vanillas. It begins with giving people small tastes and building up their tolerance for the supernatural over a stretch of time." He turned to Chef Levy. "I can go over more of the specifics with you later, but I really think my parents' plan will work if it's implemented properly."

"You volunteering?" Chef Levy asked.

Reuben nodded. "We can definitely do that," he said, gesturing to himself and Zack. Then, he looked at Zack with an owl-eyed expression as though just realizing what he'd said. Reuben turned bright red, from the base of his throat to the tips of his ears. "I mean, if that works for Zack. I didn't mean to speak for both of us."

Zack looped his arms around Reuben's waist and drew him against his side. "Hmm," Zack said, pretending to think. "That job is probably going to involve a lot of travel."

"Yeah, probably," Reuben mumbled. "If you don't want—"

"Probably going to mean a lot of time spent trapped in a car with you," Zack continued, talking right over Reuben. "Or on a boat. Or in a plane. Regardless, lots of time when you're trapped in a confined space with me."

Reuben grew impossibly redder, but he was smiling as he leaned into Zack.

"How do you know I'm not the one trying to trap you?" Reuben asked.

"You guys know you're not alone right now, right?" Sofia teased.

Kenzie tried and failed to stifle a laugh at the look that crossed Reuben's face. Zack, of course, just offered them an unrepentant shrug before loudly kissing Reuben's cheek.

"So, am I to take that as your agreement to lead this initiative?" Chef Levy asked, scowling. It was her I'm-trying-really-hard-to-stay-grumpy scowl, as opposed to her you're-in-danger-of-dying-painfully scowl. By now, Kenzie knew the difference.

"Yeah, Chef," Zack said. "We're agreeing."

When the meeting ended and everyone else started to disband, Chef Levy stalked over to their little group.

"Well, that didn't go terribly," Chef Levy, the eternal optimist, observed.

"You know, Chef," Braxton said. "I have to say, I'm surprised you accepted the role of becoming our fearless leader."

"Oh?" Chef Levy raised an eyebrow that somehow managed to communicate impatience and mild scorn. "Why's that?"

"Well." Braxton's lip twitched like he was trying really hard not to smile. "You got the revenge for Hanna that you wanted. So, it's kind of starting to look like you're hanging around because you actually give a damn about what happens to all of us. Better watch out, or the next thing you know, you'll be referring to us as *friends*."

"Hmph," Chef Levy hmphed. "I suppose spending too much time with you four has made me soft." She started to walk away and turned back. "Don't blow my cover, or I'll have to kill you. Slowly."

Kenzie and the others somehow managed to suppress their chuckles until Chef Levy was out of earshot.

* * *

It was hours later when all the chefs who had come to fight with them had said their goodbyes and were heading home. Kenzie's dad had gone ahead with Chef Levy, Zack, and Reuben in the first car that was headed back to Manhattan. Sofia and Graham would be staying in Maine with Raina, Baby Hiroto, Clementine, and the ex-Gourmands. Kenzie didn't envy their task of restoring the Reaper's garden.

That left Kenzie and Braxton. They were going back to New York to stay with Kenzie's dad until they figured out what they were doing next. They'd be on their way, just as soon as they finished the conversation Braxton had insisted they have the moment they were alone.

Kenzie sat at the Reaper's rickety kitchen table as Braxton's deep voice washed over her. She had just taken a sip of rich, velvety coffee, when—

Braxton's words sank in. Kenzie promptly spat her mouthful of coffee all over the table. She peered at her boyfriend as she tried to figure out if he was serious.

"Are you serious?" she asked him.

"Completely."

"But…." Kenzie blinked. "Why?"

Braxton raked a hand through his hair. "The short answer? I'm tired, Kenz. I just want to be rid of it."

Kenzie nodded, trying to simultaneously be the supportive girlfriend and listen to her inner voice that wanted her to scream at Braxton *Wait! You're about to make the biggest mistake of your life!*

"And the long answer?" she prompted, her mind reeling as she half-heartedly wiped at the coffee spray with her sleeve.

Braxton was one of the most powerful culinary magicians in the world. Why would he want to stop being one altogether?

Why would he ask her to take away his magic?

Braxton sighed and tipped his head back, staring up at the splintered ceiling beams.

"I think it started the first time you and I cooked together," Braxton said.

"So this is my fault?" Kenzie spluttered.

Braxton brought her hand to his lips and kissed her knuckles. "Maybe a little," he said, chuckling at her squawk of indignation.

"You asked me what kind of magical cooking I enjoyed." He shrugged. "It made me realize that I'd never questioned why I did what I did. Culinary magic was always so much a part of my life. But then after Aidan…and then my parents…." He trailed off, looking off into the distance but seeming not to see anything. "I like cooking," he said in a low voice. "But I don't like the magic part of it. After all the things I've done…after everything that's happened…." He swallowed. "I don't want any part of it anymore."

Anticipating her next opposition, Braxton said, "Losing my magic won't kill me now. After all the times I strained my magic to its breaking point, I destroyed some part of my connection to it. I know I can live without it."

"Okay," Kenzie said slowly. "Are you sure this is what you want, though? There will be no takebacks with this after I drain the Culinarian part of my power."

Braxton didn't even hesitate. "I'm sure."

"It's just such a waste," Kenzie said.

She instantly wanted to slap herself upside the head when she realized she'd allowed that unsupportive thought to come out of her mouth.

"Not necessarily," Braxton said, giving her a small smile. "I've been thinking—"

At that moment, the hut's door burst open, and Sofia strode inside.

"Speaking of the devil," Braxton muttered under his breath.

When Kenzie narrowed her gaze in question, Braxton responded with a smile and shake of his head.

"Okay, here's the deal," Sofia said, tossing a set of keys at Braxton. "I got you a car, but if you're expecting something fancy, you're going to be sorely disappointed. It drives, though. Mostly. Okay, there is this little problem with the transmission, but the bloke I rented the car from swore up and down that—What?"

Finally noticing that both Braxton and Kenzie were grinning at her like a pair of idiots, Sofia's expression turned all suspicious-like.

"Brax," Sofia said, crossing her arms and tapping her foot against the floorboards. "The last time you had that look on your face, it was because you and Aid figured out a recipe to make everything my ex-boyfriend ate turn to mud in his mouth."

Kenzie guffawed at that.

"That was epic," Braxton said. "But I've got something even better."

Sofia perched on the corner of the table, since there weren't any other chairs.

"Okay," she said. "I'm all ears."

"How would you feel about becoming a culinary magician?" Braxton asked his sister. "For real this time?"

Sofia gaped at her brother like a fish. Before that moment, Kenzie would have said there was a better chance of Armageddon than encountering a speechless Sofia. And yet, here Sofia was…speechless and gaping like a fish.

"How?" Sofia managed. "I mean, I can't." She leveled an accusing stare on Kenzie. "You even said so yourself. That part of me is closed off now." She thumped her chest with her fist. "I can even feel it."

Kenzie raised her hands as though she were surrendering. "I know, but this is different. I wouldn't be creating new magic for you this time."

"I'll be giving you mine," Braxton said. He sat forward, leaning on his elbows as he faced his sister.

"I'll transfer it to you," Kenzie quickly explained, because Sofia was getting a glazed look in her eyes. "If I'm right about how this is all going to work, his magic will recognize you the same way it did him since you're siblings. So, instead of the magic you had before, this magic will fully bind with you and become a part of you. You'll be as real and powerful of a culinary magician as Braxton is. Was." Kenzie cringed.

"Don't feel too sorry for me," Braxton said, reaching out and stroking his thumb across Kenzie's knuckles. "Whenever I'm craving something magical, I can just have my girlfriend cook for me."

"Chauvinistic pig." Kenzie stuck her tongue out at him, which prompted Braxton to try and capture her tongue between his fingers.

"No," Sofia said, finding her voice and shaking her head hard enough to rattle her brain. "You can't. I won't let you."

"I don't want my magic anymore, Sofe," Braxton said. "It's yours if you want it. Otherwise," Braxton shrugged, "Kenz can let it go."

"Fuck that," Sofia exclaimed, surging to her feet. "I want it!"

Braxton chuckled. "Then it's yours, little sis."

* * *

By the time daylight broke, Braxton's magic was reinstated inside Sofia. The two were saying their goodbyes outside the clunker that Sofia had commissioned to take Braxton and Kenzie back to Manhattan. Kenzie was giving them their privacy and packing up the rest of her meager possessions. On her way out of the Reaper's hut, she picked up Kiwi's unoccupied habitat and nudged the door closed behind her with her foot.

The habitat's prior occupant, now about five-hundred times bigger than his home, was waiting outside. Kiwi opened one ginormous eyeball and yawned widely enough to swallow Kenzie's entire head if he so desired. He didn't, fortunately for Kenzie.

"How you doing, bud?" she asked, patting Kiwi's scaly snout.

Kenzie felt like her relationship with her pet had reached new heights after he'd eaten Nurse Ratched.

If only Kenzie could figure out how to make him pint-sized again….

"Kenz, come on," Braxton shouted. "I don't want to shut the car off because I'm pretty sure I won't get it back on again."

"Oh, bite me," Sofia said.

The two of them devolved into more good-natured arguing. Kenzie stepped over some tangled roots and dead shrubs to reach the unpaved driveway. She seriously didn't envy all the work that lay ahead of Graham with this garden. The place was a mess.

Hmmm….

Kenzie set down everything in her arms and knelt so she could get a better read on the garden's magic. She couldn't connect with it the way Graham could, but she could feel the power lying dormant and shattered beneath the soil.

Kenzie pressed both of her palms to the ground. She closed her eyes and let her Culinarian magic fuse with soil. Then, she let go.

* * *

The next time Kenzie opened her eyes, two things had changed. Kenzie was no longer a Culinarian. And Kiwi was a normal-sized chameleon again.

Kenzie scooped up the little guy, marveling at the way he fit in the palm of her hand, and deposited him safely back in his habitat.

"What do you think, bud?" she asked Kiwi, who was scrambling on top of his favorite rock. "Happy to be home?"

Kiwi didn't respond. He was already asleep.

CHAPTER 41

SOFIA

SIX MONTHS LATER

Sofia slipped into her devil-red dress and checked herself in the mirror.

"How do I look?" she asked Kiwi, whose habitat was perched on a table Sofia had commissioned specifically for that purpose. Since Kenzie was always in the kitchen, which was full of loud noises and smells that would be abhorrent to a chameleon, Sofia had begun sharing custody of the reptile.

Kiwi was back to eating mealworms instead of nurses, but Sofia liked knowing that if she ever had any enemies that needed taking care of, she could sic her chameleon on them.

Kiwi responded to her query by turning the same blood-red shade as Sofia's dress, which she took as a wholehearted approval.

The outfit might be a little over the top, considering she wasn't the star of the show, but whatever. She'd worked just as hard to make tonight a reality as anyone else, even if her name wasn't embossed in gold print on the menus at their highly-anticipated, non-secret culinary magic restaurant.

Sofia had done most of the behind-the-scenes work needed to transform Polly's defunct food bank into a gourmet restaurant that was already the talk of the Manhattan food scene…despite the fact that it hadn't even opened yet. Tomorrow would be their grand opening. Tonight was just for friends and family.

As it turned out, Sofia had a real magical specialty for recipes that related to forging documents…which was how Polly's superbly-located food bank had become property of the McKaids and Ashners. Legally.

Sofia had also taken the liberty of signing over the adjoining hotel to herself and transforming that into an actual food bank and shelter that served both culinary magicians and Vanillas in need. Now, the profits went to funding the people the establishment was supposed to help instead of lining Polly's own pockets. What a novel concept….

Sofia's parents, ever the law-abiding citizens, never would have condoned the use of magic to illegally acquire property. But Aidan would have applauded her creative spin on his rice paper recipe. So, on the whole, Sofia figured she was in the clear.

It was a pity Graham couldn't be here tonight. Raina had called him earlier in the day talking his ear off about moles burrowing in the magical potato fields. Apparently, the Gourmands had set traps and Clementine was holding a sit-in to protect the moles. So, Graham had needed to go deal with that.

His absence made this sexy-as-sin ensemble feel a little wasted. The shoes in particular made her legs look even…leggier than usual. With that astute observation in hand, Sofia snapped off a quick picture on her phone and texted it to Graham.

Her phone buzzed five seconds later.

"The next time we're together, I want you in nothing except those shoes."

Sofia snorted. She was in the process of writing back, when her phone buzzed again.

"Also, I'm crazy in love with you."

Sofia's heart missed a beat, and then picked up double time.

She should be used to hearing these sorts of things from Graham by now, since he'd been telling her with words and actions every day for the last six months, but it still felt new. Exciting.

Graham had been splitting his time between Sofia's New York apartment and his garden in Maine. Between Sofia's schedule with the restaurant renovations, and her less than admirable driving skills, it had made more sense for Graham to do the commuting. Still, as much as she'd enjoyed transforming a near-empty building into something, well, magical, Sofia was ready for her next big project. After tonight, the restaurant would be firmly in the hands of its chefs—Braxton and Walter on the nonmagical side, and Kenzie doing the magic preparations.

Sofia's phone buzzed again. Graham had sent her a file attachment. She clicked on it and waited impatiently for the image to load on her screen. When it did, she frowned at the picture, trying to make sense of it.

It was a sketch of a house. No, a mansion. Flowers growing up from the ground covered the entire outside of the structure, making it look almost as though the house were made out of flowers.

Before Sofia could begin to puzzle out what this sketch was for or why Graham had sent it, he was calling her.

"Do you like it?" Graham asked as soon as the call connected.

Sofia smiled to herself. Unlike her penchant for bossiness, her disdain for unnecessary salutations seemed to have rubbed off on Graham.

"It's gorgeous," she replied honestly. "What is it?"

"Well." Graham cleared his throat, sounding suddenly nervous. "I was hoping it would be our house."

Sofia stopped fiddling with the bracelet she'd been in the process of clasping around her wrist.

"I think I blacked out for a second," she said. "Could you repeat that?"

"That would just be the outside," Graham said, his voice gravelly. "There'd be electricity and running water and all the normal house stuff inside. You'll have an office to work in, and we can take trips to New York any time…." His breath whooshed out of him. "And we'll have a guest room for Zack and Reuben, so they can stay here while you figure out what to do with the next batch of ingredients. And we'll have a room for Kenzie and Braxton whenever they want to come visit. I was thinking…. Um. Sofia? Did I lose you?"

"Still here."

Sofia's smile was so wide her cheeks were starting to hurt.

"It was just an idea," Graham said quietly. "If you'd rather do what we've been doing, then we can do that. Honestly, I don't care where I live as long as it's with you."

Damnit. She had already applied her makeup and didn't have time to fix it if she started tearing up.

"Graham." Sofia sniffed and stopped smiling long enough to put the poor man out of his misery. "This house looks perfect, and I want to live there with you."

"Really?"

"Really."

Sofia could swear she heard his smile coming through the phone.

A knock on Sofia's door stopped her from saying anything more.

"I've gotta go," she said, grabbing her purse.

"Just answer one question before you hang up," Graham said, his voice deepening. "Tell me what you're wearing under that dress."

Any sexy responses crashed and burned as she opened the door to find Braxton standing on the other side. He was wearing…jeans?

Sofia said something to Graham before hitting Braxton with her infamous stink eye.

"You realize we're supposed to be there in half an hour?" she demanded. "Where the hell is your tux?"

"In the car," he muttered, raising a hand to rake it through his hair. Then, seeming to remember that he'd actually deigned to comb it tonight, dropped his hand to his side.

"Oh my God. You're nervous," Sofia accused. "Brax, chill. It's just a restaurant opening. Not our first rodeo."

"That's not the issue," he mumbled.

"Then what is it?" Sofia asked, running even lower on patience than usual…so, negative patience.

"It's about Kenzie."

Sofia waited for the surge of resentment she used to feel at the mere mention of that name. She waited for the corresponding assault of memories of Aidan's last moments. Neither came.

All Sofia saw was Kenzie sacrificing her own life to save Braxton's.

"Okay," Sofia said. "What about her?"

"I need your help cooking some magic," Braxton replied, looking even more flustered than he had a few seconds ago.

"Now?" Sofia held her phone in front of her brother's face and tapped the time.

"Now," Braxton said, batting her phone away.

Sofia huffed, refusing to let her brother know that she might be just a little bit flattered.

"You going to knock down my door every time you need some magic?" Sofia fake-grumbled as she trailed her brother into the kitchen, where he started helping himself to ingredients from the well-stocked cabinets.

Her skills still weren't what Braxton's had been, but she was getting better. Having Braxton's power inside her certainly made the whole learning curve less steep.

Sofia felt the magic moving seamlessly inside her, just like her blood and everything else that made her who she was. It was completely different from the way it had been when she was using the magic Kenzie had gifted her. This felt familiar. Natural. Permanent.

"What are we making?" Sofia asked, looking at the assortment of ingredients on her counter.

"Sugar glass," Braxton replied, a mischievous grin splitting his face. "A lot of it."

* * *

"You're late, McKaids," Chef Levy announced.

"Noted, Chef," Braxton said.

Chef Levy scowled. "I hope you idiots know I'm not going to go soft on my review just because we're…friends." That word seemed to cause the culinary magic leader some serious discomfort.

"Careful," Sofia cautioned with a laugh. "Keep using words like that and you're liable to give yourself an ulcer."

Chef Levy put her hand in her pocket, possibly to extract a deadly weapon. Sofia took that as her cue to pinch her brother on the cheek, whisper, "Good luck," and scamper off to her table.

"Looking good, Blondie," Zack said with an appreciative whistle as she made her way over to his table.

Sofia winked. She exchanged quick hugs with Reuben and Natalie before sitting down.

Sofia let the conversations flow around her as she took it all in. To say everything had come together would be a gross understatement. The place looked fucking amazing.

They'd steered clear of the stuffy and pretentious vibe so many upscale eateries ascribed to. Instead, they'd gone for more of a homey, wine cellar kind of approach. Since the food bank had originally been built with secrecy in mind, they'd leaned into the underground theme. They'd used a combination of soft lighting and exposed brick walls to create an effect of escaping the busy Manhattan streets and winding up...elsewhere.

The table centerpieces were tall branches wound with delicate ropes of firelights. Instead of chandeliers, the dining room was lit with glass ornaments hanging from invisible wires that made them appear to be floating in mid-air.

Aidan and her parents would have loved it.

That realization didn't cause the pang of heartache and regret that normally would have come with such an observation. She still missed her family...always would...but things were different now. Somehow, over the last six months, she'd stopped thinking about all the people she'd lost. Instead, her family had begun to burgeon. It had gone from her and Braxton, to the two of them plus Graham and Kenzie. They'd also gained Walter, Zack, Reuben, Raina, and Baby Hiroto. Even Clementine...who Sofia had mostly forgiven for kissing Graham that one time.

As though she'd summoned them by sheer force of will, her phone buzzed with an incoming text. Sofia grinned at the picture that popped up on her screen. It was a selfie of Clementine, Raina, and Baby Hiroto. The text said, *"Good luck tonight! We're with you in spirit!"* Baby Hiroto was even wearing a tiny bow tie for the occasion. His pajamas were covered with purple beets and had the words *You make my heart skip a beet* printed across the front.

Sofia smiled at the waiter who presented her the label on a champagne bottle before filling her glass.

The chatter died down when Walter stood up and tapped a knife on his glass.

"We want to thank all of you for being here tonight," he began. "Everyone in this room helped bring *Bloody Delicious* together."

"To Bloody Delicious," Zack called, raising his glass.

"To Bloody Delicious!" everyone echoed back, sipping their bubbly.

Kenzie, who was looking absolutely stunning in a floor-length gray gown that brought out her eyes, raised her glass of sparkling grape juice to Sofia.

Naming the restaurant had become the most challenging aspect of the whole endeavor. They'd discussed naming it for one of their deceased loved ones, but it hadn't seemed fair to prioritize one over another. Sofia had ended the debate the first time she'd tasted the food Walter, Kenzie, and Braxton planned to serve. Sofia had always been a fan of calling things like they were, and it had seemed appropriate to let people know what they'd be in for if they managed to snag a reservation at *Bloody Delicious*…which was currently booking six months out.

Their pre-opening popularity was mostly thanks to Clementine's podcast, which she'd started to help Zack and Reuben educate the world about culinary magic. The podcast had over a hundred-million listeners every week.

"I think that's all I wanted to tell you," Walter said with a little laugh. "And I hope everyone enjoys the food."

"Now, that's my kind of speech," Zack said, toasting Walter with his champagne glass. "Short and sweet."

"Actually, there's something I'd like to say," Braxton said, stepping forward.

Zack groaned. "I knew it was too good to be true."

Sofia kicked him under the table. From the sound of it, so did Reuben. They grinned at each other. Then, Sofia turned all of her attention on her brother…and on the reason why the two of them had almost been late to their own party.

It had been no small feat to smuggle their magnificent creation into the back freezer without anyone seeing. This next part would be up to her.

Sofia let her surroundings fade away as she gathered up the strands of magic she had painstakingly woven into all one-hundred shards of sugar glass. She firmed up the magic, checked to make sure she had control of every piece, and then let her power begin to flow.

"Kenz," Braxton said, taking her hands and turning her so the two of them were facing each other. "I love you. You amaze me every single day."

Kenzie's lashes were already wet. She unwound one of her hands from Braxton's to wipe hurriedly at her cheeks. There was quite a bit of sniffling in the rest of the room, too.

Hang on, people, Sofia thought. *You ain't seen nothin', yet.*

Everyone gasped in awe as Sofia and Braxton's sugar glass phoenix swooped into the restaurant. The red, orange, and yellow translucent shards of its wings pumped as the phoenix soared once around the room before landing in front of Braxton and Kenzie.

It was Braxton's recipe and Sofia's magic. And maybe she was just getting swept up in the spirit of the night, but Sofia could swear she felt the essence of Aidan and her parents there with them.

Sofia loosed a single strand of magic so the phoenix's beak fell open, releasing its precious cargo. Braxton deftly caught the gorgeous three-carat ring in his waiting palm. The ring had belonged to Sofia and Braxton's grandmother, who had given it to their dad when he proposed to Mum.

Sofia had been thrilled for her brother when he asked if he could have it. Sofia had plenty of other ways of remembering her parents. Besides, she might have possibly overheard Graham asking Kenzie and Raina to help him go jewelry shopping on his next trip into the city. Sofia had printed out some ring designs and left them in Kenzie's locker at the restaurant…just in case the group needed inspiration.

Braxton sank down onto one knee. He smiled up at his fiancé-to-be.

"Marry me, Kenz?" he asked.

Kenzie made a sound that was half-laugh, half-sob. She didn't seem able to speak, but she was frantically bobbing her head up and down in the universal gesture for *hell yes*.

Laughing, Braxton slid the ring onto her finger. Kenzie hauled him to his feet, and the restaurant erupted in applause as the couple began making out with enough enthusiasm that oxygen deprivation was a legitimate concern.

The champagne was flowing, and one delicious dish after another was coming out of the kitchen. Sofia was reaching the kicking-off-her-shoes part of the night when she saw her phone light up. She went to silence it and saw it was Graham calling.

"Miss me already?" she asked, getting out of her chair and searching for a quiet corner.

"Sofia."

The intonation of that one word immediately sobered her. This was most definitely not a social call.

"What's wrong?" she demanded.

"You need to come to the garden right away," Graham said. "Bring Kenzie and Braxton."

✳ ✳ ✳

Suffering an eight-hour car ride with a newly-engaged couple, and with an unqualified emergency on the horizon, had not been part of Sofia's plan for the night.

Sofia loved plans. She lived for plans. Which was why she planned to kick Graham's arse as soon as they got out of the car.

What the hell had been urgent enough to pull them away from the restaurant tonight?

Sofia drummed her fingers on the leather seat next to her as she impatiently waited to reach their destination.

One of Graham's first acts as Reaper had been to repair the garden's security features. Even though the three of them knew where they were going, they still took a couple of wrong turns and had to backtrack.

Graham had ensured that the property was completely shrouded by magical plants. It would be impossible for anyone to find the garden unless they already knew it was there.

The Vanillas might know about their world, but the Reaper was still the Reaper. His garden was definitely an invite-only situation.

"Holy shit," Sofia murmured as soon as the garden came into view. Kenzie stopped the car and they all got out, silently gaping.

It was Sofia's first time back to the garden in six months, and she was utterly unprepared for what she saw.

The sky was pitch-black, which only served to make the vibrant colors even more stark. It was almost blinding.

And the magic. There was so much of it. Sofia almost couldn't catch her breath.

The three of them followed a path that was lined with fluorescent purple moss and Chinese lantern plants that were glowing like actual lanterns.

The path forked. Sofia could see that the left half led deeper into the garden. The right ended at—

"Whoa," Kenzie said. "Sweet digs."

Sofia felt a sting at the back of her throat. The flower mansion's bones were already in place. She recognized the angles and turrets from the blueprints Graham had sent her earlier that night. When they'd talked, Sofia had assumed the house was more in the theoretical planning stages.

"I was going to surprise you," Graham's smoky voice said as he stepped out of the shadows. "But then I remembered you don't like surprises." He bent and pressed a tender kiss to her lips before nodding to Kenzie and Braxton. "Sorry to interrupt your night. But this couldn't wait."

Braxton made a *lead the way* gesture. Graham laced his fingers through Sofia's and turned so the mansion was at their backs and they were heading for the main part of the garden.

The garden was bordered by a thick swath of the most intensely-green plants Sofia had ever seen. The plants had star-shaped leaves that made soft swishing sounds as they brushed together in the evening breeze. Unlike the other plants that were so carefully pruned, these ones grew in a wild tangle. Even their magic seemed a little unwieldy.

"What are these?" Sofia asked, nodding to the leaves.

Graham knelt down and brushed his fingertips over one of the plants. The leaves' green glow illuminated the soft expression on his face.

"It's a magical aralia plant," he said, holding out his hand so the leaves could snake out and curl around him. "This species will grow spiky white flowers in the fall." The leaves pulled back from Graham's arm, allowing him to stand up.

"What does the magic do?" Sofia asked in a quiet voice, giving Graham's hand a squeeze.

The sorrow in Graham's expression gave way to amusement. "These plants will kill anyone who enters the garden with evil intent," he explained.

Braxton chuckled. "Aralia would love that, mate."

"I think so, too," Graham murmured.

They passed a few moments in comfortable silence as they took in the awe-inspiring garden.

"You didn't tell me how far along this place had come," Sofia accused.

"Well." Graham chuckled. "This has mostly been a recent development."

"How recent?" Sofia asked.

"Right before I called you," Graham replied.

Sofia turned to see if he was joking. He wasn't.

"I mean, we had the garden all cleaned up and coming along as well as could be expected," Graham hurried to explain. "But most magical plants take years, if not decades, to mature.

"The last couple of weeks, I noticed everything was growing like crazy. I thought it was just because the weather was getting warmer. Then, earlier today, it was like the garden had gone through years' worth of growing overnight. I can't explain it."

"Um," Kenzie said, giving a nervous little laugh. "I can."

They all turned to look at her.

"Remember how I drained my Culinarian magic?" she asked.

They all nodded.

"Well, I kinda sorta drained it into the garden."

"Really?" Braxton asked.

Kenzie nodded. "I wasn't sure it would work, but I've been feeling the magic doing something for a while now. And today, I got the sense that it all just kind of clicked. Like roots taking hold, or something."

"That actually explains a lot," Graham said. "I thought I was going crazy."

"So, then, what's the problem?" Sofia asked, sensing Graham still hadn't told them everything.

"It's not so much a problem," Graham hedged. "Just…it's better if I show you."

He led them past the most perfect-looking white strawberries Sofia had ever laid eyes on, and through an entire orchard of magical peaches. They passed under a canopy of wisteria that smelled downright intoxicating.

Graham brought them all the way to the edge of the garden. More magical aralia surrounded a single, strange-looking pink flower. The flower had curly pink petals that ended in wicked-looking barbs. A syrupy substance collected in the petals' center.

Sofia's neck began to prickle. It couldn't be….

"These are only supposed to grow on a single mountain in China," Graham said as they all looked down at the strange flower. "They're extremely difficult to plant, and even if everything is done correctly, only one of them grows every ten years." Graham stared down at the flower. "Reaper Lee told me how he made the trip once a decade to harvest the flower."

Braxton sucked in a breath, confirming the suspicion that was making Sofia's entire body tingle in anticipation.

"This flower wasn't here earlier today," Graham said with a shake of his head. "I noticed it when I was doing my check for the night." He let out a huff of quiet laughter. "It's fully mature and ready to harvest."

"What am I missing here?" Kenzie asked, looking between the rest of them.

"Kenz," Braxton said, his voice hoarse with awe and disbelief. "Your magic grew the main ingredient in wish truffles."

Kenzie's jaw went slack.

"Wait." Kenzie held up her hand, her new diamond catching the light of a hundred different plants and reflecting it back. "No way…. I couldn't…. What?!" She was so flustered she couldn't even form a complete sentence.

Sofia couldn't blame her. Her own mind was reeling.

"Are you—" Kenzie cleared her throat. "Are you saying you could make a wish truffle? Now?"

"Yes," Graham replied simply.

"What do we do?" Kenzie whispered.

Braxton let out a low whistle.

The four of them stood there, their minds spinning with possibilities and the enormous choice that had been thrust on them.

Sofia spoke first. "I have an idea."

Everyone turned away from the flower, their expectant gazes fixing on her.

A slow grin spread across Sofia's face.

"I think it's time for another Hex Kitchen."

THE END

✳ ✳ ✳

Because reviews are so important for a book to be successful, please consider leaving a brief review on your favorite retailer if you enjoyed *Bloody Delicious*. Many thanks!

* * *

Sign up for Stephanie Fazio's e-Newsletter to learn about upcoming books at:
https://StephanieFazio.com/subscribe/

Acknowledgements

Thank you to my amazing team for helping to bring this series together. I enjoyed every minute of it!

To my editor, Ellen Schaeffer. Thank you for your attention to detail and wonderful suggestions!

To Keith Tarrier, for making such incredibly beautiful covers.

Thank you to Blanch Maze, Laure Eccleston, and the rest of my ARC team. Your incredible support keeps me motivated!

To Mom and Dad, for being the best parents ever. Thanks for always believing in me.

To my wonderful readers. Thanks for making what I do matter!

And to Andrew for being my muse, soul mate, and partner in crime.

About the Author:

Stephanie Fazio is a fantasy author. She grew up in Syracuse, New York, and prior to writing full time, she worked in the fields of journalism, secondary education, and higher education. She has an undergraduate degree in English from Colgate University and a Master's degree in Reading, Writing, and Literacy from the University of Pennsylvania. Stephanie lives in Austin with her husband and crazy rescue dog. When she isn't writing, she's getting lost in parks, hosting taco nights, or ironically and miserably losing at word games, but having fun while she does it.

Connect with Stephanie Fazio:

Visit her Website: https://www.StephanieFazio.com
Sign up for her newsletter: https://StephanieFazio.com/subscribe/

Discover other books by Stephanie Fazio

The Fount Series

The Prince's Chosen

The Forsaken's Choice

The Chosen Union

Opal Contagion Series

Opal Smoke

Opal Slayer

Opal Storm

Bisecter Series

Bisecter

Halve Human

Dusker Dark

Captain Harkibel

Mags & Nats Series

The Nat Makes 7

Mag Subject 6

Steel for 5

Hex Kitchen Series

Hex Kitchen

Cutthroat Cuisine

Bloody Delicious